Wicked
Truths

JODI ELLEN
MALPAS

ORION

First published in Great Britain in 2020 by Orion Books,
an imprint of The Orion Publishing Group Ltd
Carmelite House, 50 Victoria Embankment,
London EC4Y 0DZ

An Hachette UK company

1 3 5 7 9 10 8 6 4 2

ISBN (Mass Market Paperback) 978 1 4091 9753 9
ISBN (eBook) 978 1 4091 9754 6

Typeset by Input Data Services Ltd, Somerset

Printed in Great Britain by Clays Ltd, Elcograf S.p.A.

For Loui. My writing time isn't the same without you curled up by my desk.

Chapter 1

Where do I go from here?

Amid the crazy that has tangled my mind and twisted my aching heart, it's the loudest question of all. My forehead rests on the window of the train and my eyes watch blankly as the blackness races past and the consistent rocking sways me into a numb haze. Run home. It's what my instinct is telling me to do. Because for the first time since I left my small village, centring my attention on a past that I've fought hard to leave behind seems so much easier than trying to make sense of what is happening now.

My eyes close and the darkness I find opens the floodgates, visions of Becker and memories I don't want to have steaming forward. His face, so handsome yet angelic, his smile so wicked, his passion so addictive. And the feelings he unearthed in me, all unexpected but all thrilling. He found me. And then he lost me. He filled me with hope and drive, and then he cruelly ripped it away. He's ruined me.

Because if I don't win this battle, Eleanor, I'll feel like I've thrown away the chance of something fucking incredible.

My eyes open. Something incredible. It was. We were incredible. And that makes me hate him all the more for stealing back the gift he gave me. The gift of life.

I took you to Countryscape because I wanted you to see what no one else sees.

My swallow is lumpy, my heart in agony. I saw him. I saw what he doesn't want anyone else to see. He let me in. Becker didn't only expose his desperation to find the lost sculpture, his sweet con-artist skills or his crooked business dealings, he exposed his weaknesses. His vulnerabilities. His secrets. His pain.

It was a potent mix that when all combined made me fall head over heels for him. And loving him made every wicked facet of him acceptable.

Trust me, Eleanor. Please, you need to trust me.

'But you scared me,' I say to myself, like he might be able to hear me from London. I thought I had figured out who Becker Hunt was. All of it shocking, but more so thrilling. And then . . .

My hand goes to my wrist and rubs, feeling his harsh hold pinning me to the floor. I close my eyes and see his balaclava-covered face. I hear myself begging for my life.

Please don't hurt me.

He told me he would try not to break my heart. He didn't say he would try not to break *me*. He never warned me that by being involved with him, I could be in danger.

I dived in feet first. I knew the risks. His reputation as a modern-day Casanova didn't scare me away. His ruthless con-artist skills didn't have me bolting like they should have. I felt too alive. Too drawn, too deep. I was blinded by his bold, fearless approach to life and business.

And now I'm more lost than the piece of treasure he so desperately needs to find. And just like the sculpture, I hope he never finds me. I reach up to my chest and try to massage the hurt away, knowing deep down that if Becker wants to find something, he'll find it.

The brakes of the train kick in, screeching and jolting me from my whirling thoughts, and I glance up as the darkness ends and the grimy platform of a station appears. The thought of moving, of talking some life into my muscles, brings on another level of despondency. Because moving requires energy, and I feel drained dry.

On a sigh, I disembark with the rest of the passengers. I tell myself that daughters naturally run to their mum when they're in a crisis, no matter what their age or what the crisis. I hate that I'm in a crisis, and I hate that it feels like such a mammoth one. It's time to go home.

The taxi drops me off at the ATM, and I withdraw some cash to pay the driver, deciding to brave the short walk down the road to our house. I could do with the time to psych myself up, come to terms with the fact that I'm back here, and think about what I might say to my mother. How will I explain why I've abandoned my new, exhilarating, happy life in London?

It's quiet, the streetlamps still glowing in the dark winter morning, as I stroll leisurely down the high street, mindlessly slowing to a stop when I reach my father's shop. I look up at the sign that says 'FOR SALE', and my heart breaks that little bit more.

I let myself in and breathe in that old, damp smell. It's comforting. Something familiar in a world I don't recognise.

Nothing has changed. Every single piece of old furniture is exactly where it was the last time I was here. There's hardly any floor space to move, and no trace of walls in between the masses of clocks and paintings hanging from the bare brick. I slowly turn until my eyes fall to the bench where Dad used to sit for hours working on his treasure. 'What are we going to do with all this junk, Dad?' I ask the silence, shuffling through the dusty furniture.

I bend and blow a small puff of air over the surface of a reproduction Victorian sideboard, creating a plume of particles that bursts into the air. The tiny fragments get up my nose, and I sneeze as I hurry to the back room to find some tissue, but the noise of a handle shifting pulls my searching to a stop.

The shop door handle.

I whirl around fast. The sun hasn't even risen yet, and no

one could possibly know I'm back home. News travels fast in Helston, but not *that* fast.

'Eleanor?' The voice sounds distant and grainy, but I'd know it anywhere. My despondency vanishes, and in its place . . .

Anxiety.

He's standing by the door, looking across the room at me. And he's smiling. *Smiling?*

'Brent.' There's no denying the shock in my voice, even if it's tinged with fury. My muscles come to life, straightening my back and holding me up without the need for support from the worktop behind me. 'What are you doing here?'

He shuts the door softly, keeping his eyes on me, letting them roam up and down my body. 'I thought I should check up on you after your incident with Hunt.'

'Excuse me?' He's just turned up in my hometown, hundreds of miles away from London, and he knows there's been an *incident*? How?

'You looked distressed when you ran away. I was worried.'

I back up some more, my wariness intensifying. He saw me run away? 'You were there?' I mumble mindlessly, trying to bully my mind back into something close to straight. Impossible. There are too many things tangling it, and now this? I've been nothing but a pawn in Brent's and Becker's exploits. A naïve, stupid idiot who underestimated their rivalry and the seriousness of the game they're playing.

'What on earth caused you to be so upset?' he asks, ignoring my question. 'What did he do to you?'

I hold my tongue, suddenly hyper-alert. He's digging. Why? Is he suspicious of the fake sculpture that Becker tricked him into paying a stupid fifty million for? I don't know, and I shouldn't care either. I can't get involved. I don't *want* to get involved. I've implicated myself enough already. 'How did you get in?'

Brent holds up my keys before placing them on a nearby

sideboard. I left them in the lock? 'You knew of his reputation, Eleanor.'

That statement doesn't make me wilt like it should. It makes me angry. 'You should leave,' I declare, sounding sure of that. I am. I trust him about as much as I trust Becker. Not at all.

'I think we can help each other,' he says, coming at me, making me back up. Help each other? I'm not even going to ask. 'Becker Hunt can't be trusted. We should be looking out for each other.'

'I want nothing to do with him *or* you.' Unease starts to make my voice wavier in its sureness, and that alone makes me angrier. 'Get out.'

Brent suddenly stops, his eyes widening as he looks past me. It takes a few confused seconds to realise why.

Then all hell breaks loose.

Chapter 2

'You fucking snake,' Becker snarls, tackling Brent from the side and sending him crashing into the nearby wall with a gruff bawl.

My stomach flips.

'You fucking underhanded wanker.' He has his hand around Brent's throat to keep him in place, his body quaking with fury, constantly lifting and slamming Brent against the bricks. 'I fucking told you.' He hoists him up and swings him around, shoving him up against another wall, knocking pictures everywhere. 'I told you to stay away from her.'

Every muscle in my body ceases to function, and I remain like a statue, watching Becker go bananas all over Brent's surprised arse. My eyes could bleed. My mind could explode.

Brent wrestles Becker off and shoves him away, shrugging his suit jacket back into place while he snarls, 'So you can get your lying claws back into her?' He swings a fist quickly and cracks Becker on the jaw, sending him staggering back a few paces. My hands come to my mouth, but my gasp can't be contained.

Becker quickly gathers himself and dives at Brent's midriff, tackling him to the ground and straddling his torso. He lands an ear-piercing, precisely delivered punch to his face, splitting his lip. 'I'll blind you so you can't even fucking look at her.'

The loud clout and Becker's savage promise shocks me to life, brings me back into the shop where two arseholes are rolling around on the floor, wrestling, grunting and throwing punches all over the place. They've already bulldozed my life; I'll be damned if I'm going to let them bulldoze my dad's shop, too.

'Stop!' I shout, finding my feet and flying across the shop. I grab the first thing I can lay my hands on, Brent's jacket, and dig my fingers in, getting the best grip I can. Then I heave with all my might, shouting as I do.

I'm not sure what happens next. One minute, I'm playing tug of war with Brent's suit, shouting and screaming like an unhinged madwoman, and the next my feet have been swiped from beneath me, sending me crashing to the floor. I cry out as my head ricochets off the dusty wood, tossing stars into my hazy vision. I'm forced to close my eyes to stop the room from spinning.

'Eleanor.' Shaky hands cup my cheeks, and my eyes flutter open, trying to turn ten Beckers into one. My face is being stroked, my arm, my leg, my hair, while I try to blink my vision clear. 'Take your time, princess,' he murmurs, lifting me to cradle me in his lap. 'Shhhh.' The familiar sound is softer than his usual sexy shush, more soothing and loving. It prompts too many memories of when he's unleashed it on me before. It makes me panic inside, makes me want to push him away before he infiltrates my defences. But I'm not incapable of doing anything while I'm dizzy. I'm mumbling nonsensical words to the air, words that make perfect sense in my head.

Leave me alone. Get away from me. Fuck off, you lying, deceitful, wicked arsehole.

Then his angel eyes appear, those gorgeous, deceiving hazel orbs, gazing down at me, pouring with remorse and guilt. The green flecks are dull. He looks tired.

I snap my eyes closed, hiding from him. It's all too much. I'm being attacked from every direction by his energy, and I refuse to fall victim to it again. I start trying to remove myself from his clutches, trying to escape. 'Get away from me.'

He fights with me, winning with ease and pulling me back to where he wants me. 'Eleanor, please, you're hurt.'

'She doesn't want your help.' Brent's sneer breaks into our little scuffle, and I mistakenly relax, giving Becker the opportunity to lock his arms tightly around me.

'She's confused,' he says quietly and unsure, like he so desperately wants to believe that himself.

I might have had the ability to move taken away from me, but my mind is still working perfectly well, and I know I'm not at all confused. Becker is a dishonest arsehole. Fact.

Becker's chest begins to throb. 'You have what you wanted. You have the sculpture. You don't get Eleanor, too.'

Brent has the sculpture. A fake sculpture. The reminder aligns my perspective totally. Brent isn't here for any other reason than to try and win *me* over? It would be another score for him over Becker. I'm still a fucking pawn.

'And you get her?' Brent asks, clearly interested.

'Get out, Wilson, or so help me God, they'll be carting you out in a body bag.'

Brent sniffs and hovers in my field of vision for a few moments, while Becker continues to bristle and twitch, his jerky movements being absorbed by my head and shoulders. I don't doubt for a moment that he'll attack. The fury consuming Becker is growing by the second, dripping from his maniac stare, drizzling from every pore. He believes this man's family is connected to his father's death. That time on our way to Countryscape when I foolishly asked about his parents gave me a hint of the anger residing deeply inside Becker Hunt, but it was nothing compared to what I'm witnessing now. The roguish, supercilious womaniser has another side. A deadly side. Memories of the joker, the wind-up merchant, the playful, egotistical man that had me falling for him are fading fast.

'Stay. Away.' Becker says each word through his clenched jaw. 'I'm done. You've got the sculpture. You win. Your family has taken too much from me already, Wilson. I'll die before you take Eleanor, too. Now get the fuck out.'

My internal alarm bells are screaming, demanding I spring to life and slap Becker's face for his nerve. His statement stands for shit because I know that damn fucking sculpture is still out there, and Becker still wants it. I start to squirm, trying to free myself from his hold. Nothing will cooperate. My limbs are tingling with lack of feeling, making my movements clumsy and uncoordinated.

'Get off me.' The harsh demand fights its way past my thick tongue and dry lips, my arm breaking free and swinging behind me, catching him on the shoulder. I push myself away from him, but I only make it a few feet, dragging myself to a fake Queen Anne cabinet and using it to pull myself up. The feel of Becker's determined eyes boring into me as I put as much distance between us as I physically can only increases my fear. He's not going to make this easy. Neither is my stupid hurting heart. And that adds a drop of anger to the fear.

'Get out,' I seethe. 'Both of you get out!'

'You're smart, Eleanor,' Brent rasps, a dash of victory in his tone. 'Don't let Becker Hunt make you stupid.' The door to the shop opens and closes softly.

Brent's gone, but I don't relax because Becker remains slumped on the floor a few feet away, staring at me. 'Go,' I demand.

'Eleanor, please, let me explain,' he begs. 'You weren't supposed to be at your apartment.'

'That doesn't make it okay!' I yell. 'Why the hell would you break in?' It doesn't make any sense.

'I needed to know who broke in the day we were at Countryscape. I was looking for clues. Anything to tell me who it was.'

'I would have let you in. I would have given you my key.'

'I didn't want you to know.'

'Know what?'

He looks at me, a million woes in his eyes. 'That you're in danger.'

I recoil, stunned. 'What?'

'Your employment at the Hunt Corporation caused a stir in the industry, princess. You know that. You know how corrupt this business is, and people will do anything to get information. I've pulled you into my world; I've put you in the middle of it all.' Regret pours from every word. It's hard to see. Hard to hear. 'When we left Countryscape and found your apartment broken into, I knew I'd made a mistake by getting close to you.' His jaw clenches as he stands, taking one measured step towards me. 'But I didn't want to let you go. And I still don't.'

'It's too late.' I look away. My father was right. The high-end world of antiques and art isn't worth the hassle. It isn't worth risking your life for.

'Don't push me away, Eleanor.' He reaches for my arm, and I whip it out of his reach, trembling with fear. It's definitely fear. Problem is, I don't know if I'm frightened by what Becker has told me and the potential danger, or if I'm afraid of what he can do to me, how he can make me feel, how he blankets my wretchedness with a happiness that blinds me. 'Don't *ever* come near me again.'

'I can't do that,' Becker retorts quietly, heightening my fear and confirming exactly what it is I'm frightened of. Him. I'm frightened by how easily he carries me into his fascinating world. How easily I accept him. I'm frightened by how easy it would be to crumble and give into him, to let him take me in his arms, to let him apologise for frightening me, to let him swallow me up in his smiles and cheek. To return to The Haven, the place I love most in the world, and bathe in the bliss and serenity it offers me. To fall under Becker's spell again.

I look at him, the passionate, empowered treasure hunter, and all I can hear are Brent's words. True words. *Don't let Becker Hunt make you stupid.* I need to be smart. Stay smart.

It's head over heart now. I raise my chin and force my eyes to remain on him. It's freezing outside, but his only protection from the chilly winter air is a grey T-shirt and sweatpants. He looks bedraggled. Tired. Stressed. 'You don't have to worry any more, Mr Hunt, because now I have nothing to do with you, I should be safe, right?' I don't give him a chance to answer. 'And don't worry. I won't ask for a reference.' My words are calm, not backed by panic, but backed by a pure certainty that not even Becker can question. And when his lips part and his eyes glaze over, I know that he won't. He spends a while staring at me, possibly waiting for me to stop him from leaving. He'll be waiting a long time. 'Go find your precious treasure, Becker. I'm out.'

I get a sick thrill from his flinch, but he quickly gathers himself and slowly nods his head yieldingly as he backs away, before slowly turning and taking the door handle. His acceptance stirs remorse inside me that I fight to ignore.

He pulls the door open and hovers on the threshold, his back to me. I can literally hear his mind race, probably thinking of anything to redeem himself, anything he can say to win me over. There's nothing.

He opens the door. Pauses. Breathes in. And then he closes it again, his fists clenching by his sides.

I still, anticipating his next move, my mind not working nearly fast enough to tell me what that might be. He swings around fast, and I back away. 'Actually, no.' He points a finger at me. 'No.'

He stalks forward, and I kick my feet into action, feeling my way through pieces of furniture, trying to keep the distance between us. There's nowhere for me to go and my silly move now has me standing in the corner, trapped. A few paces has him right up close. 'No,' he shouts again, his angry breath hitting my face. 'No.' He slams a palm into the wall beside my head, making me jump. 'No.' Then the other hand on the other side of my head.

'Yes.' I fire the word mindlessly in a panic, with no faith that it'll have any effect. I'm virtually a prisoner in his arms. I turn my face in a cowardly tactic to avoid his stare.

'No, princess,' he breathes softly.

'Don't call me princess,' I snap, hating how the reminder brings back memories of our verbal tangles.

'Princess,' he whispers the word against my ear, dropping to an all-time low. My bloodstream ignites and fizzes.

'Go.' My voice is barely there.

But he hears it. 'Make me.'

I shake my head. I know what he's doing. He's going to make me touch him.

'Put your hands on me and push me out, Eleanor.'

'Stop it.'

His hand leaves the wall next to my head and he grabs my jaw, forcing my face to his. I fight him with all my might, terrified of the consequences should he win. So I slam my eyes shut when my muscles refuse to man-up and sustain his force.

'No,' he breathes, stepping in, pushing his body to mine. Our chests meld, my heart rate rockets. 'Open your eyes.'

I shake my head in his clench, stubbornly refusing to give him what he wants – what he knows will break me. What *I* know will break me. He's clever. He's also a ruthless bastard with no fucking morals. But I always knew that. Loved it to a certain extent.

His hold of my jaw slides around to my nape and massages firmly, his other hand joining it so my head is captive in his big palms. He tilts, getting my face at the angle he desires, then I feel the tell-tale signs of fire-filled air hitting my lips. He's moving in. My mind is going into meltdown, shouting and screaming orders at me, rolling them out one after the other in the hopes that I'll catch one and fulfil it. I can't. My body is refusing to move and my heart is being reminded of the twisted joy it was filled with each time he infiltrated my defences. I'm fucked.

'Please.' He blows the word across my skin and gently rolls his groin into my lower tummy. My eyes flutter open with no instruction, and he releases a long breath of air. It's a relieved breath. 'You complete me, Eleanor.' His stare hits me like a bullet to my forehead, his eyes wide and pleading, sincere and distressed. 'I fucking despise myself that I've done this to you. To *us*. I was trying to protect you. I *need* to protect you, and I fucking will, whether you like it and accept it or not.'

I stare at him. Lost. My heart and my head at war. *Make me understand.* There's more to understand now than there ever was before. But one thing I do understand without question is the risk of my heart being destroyed at the hands of this man is now greater.

No, not greater.

Inevitable. *Head over heart, Eleanor!*

I take my hands around to the back of my neck and rest them over his. I don't need to force them away. Becker flexes under my touch and gradually lifts them. My fingers weave through his, playing fleetingly, feeling them and stroking, before I take a gentle hold and bring them between our bodies, forcing him to break the connection of our chests. The whole time, our eyes are glued, a silent message passing between them. Me telling him that I'm through. And him accepting he's lost.

'You made me feel so alive,' I want him to walk away from me knowing what he's done. But more than that, I want him to walk away knowing that I can and I *will* move on.

Becker squeezes my hand lightly and brings his face to mine, nuzzling into my cheek. He's searching for reassurance that I can't give him. I take a deep breath and call on my newfound fire and spirit. The fire and spirit Becker Hunt discovered. 'I will find passion and devotion in my future again. But you will never find loyalty and acceptance.'

He winces, standing before me with his head dropped and hands hanging lifelessly by his sides. Seeing him struggle to face his wrongs, seeing him hurting, facing the truth, offers me comfort in my desolation. 'You pulled me in and pushed me away, pulled me in and pushed—'

'I pushed you away because I knew being involved with you would put you at risk!' He snaps to life, gulping down air as he swings away from me, stalking over to the window and slamming his palms onto the ledge. His back is heaving violently, rising and falling in extended, strained motions. 'I felt something stir inside of me each time I saw you – the taxi, at Parsonson's, the cafe. But the second I laid eyes on you in my grand hall, when I was staring down from my apartment, I knew what I had to do.'

'What?' I ask, peeling my back from the wall and standing firm. 'What did you *have* to do, Becker?'

'I knew I had to let you walk away.'

Walk away? He did the exact opposite. 'But you didn't. You gave me the job.'

'I wanted you.'

'You had me.'

'Then I just wanted you more.'

'And you had me more,' I remind him, gritting my teeth as I fight back the memories of our electric encounters.

He pushes himself from the ledge and turns around. 'And then I wanted you even fucking more. I lost sight of my objective, Eleanor. You distorted everything.' He keeps his distance, but his eyes don't waver from mine. 'I had the strongest urge to push you away, but an even stronger fucking urge to pull you closer.'

I'm unable to process what he's telling me, and definitely unable to speak. So silence falls and fills the empty space, while Becker trembles, and I try to wrap my mind around what he's saying. 'You fitted in perfectly.' His words are steady and strong. 'Not with Mrs Potts or my grandfather. You fitted in with *me*. In my sanctuary. In my world.'

I look away, fighting off the power of his words. My mind can talk reason. It can tell me that I shouldn't trust him. My heart, however, will betray me. And so will my body.

'I've fucked up, Eleanor. Let me fix it.' He approaches me, slowly and cautiously. 'Please.' He whispers his final plea, reaching for me again, begging for my permission. His open hand hovers, quivering like a leaf, as he waits for me to say something. I don't know what to say. My thoughts are centring on one thing, because it's the most obvious.

His regret.

But it's nowhere close to mine. 'Goodbye, Mr Hunt.' I turn and walk through to the back room, my breathing short, my head spinning.

And when I hear the door close, my coiled muscles relax.

But the hollowness returns swiftly.

Chapter 3

The sight of our cottage offers a twinge of comfort when it comes into view. Nestled in the middle of two other cottages, each bigger than ours, it looks like something out of a picture book. Cute and cosy with tiny windows and a thatched roof. It's idyllic, not a façade. There are no wicked truths hiding behind its perfection.

I slide my key into the lock, making extra quick work of it when I hear movement from Mrs Quigg's house next door. The town's busybody, there's nothing that escapes her notice, and she makes a point of making sure everyone knows, too. The whole town will hear I'm back before Mum has a chance to put the kettle on.

I push my way through the door and slam it shut behind me. Then I drop my bag to the floor and fall against the hallway wall, feeling like I've just run the gauntlet. Then I laugh because, technically, I have. I'm still not sure what I was thinking coming back to Helston. But of all the things I feared I would find here, Becker wasn't one. Nor was Brent. But I've handled them. Set the record straight. While they continue with their pathetic games, I have a life to get on with.

'Don't move, motherfucker!'

I yelp, whirling around to find a baseball bat being brandished in my face. 'Shit!' Staggering back, I blindly grapple for the front door as my heart smashes against my chest. Then the dim, natural light is suddenly replaced with a harsh, artificial glare.

'Eleanor?' The sound of the gruff voice halts my frantic attempt to escape, and my grappling hands freeze on the door handle. I give my body a few moments to stop pulsing from adrenalin, my mind trying to place the voice. It doesn't take long.

'Paul?' I say, slowly turning, my mind all knotted, as if it wasn't twisted enough already. The baseball bat lowers, and I finally allow my eyes to take a good long look at the landlord of our local pub. He's a big man, tall and round, and his head is skimming the low ceiling of our hallway. He's in a pair of underpants, his grey hair mussed, his big nose squished from endless breakages, and his pot belly is displayed loud and proud. The ex-pro boxer is out of shape but still pretty formidable. 'What are you doing here?' I ask mindlessly, trying to keep my eyes on his usually happy face. It's not happy now. *Now* it's somewhere between surprise and awkwardness.

Paul laughs under his breath, backing away. 'Um . . . yes . . . well . . .' He stutters and stammers all over his words, and my frown lines deepen with each confusing second that passes.

There's a sudden burst of activity behind him, and someone crashes into his back, sending him staggering forward a few steps. 'What is it, Paul? What's going on?'

I don't need a nanosecond to place *that* voice.

Mum.

'It's okay, Mary,' Paul soothes, calming my alarmed mother.

She's pulling in the sides of her dressing gown, her eyes darting, alarmed. Then she finds me standing by the front door, mouth hanging open. I'm blank.

'Eleanor!' she squeals and dives forward, ready to tackle-hug me. I'm not sure if she suddenly comprehends that something is amiss here, or whether my face tells her so, but she skids to a stop before she makes it to me. Then she takes hold of the wall next to her. 'Oh . . .' she breathes, her eyes widening.

Oh? I can feel my face muscles twisting, yet I find myself chuckling. I don't know why. 'What's Paul doing here, Mum?' I already know. Something close to an explanation is developing in my tired mind and I seriously do not like what I'm coming up with. Or maybe my mind is playing games with me. *Please say my mind is playing games with me!*

Mum starts chuckling, too. It's a nervous laugh. Just like mine. 'You never said you were coming home, darling.' She takes a step back and collides with Paul's naked pot belly, and his hand comes up and rests on my mum's arm, steadying her.

My eyes root to his hold of her and don't move when I answer my mother's wary question. 'Thought I'd surprise you,' I say quietly, watching as Paul's hand releases her. I look up at him. He's evading my questioning stare. The explanation that was developing in my tired mind is suddenly complete. My eyes drift across to my mother. 'Mum?'

Her lips straighten, and she exhales. 'I've wanted to tell you for months.'

'Months?' I cry, my mouth dropping open. 'But . . . how?' I'm at a loss. 'Months?'

Her whole body deflates before my eyes, and Paul's hand is back on her arm, this time offering support of another form. 'Yes, months,' she sighs. 'I didn't want to upset you.'

'Upset me?' I ask, my fingertips coming up to my head and pushing into my temples. I start laughing hysterically as I stand before my mother and her . . . whatever he is, and study them shifting and squirming before me.

'Tea?' Mum asks, a little high-pitched as she points to the kitchen, backing away.

'I'll leave you girls to it,' Paul says. 'Just as soon as I'm dressed.' He disappears up the stairs, and my misplaced bout of laughter dries up.

I follow Mum into the comfortable kitchen and rest my bum on one of the ancient wooden chairs, watching as she flies into action, busying herself by preparing a pot of tea. My clasped hands rest on the table, my back straight, unable to relax. What do I say to her? What will she say to me? I start to nibble on the inside of my cheek as I contemplate it all. Paul? I can't make any sense of it amid the fog of crazy that's clouding my mind right now. 'How long, Mum?'

She stands still across the kitchen, and a few lingering seconds of silence falls. 'Five months,' she says quietly, turning to face me.

I let out a stunned exhale of air. 'Wow,' I say, wondering how I missed it. I only left for London a couple of months ago. This was going on while I lived here?

Her lips purse and the sparkle in her eyes dulls a little as she glances away. I can't understand why I'm disappointed to see the glimmer of happiness disappear. It's guilt. More guilt added to the guilt I feel where my dead father is concerned.

She takes a seat, an unsure smile on her face. 'You know your father was hardly an attentive husband, Eleanor,' she says, waiting for me to confirm it. I can't. I'd feel like a traitor. 'He had a love affair with his shop.'

'I know,' I whisper. He used to caress the old furniture he restored like he was caressing a woman's body. Except he wasn't, God love him.

'I never *ever* betrayed him,' Mum says resolutely. 'You have to know that. Not once in our forty years of marriage. I was devastated when he passed, Eleanor. Broken.' She reaches across the table and takes my hand, squeezing gently. 'I'll never stop loving your father, darling. But I can have room in my heart for another love.'

I squeeze my eyes shut and try to reason with myself, and in my darkness, I see that sparkle in my mum's eyes. Because it is *that* bright. Almost blinding. She's happy. Who the hell am I to take that away from her? She was a good wife. Dutiful. She accepted that Dad's passion was his worthless treasure. She accepted that she came second to that.

'I felt so guilty,' she says quietly. 'Felt bad for feeling happy.'

'Mum, stop.' I shake my head, cursing myself. I know how that feels. 'You don't have to explain.'

'But I need you to know, Eleanor. I need you to understand.'

'I understand,' I say softly, fighting to appreciate just how content she is. She might be my mother, but she's still a woman. A beautiful one, who was never really made to feel that way.

'Thank you,' Mum says, spiking even more guilt. 'Paul's really a very lovely man. Big, strong, sociable.'

It doesn't escape my notice that my father was none of those things. Paul is the polar opposite to him. 'It's nice to see you smile.' I force the words through my inner turmoil – more turmoil, different situation – striving to sound as sincere as possible.

She blushes. In my twenty-eight years of life, I don't think I've ever seen my mother blush. It takes a decade off her sixty-three years. I also notice now that her hair is different. More shaped and with lots of swishing layers, and it might be morning, but she has make-up on. She's like a new woman. Reborn. 'Anyway,' she says. 'What are you doing home? You never said.'

I clam up automatically. 'I was homesick.' I grimace and mentally kick myself for not thinking of a more feasible reason. I've spoken to her often and never once given any indication of missing home. Add the minor fact that I couldn't wait to get out of Helston, she's quickly all over me with a questioning look. She's also picked up on my stiffness. Her constricting hold of my hand tells me so.

'Homesick?' she repeats, watching me closely.

'I missed you.' I try again.

'You missed me?'

'Yes.'

'You turn up out of the blue at the crack of dawn, and you expect me to believe that it's because you missed me?'

I snatch my hand away from my mother's, feeling like she's

delving into my mind through our touch. 'Yes, exactly that.' I slide my chair back and get up, heading for the sink to wash my mug. The drama since I walked through the front door of Mum's cottage has been the perfect distraction. Now that I've had a sharp reminder of how I came to be here, I can feel the hurt churning in my gut again. 'And I need to sort Dad's shop.'

'Okay,' Mum says easily, making me pause with the mug under the tap until it overflows and the hot water scalds my skin.

'Shit!'

'Come here.' Mum sighs, pushing me out of the way and turning off the tap. She retrieves the mug and sets it on the drainer. 'Let me see.' Claiming my hand carefully, she has a good inspection. 'You're fine.' She gives me high eyebrows. 'At least, your hand is fine. I'm not so sure about this.' She taps my forehead before wandering out of the kitchen. 'You can tell me why you're really home when you're ready,' she calls.

My chin drops to my chest, and I only just manage to stop myself from telling her that I'll *never* be ready.

I take myself upstairs to my old room and fall on the bed, dialling Lucy. I doubt my vagueness will be as willingly accepted by my friend, which is why I don't plan on mentioning anything to do with Becker. I can't face it.

'Morning,' she chirps, all happy. If I could see her, I know she'd have a skip to her step. It feels like eons since I last saw her, when in actual fact it was only last night that I left her with Mark. It's been the longest night ever.

'How was last night?' I ask, getting comfy on my pillow, gazing around at the familiar surroundings of my old bedroom. Everything is exactly as I left it.

'Perfect,' she pants, and I smile. I'm happy for her. 'He's perfect, I'm perfect, we're perfect.' More panting comes down the line and I wait for her to gather air and spit out an explanation for her heavy breathing. 'The stupid lifts are out of order at Covent Garden station. I've just passed step seventy-five.'

'Ouch.'

'Yeah,' she huffs. 'Shoes are coming off now. Still on for lunch? Or shall we do dinner?'

'Ah.' I snap my mouth shut and rummage through my cluttered mind for an excuse. 'You see . . . um . . . I'm out of town.'

'What do you mean, you're out of town?'

'I'm at my mum's.'

'What? In Helston?'

'Yeah, family emergency.' I cheer to myself for my quick thinking. Also because, technically speaking, it isn't a lie.

'What's happened?'

'Mum's got herself a new boyfriend.'

There's a slight pause. 'Huh?'

'My mum, she—'

'Yes, yes. I heard you, Eleanor. How is that an emergency?' Now I'm stumped, because, technically speaking, it isn't really an emergency at all. A shock, maybe, but it doesn't warrant me fleeing London late at night. 'And what about your job?' she asks.

'What job?' My voice is like a robot now, automatic and emotionless. It's the only way to be.

Lucy gasps down the line. 'He fired you?'

'I quit,' I correct her. I realise there is only so much I can share, or so much I *want* to share.

'Tell,' she demands, her laboured breaths now under control. This means, unfortunately, she has enough steam to grill me. 'You sat in my apartment last night talking with a bucketload of optimism, and the next morning you're hundreds of miles away sounding like someone's died. What's happened?'

My throat dries up with dread at the thought of talking about it. I breathe in, swallow and repeat, breathe in, swallow and repeat, searching for a scrap of strength to spit out the words and share my woes. 'I can't,' I croak, brushing at my cheeks roughly when I feel a tiny bead of wet trickle down my skin. Goddamn it, why am I crying?

'What did he do?' She sounds mad.

'He ...' I hiccup, covering my eyes like it might stop the mental images of him in my apartment. I can't tell Lucy what he did. I can't tell her he broke into my apartment and scared the ever-loving shit out of me. I can't tell *anyone*, leaving me to shoulder the truth alone. 'I can't talk about it.'

'The arsehole,' she spits, growling down the line for a few moments before a lingering silence falls, and I wait and hope that my friend can leave it there. 'Okay,' she finally says softly, though obviously forced for my benefit. 'That's fine, just know I'm here when you're ready to talk.'

I gaze blankly at nothing across my room. 'Thank you.'

'Oh, Eleanor,' she sighs. 'Why didn't you stop me from harping on about Mark? I'm sorry.'

'Don't. He's not an arsehole.'

'Come home,' she says softly. 'We'll buy a voodoo doll and stick needles in it.'

I smile a little, thankful that I have Lucy, and I honestly don't know what I'd do without her. 'I just need a timeout for a few days while I think about what to do next. And I may as well take care of my father's store while I'm here.' I never imagined I would actually look forward to clearing out his shop. It's going to distract me for a good few days.

'Okay. Call me if you need me.'

'I will.'

'Hey, has your mum really got a new boyfriend, or was that a bare-faced lie?'

'She really has.' I fight off flashbacks of Paul in his underpants as Lucy whistles down the line.

'And how do you feel about that?'

'I don't know,' I admit. 'She's happy, and that's the most important thing.' I could never deny her that. 'I'll let you know when I'll be back.'

We say our goodbyes and I hang up, snuggling down in my

bed, intending on shutting my mind down and finding sleep.

But an hour later, I've tossed my body over for the hundredth time and that needed sleep is nowhere close. My restlessness would be easy to put down to being uncomfortable. Except I'm not. I'm just struggling to clear my mind and zone out. And I'm getting distressed as a result, because it isn't Mum's bombshell that's got my mind racing. Neither is it the fact that I'm home and I might have the imminent pleasure of seeing a few old ghosts. It's the phantom that is Becker Hunt keeping me from finding peace in my darkness.

I close my eyes and see him. I breathe in and smell him. I feel the sheets skimming my skin and imagine it's his touch. I shut my brain down for a split second and hear his sexy shush. I swallow and taste his tongue in my mouth.

He's imprinted on every part of me.

Chapter 4

After spending my entire Sunday moping and avoiding my mother so she couldn't squeeze me for information, I wake on Monday determined not to waste another day. I need to get back to London. I need to be getting myself a new job. The alternative is remaining in Helston at the mercy of my regrets and my past. No. Not today.

I jump up and rummage through the chest of drawers in my room, searching for anything I can wear. I settle on some old leggings and a big jumper. After showering and dressing, I make my way downstairs, finding Mum in the kitchen making tea.

'Sleep well?' she asks, handing me a cup.

I hum my answer and take a sip. 'I'm going to Dad's store.' I tell her, and she looks up at me. I can see the fear in her eyes – fear that I'm going to ask her to come. I smile and reach for her hand. 'I've got it,' I assure her. I know she's avoided the shop, and I understand why. It's the same reason I've avoided it myself. Yet, in order for me to move forward, I need to clear up the remnants of my past. And Mum seriously needs relieving of the financial strain. It's time to pull my finger out.

'Thank you,' she seizes my hand and squeezes it. 'Now, are you ready to talk or am I to continue pretending you've really missed me?'

I roll my eyes. 'I did miss you,' I say, setting my tea down and pulling on my jacket.

'So you're on leave, are you? From your job?'

'Something like that.' I swing my bag onto my shoulder and kiss her cheek. 'Just know I'm fine, okay?' I do not need my mum worrying about me. *Because, Eleanor, there is nothing to worry about.*

She sighs. 'Not really, but I can hardly beat it out of you, can I?'

'No.' I head for the door. 'What are you doing today?'

'Paul and I . . .' She fades off as I turn back to look at her. Her smile is awkward. 'He's taking me shopping.'

I smile, seeing that bright sparkle in her eyes. It suits her. 'Have a lovely time.'

She nods, and I'm pretty sure I see tears cloud her eyes. It tugs at my heartstrings. And it makes me realise that the best gift I could give my mum is my blessing.

I leave the house and take a moment on the step to drink in air. Then I start the short walk into town. I can practically feel the whispers following me the whole way. 'Eleanor, you're home,' Mr Keller, the local carpenter, calls from across the road as he loads a ladder onto his van. 'Good to see you.'

'Just temporarily,' I say as I wave.

By the time I make it to Dad's store, I think I must have seen just about every resident of Helston. All except my ex-boyfriend and ex-best friend, which suits me fine. Hopefully I can do what I need to do and leave without any chance encounters.

I let myself in and glance around, wondering where I might start. 'God, could you have crammed any more junk in here, Dad?' I set my bag down and pick up a watercolour that's propped up against a wall. I smile, remembering when Dad acquired it in a house clearance from the next village. That day, years ago now, he came back with a van load of new 'treasures'. He was thrilled, while I was wondering where on earth he planned on storing it all. The shop had always been set to burst at the seams, yet Dad always found more space. And now I have to clear it.

I get my phone out and pull up Google, searching for local clearance firms. I find one a few towns away and call them to arrange a collection. 'Later today is perfect, thank you.'

It's time to roll my sleeves up. Over the next few hours, I think I must burn a million calories moving everything I can manage into the courtyard out back. It's only when the larger pieces of furniture remain that I realise I haven't quite thought this through. There's no way I'll shift it all on my own. I take a seat on a nearby reproduction cabinet to catch my breath and blow away some cobwebs from the sleeve of my jumper.

'Hi, Elle.'

I look up. 'David,' I breathe, finding my ex standing on the threshold of Dad's store.

'I heard you were back.'

I laugh under my breath. This place. You can't fart without the whole town knowing. 'Only temporarily.' Let's make that clear. 'What are you doing here?' I get up, needing something to do, and start shifting a table towards the back entrance of the store.

'You never answered my calls. My messages.'

I stop pushing the table and turn to face him. It's only now I notice he's lost a bit of weight. His tall frame is slighter than usual. 'Why would I?' I ask. 'Why rehash things? You did what you did, with my best friend, and I left Helston. What did you want? For me to shout and scream? Cry? We've both moved on.'

'Have we?' he asks, and it throws me.

'Mum told me she's seen you with Amy. So yes, I assume you have, and I know I have.' It's a slight stretch of the truth, but David doesn't need to know the ins and outs of the crazy happenings in my life since I left Helston.

'I've seen Amy, of course. It's hard to avoid anyone in this town, Eleanor. You know that.' He moves into the store, looking around. 'You might not believe it, but we both regret what happened. We're both sorry.'

'Well, thank you for your apology.'

He blinks in surprise. 'Welcome,' he replies, unsure.

I start pushing the table again, grunting a bit with the effort. It's odd. I thought I'd disintegrate in the presence of my ex, get angry and upset. It's quite the opposite, in fact. I feel . . . closure. Weird. I stop trying to wrestle the table through the doorway and brace my hands on the edge, puffing and panting like a loser.

'Want some help?'

I turn back to David and find him flexing his non-existent muscles and giving me a small smile.

'Call it a peace offering.'

Laughter rises, and it feels good. I chuckle and move aside in invitation, and he comes over, taking one side as I take the other. 'This means nothing except I'm fed up hating you,' I say, needing that to be clear. But I'm not fed up. I simply haven't got the energy to hate him.

He smiles. 'Have you really moved on, Eleanor?'

I nod, forcing sureness into my expression. 'Yes.'

'Then I'm happy for you.'

Don't be, because my life is upside down right now. 'Thanks,' I smile meekly. 'Ready?'

'Yep.' He bends and we lift, negotiating the table out of the store and setting it down on the ground in the courtyard. We wander back inside. 'God, I forgot how much junk your Dad hoarded,' David says, looking around, a little bewildered.

I laugh a little, completely unoffended. It's like I can't be angry with anyone right now, except Becker. Even my ex, who royally turned me over, and, technically, sent me to London and into the clutches of Becker Hunt. Yet as I'm standing here, in my father's store, doing something I should have done weeks ago, I feel almost at peace. Anger's eluding me, and in its place is acceptance.

'What are you doing with it all?' he asks as he casts his eyes over the clutter.

'I have a clearance company collecting it later.' I point to a cabinet and David moves in, taking one side and lifting as I take the other.

'And what will they do with it?'

'Skip it, I suppose.'

'That's such a waste.' We both go red in the face as we lift and start shuffling along. 'My company is doing a community drive incentive,' he puffs. 'Would you mind if I take some of it for the homeless shelter?'

I grin through my straining. 'Since when did you become a saint?'

David hits the doorframe with his elbow, the thwack loud. 'Fuck!'

I laugh, having to quickly lower the cabinet before I drop it on my toes. 'That's karma, that is.'

He grimaces and releases his end of the cabinet, rubbing at his elbow while I continue to titter to myself, the laughter rolling from me in waves. It's not even that funny, but this laughter? It feels good. And this moment, this distraction? It's masking everything I need masking.

I fall through the door later that afternoon looking like I've been rolling in cobwebs and dusted in flour. I brush myself down as I wander into the kitchen.

'I was just going to call you,' Mum says as she stirs a pot on the stove. 'Thought you might have got lost in a worthless vase.'

I dip my finger in the stew and suck off the gravy. I'm famished. 'David helped me.'

Mum's stirring stops and she looks at me gone out. 'He did?'

I dump my bag on a chair and get a glass of water. 'It's not like that. He apologised, I accepted. End of story.' I take a quick swig of my water, parched. 'We've left a few pieces in the store that David wants to donate to a homeless shelter through his company. I've given him the keys so he can let himself in to collect it all. The rest is in the yard ready to be collected.'

She smiles. 'Thank you.'

'Don't thank me.' I finish my water and set the glass by the sink, falling into thought. Empty. Dad's store is empty. But my heart is full of the memories. I smile, feeling warm inside. Like a weight has been lifted.

'I'm going for a few drinks this evening,' Mum says, returning to her pot. 'Coming?'

'I was thinking of going back to London tomorrow,' I say quietly. I'm on a roll. May as well keep up the momentum.

'Then tonight can be your leaving party.'

I glance down at my bedraggled form. I feel manky. 'I have nothing to wear.'

'Then we'll pop into town and find something.'

I gape at her. 'I doubt I'll find anything in town, unless I fancy a trip to the local bingo hall.'

'Don't be such a pessimist,' she scolds, pouting. 'There's a new little boutique store. I bet they'll have something.' She looks down at her watch. 'It's four o'clock. We have an hour before they close.' She whips off her apron and wipes her hands on a tea towel. 'Come on.' I'm claimed and guided out the door, Mum grabbing her coat and purse on the way. 'My treat.'

'No, Mum,' I argue. She's not exactly flush with money. I won't have her splurging it on me.

She pulls the door closed behind her and links arms with me. 'I know my daughter is a hot-shot in London, but I would like to treat her.'

A hot-shot in London? I inwardly snort. Maybe an idiot in London. 'Mum, you really don't have to.'

'No, but I want to. And that will be the end of that.' She pouts, an overexaggerated gesture that's meant to make me feel guilty. It works. I sag, defeated, as she leads us towards town. I should be supporting her newfound spirit, not raining on her parade.

'We'll drink wine while we get ready, too,' she adds.

I laugh to myself, thinking this woman is a flipping stranger. And, actually, I quite love her.

I gape as Mum sashays into the kitchen, totally astounded by what I'm looking at. A fox. 'Jesus, Mum.'

She giggles and performs a carefully executed twirl. 'What do you think?'

What do I think? I think she's going to the local pub, not to the Royal bloody Opera house. 'Amazing,' I say instead, because she really does. Her curvy body is encased in a beautiful deep blue wrap-around dress with a silver shrug. 'Heels?' I look down at her feet that are graced in a pair of stilettos. I've never seen her in heels. She has always blessed her feet with squidgy-soled flats.

She points to her toes and admires them. 'I'm getting used to them now.'

I felt okay until a moment ago, when my stranger of a mother flounced in. Now I feel a little underdressed. 'Sorry, you did say we are going to the Saracen's Head, didn't you?' I glance down at my simple black dress, a surprising find on our shopping trip.

'Yes.' She takes her wine glass and sips, all ladylike. 'Paul bought me this dress.' She brushes down the front, eyeing me closely for my reaction. 'A man's never bought me a dress before.'

I half melt, half wince. She looks so pleased. She *should* be lavished like she deserves to be lavished, but I can't help feeling like I'm betraying my father's memory by being happy for her. 'You look beautiful, Mum.'

Her cheeks flush and her red lips stretch into a wide smile. 'Thank you, darling.' She scrunches her dark-blond hair, boofing it up. 'Ready?'

Every head turns as we enter the Saracen's Head. Mum marches to the bar like she owns the place, setting down her purse and smiling brightly as Paul drops everything to tend to her.

'A glass of your best house white, landlord,' she says confidently, resting her bum on a bar stool. I join her, unable to stop myself from cringing as Mum and her new boyfriend flirt outrageously.

'Anything the lady wants.' Paul grins, a gleam in his eye. 'You look stunning, Mary.' Mum chuckles as Paul pulls down a wine glass. 'And for you, Eleanor?'

'Same,' I squeak, looking around the bar to avoid seeing them giving each other lusty eyes. The old English pub is bursting at the rafters, and surprisingly up-to-date music is blasting from the jukebox. Right now, 'Giant' by Calvin Harris and Rag'n'Bone Man is gracing the speakers, and there's even a few people jigging in the clear space across the pub that serves as a dance floor.

A glass of wine slides across the bar, and I look up to find Paul smiling at me. 'Thank you,' I murmur.

'I'll be back.' Mum jumps down from the stool and heads off, waving and smiling at a collection of women across the way. It's a tactical move to leave me alone with Paul. Damn her.

He's lingering behind the bar, waiting for me to say something. I take a sip of my drink, wondering what on earth I *could* say. And that guilt is rising, thoughts of my dad poking at my mind.

'I understand it must be hard for you,' Paul begins when it's obvious I'm not going to initiate conversation. He pours more wine into my glass when I place it down, like he's cottoned on to the fact that feeding me wine might loosen me up. 'With your dad and all.'

My glass is back at my lips again, anything to keep my mouth busy with a lack of words coming to me. I really have no idea what to say.

'He was highly thought of around town.'

I pause, holding some wine in my mouth as I look at Paul.

Highly thought of? I swallow and clear my throat. 'You mean highly thought of as a bit eccentric?' I appreciate Paul is trying to be diplomatic, but it's no big secret that most people around these parts thought my dad was a bit cray-cray.

Paul withdraws, a little embarrassed. 'I just want you to know that I have the utmost respect for him.'

'He was a good man,' I reply quietly, glancing over at my mum, who's developed a bit of a sway as she chats. If she starts dancing, I think I might pass out. 'But he never really gave Mum the attention she deserved,' I add thoughtfully.

'She has my full attention,' Paul replies, and I look to find him smiling as he backs away and serves someone else across the bar. But his interest is constantly straying to my mum's arse. I want to dive across the bar and slap my palm over his wandering eyes. I definitely inherited my mother's arse. Becker's fondness for mine is suddenly all I can think of, and I shift on my stool, waiting for the familiar discomfort from a few good spanks to kick in. It doesn't, and I admit to myself that I miss it. I miss *him*. For the first time today, I lose my battle to keep my thoughts in check. I may have closure on my dad's store and even my ex, but I don't think I will ever really have closure on Becker Hunt. He's got too tight of a hold on my dumb heart.

An hour later, my mother is dancing, and I'm still propped on my stool coming to terms with it. I've declined her offers to join her on the dance floor and have spent the best part of my evening smiling sweetly and chatting with many of the locals. Feigning contentment and convincing them how amazing my new life is in London is exhausting me, and I'm just about done with it when I'm certain that I must have spoken to every single person in the Saracen's Head.

Sliding from my stool, I slip past Mum on the dance floor, laughing when she grabs my hands and twirls me. 'I'm just going to the toilet,' I shout over Prince as he croons 'Kiss'.

'Spoilsport.' She laughs, releasing me and shimmying on over to Paul, who promptly hands her another glass of wine.

I make my way to the ladies, and once I've used the loo, I lean into the mirror and brush at my pale cheeks. My brown eyes look a little heavy, and I can't work out if it's tipsiness or tiredness that's the cause. 'She's happy,' I say to my reflection, batting off the silly twang of disappointment the admission stirs. All of the time I spent worrying and making sure I called to check up on her seems like a bit of a waste. It's both gratifying and a little wounding. Not to mention guilt-inducing. I never once considered the fact that she might move on. I never pictured her with anyone but Dad. What would he make of this? Of Mum and Paul?

I shake my head and those thoughts away as I collect my purse, square my shoulders, give my hair a quick ruffle, and then pivot, taking the handle of the door and pulling it open.

'David,' I screech, jumping back. 'Jesus, you startled me.'

He shrugs sheepishly. 'Sorry.' And then he seems to turn a bit awkward, shifting uncomfortably. 'Elle, can we talk?'

Something about the way he's looking at me, like in apology, makes me wary. 'What about?'

'It was nice seeing you today.'

Oh no. 'David—'

'We had fun, right? Like old times?'

Oh Jesus. 'Accepting your apology wasn't an invitation,' I say, standing firm. 'I can forgive you, and, trust me, that's for my own selfish reasons, not to make you feel better about what you did to me. But I won't forget, David.' I skirt past him, breathing in deeply.

'Please, Elle.'

'Please don't, David.' I fight my way through the crowds, not prepared to get into this. I'm done.

'You were so distant,' he calls, following behind. 'It was like you weren't really here any more.'

What? No. He doesn't get to push this back on me. I swing around, livid. The confrontation that was avoided earlier in Dad's store? It's happening now. I don't know why I'm feeling the need to suddenly rip a strip off him. Maybe because I'm tired. Or maybe because my earlier resolve has wavered this evening with Becker playing on my mind. 'That's your excuse?' I ignore the fact that he's right. I was in Helston in body, but my mind was elsewhere, dreaming of . . . my dreams.

He pulls to a stop, and I realise all of the attention is on us. The pub is quiet. No music either, like the jukebox has shut up and wants in on this, too. 'I'm sorry,' he murmurs.

'You already apologised and I already accepted. Let's leave it there.' I turn to leave but find myself swinging back around, suddenly full of words I want to unleash. I'm blaming the wine, too. 'Actually, let's not leave it there. You did me a favour, David. When you shagged my best friend, you did me a favour.'

Paul appears with a fresh glass of wine for me, and I take it gratefully with a smile.

And throw it in David's face.

The collective gasps in the pub seem to stretch for ever as he stands with his mouth hanging open, stunned, blinking, wondering what the hell has gotten into me. Because little meek Eleanor Cole would never do such a thing. Yeah, well, Eleanor Cole has changed. Eleanor Cole won't stand any shit any more. Eleanor Cole has fire in her belly.

'You've changed, Elle.' David's persona shifts, and he frowns, looking at me like he doesn't recognise me any more. Good. I don't want him to recognise me. Because I'm not the same girl he dated for years. 'What, you think you're better than us now?' he asks. 'Think you're all big and superior with your London job and your city lifestyle?'

And there he is. My ex-boyfriend, the insensitive arsehole. He couldn't say anything worse to me. And to think I was at peace forgiving him? I'm an idiot in more than one way.

'I think it's time to leave, David,' Paul says diplomatically, nodding to the door as he refills my glass, giving me a look to suggest this one should not be wasted.

'Oh,' David laughs. 'Should have known you'd side with Elle since you're fucking her mother.'

The gasps that flood the bar this time are horrified and justified. Mum's new boyfriend is a burly bloke and an ex-pro boxer – no one messes with him. The years he has on David won't faze him. 'Be careful, son,' he warns, leaning across the bar. 'Don't think I won't throw you out of here.'

David ignores the threat, sighing and rubbing at his head. 'Elle, I'm sorry. Can you just give me a minute to explain?'

'What's to explain? You did what you did and I'm over it.'

He rests his hand on my arm, and I shrug him off, slamming my lips shut for fear of turning the air blue with my bad language. 'You've not moved on,' he says. 'Neither have I. You can't ignore how great we were together today.'

I ignore him. It takes every scrap of willpower I have. I sit myself back at the bar and drink my fresh glass of wine, glugging it down irresponsibly. The quiet around me should be making me squirm on my stool, but my fury is halting any discomfort that I could feel under the interested attention of the entire pub. I bet they're all loving this. The drama, the gossip. The town jungle drums will be going wild.

'David,' Mum says, her heels clicking as she makes her way over. God love that woman. He's just insulted her, and she's not showing the slightest bit of offence. 'Let's step out—'

She's interrupted when the door to the pub slams shut, sending a cool breeze gusting through the bar. There are a few more collective gasps. And then whispers, too.

Like something magnificent has just walked in.

Then I hear a familiar voice saying a polite, 'Evening.'

And I know immediately that it has.

Chapter 5

Every single one of my nerve endings begin to tingle, my grip tightening on my glass as I stare at the top shelf of the bar. It's silent – unnervingly silent. I keep myself facing forward, my heart now working up to a steady staccato, and peek to each side of me, seeing everyone in my field of vision looking towards the door – eyes wide, mouths hung open, hushed.

'I believe you were asked to leave.' Becker's tone is dripping with threat that not even *I* would challenge. My round eyes shoot to my wine glass, which might shatter at any moment under the pressure of my grip. I need to loosen my hold, but this glass feels like it's the only thing stopping me from tumbling from the stool in a flat-out panic.

'Who the hell are you?' David is on the defensive immediately, and I'm not at all surprised. I know I'm going to turn around and find Becker adorned in a fine suit, his scruff perfect, his specs resting on his perfect nose. David will feel threatened. No man appreciates Becker's unholy godliness.

I sip more wine, despite knowing I need to stop drinking. Tackling David is one thing; Becker is a whole new level of willpower. Getting blind drunk won't help me.

The silence is tangible, everyone's interest obvious by the quiet and thick atmosphere.

'Who I am is not your concern.' I hear the even beats of Becker's brogues coming closer and see Paul in front of me watching as something approaches behind. Or *someone. Someone* tall. I see him out the corner of my eye perch on a stool next to me, his knee close to mine. 'Haig on the rocks, please.'

David is bristling behind me but, right now, I'm in no position to address the situation. I want to cut off both of their balls. I just can't decide which one I want to hurt more. 'What are you doing here?' I hiss out the side of my mouth, refusing to look at him.

'I've given you plenty of time to come to your senses,' he states matter-of-factly, confidence oozing from his entire being. 'Time's up.'

'You cannot be serious?'

'Oh, I've never been more serious about anything in my life. Not masters of art. Not priceless treasures. Not even Gloria, and you know how I feel about my precious, priceless Aston.' There would be nothing to stop my eyes from finding his after those words. His face is straight, serious, as he accepts his drink from a quiet Paul and raises his glass in thanks before taking a healthy swig, his hazel eyes on me. 'And since old boyfriends seem to be on the prowl, things just got a whole lot more *serious*.' His face remains impassive, though I sense the threat there. 'I'm not giving up, Eleanor.' He turns to David, who's standing quietly behind us, probably gawping in disbelief. 'You still here?'

'Who the hell are you?' My ex splutters again, somewhere between anger and genuine curiosity, trying to straighten out his soaked shirt.

'What are you, deaf?' Becker asks, and I cringe. The pub is still super quiet, all attention pointing at us. 'I already told you, it's not your concern. Run along now.'

'I'm going nowhere.' David laughs. 'This is *my* local.'

'Time to leave, David,' Paul pipes up, walking around the bar. I follow his path and watch him open the door.

'This isn't done, Elle.' David says, and I look at Becker briefly, as if checking he's listening. 'You know it, and I know it.'

I remain quiet, but Becker shifts on his stool, drawing breath. 'Trust me,' he says calmly, giving my ex a death stare. 'It's done.'

He's his usual beautiful self, dressed to impress in a dark grey charcoal suit. I wish I'd never looked at him.

I turn back to face the bar and close my eyes to gather some strength, guzzling some more wine, hoping to douse the building unease simmering in my gut. 'Please go,' I murmur, hearing hushed whispers beginning to break out, no doubt everyone surmising who Becker is.

'I'm going nowhere until you agree to come with me.' I can feel his eyes drilling into my profile.

'You'll be waiting a long time.'

'I'm in no rush,' he whispers as his hand drifts over to my leg and rests on my kneecap. I whip it away, furious with my body for heating up with only a brief skimming touch. 'I've spent years searching for a lump of marble that probably can't be found, Eleanor. Do you think waiting for you is going to faze me?' He finds my knee again and squeezes. 'Especially since you *want* to be found, princess.'

'I do not want to be found. I want to forget I ever met you.'

'Liar.'

Paul presents himself behind the bar, eyeing my companion warily. 'You okay there, Eleanor?'

'Fine.' All that held air in my lungs billows out. 'He's just leaving.' I want to crawl into my wine glass and drown myself, especially when my mum hurries over. Oh my days, how am I going to explain him?

'Eleanor, aren't you going to introduce me?' she asks, putting her hand out to Becker.

I watch as he takes it gently and shakes. I've lost the ability to speak, so I resort to watching helplessly as Becker bamboozles my mother with one of those disarming smiles and a flash of his sparkling angel eyes. 'I'm Becker Hunt,' he declares softly. 'Eleanor's boss.'

Mum breathes in her surprise and darts her eyes to me. The arsehole. I want to correct him, but my ability to talk doesn't look like it's returning anytime soon. I know what she's thinking, and she would be right. I've managed to evade her questions but, thanks to Becker, I'm not going to be sidestepping them any longer.

'Well, what a surprise,' she gushes, nudging me in the shoulder. 'Eleanor has told me so much about her new job, but she never mentioned you.'

Becker hums, and I contemplate ordering a bucket of wine so I literally *can* drown myself. 'She likes to keep things business,' he muses quietly, pulling my startled eyes to him.

'And what about you?' Mum asks cheekily. I'm suddenly swinging my incredulous look her way. She totally ignores my discomfort. *What is she doing?*

'Mum,' I prompt, but she flat out ignores me, too intrigued by the handsome man in our local. 'Mum, it's time to go.'

'Well?' Mum asks again, and I look at Becker, silently passing a message across, begging him to not feed her interest.

He looks at me and smiles, thinking hard about what he might say. It worries me. Then he sighs and returns his attention to my mum, who is still waiting for an answer. 'I don't want to keep it business, Mrs Cole. I want to be more than her boss.'

I should drop-kick his cheeky arse back to London. What the hell is he playing at?

Mum looks set to faint, her face going red with the pressure to keep her squeal of delight contained. 'Get me another wine, Paul,' she calls, patting the back of Becker's hand. And I just stare at him, at a loss. 'Eleanor, darling.' Mum winks, her lips twisting into an excited smile. 'You little bugger, you,' she whispers, flouncing off to get her wine, lapping up the attention as she goes.

My body goes limp on my stool, and Becker leans into me, pushing his lips to my ear. I only just restrain my whimper as he breathes shallowly. 'I'm going to wait outside for you, princess. If you're not there in ten minutes, don't think I won't come back and collect you myself.' He kisses my cheek gently and squeezes my knee. 'Time's up.' He stands and walks away, fastening the button of his suit jacket as he goes. And what do I do? I join the rest of the women in the pub, including my mother, and admire his perfectly formed backside as he saunters away.

He pulls the door open and looks over his shoulder, finding my eyes. 'Stop looking at my arse,' he murmurs, and then exits, leaving behind a load of potty female hormones dancing around the bar.

'What a darling!' Mum sings, stumbling over to congratulate me. 'Oh, Eleanor, he's perfect.'

I wince as she hauls me in for a hug. Perfectly sinful, that's what he is. 'You don't know him, Mum,' I sigh, breaking her hold.

'So tell me, then.'

I give her a look, one tinged with worry, and thumb over my shoulder. 'You saw him.' How pathetic. I can't come up with something better than that? Actually, no, I can't. Unless I tell her the truth. Which I can't.

'So why have you come running back to Mummy?'

'Because . . .' My words fade, and I frantically search through my mind for the plausible explanation I need. 'I can't get involved with my boss.'

'That doesn't seem to bother *him*.' She clucks my cheek. 'He seems wonderful.'

She's known him for all of three bloody seconds. Good God, if only she knew. I really can't share, and it has nothing to do with my signature on Becker's NDA.

She rubs my arm comfortingly. 'Did he cheat on you?'

'No,' I blurt out, and immediately regret it. I should have said yes. That would have swayed Mum's opinion of Becker perfectly. She saw what I went through after what David did to me.

'Not every man will betray you, Eleanor.'

I adopt something close to a sulky face and turn towards the bar. What does she know? He already has, albeit it in a totally different way. 'Another, please, Paul,' I grumble. 'A big one.'

'Coming up,' he agrees easily, swinging into action. 'Want something stronger?'

My ears prick up. 'You got an anxiety pill?'

Paul laughs, gesturing to the top shelf. 'Take your pick, sweetheart.'

My eyes drift from one end of the top shelf to the other. Yes, I should get plastered so I can't physically walk outside to him. 'Any recommendations?'

'Limoncello,' he suggests, pouring me a shot and passing it over. I neck it at once and slam the glass down, wincing, before I'm quickly baulking at the sight of my mother leaning across the bar kissing Paul.

'Mum,' I cry, watching, totally horrified, as she eats Paul alive. 'Oh God.' I help myself to the bottle of limoncello and pour another, throwing it back, then immediately another, anything to keep me busy. I come up for air and find she's still at it, so I carry on downing the sweet stuff like it's going out of fashion, hoping it might scrub my brain at the same time. Oh my days, this is too much. Trying to accept that she's found a new lease of life is one thing, even if I'm struggling like hell. Watching her gobble the face off that new lease of life is a whole different story.

I'm all out of limoncello.

'Mum, please.'

It takes Paul to detach my mother from his shirt and push her back onto her stool, and she doesn't make it easy for him. 'Sorry, Eleanor.' Paul laughs, a little embarrassed. I want to run away but lurking outside is another brain burner.

I signal to a bottle of limoncello behind the bar, but quickly snatch my hand back, thinking I could do with something even stronger. 'Actually, give me a Jäger.'

Paul fulfils my request quickly, sliding it across the bar

saloon-style. I catch it accurately and throw it back, gasping. 'Perfect.' I cough, wiping my mouth. I just want to get absolutely shit-faced and forget . . . everything.

'I'm not sure getting blind drunk is such a good idea, darling,' Mum pipes up. 'He looked like he wanted a serious talk.'

I laugh loudly and point to my glass again. Paul obliges, and after I've downed another shot, I flop forward and let my forehead meet the bar. Hard. Then I lift and let it fall back down again and again, taking pleasure from the consistent thuds shuddering through my brain. I'm hoping to physically knock some sense into me, because there's a man waiting outside and I'm having to lock down every muscle in order to stop them from engaging and taking me to him. It's like a bizarre magnetic pull hauling me backwards, and it defies everything my pounding head is telling me.

I let loose with a few more head thwacks on the bar, causing an audible bang each time, which I'm sure Becker can probably hear from outside the pub.

'Eleanor,' Mum cries, pulling me back up and checking my forehead. I let my body sag on the stool while she faffs all over me. Then she takes my chin and holds it firmly. 'Now, then. Enough of that,' she says, jiggling my face a little, probably because my eyes are wandering through drunkenness. 'Paul, water, please,' she orders as I blink rapidly. 'Here.' Mum tips a glass to my lips, and I gulp it all down ravenously, joining her in the urgency to cancel out the alcohol that I've just purged on. What was I thinking? Getting drunk would be stupid. I'm better than this recklessness. I pause for thought. Am I really? After all, recklessness got me in this mess in the first place.

I take my palms to my cheeks, rubbing furiously before revealing my face to Mum. 'How do I look?'

'Drunk,' she says on a laugh, brushing my hair from my face. 'How do you feel?'

'Drunk.' I grab another water and chug it down.

'You've had eight minutes.' Paul looks down at his watch and taps the screen. 'You've spent eighty per cent of the time he's given you trying to get blind drunk and the remaining twenty trying to sober up. I don't fancy your chances.' He passes a tequila over. 'If you're unconscious, he can't make you talk, right?'

I gasp at his genius idea and swipe up the glass, but it's intercepted by my mother. Traitor. 'No more,' she snaps, shooing Paul away.

Paul holds his hands up in surrender. 'Sorry, Eleanor. I tried.' He's well and truly under the thumb. *Pussy.*

'It's fine,' I grumble as I stand, surprisingly stable. '*I'm* fine.' I drink in air and take a quick glimpse around the pub, noting that everyone is back to chatting and dancing. 'I'm fine.' I breathe in and out, in and out, in and out. 'I'm really fine.' *Head first, Eleanor. Ignore your stupid heart.*

'One minute left, Eleanor,' Paul calls, and I start to tremble, because one thing I know for sure, beyond all things I know for sure, is that Becker Hunt will be coming to get me if I don't go out there. I'll show strength. He won't break me down. 'Thirty seconds.'

'Oh God.' My shakes intensify as I look at Mum. She smiles. It's a knowing smile. One that tells me she has me all figured out.

'Don't be a fool, darling,' she warns encouragingly.

A fool? Been there, done that. I look away from her before I spill it all, every little detail, so she can really gauge what kind of shit I'm in. This isn't a simple *boy meets girl, girl meets boy, boy messes with girl, girl falls hard for boy, boy fucks up* kinda scenario. I fucking wish it was.

I manage another step, and another, until I'm in my stride and talking some courage into my drunken bones. When I reach the door, I click my neck on my shoulders before straightening them and pulling it open. *Show strength*, I tell myself. Be bold and strong.

Then I see him.

And all of those demands sink like they've fallen into quicksand.

Becker Hunt doesn't lose.

And that fact douses down the fire in my belly.

Chapter 6

He's leaning against the side of his beautiful red Ferrari, legs crossed at his ankles, arms folded across his chest. My head starts to spin, and it has nothing to do with the stupid amount of alcohol I've purged on.

He watches me from across the pavement, his head cocked slightly to the side. 'Just on time,' he says quietly, glancing down at his watch. There's victory leaking from every single delicious pore of his delicious body. I fucking hate him. I fucking adore him. They're conflicting feelings that are driving me positively insane.

'What do you want?' I ask, keeping my distance and grabbing onto my waning determination. I like his confident persona about as much as I like psychological thrillers. Not a lot. They screw with your mind and make you second guess everything.

'What I want,' he murmurs quietly but surely, 'is standing six feet away pretending she doesn't want *me*.'

Time stops still as my mind sprints, reminding me of all the encounters we've had, all of the clashes, the kisses, the touches. 'I'm not pretending.' I could get over the map business, the fact that he's on a desperate treasure hunt that his grandfather has forbidden him to pursue. I even got over his con move on Brent. It's the breaking in and making me fear for my life that I have a problem with. The fact that I'm potentially in danger by association. Funny that.

'The NDA.' His lips barely move as he utters the letters quietly, but he may as well have thrown them at me, because

I feel like they've just slapped me in my face.

'We both know that stupid NDA is a pile of crap.' I laugh, but his expression remains stoic, totally unfazed. 'Do you honestly think it's going to have me running back into your arms? Forgiving you?'

'It was an agreement we made together. Are you breaking it?'

I lob him a filthy look that says more than any words I could spit, and once I'm sure I've burned off a layer of his skin with the fire in my disgusted stare, I make tracks, walking on surprisingly stable legs down the street towards home. 'Yes, I'm breaking it.' I should have stayed at home tonight. Yes, I may have given David the proverbial finger, but I've also rid myself of one arsehole and found myself another to deal with. Except this one is so much harder to tackle – challenging on every level.

'You know I'm going to come after you, Eleanor,' he calls, his feet kicking in as soon as the last word leaves his lips. I speed up. Yes, I know that. I also expect he'll be brushing past me any second and blocking my way. Then we'll do our usual silly dance, me stepping one way, Becker following suit. And then he'll touch me. The thought quickens my heartbeat as well as my feet. 'Life's too short, princess.' He's close, and my deter-mined march turns into a steady jog. 'And you're too—'

'No!' I flip out, skidding to a stop and swinging around to confront him, but Becker doesn't anticipate my move and fails to stop in time. He crashes into me, our chests slamming to-gether, his arms locking around me to steady me. An electric current sails through me, sizzling and robbing me of breath. How? How, after everything that's happened, do I react like this?

Our hearts are pounding into each other. The front of our thighs are pressed together. His groin is pushed into my lower tummy. We're welded together. Everywhere. Stuck. Negative on positive. My heated breaths are ricocheting off his suit jacket, my eyes fixed on his stubbled throat, watching him swallow repeatedly as he holds me. It's not Becker's firm grip keeping us locked together. It's something else, something powerful and unrelenting.

Something I positively hate. Because it feels like it is out of my control.

'Curious not to,' he finishes on a shallow breath of air, his hand sliding onto the back of my head and fisting my hair. He pulls me out of his chest and gazes down at me, face straight. His hazel eyes flit over every piece of my face, a slight frown on his lovely brow. 'I was meant to find you, Eleanor,' he whispers. 'You were supposed to find me.' He nods mildly, like he's instructing me to do the same.

But I don't nod, so he goes on.

'I know I need to prove . . .' His words fade, and I wait pensively for him to find his tongue.

It's a few uncomfortable seconds before I realise that he isn't going to. 'What?' I push.

He looks past me to the wall, evading my eyes.

'What?' I repeat, standing firm. 'Prove what?' I have to force my breathing to become steady, have to force myself not to hold my breath. The lingering silence leaves space for my mind to warp, to think of what he might say.

'I . . .' His mouth opens and closes, his face twisting as the visible evidence of his internal battle holds my attention. 'I . . .' A long inhale of air swells his chest and puts extra pressure on mine. 'It's . . .' He shakes his head in frustration, mussing his hair, closing his eyes tightly behind his glasses. 'Damn it,' he sighs, his refined body going slack. Everything against me softens. The muscles beneath his suit seem to lose their sharp edges, his tense arms fall limply to his side, his face drops, and his eyes take on an edge of desperation. 'I need to prove to you that I'm not the bad guy, princess. And I'll do anything to make you see that. *Anything*.'

Anything? Would he lie? I don't know, and that's a serious problem. Every time I thought I'd figured him out, felt a fraction closer to being safe by putting my heart in this man's hands, he proved me wrong.

'I should have told you about my suspicions. I should have told you I thought the break-in was connected to me. You'll never know how much I regret that, Eleanor.'

'Do you know who did it?'

'No,' he answers assertively. 'We couldn't find a thing – no fingerprints—'

'We?' I recoil, and Becker bites at his bottom lip nervously.

'Percy,' he murmurs, blinking and looking away. 'Percy was there, too.'

My eyes widen. The geeky tech dude? 'Where?'

His expression takes on an edge of shame. 'Behind your front door. He got out undetected.'

'But why?'

'Because he studied forensics. If there's anything to be found, he'll find it.'

'So you dragged him in on your crimes, just like you dragged me into them?'

Becker laughs, and it's all I can do not to slap him for it. 'I dragged Percy nowhere. He works for me. Think Q.'

For a moment, I'm completely confused, but then . . . 'As in James Bond?'

'Yeah, except he's more qualified.' He shrugs. 'I met him at university. Been friends since, although he's somewhat of a recluse.'

Oh my days, someone wake me up. 'And your high-tech genius forensic expert employee friend found nothing?' I ask, and Becker shakes his head. 'And you expect me to believe that?' I move back. 'Like I believed you called the police. Like I believed your pile of horseshit about opportunist thieves?'

'What the hell did you want me to say, Eleanor? That I was

worried one of my enemies had infiltrated your home?'

'Yes! At least then I would know what I was dealing with, Becker. You can't drag me into your corrupt fucking world without giving me the ammo I need to survive it.' *Or the ammo to survive you!*

'You don't need to survive,' he retorts, almost angry. He has a nerve. 'You just need me by your side.'

'Oh, I do? Because since I've had you by my side, I've become a fucking victim, Becker.' My head could explode with stress, but more so with anger. I think, remembering the interest in my position from so many people who I've met since I started working for the Hunt Corporation. Brent, the man who grilled me at Countryscape, Alexa, Paula, various people who I've dealt with on the phone. The list is endless. But what on earth do any of them think they'll find in my apartment? I'm not stupid. Everything I know is in my head, safe, and that's where it'll stay.

The gravity of my situation suddenly feels suffocating. How many people will try to break into my apartment in an attempt to get information? How much danger have I put myself in? Or, more to the point, how much danger has Becker put me in? And what the fucking hell do they think they'll find lying around my home? A long-lost sculpture? 'I am not a victim, Becker. And I won't let you make me one.' I barge past him and get precisely nowhere. I flinch when his hand meets my arm and whirls me around, and an electric charge materialises from nowhere and assaults my nervous system.

'If you think I'm going to make this easy for you, Eleanor, you can think again,' he grates. 'I haven't re-evaluated my entire life and purpose for nothing. I haven't changed all my plans, just for you to walk away from me. No fucking way.' He moves in closer, bringing his mouth uncomfortably close to mine. 'You know in your heart that we were always meant to be,' he whispers. 'You know you can tackle me and everything I throw at you, and I know it too. Do not give up on us, princess. Quitting doesn't suit you.' Becker pulls back a fraction, searching my eyes, swallowing. 'And if you want brutal honesty, I'm fucking lost without you. And though I can find anything in this world I put my mind to, I know I won't find myself if you leave me.'

My backbone goes ramrod straight. My lips part. His angel eyes holding mine are devouring my resilience, eating away at my invisible layers of protection. His words are denting my resolve. Reason is being distorted by the pleading look on his face. Sensibility is being crushed by a familiar riot of relentless hope.

Becker Hunt is utopia. He's a fucked-up kind of ambrosia. He's the only wisp of joy that I've been blessed with in too long. He was meant to find me; I was supposed to find him. Is Becker Hunt my fate? Him and everything that comes with him? His thrilling, dangerous world. Is it where I've always meant to be?

His jaw tightens, and he takes my hand, pushing my touch firmly into his pec. His heart bucks wildly beneath my palm, sending pulses rippling up my arm. 'You know what makes me tick. You know my passion. No woman has ever stirred move-ment here beyond a regular, necessary beat.' He starts to guide my palm around in slow, firm circles. 'But you have. You've opened my eyes and pushed my boundaries. You accepted me. Stood by me. Comforted me. You've given me something besides my work to feel passionate about, Eleanor. And that makes you my most prized, priceless treasure. And you know how I feel about my treasure.'

Tingles. They spring up onto every inch of my skin. Breath. I fight hard to find it. Hope. It's back with a vengeance, and the wall around my heart starts to crumble. This womanising, arrogant player isn't playing any more. I've never seen him look so serious or vulnerable.

I'm in control here. And all I've ever wanted to know is that I'm not wasting my love. To know that if I'm to risk it all,

Becker has to give me something in return. Him. All of him.

This is a guy who fucks like a god on steroids and looks like a god, too. He's a proper man – all masculine, toned, and rough behind those deceiving Ray-Ban spectacles. And he's shaking before me, pouring his heart out, waiting with fear and anticipation for me to speak. I should run fast, leaving a cloud of dust in my wake.

I should.

But I won't.

Because ever since I ran away from him, ran away from London, I've felt misplaced. I've not been *me*. I've just been . . . existing again. I don't want to exist. I want that sense of belonging back. I want the thrilling, exciting adrenalin. I want him. Goddamn me, I want him so much. He's validated all of my hopes. His words are golden.

He's been honest with me.

I steel myself to take a gigantic leap of faith, never letting my eyes stray from his. I'm not out of fight – I have plenty of fight – but am I fighting the wrong thing here? I can't ignore my heart. It's telling me to believe. 'I'm miserable without you,' I admit. 'Empty. Lacking purpose. Unfulfilled.'

Becker deflates before my eyes and moves, taking my chin and getting nose-to-nose with me. 'You never have to be without me.' He takes my mouth gently, kissing me with a tenderness I've never felt from him before.

I whimper. It's a sound of surrender.

Becker growls. It's a sound of power.

And those two signs pave the way for my future.

Is it wrong to want him this much after everything? I don't know, but I feel like a valve has been released on my head, relieving my mind of the pressure of thinking. All I can focus on is my heart, and it's telling me I've chosen right.

I meet his soft rolling tongue and cling onto him. 'I've missed you,' he whispers, working kisses up to my ear and back down again. 'Jesus, Eleanor, I've missed you so much.' He bites my bottom lip and drags it through his teeth, watching me as he does. 'I want you to repeat after me,' he says, pushing his groin into my lower tummy, hiking that unrelenting desire for him. 'Becker Hunt owns me.' He watches me closely. 'Say it.' His jaw pulses from constantly biting down on his back teeth, his angel eyes darkening as they stare me down. 'Say it, princess,' he breathes, desperate and hungry, every part of him spilling with need. Need for *me*. It only enhances my fortitude and reinforces my decision. Becker Hunt needs *me*. And this, this thing he's doing now, demanding I confirm he owns me, is his way of acknowledging that he doesn't have the control here.

I breathe in his face, the strength of his body compressed to mine feeling natural. His weakness makes me feel stronger. 'You will never own me.' I strain the words into something close to a promise, and he smiles. We're still playing that game, except both of us now know the rules, and I definitely know the consequences. Becker is more unpredictable than ever before. More exciting. More irresistible. More magnetic. He's also more desperate. I'm in. Because *out* isn't an option. I've made my choice. I love him, and his wicked truths can't change that.

He drops a soft kiss on my abused lips, and then licks across the seam, from one side to the other. Slowly. 'Your ride awaits.' He weaves his fingers through my hair gently 'Do you need to speak to your mother?'

I glance to the side, seeing the lights from the pub glowing through the windows into the darkness. She's fine, I tell myself. She doesn't need me. But it seems Becker Hunt does.

Chapter 7

I don't remember the drive home. I can only assume the stupid amount of alcohol that I consumed caught up with me and knocked me out. I called Mum as soon as I was deposited in Becker's car, telling her where I was going and why. She dashed out of that pub in those heels like a pro and pretty much dragged me from the car. I was worried for a moment. Until she squeezed me tightly and told me to show Becker what I'm made of. I smiled, because this time I know exactly what I'm made of. And so does Becker.

I conked out within minutes, hearing Becker in my subconscious humming along to Ed Sheeran's 'Shape of You'. I know I was smiling in my semi-conscious state.

I'm in his bed. It's dark, my body warm, the smell oh so familiar. As is the sense of belonging. Rolling onto my back, I stare up at the ceiling, my mind a storm of thoughts. I drop my head to the side, finding I'm alone. Where is he?

I sigh and get up, taking the sheets with me, set to go find him. As I break free of Becker's bedroom space, my steps falter when I register music playing. Soft music. It's familiar, one of those tracks that you know but can't name. Glancing around, I spot a strip of blue illuminated light glowing in the wall, and I pace slowly over, finding a music system built into the wall. The neon display has the name of the track drifting across the window on loop. The Beloved's 'The Sun Rising'.

I watch the letters pass across the lit window for an age, the hypnotic tones making my skin tingle and my heart skip one too many beats. I swallow hard and look over my shoulder, my senses going into overdrive, all the while the words of the track stabbing at my mind, speaking to me, trying to tell me what Becker's state of mind is. He's close by. But he's not here.

My feet are moving before my brain engages, taking me slowly and mindlessly towards the glass wall that guards his grand hall. I hold the sheet close to my body, like it can protect me. But I don't think there's anything that can protect me from Becker Hunt and his debased world. Not my conscience, not my sensibility, and definitely not my heart.

The Grand Hall comes into view below, and I drink it all in, every exquisite inch of it.

And then I see him. He's the most beautiful thing in a room full of some of the world's most stunning treasures. He's naked, sitting in a Louis XIV armchair, his body slumped, his elbow resting on the arm, his heavy head propped on his palm. Every muscle on his torso is accentuated by his position. For once, they don't keep my attention for very long. I look up at his blank face staring at nothing, his glasses resting on his perfect nose. He looks ... lost. Because he is. He's lost in our maze, and it is unfamiliar territory for Becker Hunt. My hand comes up to feel the glass, like in a strange sense I'm telling him I'm here. He left me in his bed to immerse himself in the chaos of the Grand Hall. To find calm amid the bedlam. I know that. Because I know him.

I smile, ignoring the irony of me standing here looking down on him. He's a statue, unmoving for ages, but then his head tilts and his eyes slowly climb the empty space under the mezzanine floor beneath me until they reach the base of the glass wall and take their time creeping up my legs.

Something inside of me explodes when our stares meet. I struggle to catch my breath, my hand dropping from the glass, my body discreetly heaving.

That bang was my heart. It's his, there's no denying it. I'm all his, and it is the best thing that has ever happened to me.

His face is still straight, the contours of his jaw sharp, almost annoyed as he stares up at me like I'm an intruder. I guess I am. To Becker, I'm the worst kind of intruder. I smile knowingly down at him, and he starts to rise from the chair. I watch as he straightens to his full height, taking his sweet time about it, extending the torture of his muscles stretching out with the movement. He's bare. Beautiful. A piece of art.

And I own him. He is my most treasured possession. I love him.

He must see it in me now. It must be written on every inch of my skin. In my eyes every time I look at him.

His lips slowly curve.

It's beautiful.

It's rueful.

It's my Saint Becker Boy Hunt.

I smile right back, watching as he flicks his head a little, indicating for me to join him. I shake mine and do something on impulse, opening up my sheet and exposing my naked body to him. His smile stays firmly in place as his eyes journey down and back up, his head bobbing mildly, silently appraising me. Then he points at his chest before flicking a finger up to the glass, asking if he should come to me.

I nod.

He moves fast, virtually sprinting to the wooden door, and I race to meet him. My heart sings with frantic beats as I dash for the door, throwing it open and charging down the stone steps. The cool air tickles my skin for a few seconds before pure elation snuffs it. That smile. It said nothing and everything.

I hear the slaps of his bare feet hitting the steps, his heavy breathing drowning out my own gasps for breath. And then I see him for a split second before he crashes into me, grabbing me and throwing me against the wall. He says nothing, just attacks my mouth with an unfathomable force, swallowing me up in the passion of his kiss. His tongue stabs and laps greedily, and we moan – desperate, impatient, hungry moans.

He lifts me from my feet and starts to take the stairs, our mouths still sealed, my legs coming up and seizing his waist. My hair is being tugged, his hand is squeezing my bum, and my own hands are going wild, grappling at his naked back. We're frenzied. Mindless. Clumsy and loud. My back meets something soft, Becker coming down with me, his mouth breaking from my lips and nibbling its way down to my breasts as his hand climbs the inside of my thigh.

My head starts to shake from side-to-side as I writhe on his bed, my hands coming up to cover my eyes. His fingers push into me. 'Becker.'

He hums, nipping a nipple in turn, at the same time dragging his hand slowly from between my legs. I bite back my scream, squirming beneath him. 'Over you go.' He takes my hips and flips me onto my front, then starts to pull me to my hands and knees. The gesture snaps me from my euphoria like a bucket of ice water's just been poured over my head.

He wants me from behind? Again? Always from behind. It's never occurred to me before now to wonder why.

Everything inside of me is screaming for me to stop him – to make this time different. Why? Why does he always want me like this? My hands push into the mattress, holding me up, my knees trembling as he tickles a perfectly straight line with his fingertip down my spine. Cognitive thought is near imposs-ible, the sensations and anticipation building under his touch. 'Becker,' I croak, dropping my head, clenching my eyes shut.

'Shhhh,' he hushes me, then knocks all protest out of me when he replaces his finger with his lips, kissing a path down my back, his hand cupping my boob, moulding it meticulously. He's bent over me, devoting his attention to any part of me that he can lay his hands or lips on, driving me insane with need. Then he's gone for a moment. The tear of something tells me why, followed by a sharp inhale of air. 'Ready for a good-fucking-morning?' he asks gently, stroking my bottom.

'Becker.' I'm not sure what I'm begging for. Penetration or an explanation as to why it always needs to be like this. 'Becker, please.' I feel the hot head of his erection meet my sodden flesh, rolling around. I smash my fist into the mattress on a broken scream.

And then he pounds forward on a guttural yell and digs his fingers into my hips. His force nearly has me collapsing to my tummy. I don't know what's wrong with me. I feel weak and unsure whether I can sustain his brutal fucking right now. 'Becker!'

He crashes into me once more, working his way up to a steady rhythm. 'Shit, Eleanor, you feel fucking good.'

Bang!

'No!' I scream, scrambling to escape his power. I free myself from his brutal clutches and swing around, gasping for air as I find my balance and kneel by the pillows.

Becker's arse drops to his heels, panic flooding his features. 'Shit, Eleanor, did I hurt you?' He goes to move forward, to comfort me, but I hold up my hand, forbidding him to come close.

'I want to see you,' I tell him, my voice even and determined.

His brow wrinkles in confusion. 'I don't understand.' He looks away.

Makes two of us, I think, my body going slack. 'I want to see you when we're making love. I want to kiss you.'

His eyes snap to mine, and I can literally see him trying to wrap his head around my declaration. It's not hard. Becker above me. Or even me above Becker. I don't care which. 'Right.' He seems to shake some life back into himself, and slowly, tentatively, like he's scared, he begins to move forward, wrapping a forearm around my waist and pulling my front to his. 'I can do that,' he says quietly. I feel a small, amused smile tug at the corner of my mouth, because that statement was telling himself. Not me.

He slowly lays me down, so gently you'd think I was glass, and I bring my palms up to cup his cheeks. Thoughts run rampant in my mind. Has he never taken a woman like this? Let her see him when he's making love to her? And it's in this moment I consider the possibility that he's never actually made love to a woman at all. He's fucked. There was no sentiment or feelings for him, just raw hard screwing. It's all he knows how to do.

My hands slip from his face when he pulls back. He pushes my legs apart, spreading me wide, then spends a few riveted moments staring down between my thighs. I keep quiet, quite riveted myself by his approach. It's not like he doesn't know what he's doing, more like he's unsure about doing it.

Taking deep drags of air, he reaches down and takes hold of his cock, stroking down the shaft with his fist slowly as he kneels between my thighs. Then he's lowering to me, guiding himself to my entrance, the whole time watching his own actions instead of me. The dash of contact when the tip of his arousal meets my flesh has my hands flying to his shoulders. Becker begins to physically shake. He's beginning to sweat. His face is cut with concentration, his Adam's apple pulsing from his constant swallows. He pushes in a little and closes his eyes, letting his head hang limply. I send my hands on a feeling mission, keen to touch every place I can now that I have the opportunity. My palms slip up each side of his neck, onto his jaw and come to rest on his stubbled cheeks. But his eyes remain closed.

He's half-submerged, tinkering on the edge of full penetration. He's steeling himself, working up to that final push. And then it happens, and my back bows violently, my cry welcoming him into me.

'Good God,' he says quietly, dropping to his forearms, his

head remaining low. His face is so close to mine, but I don't get his eyes. Becker chooses to bury himself in my neck as he starts to pump his hips, gasping each and every time that he enters me. I wrap my arms around his shoulders, holding him to me. He's strong and still so powerful with his drives, albeit more calm and controlled, but I sense he needs the comfort. We moan collectively, slip together perfectly, the feel of him crowding me almost too much. But he still refuses to look at me, so I stroke my way up and take the side of his head, trying to pull him from his hiding place. He won't budge. I give up for a moment, and he continues to plunge deeply, continues to spike all of the sounds of pleasure from both of us. God, I need to see him. So I try again . . . and fail, except this time he doesn't just hold firm, not allowing me to pull him back. He actually shakes his head, like he's shaking me off.

'Becker?' I question, but he ignores me, working up farther still, increasing his pleasure and mine. 'Becker, look at me.'

Nothing. Just more drives and more incredible friction, but the gratification is slipping away with every second he refuses to give me his eyes. Yes, I can feel him, but I want to *really* feel him, see him, read his thoughts.

'Becker.' My frustration is growing with his persistent, stubborn refusals. 'Becker, please,' I yell.

He stops thrusting, freezing above me, panting into my neck. He's still buried balls deep, throbbing within me. But he says nothing.

'Why won't you look at me?' I ask, trying to wrestle him from my body. It's impossible. He's too heavy. 'Damn it, Becker.' My wriggling becomes chaotic and before I know it, I'm jacking my body violently, starting to lose my mind. He has me pinned in place. I'm going nowhere unless he lets me. 'Let me go.'

'Stop.' His soft order breaks through the bedlam of my thoughts. 'Please, stop.'

I do, immediately, his quiet plea assisting in settling my

building frustration. My internal walls are hugging his cock, my muscles contracting without instruction, inviting a counter-pulse, but there's no pleasure now. Just confusion. 'Why won't you look at me?' I repeat, slipping my hands around his back. I can distinguish the tips of ink over his shoulder, outlining the compass of his giant tattoo. I feel compelled to trace the edges softly, ghosting my finger over the ink, still so fascinated by the mammoth piece of art.

'Because.' He breathes heavily, deeply and uncontrolled. Then he growls and lifts, pulling out of me so fast I wince and pull my legs together. 'Because ...' He gets off the bed and starts pacing, irritable and stressed. I watch with concern.

'What?' I ask. 'Am I not easy enough on the eye for you?'

He scoffs, sounding disgusted by my suggestion. 'Don't be stupid, Eleanor. You're beautiful. Everywhere.'

'Then what?' I shout, feeling my control slipping again.

He stops and drags a frustrated hand through his hair, looking up to the heavens for help. 'Fucking hell.' He lands big round eyes on me. It makes me recoil, wary. 'Because,' he begins again, pointing an accusing finger at me. 'If I look you in the eye while I'm inside you,' he heaves, swallowing and sweating. He's getting more and more agitated by the second. Then he roars and flips right into the realms of madness, his fists clenched and coming up to his head, bashing violently on his temples. My eyes widen as he levels a face full of stress on me. 'Because if I look you in the eyes when I'm inside you,' he yells. 'I'm going to fall in fucking love with you!'

If I was standing up, I'd fall over.

'And neither of us need that,' he finishes as he starts to pace again, his anger turning into laughter, his hysterics crazy-like. He's amused at the absurdity of such a thought.

I bubble with resentment, with anger, with pain. What the fuck does he think all this is, then? Why the fuck did he drag me back to London? All those words and the gestures? They meant nothing? He's in fucking denial, and *I'm* fucking livid.

'It's too late!' I scream, all of my emotions bursting out of me before I can stop it, spelling it out for him, sending myself dizzy with the decibel level of my own voice.

He snaps out of his moment and looks at me vibrating on the bed. He's shaking pretty badly himself. Then he bashes the side of his fist on his chest, making me jump. 'I fucking know!' His arms go up in the air manically before dropping limply to his sides, his whole body going lax. 'I know,' he says more calmly. 'I fucking know, Eleanor.'

I try to stop the tiny sob escaping, but it's not a battle I can win. My emotions are in tatters. My shoulders jerk uncontrollably under the strain of it all, the tears just pouring right out of me. I cover my face, ashamed for letting myself fall apart, but they're quickly removed with force, preventing me from evading his probing eyes.

'I love you,' I say, almost apologetically. He doesn't say anything, just smiles and gently takes my arms, pushing them down to the bed, lightly holding them above my head. He seems to have gathered himself, while I've taken over in the wild department, unable to get a hold of my fraying emotions.

'Shhhh,' he whispers softly, resting his lips on my forehead, calming me down. 'Just breathe, baby. Deep breaths.'

Following his soft order, I drink in as much air as my lungs can sustain, fighting to get my sobbing under control. It doesn't escape my notice that he's also sucking in air, fulfilling his own order. His lips are held firmly to my forehead while he waits for both of us to settle, and when that time eventually arrives, he rests his forehead on mine.

And I finally have his eyes. They're dark, swimming with as many emotions as I'm feeling myself – fear, doubt, wonder. 'I know it's too late, Eleanor,' he whispers, breathing in my face as he shifts his hips. My legs spread and relax, inviting him to me. 'What the hell have you done to me?' He swivels and enters me on a meticulous, calculated plunge, and I whimper, my breaths jagged from my fraught state. Becker swallows hard and clenches his teeth but refuses to break our gaze. He doesn't even blink. 'Okay?' he asks, threading his fingers with mine.

I nod, scared to speak for fear of sobbing on him. He mirrors my nod, accepting and satisfied, then brings his lips down to mine. The soft warmth of his mouth brushes gently over mine as he watches me, rearing back slowly and driving forward with equal care. 'Open up to me,' he murmurs against my mouth, kissing one corner. 'Kiss me while I'm making love to you.'

I melt beneath him as he coaxes my mouth open with his tender pecks. We kiss passionately, our exploring tongues rolling and lapping deeply. My hips start to rotate, meeting his grinds, and the whole time our eyes remain locked, gazing at each other while our bodies create sensations like I've never experienced before, and our lips uphold the forever kiss. I'm tingling everywhere, relishing in the feel of our combined sweat making us slip together. The tempo is perfect, accentuating every stroke, his groin creating friction on the tip of my clit which is working me slowly and steadily towards release.

He moans, like he could be in pain, and separates our mouths, but never our eyes. Bursts of air are heating my face, his deep gasps loud. And then he takes a long breath and holds it, and I know he's on his way. My stomach muscles are beginning to ache, but the intense waves of pleasure won't allow me to give them a break. I'm on my way, too. His pace increases, his fingers tighten with mine, and he nods at me, his eyes widening. He's close.

I pant, catching a deliciously deep plunge, flexing my hips to emphasise it. Every muscle tenses and he releases the stream of stored air that he's been holding before gasping for some more and filling his lungs again. 'I'm coming,' I whisper in his face, and he pumps harder as a result, tossing me to the brink. It scizes me from every angle, taking hold of my body and bending it into a violent arch.

His palms are suddenly encasing my cheeks, holding my face. He's staring at me so intensely. 'I want to see,' he pants. 'I want to see the wonder on your face and see if it's anywhere close to how I feel.'

I breathe up at him, my hands grappling at his back as stabs of pleasure attack me, my face contorting, my body tensing.

'Yes, it's that good.' He thrusts one last, firm time and holds himself within me, throbbing dully, my internal walls squeezing him fiercely.

The waves of pleasure keep coming and coming, taking their time to pass over me, sending flurries of goose bumps all over my wet skin. I'm exhausted but bursting with energy. Scared but excited. The man looking down at me has sent my poor mind into a tailspin and my life spiralling into the unknown. My only consolation and comfort comes from the knowledge that I have had the exact same effect on him.

And like he's read my thoughts, his lips twitch and his eyes sparkle. 'Welcome home, baby.' He kisses my cheek tenderly, and then collapses, swathing me in his body. His tongue meets my neck and licks away the sweat, and my chin rests on his shoulder, my arms surrounding him. His weight atop of me feels good. Sharp, heavy, protective, and good.

'Good fucking morning,' I sigh, feeling the weight of the world lift from my shoulders.

Understanding.

We lay there for an age, silent, until I can't take his heaviness any longer.

I wriggle until he lifts from me, looking at me in question. I answer by forcing him to his front. He goes willingly, easily, and I straddle his thighs so I get the whole of his back in view, including his arse. For the first time ever, I'm not drawn to his delectable derrière. My eyes are on his glorious tattoo. I ignore the scratches that I put there.

The elaborate art brings a smile of wonder to my face. I see everything I saw before, all of the intricate detail, it all swelling before my eyes. Tilting my head, I ghost my finger through the UK, letting it drag south until it's drifting through the Mediterranean. There are even dashes of ink that represent the waves of the sea, the names of countries blended into the shaded areas here and there, making you need to cross your eyes in order to see the words more clearly. It's truly incredible.

'Eleanor, I . . .' Becker's words fade to nothing, and my eyes climb the artwork until I have his perfect profile in view, waiting for whatever he's trying to get straight in his head. He sighs. It's a frustrated sigh. 'You irritate the shit out of me.'

I roll my eyes. 'I know.'

'I love it.'

I smile and continue with my studying of the elegant tattoo blanketing his broad back, moving my eyes across the disguised numbers buried in the waves. My lack of response must make him curious, because after only a few seconds, he turns over beneath me and pulls me down by my upper arms until we're nose-to-nose. He narrows his eyes on me, his mind clearly racing. But I remain silent, just staring at him. His lips press together, then he bites on his bottom one, then he flips his eyes up to my red hair, then down to my flushed cheeks, and then, finally, back to my waiting eyes. He practically scowls at me, turning my fixed frown into a hesitant smile. 'How did this happen?' he asks, showing genuine wonder.

'I don't know,' I admit. I did everything to stop it, but it proved unstoppable. I'm just so happy that it's something Becker is equally perplexed by.

'I told you not to fall in love with me.'

'Did you tell *yourself* not to fall in love with *me?*'

'Every fucking second of every fucking minute of every motherfucking day.' He's truly exhausted by it.

I grin. 'And how did that work out for you?'

He laughs under his breath and bites the end of my nose softly. 'Work it out for yourself, princess.' He sighs on a shake of his gorgeous head, as he pushes me up so I'm sitting, straddled on his lap. Then he takes my hands and starts to play with my fingers, weaving and fiddling while he watches. 'This is huge, Eleanor,' he says quietly. I could laugh, but I don't because he's so right. For Becker, the man who'll never allow anyone in, this is fucking colossal. Like ground-breaking huge.

'I know that.' I try to pacify him, like I'm holding his hand so he can get through this revelation. I can only hope he holds my hand, too.

'But if you feel like I do,' he goes on, keeping his eyes on our hands. 'Then that's good, right?' Looking up at me, he gives me a tiny smile. An unsure smile.

'Right,' I exhale, and his twiddling fingers stop with their playing.

'How do you feel?' he asks. This is so strange. He's like a child who has found they're in an unfamiliar situation and is seeking reassurance – any comfort to put them at ease. And I realise, that's exactly what this is. He's frightened, and it's understandable after all of the losses he's suffered. His mum, his dad, his nana.

The anger.

The deep-seated fury that's eating him alive from the inside out. Mr H's blind fury, the words he yelled at Becker when he found out he'd ripped off Brent Wilson. *Revenge.* I want to know about his father, ask *why* he holds the Wilsons responsible, but I'm also very wary of the nerves I might hit. The pain I will spike.

You've taken enough from me already. You're not taking Eleanor.

The revelation I'm faced with right now, the fact that Becker's in love with me, is causing him enough stress. I need to let him get used to it, get used to *me*, before I ask any more about the Hunt family legacy. Shit, I need to wrap my own head around this, too.

A sharp flick of Becker's hips upward knocks me from my daydream, and I blink my eyes, finding him regarding me closely. 'How do you feel?' he asks again.

I smile and flex my hands, prompting him to release his hold so I can trace the sharp edges of his lean chest. I concentrate on my slow drifting finger as I ponder what I should say. 'I feel light,' I say quietly, circling his tight nipple, smiling when it stiffens under my touch.

He flicks his hips up again, jolting me. 'You don't feel very light to me.'

Pinching his nipple, I twist, throwing him a dirty look. I don't take it to heart. He loves my arse.

Becker seizes my hand, eyebrows high in warning. 'Don't make me spank you,' he says seriously. I wriggle a little, missing the delicious warmth that his spankings leave behind.

'You have an arse fetish,' I say coolly, holding back my grin.

Becker doesn't. He gives me a blinding, adorable, cheeky smile and slides his hands onto my bottom, squeezing gently for a few teasing seconds, watching me. Then his hands leave my skin and I suck in breath, holding it, waiting. And damn if I don't lift a little, giving him better access, inviting him.

Slap!

Both hands come down hard, knocking me forward a little. 'Only a fetish for *your* arse, princess.'

My hands plant into his pecs, bracing myself, and my hair falls forward onto his chest as I breathe through the discomfort. 'Holy shit,' I whisper brokenly.

He performs a calculated swivel of his groin and takes the tops of my arms, pulling me down to him. 'What else do you feel?' he asks.

'Like my backside's on fire.'

'Shhhh . . .' His pouting lips nearly touch mine, the low sound of his sexy shush sending a flurry of tingles down to my toes. 'Tell me how you feel about *me*,' he pushes.

'Right now, I want to slap you.'

'I feel like that about you *all* the time.' Becker's grip of my arms clamps down some more, encouraging me to spill. His eyes are close to mine, curiosity on hesitation. I'm holding back – a crazy thing to do given where we've found ourselves this morning. All of the confessions, the revelations, the feelings. 'I feel light,' I say again, but this time he doesn't make any sarcastic wisecrack. He just holds me suspended above him by the tops of my arms, my hair spilling around his head, forming a kind of private veil around us. 'Like I'm floating.'

He holds onto his smile, keeping it back, but his angel eyes are firing off sparks of happiness. 'Go on,' he prompts, desperate for more. It's all reassurance to him, like I'm confirming what he's feeling himself. That it's okay to love me.

'I feel like I'm lost in a maze,' I whisper, my gaze falling to his lips, seeing them parted and wet, full and ready to taste. 'And I have no desire to find my way out.' I look up at him when I hear a tiny hitch of his breath, seeing his eyes have glazed slightly. He gets it. He knows just how I feel.

'Like every corner you turn is a surprise?' he murmurs, swallowing. 'Like you can't figure out if each step is an exciting stumble or a petrifying stagger?'

I bite my bottom lip. Yes, that's exactly it.

'Like,' he blinks slowly, keeping his eyes shut for a few moments, before dragging them open and flexing his fingers, releasing me a little before squeezing, as if to reinforce his point. 'Like none of that shit matters as long as you're stumbling and staggering with me?'

I'm done. I can't hold back any more. The lump in my throat swells and chokes me, and a drop of my emotions trickles down my cheek. It's relief, and I nod, unable to speak through the bulge that's blocking my throat. This is everything. This is acceptance, and it looks good on him. He smiles, a true happy smile, and releases my arms, letting me fall onto his chest.

'Me too, princess.' He pushes his mouth to my ear, kissing me hard and squeezing me until I think my bones might crumble under his power. 'Me too.'

My cheek rests on his shoulder, my upper arms sprawled above, encasing his head. I feel small in his hold. Safe in his hold. I shouldn't entrust my heart to this man, but the fact that he's entrusting his to me makes this even ground. And now I'm trusting him to protect me from his debasing world.

'Eleanor?' he says, turning his face into my neck and breathing in. I hum, and he goes on. 'Will you be my girlfriend?'

I feel his grin stretch against my neck, and, I swear, I smile the widest I ever have. 'I will.'

'And Eleanor?'

I hum again, and this time he pulls himself free from my neck and gazes at me. 'I love you.' His voice is barely a murmur, hardly heard.

But it's the loudest thing that anyone has ever said to me.

And the most significant.

Because Becker Hunt said it.

Chapter 8

Becker left me to snooze while he took a shower, and I don't think my secret smile left my face the whole time that I listened to the water raining down on him. After smothering my face in kisses that had me giggling like I've never giggled before, then flipping me over and giving my arse a welcome-back slap, he dressed and left me in his bed.

That smile of mine was still with me while I showered and dressed, but it slowly dropped away with each step I took down the stone staircase. And now it's gone completely, and I'm sitting on the bottom step, spinning my phone in my hand, a little nervous. I can hear activity in the kitchen from two old people that I can't wait to see . . . but also can.

It's only just occurred to me, after leaving the blissfulness of Becker's apartment, that I have no idea what to say to Mrs Potts and old Mr H. What has Becker told them? Do they know why I wasn't in work yesterday? My thumb replaces my lip for something to nibble on, and I peek down the corridor to the kitchen door, wondering what to do.

My phone jumps to life, ringing in my hand, and my arm jolts upward in fright, sending it sailing through the air. 'Shit,' I curse, scrambling to gather it up when it lands a few feet away. Lucy's name flashes up at me, and my hand retracts like it's been electrocuted. My fist balls and comes up to my mouth, my teeth clamping over it as my face screws up in dread. She doesn't know I'm back. How am I going to explain? I don't know, but speaking to Lucy means delaying having to face Mrs

Potts and old Mr H. So I take the call.

'Hello.'

'Morning,' she sings. 'When are you coming home?' Home. The small word makes me smile, but every muscle in my achy body tenses, and my arse is suddenly burning again. Oh yes, I'm home.

'I'm back.'

'You are?' she blurts out, surprised.

I hum my confirmation. It's a cop-out. A guilty sound. And she doesn't miss it.

'Where are you?' The suspicion in her tone cuts right through my conscience. I can't lie.

I wince before I answer, preparing myself for her reaction. 'At work.'

'What?' she shrieks, and my face screws up again, knowing she isn't done. 'For the arsehole?' she asks. 'The womanising prick?' She goes on. 'The—'

'Yes,' I grate, clenching my phone so hard to my ear, I'm in danger of crushing it with my bare hand.

There's a brief silence. She's thinking. 'We need to talk,' she says, and I laugh sarcastically because she's right. There's no way I can analyse this crazy shit storm alone. I need her. Even if just to hug me. 'Lunch?'

'Um,' I look towards Becker's office, then back to the kitchen. I have no idea how today is going to pan out. I need to talk to her desperately, but I also need to figure out some stuff here, namely Mrs Potts and old Mr H. I also have work to catch up on.

'Please,' she murmurs dejectedly.

I frown down the line. 'What's happened?'

'I'm just feeling needy.'

'Because?'

'Because Mark's department is having a night out, a certain someone is going, and I'm not.'

A certain someone. 'Printer-room girl from floor eighteen.'

'Yes,' Lucy squawks. 'Yes, she's fucking going, and I don't trust her one little bit, Eleanor. Not one little bit. She's been sniffing around, making excuses to be near Mark's desk, and it always happens to be when I'm not around. I come back, and the girl on the desk next to me tells me. Every fucking time. I've started to hold in my pee all fucking day so I don't have to leave my desk, and I only go out for lunch when Mark does. I'm going fucking insane.'

I recoil, keeping my phone at a safe distance while I let her rant settle. She sounds borderline psychotic, but I hold my tongue, keeping my thoughts to myself. 'But Mark's really into you,' I point out the obvious with nothing better springing to mind, and anyway, my observation is valid. I've seen how he is with Lucy. She's just being paranoid. 'Talk to him. Tell him it's bothering you.'

'I'd rather talk to her,' Lucy gripes. 'With my fist.'

An unattractive snort of laughter shoots from my mouth and echoes around the corridor, and I quickly look from left to right, ensuring no one has come to investigate the noise. 'I'll meet you outside your office.' She needs me. I can't deny her a needed pep-talk, especially after all the moral support she's given me over the weeks. 'One o'clock?'

'Thanks,' she breathes, relieved.

'See you soon.' I hang up and stand up, ready to face Mrs Potts and Mr H, but my steps slow before I reach the kitchen until I'm at a standstill. Then I start backing away, my bravery deserting me. I need information. I need to know the score. I need to know what they know.

I turn and go to Becker's office. We've covered significant emotional ground, but now it's back to work. Now he's my boss again – my arrogant, testing boss. The boss I just confessed my love to. The boss who just confessed his love to me. My nerves intensify while my eyes journey across the intricate carvings of the door, the Garden of Eden and that huge fucking apple glaring at me. Forbidden fruit. The devil.

Stabilising my breathing, I push my way into his office, finding his work space empty. Oh. So where is he? I wander in and decide to call him, rather than search every possible room in The Haven, but a noise from behind has me whirling around, surprised.

I find nothing, just the wall of ceiling high bookshelves. 'What was that?' Keeping still and quiet, I listen carefully as my eyes scan Becker's palatial office. I'm not liking the goose bumps that have jumped onto my skin. Nor the increased beats of my heart.

Then I hear it again – something like a shifting of wood. It's faint, but I still jump like a scared cat. My feet are in action before I can tell myself to be rational. If my senses want to get me away now, then I'm not going to argue with them. I zoom from Becker's office and shut the door behind me, immediately dialling him. His silly little rule in the NDA – the one that states I must answer within five rings, better apply to him, too.

He answers in two. 'Princess?'

'Where are you?' I ask, my jumpiness mixing with a bit of impatience. I sound plain wound up. Or spooked. Or both. Is this place haunted?

'You okay?' He's obviously sensed it.

'No, I think there's ...' I drift off, quickly reasoning with myself. I think there's what? A ghost in his office? He'll think I've lost my mind. 'Where are you?' I breathe.

'In my office,' he states, nonchalant and calm, prompting a massive frown to wriggle its way onto my forehead.

'What?' I turn and come face to face with Eve and the gigantic apple again.

'I'm in my office,' he repeats, still super cool.

I turn the handle and push the door to his office open, remaining on the threshold, wary. 'But I ...' My words fade to nothing, because, low and behold, there he is, sitting at his desk. *What the hell?*

Becker looks up at me, smiling coolly. He looks pristine, suited and booted. Deliciously sinful. My phone is still held limply in my grasp, hovering at my ear, whereas Becker has taken the initiative to disconnect the call.

'You okay?' he asks, taking his glasses from his face and cleaning the lenses.

I crane my neck so I can scan his office, rather than stepping inside. 'Fine,' I murmur mindlessly.

'You coming in, or are you just gonna hover on the edge of my Garden of Eden?' His silly joke doesn't have the desired effect, my mind too puzzled, though an appropriate, very vivid image of Becker munching on a ripe, juicy apple does tickle the corners. Tossing it aside on this occasion is easy.

'How long have you been in here?' I ask, taking tentative steps as I let my phone drop from my ear.

'Since I left you in bed.' He watches me approaching him like he's dangerous, a questioning look on his face. I can't blame him; I must look super suspicious, but I'm not at liberty to feed his obvious curiosity because I haven't a clue what's just happened. I must be losing my mind. He wasn't in here. I'm not asleep and dreaming, though I nearly pinch myself to check. So what the hell is going on?

When I arrive at Becker's desk, he raises his eyebrows in prompt for me to enlighten him on my peculiar behaviour. 'All right?' he asks when it becomes obvious that I'm far from forthcoming. He slips his glasses back on, blinking a few rapid times as he does. His action draws my attention to something on his eyebrow, now half concealed by the thick frames of his glasses. I reach over his desk, and his eyes follow the path of my hand, until I press the tip of my index finger onto the edge of his well-defined brow.

'You have something here,' I say, wiping at the grey smudge.

The smear is large, and it doesn't disappear with one swipe of my finger.

Becker withdraws from my reach, his hand coming up and dusting away the remnants of . . . whatever it is. 'Probably soap.' He dismisses it easily, not even looking at what he's wiped from his face, before taking his attention to something on his computer screen.

Silence falls. An awkward silence. I haven't made it awkward. He has, by the way he's blatantly feigning concentration on his screen. I start to chew on the inside of my lip as I unbend my body from over the desk, bringing my thumb to meet the tip of my index finger and rubbing what I've wiped from Becker's brow between them. I try to be as casual as possible, glancing around the office as I do. Whatever I wiped away feels . . . dusty. Abrasive. Not soapy.

He's being all shifty and it's bothering me. 'I don't think it's . . .' Something catches my eye near the bookcase adjacent to Becker's desk. I frown, tilting my head thoughtfully.

'What?' Becker asks. He doesn't sound too cool and collected now. *Now* he sounds a little worried.

'What's that?' I ask, making tracks towards what's holding my attention on the bookcase. It's a sliver of light running from top to bottom of the old wood, straight down the middle. It becomes more obvious the closer I get, the gap widening to about a centimetre. My feet speed up instinctively, but just as I engage my arm to reach for the protruding wood, Becker barges past me and lands in front of the bookcase, leaning back against the unit. The gap disappears, assisted by his weight pushing into it, and I pull back my outreached arm on a tiny gasp of alarm. The noise of the dislodged piece of bookcase locking into place is a similar sound to what I heard when I was alone in here a few minutes ago. Or, apparently, not alone.

'That's nothing,' he spits out fast before slamming his lips together, a silent sign that he won't be forced to say anything more on the matter. Is he fucking kidding me? I know my current facial expression pretty much spells that out for him. I must look like someone's just told me that the government's upping the age restriction on alcohol to sixty.

He glances away guiltily. He shouldn't have. I've just spotted another speck of powder under his earlobe, but instead of telling him so, I simply reach forward and wipe it away again, this time holding my finger between us instead of dusting it off. His head doesn't turn, but his eyes do. They fix to the tip of my finger and remain there until I decide he's had enough time to look at the offending flicks of . . . whatever it is. *What is it?* I don't know, but it's adding to my boyfriend's nervousness, and it's rubbing off on me. There's a room behind this towering bookcase, and I want to know what's in there.

'Open the door,' I demand, jaw tight.

Becker looks as guilty as sin. Appropriate. He's not going to budge. Fine.

I start to pull books out from the shelves, one after the other, waiting for one to click and release a secret door. I feel stupid, but how else will it open? This is how it's done in the movies. One has to work.

'Eleanor, stop.' He grabs me and pulls me away.

'Then open it.'

'For fuck's sake,' he grumbles, positioning me to the side, his muttered curses coming thick and fast. Giving me a scowl of epic proportions, one that I return, probably fiercer, he reaches past a book and pulls. 'Have it your way.' Something clicks, and a whole section of shelving releases, creaking open a few inches.

I inhale, stepping back, as does Becker, giving me free access. I look at him, and his eyebrows raise, his arm swooping out in sarcastic gesture to go right ahead. I bite my lip and tentatively reach forward, taking the side of the wood and pulling it towards me. It's heavy, but Becker doesn't help me out, just stands to the side, watching me struggle. *Arsehole.* Does he think I'll give up? Of course he doesn't. Using my free hand, I haul the huge door open, the hinges creaking eerily.

My mouth falls open when the small room comes into view. Lumps of metal, wood and stone litter the space, as well as chisels and hammers of every shape and size. There are shelves, all packed full of sculptures, all different kinds – busts, animals and figurines. None of them are familiar, but they're all amazingly well-carved pieces. And then I frown when I see a drawing of a sculpture that I recognise, the surface dusty, the edges curling. '*Head of a Faun*,' I say to myself, tilting my head, reaching for the tatty piece of paper.

And then I gasp, retracting my hand like the sketch could have just burst into blazing flames before me. Thoughts, lots of them, rush around in my head. His con-move, *Head of a Faun*, the unidentified dirty mark I've just wiped from his face. The fact that my boyfriend is a sweet con artist.

And just like that, the obscenest thought of all starts to poke at the corner of my mind. It's so crazy, it should be easy to push it aside, disregard it. It's outlandish. Ridiculous. Yet I can't shake the suspicious feeling, because many things about The Haven, the Hunt Corporation, and Becker Hunt are ridiculous. And now this hidden room? And these tools? And that picture of the long-lost sculpture?

I study the man before me closely, the poke on my mind becoming more of a vibration as I mentally revisit our time at Countryscape. How composed and prepared he was during the bidding of *Head of a Faun*. How he knew it was a fake.

Becker's jaw clenches, his eyes locked on mine, unwavering. 'Say it,' he whispers demandingly, face straight. 'Say it, princess.'

I'm transfixed by his depraved beauty. Someone so shady shouldn't be this good-looking. It's like a fucked-up kind of bait. A dangerous temptation. I'm getting mad just thinking about how damn alluring Becker Hunt is as my brain is trying to piece together what I'm about to ask and how I should position it. There's no right way. However I ask, it won't change the answer.

So I dive in feet first and ask my question. My ridiculous, outlandish question. 'How good are you at sculpting?' I immediately drag in air and store it, bracing myself.

He smiles, amused by my approach. 'A fucking master,' he replies clearly, no holding back, as plain and simple as that.

The fucked-up, corrupt world I'm in stops spinning.

Chapter 9

'Oh my God.' I reach for the bookcase, drinking in air, my heart going from nought to sixty in a second. 'Oh my God, oh my God, oh my God.' My world might have stopped spinning, but my head is making up for it. I'm dizzy. I can't see, can't breathe, can't form a coherent sentence. I feel like I'm suffocating. My hand grapples at my neck and my body rolls with waves of panic.

'Eleanor?'

I blink, trying to gain focus, trying to see him, as a tidal wave of information pours into me, making everything clear. 'You're a forger,' I hiss. 'You forged the fake *Head of a Faun* and made sure Brent bought it!'

'Shhhh.' Becker moves in close, taking my arm, but I doggedly brush him off. That wasn't his usual sexy shush. That was a short, sharp gust of breath. He's mad with me. The nerve!

'Don't shush me,' I wail, but then I slap my own hand over my mouth before Becker does, because I've just realised that his granddad is in the kitchen down the hall and he won't know this. He can't know this. It'll finish him off. God, I remember him asking Becker if there was any clue to who crafted the fake that he was supposed to call out as a forgery. Little did Mr H know, his grandson fucking sculpted it. Oh . . . my . . . God. Of course Becker wasn't going to declare it a fake. He made it. He plotted the whole damn thing from beginning to end.

'Eleanor, calm down.' Becker practically shakes me from my meltdown and my morals suddenly appear from nowhere and bite me on my sore arse. I don't know where they've been all this time, leaving me to get wrapped up in all of this . . . this . . . this . . .

'Oh my God.' Tricking someone doesn't seem so bad now. Even ripping someone off for a whopping fifty million seems quite tame. But forging a long-lost treasure? What else has he forged? I'm a criminal if I stay here. Already am if I escape. Just being here, working here, implicates me. I'm Becker's Bonnie. He's my Clyde. Okay, so we don't shoot people, but some people in the antiquing world might see this as equally immoral. Because it is. Another crime. They're building by the day. What else is there?

Fucking hell, pull yourself together, Eleanor.

'How many priceless treasures have you forged?' I ask.

'Just the sculpture,' he answers easily and willingly, shutting me up. He shrugs a little, shyly. 'I sculpt as a hobby. It relaxes me. And I'm quite good at it.'

I'm speechless. Nearly. 'I need air.' I turn, but he catches my wrist, holding me in place.

'Eleanor, you're not leaving,' he says with a determination that snaps me from my spiralling thoughts.

'You'd better tell me everything,' I whisper-hiss in his face. 'Everything, Becker Hunt. I want to know it all – your mum, your dad, your vendetta against the Wilsons. I'm not leaving until I have every scrap of information in that fucked-up, corrupt mind of yours.' I rap on his temple, like a copper knocking on a door. Good Lord, the police.

'What do you mean, *you're not leaving until you know everything*?' He hones straight in on that part of my rant, which should probably ease me a little. 'You're not leaving full stop.' He's worried about me running away again. Good! I'm a gangster's moll. Sculpting a fake, paying someone to authenticate it? Planting it in a house so it's found, the auction, the act . . .

'Talk, Hunt. Talk now.'

He matches my determined stare, his chest puffed out, his jaw tight. It's a standoff. He better be prepared to lose. 'Fine.' I pass him and get precisely nowhere.

'Eleanor,' he breathes, catching me around the waist and lifting me from my feet.

'You'd better start talking,' I hiss, wrestling with his hands around my waist. 'I didn't come back so you could carry on with the lies, Hunt.'

On a bark of irritation, he dumps me on my feet harshly, his frustration getting the better of him. 'Keep your voice down, Eleanor.'

I'm quivering with fury, and I have a boatload of determination backing it up. He better not underestimate me. 'Talk!'

I see the moment he comprehends that I'm not backing down because he clams up. That angry look, the unique one that only shows when his parents are mentioned, is present, but it's not scaring me away this time. His hesitance isn't because he's reluctant to spill about his crimes. He's actually more reluctant to share the story of his parents. He doesn't want to talk about it, wants to avoid the pain. But he's putting me in the centre of his corrupt world. He can't be selective with the information he provides to help me survive it. 'All or nothing,' I say.

He balls his fist and brings it to his forehead, banging repeatedly as he clenches his eyes shut. 'Fine, I'll tell you about my mum and dad, and then you'll understand why I forged *Head of a Faun* and made sure that arsehole bought it.' He stomps off across his office, leaving me stuck to the carpet where he plonked me, and on a roar of agony and grief, he throws his fist into the back of the solid wooden door.

I flinch, watching as he pulls his arm back, ready to hit the door again. 'Becker, stop.' I hurry over to him and seize his balled fist before he can land the door with another brutal punch, though he doesn't make it easy for me, resulting in a tug of war that I refuse to lose. 'Stop!' I yell, wrenching at his arm. His eyes are wide, revealing all of his anguish as he heaves before me, more through emotion than physical exertion. 'Just stop it.'

He gasps for breath and throws his arms around me, squeezing me to his chest. I'm struggling to breathe, being suffocated, but I endure his fierce hug, let him swathe me until he's ready to let go. 'Mum was in a car accident,' he spits the words into my neck urgently, his voice rough and broken. But he isn't telling me anything that I don't already know. It was front-page news. The whole world knows his mum died tragically in a car accident.

I try to wriggle from his hold, failing miserably. 'Becker, let me see you.'

'No, just stay where you are for a minute.' His strong arms lock down some more, making escaping impossible. 'She was on life support for three weeks. Almost every bone in her body broken.'

I wince and swallow.

'Her brain showed no signs of activity.'

'Becker—'

'Dad signed the papers to switch off the life-support machine. I didn't want him to, but he said even if she survived, she wouldn't be his Lou any more. Wouldn't be my mum.' I want to tell him to stop, but I realise that sharing this with me, albeit almost robotically, is a huge breakthrough for him. I need to let him do it, no matter how hard I'm finding it to listen. Hard, but not as hard as it would be to live it. I've had my own loss, but the burden of such a decision to turn off your loved one's life support doesn't bear thinking about. Or, more to the point, *not* having that decision. Becker didn't want to give up on her. 'I couldn't watch,' he whispers.

My eyes flood with tears that I'm fighting so hard to hold back. 'I'm so sorry.'

I feel his head nod a little. 'She was on her way to the bank to put the map in Dad's safety deposit box.'

This piece of information comes from leftfield, and I spring from his arms, looking up at him with all the shock that statement deserves. 'What?'

'Dad kept the map here at The Haven,' he tells me, void of emotion. 'Mum found it and wasn't happy. She said it should be somewhere secure and took it upon herself to take it to the bank before Dad could stop her. Someone went into the back of her car at the lights. Pushed her onto the crossroads.'

I don't like his vacant expression. Or what he's just said, because after everything I've just heard, my mind is spinning with where this is leading.

'She didn't stand a chance.'

I flinch. It would be so wrong for me to cry when Becker's forcing himself to keep it together.

'When Dad got her belongings back from the hospital, the map was gone.'

My stomach bottoms out, and I gawp at him as he watches me, totally stoic. So many questions are whirling around in my head, but I'm not sure which one to fire at him first. Plus, I need to be able to string a sentence together, and I'm incapable of speech right now. But my vision seems to have become hypersensitive, and I can see with frightening clarity what's lingering behind Becker's angel eyes. All of that anger and hurt, resentment and turmoil, it's all there and it's more potent than ever before.

'The Wilsons,' I only manage those two words, but it's all I need. Becker nods his head, and as if I need the horror story to continue, he goes on.

'I know it was Brent's father. He killed my mum and took the map.'

'How do you know?' I whisper, worried.

Becker watches me closely, doubling my worry, because right

now he's monitoring my face for a reaction to what he's going to say next.

I step back, swallowing. 'How?' I ask. I'm ready.

'Because my dad stole it back.'

Or not ready. 'Oh God.' I grab the nearby clock for support, but my evident shock doesn't hold him back. He's on a roll now, bombarding me with it all.

'After Mum died, Dad may as well have been dead, too. He was ruined. Consumed by guilt. The police put it down to a tragic accident. Case closed. They refused to look into any of the evidence we gave them.' His lip curls at the mention of the police. 'Dad went away for a while. Said he needed to be alone. That's what he told me and Gramps, anyway.'

I look at him in silent question.

'He followed Brent's father to Florence.' He speaks with a hatred that's terrifying. 'Why do you think Brent's father was in Florence, princess?'

Fuck me, I'm shaking, and there's nothing I can do to stop it. 'Because the missing piece of map includes Italy. Florence is in Italy. The garden of San Marco was in Florence.' I mumble it all mindlessly. 'And the Garden of San Marco is where the Magnificent discovered Michelangelo's talent for sculpting. Brent's father was taking an educated guess without the missing piece of the map.' Good bloody God, this is getting more real by the word. 'But there's Rome, there's Bologna, there's Venice. Michelangelo travelled with his commissions.'

Becker nods his agreement. 'I told you. They're amateurs. I spent three years between the three cities and found nothing. Dad tracked Brent's father to Florence. Found him chasing his tail. He stole the map back and posted it to me.'

I drop my eyes to the carpet, trying to rummage through the chaos in my mind, trying to get it all straight. That missing piece, so small but so significant. *Head of a Faun* can't be found without it, if it even exists. It might not exist. Chances are it doesn't. But only the missing piece can clear up the mystery. I consider, just for a moment, whether I should tell Becker that I know where he's hiding the map. The words tickle the tip of my tongue, but I suck them back. His mother and father died because of that map. I can't blame him for wanting to keep it secret and hidden, if only for his own sanity.

'That was the last we heard from Dad,' Becker exhales and takes his fingers under his glasses, rubbing into his eye sockets. 'Then the Italian authorities found him.'

I blink my wide eyes, my mouth drying up. 'Mugging gone wrong,' I whisper, everything falling into place. I need to sit down. My legs are wobbly, and my head could explode with information overload. Stumbling across his office, I land in a chair with a thud. The families' rivalry, the hate, the suspicion, the ramifications of it all.

'No police help *again*,' Becker grinds on. 'The only thing that would have brought my father back to life after my mother died would have been finding the missing piece of the map and finding the sculpture. It gave him the purpose he needed. He felt she died for nothing.'

I get that, but more frightening is the fact that Becker feels the same as his father, except probably on a more intense level. He's lost both of his parents. He has double the resentment. And old Mr H's fear is now all too reasonable. He doesn't want to lose his grandson – his only living relative – like he did his son, daughter-in-law, and his own wife, albeit in different circumstances. But it all boils down to that map. Mr H is prepared to sweep all of the awful circumstances under the carpet, try to make peace with the Wilsons, in order to keep his grandson safe from the curse of the map? No wonder he was so mad with Becker when he found out he'd conned Brent. Becker's lied to him. He promised his gramps he was letting it go, but he did that to protect the old man. My Lone Ranger wanted to find that sculpture to avenge his parents' deaths and to fulfil his dad's wish. He wanted to do it with no risk of further heartache to his grandfather. So he closed himself off, limited any emotional attachment to his gramps, and anyone else, for that matter. My poor, vulnerable, complex man.

'The Wilsons are the immoral ones here, princess. Not me.' Becker's eyes cloud over. He goes to his desk and slumps in the chair, his tall body reclined back. He looks so tired all of a sudden, worn down, as he pulls something from his pocket and studies it, soon becoming lost in a daydream. 'She was so beautiful,' he says quietly, taking his index finger to his top lip and brushing lightly from side-to-side, deep in thought. 'My dad worshipped the ground she walked on. Was broken when he lost her.'

My tummy flutters with nerves that befuddle me. He looks peaceful now, at ease and stable. It throws me. I should be relieved that he's finally sharing his heartbreak with me, but while there's gratitude, there's a massive cloud of apprehension fogging it.

I watch him as he studies what I assume to be a photograph of his mother. 'You're beautiful,' he whispers to himself, and then he looks at me. The hurt in his eyes nearly knocks me from the chair to my arse, and I realise that statement was meant for me. 'Just the thought of not having you around feels unbearable.' His face twists, like he's pissed off that he's found himself thinking like that, let alone feeling like it.

This should spike the most incredible sense of satisfaction in me. But it doesn't. Becker Hunt prides himself on being impenetrable. He's a lone wolf. Lets no one get close to his heart in an extreme attempt to prevent himself from getting hurt, to stop him from experiencing the same devastation that his father did when he lost his mum. To let nothing get in the way of his mission to find that sculpture. It would be easier for him to walk away from me, rather than deal with these feelings that have caught him off guard. It would be easier for him to let me go and continue his search for the sculpture. I thought he'd turned a corner, come to terms with me and what's evolved between us, but seeing his turmoil, seeing the despair on his face, makes me realise that accepting this is a constant challenge for him.

'I feel like you've performed a smash and grab on my heart, princess.' Becker pulls his glasses off and chucks them on his desk, along with the picture, before taking his palms to his face and rubbing furiously. 'You've proper screwed me over. You weren't part of my plan.'

'And you weren't part of mine, either.' It's true. There have been plenty of times I could have walked away – and sometimes did – but Becker always brought me back round, or simply brought me back. It's instinctual. For both of us. Like a magnetic force keeping us close. I'm so over fighting with what nature intends. And it clearly intends that we be together. No matter who he is and the secrets he has to tell, I'm supposed to be here with him.

His face appears from behind his palms. 'I have a question for you,' he says, startling me.

A question for me? Lord, I could think of a thousand for him. 'What?' I ask warily.

He points to his secret room, indicating to the place where he carved the forged treasure. 'Do you love me any less?'

'No.' My answer topples past my lips with not a shred of hesitation, and he visibly loosens up in his chair.

'I'm still me, princess,' he whispers. 'I realise this is a lot for you to take on board, but you need to always remember one thing. The most important thing.'

I don't ask what that is. I already know, but he tells me anyway. 'I love you.'

I nod mildly. I never doubted it. I've been corrupted for love. He must know that nothing will chase me away. As long as he gives me his all, I'm going nowhere. All of him, all of his secrets. Beneath his confident outer layer is a scared boy. A man who dreads losing anyone close to him, so he's always kept himself emotionally detached and worshipped inanimate objects instead, and given no time to anything that could make him waver in his determination to find what he's looking for.

And, God, if all that doesn't make me love him even more.

I stand and wander over to him, feeling the tug between us getting stronger the closer I get. He pushes away from his desk in his chair and pats his lap. 'Jump on.'

Offering a small smile, I sit on his lap and rest my back against his chest, melding myself to him on a sigh. Strong arms come around me and hold me tightly, his face disappearing into my neck. 'I've been searching for that sculpture for years, Eleanor. But I've found something more precious. More valuable. Something I want to cherish more, admire more, love more.' He squeezes me. 'I found you. And you're far more important than a piece of stone.'

This moment in time. This is magic. The fact that all of our turmoil and conflicting feelings were worthwhile. That I have something to show for it after going through so much. I have Becker. And he has me. It's a win–win, but something else is frightening me now. He wants revenge, not by hurting anyone, but by finding what his father searched for and what both his parents died for. It's like a strange kind of peace-finding mission. I'm scared he'll never be able to move forward, get on with his life with me, until he finds what his whole family has searched for. Everything he's done to this point would be meaningless if he gives up now. I understand the deep part of him that needs to find that treasure or find out if it even exists. Not wants to but *needs* to. But I love him too much to risk losing him. Like his father lost his mother, like his granddad lost his son . . . like Becker lost his parents. While he's willing to put himself in the thick of danger, he's not willing to expose me to it. And that's another reason why he's stopped.

That's the crux of it. The danger. He fears for me. It should comfort me. Should. It doesn't, though. Because I have serious doubts that Becker can walk away. I see the longing in his eyes, no matter how much he fights to hide it from me. I'll always see it and always wonder whether he regrets making his vow to abandon his search. Will he come to resent me?

I don't want to be a regret. I don't want him to look back and wish he'd chosen the treasure and not me. But . . . could he have both? I hold my own breath, pondering that. 'Promise me something,' I order, lifting from his lap and turning around, straddling him. He looks wary. It's a bit insulting. 'Promise me if you change your mind, you will tell me.'

His head tilts, interested. 'Change my mind?'

'About finding the treasure.'

He breathes in, looking a little shocked. 'I'm telling you I don't need to find it.'

'And I'm telling you I think you do. I don't want you to hate me.'

'How could I hate someone who's shown me how to love?' He leans in and kisses my shoulder, smoothing my red hair with his palm. 'I adore you, woman. Your strength, your bravery, your devotion.' On a smile, he ghosts his finger over my eyebrow and down my cheek, reaching my chin and tipping up my face. Dropping the gentlest of kisses on my lips, he hums quietly, '*You* consume my thoughts now, Eleanor. My mission in life from the moment you hijacked my heart was to love *you*. Cherish *you*. To devote all of myself to you. It's all that matters to me now. You are the most priceless, precious treasure of them all.' Another sweet kiss lands on my open mouth. 'I don't need anything else.'

I could cry for him. 'I love you.'

'Super.' Becker hauls me forward and holds me tightly. 'I feel like I've been for a double session with my therapist.' He nuzzles in my neck as he stands and detaches me, using brute force when I put up a fight. 'Are we good?' he asks.

How could we not be? He's just spilled his heart; told me things I know he hates to even think about. It's a massive step for him. Nevertheless, I need to make one thing clear. 'No more sneaky stunts.'

'What's classed as a sneaky stunt?' he questions, smirking as he dips and munches on my cheek ravenously.

I giggle, squirming, relishing in his lightened mood. I feel enlightened and relieved, and I know Becker must feel the same. 'Secrets, Becker. No more secrets.'

'Right.' After kissing my cheek, he takes his chair back up, and I settle opposite him, hands in my lap. A lovely eye is narrowed on me before he goes to his computer and starts typing. I wait patiently for him to finish, remembering why I came here in the first place.

'I was heading for the kitchen, but it struck me that I didn't know what I might be faced with.'

'Dorothy and Gramps, I expect,' he answers easily, reclining in his chair.

I lob him a tired expression. He knows what I mean. 'Do they know why I wasn't here yesterday?'

'What do you think?'

Okay. Stupid question. 'Do they know ...' I mull over my words, unsure how to say what's on my mind. 'Do they know ...' My finger waggles between us, trying to help me along with actions rather than the words – words that I'm struggling to find.

'They know you're back. They know you're sleeping in my bed.' Becker helps me out, but only a little. Sleeping in Becker's bed wasn't quite along the lines I was thinking. 'And that I haven't behaved like this with a woman ever,' he finishes tentatively.

I smile. 'Okay.' I sound smug. I am. 'And is your gramps talking to you yet?'

His hands come up and scrub at his face. 'Hardly.'

I'm not surprised. While Becker's beloved granddad has

hoped all this bad feeling regarding the Wilsons was in the past, Becker was keeping it very much in the present. 'I won't tell him,' I say, nodding to the secret room behind the bookshelf, feeling the need to voice it. Regardless of Becker's instinct to distance himself emotionally from his only living relative in a silly attempt to protect himself from heartbreak, he still cares enough to shield his gramps from the stress or anger that will be stoked if he knew his grandson sculpted the fake that Brent Wilson paid fifty million for.

When I think he might toss his NDA in my face, Becker smiles at me. 'I trust you, princess.'

I beam my understanding, fully comprehending how big a deal that is. My Lone Ranger doesn't want to be a loner any more.

I stand. 'I should go say hello to them.'

Becker stands, too, placing his palms on the desk and leaning across. I regard him with interest, loving the serious edge his stare takes on. A small cock of his head tells me to go to him, and I mirror his pose, leaning into him. Reaching forward with his lips, he plants a gentle kiss on my mouth. I breathe in, like I could inhale him into me.

'Thank you,' he says, his soft flesh vibrating against mine. 'Thank you for . . .' he tails off, searching my eyes.

'Listening?'

He nods, grateful for my prompt, even if it's not exactly what he was trying to say. His gratitude is more because I'm still here. Because I haven't run away after learning so much. He has nothing to fear. I'm staying. Love makes you do the craziest things, and you don't get crazier than this.

Becker pulls away, leaving me suspended over his desk in a daze. 'You may go.'

My trance is soon broken when the clean crunch of him biting into an apple yanks me from my happy place, dumping me right into another one of my happy places. I smile as I push myself off the desk, walking backwards with my eyes travelling back and forth to Becker's mouth with the apple.

He picks up the phone and dials before holding it to his ear. 'Percy. There's a vintage car auction coming up,' he says down the line. 'I need all the specifics.'

I leave Becker and his lucky apple to it and make my way to the kitchen.

Chapter 10

The nerves are back with a vengeance when I tentatively push my way through the door of the kitchen. So Becker tells me they know I'm sleeping in his bed? Yes, they know that, but what Becker failed to mention was how they took the news.

Woof!

I only just locate Winston in time to prepare myself for his pounce. 'Hey, boy!' I laugh, stumbling back when he launches his chunky front paws at my thighs. He's panting happily, his tail wagging so fast it's a blur. I give him all the fuss he wants, my feeble side centring my attention on someone – or something – who I know is pleased to see me, rather than face two people who I'm not so sure about. 'Glad to see me?' I ask, ruffling his ears.

He starts sniffing me, his body suddenly stilling. I fear the worst and freeze along with him. I haven't forgotten Becker's dog's aloofness when he caught a whiff of me after Becker had his way. Winston snorts a few times, getting a good hit of my scent. Then he looks up at me, and I wait patiently for Becker's cheeky British bulldog to decide whether or not he and I are on speaking terms. The relief that courses through me when he resumes excited shakes is really rather silly. The fact that I'm here has clearly overshadowed the fact that Becker's had his hands all over me.

I drop to my knees and let the big ball of muscle trample all over my lap, his wagging arse making him all unstable as he tries to sit down. 'Pleased to see you, too, boy.' I bury my nose on top of his head and inhale the comforting mild doggy smell.

Winston and I are in a world of our own, thrilled to be re-united . . . until the sound of a cupboard door closing echoes around the kitchen. That door was closed on purpose. *Loudly* on purpose.

I cringe as I peek up over Winston's head, enduring his weight on my lap like it can protect me from their disapproval. Mrs Potts is standing by the pantry door, her hand still on the handle, and Mr H is at the table, a spoon halfway to his mouth. 'Morning,' I squeak meekly, smiling nervously. Both are quiet and both are still, to the point it becomes uncomfortable, and I start mentally begging for one of them to at least say *something*. Anything. Warn me, I don't care.

'He's missed you,' Mrs Potts says, nodding to Winston on my lap, prompting me to look down, too. 'And so have we.' My head flicks up, shocked. Mrs Potts smiles and opens up her arms to me. 'Come here, *princess*.'

I laugh, but I could quite easily cry. The weight of the world feels like it's just lifted from my shoulders. I coax Winston off my lap, and he grumbles his protest, but I ignore him and straighten up, brushing down the front of my dress.

'Come on then.' She gestures with impatient hands, and I kick my feet into action, taking myself to her. I'm a little over-whelmed by the fierceness she injects into her hug, squeezing me tightly. 'I want you to do something for me,' she whispers, tightening her crush so I can't retract. I remain trapped in the old lady's round body, waiting for her to continue, dreading it, too. 'Handle him with care, Eleanor,' she says quietly in my ear. The pressure of her request hits me like a kettlebell in the face. These feelings are all pretty new to me, too. Alien, scary and overwhelming. I feel captured by a strange mixture of happi-ness and trepidation. I can only imagine how Becker must be feeling.

Like he's trapped in a maze. Like each step is terrifying.

Handle him with care? We should have a chat about how carefully Becker handles my arse.

Mrs Potts eases up and allows me to pull away, but she keeps her hands on my shoulders, smiling fondly. 'I don't know why you weren't here yesterday,' she says, and I divert my eyes, worried she might read the secrets hiding in their depths. 'But you're back, and that's all that matters.'

I smile awkwardly and glance to my right, finding old Mr H approaching gingerly on his stick. He might be doddery, but I can tell there's a little reluctance slowing his pace, too. He doesn't seem pleased to see me at all. He's looking over his glasses at me warily, like I'm an imposter. 'Do you remember that spirit we spoke about?' he asks seriously, and I nod, recalling the conversation perfectly. 'Don't ever let it go.'

I know what he's saying. He's saying I need to keep that fire in my belly to deal with his grandson. The uncertainty of it all could swallow me up if I let it. 'I won't,' I assure him. His prompt spurs me to go on and share the news that I've recently learned. 'Becker told me about his parents.' I give both old Mr H and Mrs Potts a moment of my eyes. They don't need to know the finer details, like how we came to be having that conversation. That is another of Becker's secrets I will keep.

I hear Mrs Potts happy sigh and see Mr H's old eyes shine brightly. 'I'm glad.' He looks like the news is a weight from his shoulders. Maybe it is. Maybe he sees the development as a step in the right direction, a display of how serious Becker is about me.

'Me too,' I admit, ignoring the knowledge that his grandson was pretty much threatened to spill. But he still told me. It doesn't matter that he confessed under pressure. It just further reinforces the fact that he doesn't want me to leave. 'It's so sad.'

'That it is, Eleanor. And the circumstances . . .' He drifts off somewhere, and Mrs Potts places a gentle hand on his arm, rubbing soothingly.

'I understand why you're so adamant about Becker dropping this,' I say. 'The search for the sculpture. I understand why you're civil towards Brent Wilson.'

He laughs. It's a strained laugh, full of disdain. 'Forcing yourself to be courteous towards people you loathe is hard, but if it means I get to keep my grandson, then I'm willing.'

My respect for the old man has always been great, but it's suddenly greater. Only someone with integrity and strength could put such warranted anger aside for the sake of a loved one. The fact that it's all been a waste of energy for the old man is beside the point, since Becker has kept the rivalry very much alive.

I half-smile on a mild nod, and he takes an unsteady step forward. 'Give me one of those hugs.'

I save him the effort of coming to me and walk into his arms, feeling so bloody happy. I might join Winston and start trembling, too. Sinking into the old man's comforting embrace, I smile. That's it. I'm officially adopting these wonderful people as my family.

Our happy hugs are interrupted prematurely when the door to the kitchen opens. I break away from Mr H, and we all turn and find Becker casting his eyes over all three of us. 'Emotional reunion?' he asks. Mr H drops me like a hot potato and tosses a disdainful look at his grandson. My heart sinks a little. Becker wasn't wrong. He's still miffed.

Mrs Potts hoots her amusement and claims Mr H's arm. '*Happy* reunion, Becker boy. Very happy. Come on, Donald. You can help me water the shrubs.'

'Oh joy,' he grumbles, allowing her to lead him away. 'Rock and roll.'

I laugh under my breath, watching them walking together from the kitchen. I swear, I don't think I've ever been so happy. And for the first time in for ever, it's not accompanied by guilt. My contentment only sky rockets when two firm arms slip around my waist from behind and the hardness of his chest meets my back. A million goose bumps pitter-patter across my skin as I feel his face coming closer to mine. All of this easy affection is the best perk of all. His cheek meets mine, the arm of his glasses pushing into my temple. 'Glad to be back?' he asks, a stupid question if ever there was one. I must be glowing.

'Maybe,' I tease, laughing when he turns into me and bites my cheek. 'Your granddad really did look pissed off with you.'

'I'm working on it,' Becker says, sounding sincere, and maybe a little thoughtful. 'I know how much it means to you that I put things right, so I will.'

How much it means to me? He's a case. But his sentiment is sweet. In a backwards kind of way. He attaches his lips to my cheek and sucks, and I squirm in his tight hold as he munches on my flesh. 'Becker, stop.'

Woof!

I'm released in an instant, and I whirl around, finding Becker scowling at the floor.

Woof!

'Don't start,' he snaps, stepping forward in warning. Not that Winston takes much notice.

Woof, woof, woof!

All four of his giant paws leave the floor each time he barks, that deep, threatening tone telling his owner that he isn't messing around.

'She's mine, you daft dog.'

Woof!

'No.'

Woof!

'You can't have her.'

Woof!

My face stretches into a grin, as two of my favourite men go head-to-head, circling each other. 'Winston,' I coo, lowering to my haunches and patting my lap.

'Hey.' Becker gives me a disgusted look.

'You need to show him that he's not being replaced,' I tell him. 'Winston, come here.' But the burly dog ignores me, keeping his pissed-off glare on his owner.

'No,' Becker counters, walking over to me. 'He needs to learn that there's me, then there's you, and then there's him.' He pulls me from the floor and picks me up, claiming me. 'Mine,' he declares, earning a vicious growl from his beloved pet.

Woof!

'Fuck off,' Becker grumbles, negotiating me in his arms to get a better hold. The smile on my face is beginning to make my cheeks ache. 'He'll learn.' He marches towards the counter, but comes to a jarring halt, nearly dropping me. 'Motherfucker,' he gasps.

'Oh!' I yelp and cling onto his shoulders to stop myself from tumbling from his arms as I look down at the floor. What I find tips me over the edge of amusement into hysterics. Winston has his jaw clamped around the material of Becker's trousers. 'Oh my God,' I laugh, tears springing into my eyes.

Becker's face is savage. He isn't finding this funny at all. 'Winston!'

I shake, juddering in Becker's arms, a combination of my laughter and Becker trying to shake off his dog. 'Winston, for fuck's sake, this is a five-grand suit. Get off.'

I can hear my new bodyguard growling as he wrestles with the expensive material of Becker's trousers. He's crouched on his back legs, pushing back on his front paws. 'Just put me down.' I wriggle in Becker's arms.

'No.' His grip increases, and I give up trying to break free. 'I'm not losing this.' He starts kicking his leg out, cursing and swearing like a sailor, his face going red from his fury. I let them do their thing. Both seem rather determined.

But then the loud rip of material seems to bring the fracas to an abrupt halt.

Oh, shit . . .

Becker's neck veins are bulging as he slowly lowers me to the floor before looking down at his leg. I know it's paramount to keep my mouth shut. I cautiously follow his gaze, noticing Winston is sitting proudly at Becker's feet. Then the material of Becker's trousers comes into view. Shredded. I clamp my mouth shut and pinch my nose, trying to block off any orifice where air can escape. I can't laugh. He looks homicidal.

Calmly and slowly, Becker bends at the waist and reaches to just below his shin, poking at the ragged fabric until the hairs on his leg are revealed through a gaping hole. I think I might be going blue from holding my breath for so long.

His nostrils flare. And he swallows. And he slowly rises to full height.

'Look,' he hisses, jabbing a finger in the direction of his right leg.

My shoulders begin to jerk, and Winston raises his nose in the air on a tiny snuff.

'Five grand, Winston!'

His dog jumps up onto all four paws and trots over to my feet, Becker following his path with incensed eyes. I peek down, shouting at Winston in my head not to push his luck. He doesn't care. He's as cocky as his owner. Obviously had a great teacher. He makes himself comfy at my feet, and then he does something so brazen, I actually gasp, releasing my held breath.

He licks me. The cheeky little fucker turns his face into my leg and licks it. I give up my fight to restrain my laugh and snort unattractively all over the kitchen, and Becker's jaw drops open as he looks at me all *what-the-fuck?*

'I'm sorry,' I titter, resisting reaching down and petting Winston. That would be rewarding him. I can't do that. This is more serious than I thought. We need to get the pecking order straight, so I step away from Winston and let Becker do his thing.

'In your bed,' he yells, throwing his arm out towards the basket in the corner. 'Now.'

Winston looks to me. I can feel his doggy eyes gauging the distance I've put between us, probably wondering why I'm not fussing over him. He must realise that he's pushed the boundaries, or maybe he's just clicked that I'm not coming to his defence, because he starts to slowly pad his way over to his basket, stopping halfway and peeking over his shoulder. I bite back my chuckle, watching as he assesses how much trouble he's in before finally plodding the remaining distance and dropping heavily into his bed on a grunt.

I glance across to Becker, finding him tugging at his trouser leg. 'Ruined,' he spits, looking up at me.

I hold onto my grin and wander over to him, listening out for any signs of a dog in pursuit. 'Let me see.' I gently push his hands away and kneel to inspect Becker's mutilated trouser leg. He's right. Totally trashed. 'Maybe you can replace them,' I suggest diplomatically, looking up at him. His face has smoothed out, all of the angry lines gone.

'It's bespoke.' He sighs, reaching down and pulling me up. 'You've turned my own dog against me.' He turns me in his arms and starts walking, pushing me towards the kitchen door. 'I have competition.'

'You have an angry dog,' I say on a laugh, resting into his back. 'You should spend more time with him. Build a bond.'

'Our bond was just fine until you came along.' I'm gently nudged into the corridor and turned back in his arms. 'I can't win with him. When you're not here, he doesn't speak to me, and when you are, he assaults me.'

I grin and toss my arms over his shoulders, loving his exasperation and loving our closeness even more. 'I'm meeting Lucy for lunch.'

'Okay.' His nose nuzzles mine.

'I need to do some work.'

He reaches behind his neck and disconnects my hold, smirking when he catches the affronted state that I've tried and failed to disguise. 'Don't let me stop you.' He turns and strides off down the corridor, and my eyes drop straight to his arse. I sigh, my head falling to the side in admiration.

When he reaches the door, he pauses, looking over his shoulder. 'And stop looking at my arse.'

My eyes climb up his chest, my face stretching into a delighted smile. 'No.'

I'm back.

Chapter 11

I'm in my element again, surrounded by the things I love at The Haven. It's Friday. My first week back has been all I could have hoped for, though finding a happy medium in the workplace between personal and professional is a constant challenge. Becker distracts me without even trying.

He kindly collected some clothes from my apartment for me – I couldn't bring myself to go there – and Mum has checked in every day, eager to hear regular updates of my life, especially now that she knows Becker is in it. I'm going home again soon, to spend some real quality time with her. I'm slowly coming to terms with my mother's newfound zest for life, and that she has a new love.

I've lunched with Lucy every day, too, and she's now up-to-speed on everything regarding Becker and me. Well, not quite *everything*, of course, but she's slowly accepted that this is where I want to be. I can't allow the fact that she knows nothing of lost maps and break-ins cloud my contentment. I, however, am *fully* up-to-date with *everything* concerning Lucy and Mark – printer-room girl and all. Lucy's adamant that she's after her man. Frankly, I think she's being paranoid, but instead of telling her so, I've focused on pointing out the obvious clues that Mark is smitten with her. Like him calling or texting every two minutes when they're not together.

This morning, after lying on one of the chesterfields in the library and staring up at the depiction of Heaven and Hell on the ceiling for a while, I've literally whistled while I've worked, skipping from bookcase to bookcase. It's taking every effort to avoid a certain shelf with a certain secret compartment that contains a certain secret map, as it has each time I've been in here since my return.

But that challenge becomes harder when my phone pings with a message from Becker.

Can you grab me the 2001 (T-W) file? Third shelf up, second row behind the door x

My eyes flick up to the shelf he's stated, the shelf with the secret compartment, and butterflies erupt in my tummy. God-damn me for the thrilling feel of adrenalin that immediately starts to course through my veins. I should have told him that I know where the map's hidden. But then I remind myself why I haven't. It's his secret. A personal one. Like that secret room, the one where he masterfully chipped away at a lump of marble, producing a piece of art. The fake piece of art that he tricked Brent Wilson into paying a whopping fifty million for so he can search for the real treasure without being tailed. Except Becker's vowed his search is over. Which makes all the effort he went to in order to execute his master plan a complete waste of time. It seems like a bit of a shame. Doesn't that lost treasure deserve to be found?

I'm still pondering that a few minutes later, spinning my phone in my hand, when it starts ringing. Lucy's name flashes up on my screen, and I quickly answer to distract me from more inappropriate thoughts.

'Hey.' I drop to the couch and tidy the pile of files in front of me, hearing loud panting. 'Are you running?'

'Walking fast,' she huffs. 'I have an hour to find an outfit.'

'What for?'

'Wednesday night. We're going out.'

'We are?'

'Yes.' Her answer leaves no room for refusal.

'Okay.' I don't argue. I could do with a drink. Or twenty.

'I might even go for tits *and* legs.'

'Only one,' I laugh. 'You can't break your own rule.' I keep my eyes on the pile of files before me, resisting the enticement of the forbidden bookshelf in the corner of the library.

'I feel like living on the edge. You should try it.'

I laugh out loud. Oh, she has no idea. My amused chuckle drowns out the voice in my head a little, the curious, demanding one telling me to dive into that secret compartment again. So I laugh louder, throwing my head back.

'All right,' Lucy says, undoubtedly looking at her phone with a wrinkled brow. 'It isn't *that* funny.'

My laughter dissipates. 'Sorry,' I sniff, pulling myself together and straightening my blouse along with my face. She blows an exhausted breath down the line, making a harsh crackling sound in my ear. 'You still walking fast?' I ask.

'No, I broke out into a sprint four sentences ago.'

'Why?'

'Loose Knickers is in the office with Mark, and I'm not.'

'Ohhh,' I breathe, my eyes pulling to that damn bookshelf again.

'Hey, you okay?'

'I'm fine.' My reply is automatic, and I conclude quickly that it's also the truth. I really am fine. More than fine. There's no need to expand on that. Actually, there is. I'm hopelessly in love with the man who broke into my apartment, forged a sculpture, and meticulously carved out a plan to trick his arch-enemy into buying it. The one who he suspects is responsible for his parents' deaths. I inwardly laugh. It sounds obscene in my head, too.

'Looking forward to our night out,' I say instead.

'Me too. I'll call you.' She hangs up, and I get to my feet quickly before I can allow my thoughts to run wild again.

Problem is, they're not running wild. They're simply summing up my reality. My crazy, wild reality.

I stare down at the pile of red files before me, my eyeballs beginning to ache from the effort it's taking me not to look at that bookshelf. And my brain is beginning to ache with my constant screaming demands not to. My foot starts tapping, my thumbnail finding its way to my mouth so my teeth can gnaw on it. When my phone pings in my hand, all of my nervous actions stop dead in their tracks.

You've just breached clause 3.7. Strike 1 x

Clause 3.7. Answer a text within five minutes. Strike 1? What's he suggesting? Three strikes and I'm out? Peeking over my shoulder, I eye the bookshelf with the suspicion it deserves. Get the file. That's all. Pretend it's just like any other bookcase in the room. I'm not giving myself enough credit. I *can* control my curiosity. On a confident nod of my head, I march over to the bookcase, my eyes scanning for the file I need. I find it. Grab it. Turn away from the shelf.

Then the soles of my shoes seem to weld to the carpet. I can't physically move. I have no clue why. I've seen the map, it'll be nothing new, but I didn't know what I was looking at back then. Now I'll know exactly what I'll be seeing *and* the significance of it. Or I could just look at Becker's back. God knows, it's stunning enough, with or without the masses of ink decorating it. But I have free access to his back now. It's too easy. Delving into the secret compartment is wrong. Daring. Daring is exciting. Becker has unearthed that daring side in me.

'Damn you.' I slowly turn around and bend, peering over the tops of the books that hide the secret compartment. Then my hand is reaching forward of its own volition, feeling for the catch. 'Where are you?' I ask myself, my face squished against the wood.

'Eleanor?'

I jump, dropping the file and smacking the top of my hand on the shelf. 'Shit.'

'What are you doing?' Becker sounds as wary as he does interested.

I stare blankly at the tower of red files before me, not daring to confront him until I've nailed my poker face. That could take a while. I feel like a rabbit caught in the headlights, all wide-eyed and startled.

I clear my throat. 'Just collecting one of the files you need.' Dipping, I gather up the leather book and straighten, then faff with it for a few seconds, biding my time.

'And do you have it?' he asks coolly, his voice rising as he comes closer.

Wiping all guilt from my face, I fix an unruffled smile to it – or the closest I can muster – and turn, holding up the file. 'Yes.'

He's frowning so much he looks like he has a six-pack on his forehead. And for some reason I might never fathom, I start giggling. Why am I giggling? Guilt? Distraction? If so, it isn't working. That six-pack on his brow is now an eight-pack. It's the most impressive frown I've ever seen. 'I know about the map,' I blurt out, letting my arms drop to my side, exasperated. I can't keep it to myself. It'll drive me potty. And anyway, no secrets. That's what he said.

I feel the stress alleviate as a result of my confession. It's probably a premature feeling, given Becker hasn't shown any reaction yet. His forehead is still keeping close company with that eight-pack.

Then it vanishes from his face. 'I know.' He slips his hands into his pockets, lowering his chin as if waiting for more, but he goes on when I don't give him anything else. I have nothing else to give. He knows I know? 'You've traced it, licked it.' He's being suggestive, and it's having the desired effect. I cross my legs in my standing position, rolling my eyes. 'Played guess the country on it,' he adds.

It's almost like he's speaking in code, telling me in his own little way that I shouldn't push any further. 'I've done none of those things on the original,' I murmur. There will be no silent mutual agreement here. I know, and I'm not going to pretend that I don't. What does it matter, anyway? The map's the map, whether on his back or on paper.

'I see.' He definitely looks nervous now, and I start to mull over why that might be while Becker watches me like a hawk.

He told me it was somewhere safe but made it equally clear that he wasn't going to share *where* exactly that was. It didn't matter, I already knew, but it would have saved this awkward moment had he told me. Besides, it's not somewhere safe if little old me found it by accident. It's also plastered all over his back. That's a risk, especially considering how many women Becker has bedded. I wince at my stray thoughts.

'How'd you find it?' he asks.

'I wasn't looking.'

'So how did you find it?'

'When I was sorting the shelves,' I explain, uneasy under his interrogating presence. 'My hand caught the latch and before I knew it—'

'You'd reached in, pulled the lever, opened the door, taken the book out, opened it, and found the map?'

I swallow. It sounds wrong when he says it like that, but that's pretty much the crux of it. 'Yeah.' I can't shirk him. He has me pinned, and I practically handed him the hammer and nail. 'I won't tell anyone.'

'I know.'

'Then why are you looking at me like you want to eradicate that risk?'

A smile breaks from nowhere, throwing me for a hoop. 'I

knew you'd found it, Eleanor.' He takes a step towards me, and I instinctively retreat.

'How?'

'I could smell your perfume on the wood.'

'Are you serious?' Like a twat, I bring my wrist to my nose and sniff.

'Plus you didn't engage the catch just so.' Becker raises his eyebrows. 'If you're going to be my girlfriend, princess, you need to work on your sleuth skills.'

'Fuck off, Hunt,' I retort, full of indignation. Goddamn me, I thought I hid my tracks well.

He chuckles. 'I would have told you, had I not known you'd found it. But you did. So I didn't.'

'Really?' I ask.

'Yeah. Because loving is trusting, right?'

My mouth goes slack, dropping open as I regard him. 'You showed me the secret entrance to The Haven weeks ago.'

'I guess I was trusting you before I realised I was in love with you.'

My thudding heart skips a few beats, my teeth sinking into my bottom lip. 'God, you're adorable sometimes.' I say, moving in and hugging him as he laughs. All of my striving for a happy-medium place where work and personal are defined and understood just isn't going to work. I reach up on my tiptoes to sink my face into his neck, syphoning off the warmth of his skin.

'This isn't very professional,' Becker mumbles into my shoulder, keeping his hands to himself.

'Shut up.'

'Okay.' He quickly seizes me and lifts me to his chest, squeezing the life out of me.

We feel free and easy right now, but would I be a fool to assume that this is it, that this is how it'll always be? Becker's inexperience and his self-admission, the one that sees him immune to heartbreak, have a small space in the back of my mind. I'll never break his heart. I just fear what preventive measures he'll take in order to eliminate the risk completely.

'Gramps doesn't know about that hiding place,' he says out of the blue.

'Oh . . .' Of course he doesn't. If Mr H knew where the map was, he'd have given it to the museum himself. 'And you don't want him to know because he'll get rid of it.'

'Precisely. Then God knows whose hands it could fall into. It's safer with me.'

'But you don't want to find the sculpture?' I ask, narrowing my eyes and refusing to acknowledge the little voice in my head that's *begging* him to say *yes*. Yes, he does want to find the sculpture.

'No, I don't. *If* it's even anywhere to be found.' He releases me and raises his eyebrows, as if he's reading my mind.

'Good.' I say decisively, moving back, smiling sweetly. Besides, it's a known fact that it could be a myth. There are even tales of Michelangelo destroying it himself. 'But if it is out there, you don't want to find it but you don't want anyone else to find it either?' Namely, Brent Wilson.

'Precisely.' He curls an arm around my waist and hauls me back into him. 'The map stays with me.'

I'm kind of glad. Why? 'Okay,' I agree, and he wrinkles his nose, rubbing it with mine.

'Okay,' he counters, and we stare at each other for a while, both of us narrowing an eye on each other. *I want you to find the sculpture!* 'I'm glad you're at peace with your decision.'

He laughs, hugging me, as the library door opens. I look over Becker's shoulder to see Mrs Potts hovering at the entrance. 'Am I interrupting?'

I don't scramble free of Becker's embrace, and Mrs Potts doesn't eye us despairingly. In fact, there's a certain fondness on her old face. 'No,' I answer when it becomes obvious that

Becker isn't going to, choosing to keep hold of me with his face hiding in my neck.

'Oh good.' She pats down the violet bomb on her head and purses her lips at Becker. 'I have a call you might want to take.'

I try to break free, but he's having none of it. 'Take a message,' he orders flatly.

'It's Brent Wilson.'

That soon gets Becker moving, along with my heart rate, which goes from content and settled to speeding and stressed in the space of a second. And it pisses me off. Just the mention of Brent's name pisses me off, as well as the natural reaction it spikes in me. Becker looks at Mrs Potts. 'What does he want?'

'He wouldn't say.'

My eyes bat back and forth between them. 'I'm busy,' he spits, waving a hand dismissively.

Mrs Potts backs out of the room on an accepting nod, closing the door softly behind her. 'Do you think he knows?' I have to ask. The man paid a cool fifty million for a lump of marble that Becker lovingly crafted and unlawfully authenticated. If he finds out, the shit will hit the fan and splatter as far as Rome. Why else would he be calling Becker now?

Becker stops by one of the gold ladders and glances across the room at me. 'Knows what?'

I don't manage to retract my look of incredulity. How can he be so obtuse? 'About the fake *Head of a Faun*? The one he paid fifty million for?'

I'm even more stunned when he scoffs, laughing at my perfectly reasonable concern. 'I'm not worried about that.'

Okay, now I'm just plain confused. 'Then why are you acting like you're preparing for war?'

Now he really laughs, but it's forced. It's a condescending laugh, and his fingertips slip under his glasses and rub at his sockets. 'Probably because I am,' he mutters.

'What do you mean?' I'm lost. And then suddenly . . . 'Wait, you really do think it's him who broke into my apartment, don't you?'

Becker pulls off his glasses aggressively, giving himself better access to his eyes so he can go at them like he could be digging for gold. 'Yes. No. I don't know.'

'Okay, forget that. Why is he calling you now? He's got the sculpture. He's won. What else could he possibly want from you?'

Becker casts a *really?* look my way.

'Me?' I laugh. That's ridiculous. 'The man makes my skin crawl.'

'That man will do whatever he can to get one up on me, and now I have a sweet weak spot.' He glares at me accusingly. 'That's you, in case you were wondering.'

'I wasn't wondering,' I say tiredly. 'And has it ever crossed your mind that, actually, he might just want me because I'm me, and not because I'm yours?' The cheeky fucker.

He twitches, like he could be shaking something off his shoulders, and scowls to himself. 'Of course he wants you because you're you. The fact you're mine is a bonus. For fuck's sake,' He shoves his glasses back on and stomps towards the door.

He's leaving? 'Becker?' I call, but I'm ignored, prompting me to go after him. He's not walking away from me. No way. I catch his arm, just as he pulls the door open, and throw my palm into the wood to push it shut, hindering his escape. 'Don't walk away from me.'

I'm taken by surprise when the tables turn and it's no longer me holding Becker, but him holding me. He moves fast, whirling me around and pushing my front to the door. I gasp, my chest splatting against the heavily carved wood, some protruding parts pressing into the soft curves of my tummy.

'Shhhh.' His husky tone penetrates my hearing and his hips lock my lower body in place. He's aroused. Hard. Sharp. A quick hand grabs the hem of my dress and yanks it up to my waist. I cry out, caught in a confusing mix of guardedness and uncontrollable want. My cheek is squished on the wood, my hands either side of my head, and the quiet instruction in my mind that's telling me to fight him is being ignored. One finger traces the crease of my arse over my knickers, teasing, stroking, driving me crazy.

The soft bristle on his cheek rubs against mine, and my eyes close, feeling his hot breath spread across my face. 'Hmmmm,' he hums, turning his mouth onto my skin and licking a long, wet trail up to my temple.

My muscles lock down, tensing, my knotted mind taking pleasure from the anticipation of his touch. I'm flooded between my thighs, wet and begging, and it's all beyond my control. 'Is this your way of marking your territory?' I ask my darkness.

'Shut the fuck up, Eleanor,' he warns, taking the top of my knickers and shoving them down to my thighs. A few blissful moments are spent caressing my still tender skin before he slips his hand between my legs and finds my condition. 'You want me, baby?'

I groan, fighting the urge to scream my desperation.

'You want me to plunge deep and hard?'

My hands ball into frustrated fists, ready to pound the wood. The small collection of nerves in the tip of my clitoris are twitching, vibrating, screaming for contact.

'Or do you want me to lick you here?' He sinks two fingers into me and puts weight behind his drive, holding himself deep. My legs begin to wobble, and just when I'm about to defy his insistence on keeping quiet so I can bellow my desire, he pulls free of me harshly and slaps me clean across my arse. I jerk forward, making the huge door rattle on its hinges. 'Mine,' he growls, beginning to rub some life back into my burning flesh. 'If everyone remembers that, then no one will get hurt.' He pushes his lips to my temple and breathes through his kiss, caging me in from behind as he pulls my knickers into place and my dress back down. I'm dazed, still turned on, and absolutely staggered. There's a huge part of me that's thrilled he's staked such a violent claim, but I can't ignore the tiny piece of me that's worried. His promise, and I have no doubt that it's a promise, isn't referring to him or me getting hurt. He isn't speaking of emotional damage to either one of *us*. He's talking about physical hurt. I need to avoid Brent Wilson at all costs.

I allow him to turn me in his arms until I'm facing him, my eyes rooted on the knot of his tie. I'm worried about what I might see if I look into his angel eyes, but I'm given little option when my chin is tipped up to meet his face. 'I love you,' he says clearly, softly, a million miles away from the threat of his voice a minute ago.

I laugh. I can't help it. And God love him, he frowns at my reaction to his swinging mood.

'Have I said something funny?' he asks, stepping back, injured.

The tips of my fingers meet my forehead and press into my skin. 'No.' I shake my head, thinking better than to try and explain. He's a total novice at affection.

'Then why are you laughing?'

'You're behaving like a Neanderthal.'

His cute head cocks when I glance at him. 'Explain.'

'Possessive. Are you going to spank me every time you feel under threat?'

'I'm not under threat.'

'No?'

'No.' He snubs my claim and puts his hands on my hips, hunkering down to get his eyes level with mine. 'Because you love me.' He grins, and I mirror it. 'Don't you?'

'Yes.'

'And you love me spanking you, don't you?'

'I'd love it more if you made me come when you spank me.'

His grin stretches, spanning his entire handsome face. 'You didn't answer my text within five minutes.'

I gape at him, outraged. 'You can't punish me in our private life for something I do in our professional life.'

'I can,' he counters, reaching past me and pulling open the door. 'We'll call it a job incentive.'

I'm speechless as he ushers me from the library. Taking my hand, he walks us down the corridor leisurely, peeking down at me with that adorable grin. 'I'm loving the new dynamics of our working relationship.'

I shake my head. He's such a juvenile sometimes. 'You're a twat.'

Becker laughs and straightens the frame of a picture as we pass. 'Yes, a holier-than-thou one, apparently. And you love me.'

Chapter 12

The following Tuesday, I stroll into Becker's office to discuss the upcoming sale of a Dalí, finding the elaborate space empty. I take a seat at his grand desk and try calling him, but it rings off, and I lean back, wondering where he could be.

My eyes cast over to the bookcase where his secret room is beyond, and I bite my lip, slowly rising. It helps him relax. A couple of times over the weekend he disappeared for a few hours. And a couple of times I found grey smudges on his face. Is he relaxing now?

I narrow my eyes on the bookcase where I know the entrance to be, as I round the desk tentatively and edge towards it, listening for any sounds beyond. Nothing. So I feel up the bookcase, finding it flush. I pout, edging away, slowly taking myself back to his desk. I lower to the chair, thinking. How long did it take him to masterfully craft that fake? How long was he plotting to rip off Brent Wilson and clear the path for his treasure hunt?

The home screen on his computer seizes my attention. The Google search bar is empty. Begging to be filled. Curiosity and intrigue seems to growing in me by the day.

My fingers are tapping before I can stop them, and I hit enter. The page loads with various articles, and I scroll through them, searching. My heartbeats quicken when I see something. An article from a local London newspaper. I click it and inhale when Becker's father's face fills the screen. The Hunt men were definitely at the front of the queue when God was giving out looks. Lord, it's like looking at Becker, just a few years older.

He's wearing glasses too, and not for the first time I wonder how bad Becker's eyesight is.

Becker's dad is in a tuxedo, a brandy in his hand, obviously at some kind of gala or ball. And next to him, the most stunning woman I've ever seen. Lou Hunt. Becker's mother. Her hand is wrapped around a wine glass, her neck adorned with some serious sparklers, her body encased in a black velvet gown. She's mesmerising. Or was. I wince, a horrible pain radiating through me. Such a handsome couple. Such a waste. And all because of that lost sculpture.

My eyes drop to the article below, and I inhale.

World renowned art dealer found dead in Italy

I start scrolling, hungry for information, even if I know what the newspapers reported wasn't the truth. Then jump out my fucking skin when I'm grabbed from behind. 'Boo,' he says in my ear, and my finger finds the close icon and clicks off the screen before he spins me around and slams his mouth on mine.

'You scared the crap out of me,' I mumble against his lips.

'I know. I can feel your heart thundering. What were you doing?'

I push my mouth harder to his, ignoring his question. 'Where have you been?'

'At Sotheby's. I've acquired a new painting. Georgia O'Keeffe. We need to arrange delivery. Will you take care of it?'

'Sure.'

'The num—'

'I can take care of it,' I assure him, and he smiles.

'You gonna pay for it, too?'

Ah. Good point. I smile sweetly. 'Can I borrow some money?'

He laughs as his phone rings. 'And there's a Warhol exhibition coming up. Get me the catalogue?' he asks, and I nod as he answers. 'Hello?' Becker pulls me from his chair, kisses my cheek, and takes my place, swatting my arse as I walk away.

I go straight to the coffee table between the couches and start collecting up a pile of books and putting them back on the shelves, anything to keep my attention off my impressive man sitting at his impressive replica of the Theodore Roosevelt desk.

Impossible. I peek over my shoulder, finding his eyes rooted to my arse. I cough, and he glances up, blinking. Then he shakes his head to himself and realigns his attention. I smile and carry on restacking the shelves, but I can feel him watching me. His office is literally throbbing with our combined desperation for each other. This working relationship was always hard, but now we've leaped over the line into acceptance and understanding, it's unbearable. Keeping my hands to myself is an hourly challenge.

Peeking behind me again, I find Becker now in front of his desk, his phone to his ear, his arse resting on the edge, his spare hand braced on the wood. I gulp down some restraint and stupidly allow my relentless eyes to home in above his neck. His angel eyes behind his Ray-Ban specs are nailed to me.

I can't take it.

'I'll leave you to it,' I mutter, placing the last few books on the table and moving towards the door.

He's off the desk in the blink of an eye, jogging towards me. My hand is claimed, and he leads me over to his desk, his phone still at his ear. I'm guided to the chair and pushed into the seat, then he resumes position on his arse, on the edge of his desk, a whisper away from me.

Hazel eyes hold me in my seated position, and one of his feet slips between mine. 'Yes,' he says into the phone, tapping both of my ankles with his foot and raising an eyebrow.

My mouth gapes when I catch on, and my legs turn to steel in an effort to stop him. Becker's eyes laugh in the face of steel. He cocks his head, keeping his phone to his ear by his shoulder, and leans forward, placing a palm on each of my knees. My body temperature hits the ceiling and my teeth clench. No amount of stiffness or strength could stop him. Not mental, not physical, though I try. *What is he doing?*

The '1965 Ferrari 275 GTB,' he says, spreading my legs so I'm wide open and exposed to his appreciative eyes. My hands find the arms of the chair, my fingers clawing into the leather. 'The Long-Nose Alloy Berlinetta.' I'm still and silent as his long fingers walk their way up the inside of my thigh. Those damn fingers are leaving a trail of fire in their wake, and the thought of them reaching the apex of my thighs has me lifting my arse from the leather to escape. He's on a business call. I need to be quiet, and I can't guarantee that at all.

'Ouch!' I yelp when he pinches the delicate flesh on the inside of my thigh, my body going limp from shock, my arse hitting the chair again. I shoot him a look, finding his lips pouting and his index finger resting lightly on them.

'Shhhh,' he whispers, stretching the sound out for ever, returning his hand to between my legs. My head starts to shake frantically, telling him silently that I can't, but he just nods in response, keeping his phone held to his ear by his shoulder while he reaches for something on his desk. *A coaster?* It glides through the air towards me, and my mouth drops open, stunned by his intention. Big mistake. I've just invited him to slip it between my teeth, and he does, wriggling it a little for me to grip onto. Oh, Jesus, he's really going to do this. Is this how it's going to be? Sexual games during the working day? I want to be delighted, but I'm too worried right now. Mr H or Mrs Potts could walk in at any moment and catch me with my legs spread and Becker . . . playing with me.

'I'm only interested in the original colour,' Becker goes on, and I look up at him, his body bent to reach his target. He gives me a wicked grin and comes down to his knees in front of me. My eyes follow him all the way. Here I am, legs wide open, fingernails piercing the leather of the chair, with a coaster in my fucking mouth.

Welcome back to The Haven.

His fingers brush the seam of my knickers, and I whimper, quietly begging, which he totally ignores, looking up at me and relishing in the sight of me squirming. Then the warmth of his fingers connect with my sensitive heat, and his eyes widen, sparkling. My spine clicks one vertebra at a time until my back is poker straight.

'When does it arrive from Italy?' he asks, so calm. I don't know how he's doing it.

My jaw begins to ache from my crushing grip of the coaster between my teeth, my forehead beginning to bead with sweat. I look down, seeing his arm between my legs. I could yank it out, if it wasn't for the invisible handcuffs keeping my wrists nailed to the arms of the chair. I'm immobilised by his boldness. I close my eyes, unable to resist the urge, as he slowly slips his fingers inside me. The soft heat of me melds around him instinctively, immediately creating a maddening friction. I force myself to breathe through it, but Becker increases his pace, making my attempts more difficult by the second. This is so wrong, but that doesn't seem to be registering with my nerves, muscles, or my morals. My insides are alight. I flex my hips up, inviting him, encouraging him.

I can vaguely hear someone on the other end of the phone rambling on about imports and interest from other parties, but I'm too alert to the feel of Becker within me to feel disgrace. The illicitness of this is just turning me on more, my orgasm gaining momentum unstoppably. The force behind his caress is bordering too much, his fingers hooked and sweeping within me. Then the bastard starts pumping, introducing his thumb to my clit. My eyes snap open, and I scream, the coaster muffling it a little, but not nearly enough.

'Nothing,' Becker assures the caller, giving me a warning look. My eyes close again. He doesn't let-up. He drives on and on. I'm never going to fight my way through my climax in silence. I start breathing through my nose, feeling every drop of blood in my body rushing south.

'Look forward to it,' Becker says evenly, like he hasn't got a panting woman dripping with need before him.

Then it happens, and there is nothing I can do to stop it. The build-up of heat sizzles and burns, makes me shift and moan and sweat. I start to scream in my head as the pressure between my thighs erupts, sending every nerve ending into spasm.

My body goes slack in the chair, and I use my last ounce of breath to spit out the coaster, eager to capture some valuable oxygen. I peel my eyes open. He's smirking at me, an adorable, almost innocent grin. My angel eyes. My sinful Saint Becker.

He pulls his fingers free, then spends a few moments keeping me riveted while he licks my release away. 'Yes,' he says quietly into the phone. 'It's been a very productive call. Thanks, Simon. I'll see you soon.' Then he hangs up and slowly rises, my eyes following him until he's towering over me. 'Okay?' he asks.

I make an idiotic attempt of composure. My condition is clear. 'Super.' I gulp, closing my legs.

Becker reaches for my hand and pulls abruptly, yanking me to my feet. Our chests collide. His nose touches mine. 'You're welcome,' he says cockily, dropping a hard kiss on my lips. I'm about to laugh, but I'm being swung around before I can engage my mouth.

'Whoa!' I cry, my palms slapping onto his desk. I'm pushed down until my front meets the wood. 'Oh fuck,' I curse as he keeps me in place with a firm palm on the back of my neck and pulls my dress to my waist. 'Oh fuck, fuck, fuck.' I clench my eyes shut.

'What did you do, princess?' he asks, his voice like silk. 'What did you do while I was fucking you with my fingers?'

My fist meets the desk in frustration. 'Closed my eyes.'

'And what happens when you do that without my say so?' He pulls my knickers to the side and strokes my cheek affectionately. Oh my days, Mr H and Mrs Potts would have heart attacks if they walked in now.

'You spank me.' I don't fuck about. Why prolong the inevitable?

'Precisely.'

Thwack!

My hands lift and ball, then plummet to the desk with force as I grunt through the sting of pain, rather than scream. The burn is something I'm becoming surprisingly accustomed to. It still hurts like hell, but I'm learning to deal with it, learning to breathe my way through it. It's a good job, because I sense Becker's spanking habits are here to stay. I roll my forehead onto the desk and pant into the wood. 'Are you done?' I ask, feeling him still poised behind me.

'Just admiring my arse,' he replies happily, giving it a loving pat before pulling my knickers into place and my dress down. I let him pull me up. 'Take a seat.' He points to the chair and rounds his desk, switching quickly into boss-mode. So it'll be professional on his terms? When Becker says? I lower myself to the seat and brush at my crimson cheeks.

'Mr Hunt,' I say, following his lead. 'I—'

'Mr Hunt?' he sighs, exasperated.

'Sir?' I try, knowing exactly what response I'll get to *that* suggestion.

'Yes, if you want me to fuck you every time you use it, go right ahead. Call me *sir*.' He rolls his eyes. 'Becker, princess. To you, I'm just Becker.'

My lips stretch into a grin. 'Yes, sir.'

'Behave,' he warns, grabbing his mobile and bashing out a text. 'Pass me your phone,' he says, and I oblige, unlocking it and sliding it across his desk. He navigates a few screens, then hands it back. 'I've downloaded my private bank's app. You need to memorise the login details. There are four security questions, all of which you will know the answers to. The answers apply to me. And a facial scan is required as extra security.'

I stare at him in disbelief. 'You trust me with all your money?'

'Why, are you going to run off with it?'

I laugh, looking down at my screen, seeing the login screen. 'And what are the log in details?'

'Username is SAINT. All upper case.'

I smile as I type it in. 'Password?'

'CorruptLittleWitch1992. All lower case with an exclamation mark on the end.'

My smile widens, and as soon as I've finished entering, I'm asked Becker's favourite colour. 'Red,' I say as I type. Then another question. 'Gloria,' I murmur, my fingers working fast over the keys. The third question makes me smile, and I look up at him. 'Granny Smiths,' I say, and he smiles in return. The final question makes me baulk. 'Seriously?' I ask.

'Seriously.'

'Your favourite position?'

'Correct.'

I sigh, typing out my answer. I frown when it tells me I'm wrong. I look up at him. 'It's definitely doggy.' What gives?

He gets up and rounds his desk, coming in beside me and dropping a kiss on my cheek. 'It was. But now . . .'

I grin and type in 'Missionary', my phone scans my face and the screen opens. 'Fucking hell.' I baulk when the balances hit me.

'Don't spend it all at once, eh?'

Jesus Lord above. I don't think I could spend this money in a lifetime. But, then again, I don't make a habit of spending millions on art. 'I'll sort the transfer.'

'Thanks. I'll email you their bank details and how much.'

I close the app as Becker takes his seat back up. 'Oh, and I'm going out with Lucy tomorrow night.'

'That's nice. Where?'

'I don't know yet.'

'Okay.' He looks up at me. 'I have an appointment at Parsonson's at three.'

Parsonson's? The auction house where I turned up late for my interview because some cheeky arsehole nicked my cab? 'Do you need me to prepare anything?'

'Yes, yourself.'

'Huh?'

'Prepare yourself, princess. You're coming with me.'

Chapter 13

The sight of the glass revolving door outside Parsonson's sends me cold. I can see myself trapped in one of the quarters all those weeks ago, frozen in a shock-and-awe moment.

'After you,' Becker says, having me tear my gaze away from the doors, finding his arm is swept out in a gesture for me to lead on, his expression telling me he knows exactly what's going through my mind.

'Thank you.' I push into the glass and follow as it slowly glides around, reacquainting myself with the stark reception of Parsonson's as I go. I'm lost in my reflections, remembering the last time I was here, when I'm suddenly pushing against a dead weight. I'm trapped again, and knowing what I'll find, I turn to search him out on the other side. Except he's not on the other side. Becker's in the same section as me. Close. I move backwards until my back meets the glass.

'Imagine,' he says quietly, closing the gap between us, 'if we'd have been in *this* situation that time.'

I mull over his suggestion, thinking about the energy that sparked back then. Having glass between us wasn't effective enough. Like this? I honestly can't imagine how I would have been. Even more useless? I was pretty pathetic with a protective sheeting of glass keeping me contained. 'It's very cosy.'

Becker chuckles and reaches past me as he walks forwards, getting the door shifting again. I step out and gather myself. 'I might have slapped your face for stealing my cab,' I say, getting heightened amusement from Becker at my claim. He's right to laugh. The suggestion is funny. I was capable of nothing in that revolving door.

'Mr Hunt.' The receptionist appears from a white door that blends into the wall perfectly. She looks as pristine as the last time I saw her.

'Afternoon, Janet,' Becker says, leaning over the desk and giving her his cheek. I watch, astonished, as she pecks his stubbled jaw and he laps it all up.

Becker indicates towards me, and she looks at me, smiling brightly. 'This is Eleanor. She works for me.'

'Lucky Eleanor,' she quips, giving me her hand to shake. 'Oh, I've seen you before.'

'Yes,' I confirm, turning an accusing look up at Becker. 'Unfortunately, I was late for my interview.'

'Unfortunately?' Becker questions seriously. 'Trust me. You wouldn't want to work for Parsonson's. I did you a favour.'

'Would have been nice to have a choice.'

The lady behind reception laughs at our light banter. 'Well, Eleanor, if it's any consolation, many would kill to work for the Hunt Corporation.'

'Many *women*?' I ask seriously.

She laughs loudly, and Becker rolls his eyes. 'I'm here to see Simon,' he says, clearly bored with the banter now.

'You know where you're going.' She smiles coyly, and I quickly look to Becker for his reaction. She's flirting, and Becker is smiling at her, giving her gleaming eyes and that adorable grin. He's a tart.

'Thank you, Janet.' He strolls off to the elevator, leaving me to follow.

'I want to add something to your NDA,' I tell him as I come to a stop beside him at the lifts.

He looks down at me curiously as he reaches for the call button. 'What's that, princess?'

'No flirting.'

'I agree.' He straightens and pulls the sides of his jacket in, fastening the button. 'You're not allowed to flirt.'

'I'm talking about you,' I say on a laugh. He can't expect me to stand by and watch him lap up the drool being dribbled all over him by enchanted women.

'I don't flirt,' he protests as the lift arrives and we step in. 'I'm building good business relations.'

I snort my repugnance but decide to leave it there. Because I'm at work and I can be professional. Kind of. 'Oh, so that's how we build good relations? I'll remember that.'

He grins, nudging me in the side with his elbow. 'Don't get any ideas.'

The lift stops on every floor, people boarding or exiting, while Becker and I stand side-by-side, looking straight ahead to the metal doors. It's a ploy both of us seem happy to adopt in an attempt to ignore the sexual tension bouncing off the walls of the box containing us.

When we come to a stop on the seventh floor, Becker prompts for me to disembark, and I look up at him, stunned.

'You going to stand there all day?' he asks.

'This floor?'

'Yes.'

'This is Mr Timms's floor,' I say.

'Correct. Simon Timms.'

'You're meeting Mr Timms? That's who I was due to have my interview with.'

'Then this should be interesting,' Becker quips as I step off the elevator, not looking forward to meeting the Rottweiler of a receptionist up here. What was her name?

'Morning, Shelley,' Becker says, overtaking me after he's answered my silent question. She looks up, but she's smiling today, delighted. Of course she's fucking delighted.

'Becker.' She dives up from her seat and rounds her desk. Becker? Not Mr Hunt? I stand to the side like a spare part while they say their hellos, all smiley and *definitely* flirty. Building good business relations? Yeah, I bet. I also put money on the fact that my darling boss/boyfriend/con-artist/. . . whatever the bloody hell he is, doesn't bless his *male* associates with such charm. 'Would you like a drink?' she asks.

'No, I'm good.'

I thrust my hand forward, disturbing their fond reunion. 'Hi, I'm Eleanor.'

She flicks an interested look to me, and I assess it carefully, looking for any scrap of evidence to confirm that she remembers me. Will she acknowledge our last encounter, and more to the point, how rude she was?

There's definitely something there, some recognition. 'Hi.' She takes my hand, all friendly, but she doesn't spend too much time greeting me, quickly returning her attention to my more appealing companion. 'Simon's ready when you are.' Shelley smiles like she's never seen a man before, let alone a man like Becker.

'Great.' He strolls off. 'Come along, princess.'

I stare at his back, astounded, my fist clenching as I follow him. 'Don't push me, Hunt.' I warn, and he grins as he knocks on the door before pushing it open and stepping to one side. I don't thank him as I enter Simon's office, glancing around at the clinical space. Just like the rest of the building, Mr Timms's office is sparse, with only a minimal desk, a few chairs positioned around it, and a white couch and coffee table.

'Hunt.' The noble voice matches the man behind the desk perfectly. He's kitted out in green tweed, he has a comb-over, and a chubby round face. He gets up and offers his hand to Becker.

As expected, there's no kissing in this greeting, just a firm, manly handshake before Simon centres his attention on me. His round face lights up. 'Simon Timms,' he declares proudly.

I can't expect Simon Timms here to recognise me because

I never made it to his office for my interview. But he might remember my name. 'Eleanor.' I offer my hand and he takes it keenly. 'Eleanor Cole.'

I definitely detect a frown. 'Eleanor Cole,' he muses, looking off into the distance. 'I know that name.'

So he should. 'I had an interview with you a while ago.'

'Ah!' he sings, but quickly frowns again. 'That's right. You were late.'

I peek at Becker, seeing him looking at me, his face deadpan.

'Apologies,' I say, keeping my stare on my boss. 'I had an unfortunate incident with a taxi and a less-than-helpful man.'

Becker snorts on a grin as Simon Timms retakes his chair. 'That's a shame. I'm sorry about that.'

'Did you fill the position?' I ask.

'Actually, yes, for about a week. Turned out to be all talking no walking. Useless.'

I relieve Becker of my eyes. 'Maybe I'll reapply.' I receive a swift nudge in my side, which I totally ignore, moving forward. 'I'll resubmit my application.'

'You're not available for hire,' Becker growls.

'*Everyone* is available, Mr Hunt.'

Simon bursts into laughter, slapping his belly. 'I like you, Eleanor.'

I smile smugly as I round Simon's desk. I can feel Becker behind me literally quaking at my obstinacy. 'I like you, too, Simon.' I'm being outrageously flirtatious as I perch on the edge of his desk. I don't care. Two can play Becker's game, and I'm in a winning mood. 'That's a mighty fine watch.' I reach forward and fondle wistfully with the solid silver piece, recognising it immediately. The '1973 Oyster Cosmograph?' I muse. I know I might as well have stripped naked and offered Simon a feel of my tits when he gasps his joy.

'Yes,' he hoots, delighted. 'One of Rolex's finest.'

I smile. 'It certainly is.' I cross one leg over the other. 'A sturdy watch for a sturdy man.' I cock my eyebrow suggestively, prompting Simon Timms to dive all over his laptop in a rush.

The next moment, his printer springs to life and he's retrieving something from the tray. A piece of paper gets thrust towards me as he eyes Becker smugly. I'm learning very quickly that while women love Becker, men clearly do not. Simon here is being bold. And a sexist pig, for that matter, but I'll let it slide just this once, since I'm purposely fanning the flames. 'Why don't you reapply now,' he says enthusiastically as I take the paper by the very edge and pull it slowly from his grasp.

'Why, thank you.' I bite my lip and watch as his eyes drop to them. 'I might just do that.'

I'm moving before I can add a little cheeky wink, my body being yanked from the desk by a very determined grip on my upper arm. I fall apart on the inside but maintain a serious face as I glance at Becker. He looks murderous. Good. A dose of his own medicine won't hurt him.

He doesn't need to breathe a word. He just glares at me in warning, with molten lava that could have come from Hell itself spilling from those angel eyes. I pout and pull my arm free, giving him a fixed glare. It's a *don't-fuck-with-me* glare, and I know he catches it because he gives me a *don't-push-me* glare in return.

'She's a gem,' Simon says on a chuckle, breaking our glaring deadlock.

'She's something,' Becker mutters, ridding his face of all condemnation and turning a fake smile onto Simon as he whips the application form from my grip. I try to seize it back, but he's ripping it up speedily. And once it's in a million pieces, he grins as he hands it back to me. 'You and I both know that you get way too many perks for you to even *consider* a job change.'

I want to stuff the scraps of paper up his perfect arse. 'Like what?' I goad.

He arches a surprised brow. What? Does he think I'm beyond

hearing it out loud in front of fellow professionals? *Professional?* What a laugh. He wants bold and cocky? Let's play, Hunt.

'Well, let's see,' he muses, turning to Simon and wandering over to one of the seats opposite his desk. He pulls his trouser legs up by his knees and slowly lowers to the chair, crossing one leg over the other and resting his elbow on the arm, all casual and unruffled. Simon and I both follow every move he makes, me intrigued by what he might say, and Simon looking a little wary. Probably because of the undercurrent of threat apparent in each move Becker is making. 'Like the fact that you love me spanking your arse when you don't do as you're told.'

Simon gasps, and I roll my eyes, suddenly comprehending that Becker will pull no punches and say it exactly as it is. Flicking my eyes to Simon, I see him lean in a little over his desk, getting closer to Becker, like he wants the sordid details. What a creep. I can see from the look in Simon's eyes that he wishes I made it to his interview on time.

I wander over and take a seat next to my boss/lover/boyfriend/arse-spanker/con-artist, the bold son of a bitch.

'Like . . .?' I go on, wondering why on earth I'm encouraging this? But I can't help it. *You've met your match, Hunt. You've found this spirit. You can damn well deal with it.*

'Like,' Becker goes on, indulging Simon with a lopsided, suggestive grin. I'm forced to keep my own grin restrained. He's a bold bastard. And I love him. 'The fact that she screams loud enough for—'

'I think Simon gets the picture, Becker.' The man really doesn't give a rat's arse about professionalism.

'Like—'

'Becker,' I breathe, throwing him a warning look that he completely ignores.

'Like you are mine, princess.' He slowly casts his eyes across to me, face straight, totally serious. 'So you'll understand if I get a little narky when you get familiar with other men.'

'Touché,' I whisper in response, letting my small smile loose.

'Super,' he counters, before returning his attention to a stunned Simon. 'Now that Eleanor's status has been clarified, let's get to business, shall we?'

Simon falls into a nervous mess, faffing with papers and shifting things on his desk. I chuckle under my breath, knocking Becker's knee with mine. He peeks out the corner of his eye and tosses me a wink. '*Head of a Faun*,' Simon blurts out, and my smile drops, the mention of that damn sculpture suddenly reducing me to a fidgeting idiot. I thought we were here to talk about the vintage Ferrari?

'What about it?' Becker asks, hostility breaking his steady tone, his surprise clear, too.

Simon rests back in his chair and links his fingers across his large stomach. 'I wanted that sale, Hunt.'

'Every auction house on the planet wanted that sale. What makes you think that I could manipulate the seller's decision to take it to Countryscape?'

I could laugh. Becker manipulated every moment of the sculpture's journey from a worthless lump of marble to the fifty-million-pound price tag.

Simon's expression changes somewhat, and I have no idea what to make of it. It's a knowing look, I think. My eyes pass slowly between the two men a few times, trying to gauge what's being said without being said.

'You carry more clout in this world than you're letting on, Hunt,' Simon says, watching Becker closely. 'Don't try to kid me otherwise.'

Becker slaps on a charming smile and shifts in his chair, getting comfier. To an outsider, I'm guessing the smile currently gracing his face would seem genuine, but I'm becoming a master at deciphering his smiles, and this right here is fake. One hundred per cent, it's fake. Like that sculpture. 'You're giving me more credit than is due, Simon.'

'Am I?' he questions quickly, not missing a beat.

'Way ... too ... much.' Becker says slowly. Warningly. I'm wary of the signs of hostility, so I'm floored when Simon Timms ignores them.

'I don't think I am.'

Becker's jaw ticks, and I find myself intervening before this gets out of hand. I lean forward, getting Simon's attention. 'Countryscape wanted the sale, and they got the sale.' I smile sweetly. 'Becker bid, he lost, and life goes on. Now, Mr Timms, I thought you had some info on the 1965 Ferrari?'

Simon recoils, suddenly speechless, and Becker coughs his throat clear, disguising his laugh. 'I think you've been told, Simon.' He flashes an over-the-top smile.

I sit back, looking at Simon expectantly as he reaches blindly to the side and retrieves a file, his scowl fierce. He then tosses it to our side of the desk. 'Here.'

'Super. Thank you.' Becker takes the file and flicks through, while I keep my gleaming smile on Simon Timms. Funny. He's not looking at me lustfully now. He's looking at me like he holds me in contempt.

I'm desperately trying to maintain my poker face. Any mention of that bloody sculpture makes me nervous, annoyingly. I need to work on that. Timms is making me feel uncomfortable, and it's in this moment I consider something. Is he wondering, given Becker has just spelled out my status, if I have inside information on the Hunt Corporation, too? Have I got to add him to the list of people who will try to wring information from me? Was it him who broke into my apartment?

'It's all there,' Simon goes on, dragging his eyes off of me and returning them to Becker. 'I'm sure you'll be satisfied. I'll look forward to your bid.'

Becker nods thoughtfully, and then rises from his chair. 'Indeed. Good day to you, Simon.'

It takes everything in me to stand coolly, as opposed to

diving upwards, like an eject button has been pressed. 'Good day,' I say tightly, purposely looking him straight in the eye as I leave, hoping he reads my message. I'll hold no prisoners. Don't mess with me.

There's no farewell. Simon Timms doesn't stand and see us out. But I feel his eyes boring into me as we walk away. 'Just shout if things don't work out at the Hunt Corporation, Elea-nor,' he calls, and I turn to find him smiling. It's a slimy smile. One that makes my skin crawl. Good God, Becker really did do me a favour.

'I don't think so, Simon.' I turn and leave, catching up with Becker. 'I don't like him,' I declare, feeling Becker's warm palm slide onto my lower back.

'Me too,' Becker mutters, directing me to the right when we reach the end of the corridor.

We breach the area where Shelley is sitting, prim as can be, and Becker slaps the hugest smile on his face, knocking her back on her swivel chair. I bet he has payback planned after my BAFTA award-worthy performance in Simon Timms's office before the tables turned. I inwardly groan. This is going to be torturous. But I can be possessive, too. Bring it on, maverick. Problem is, I genuinely believe that Becker is unaware of his knockout charm. I think it's natural to him. I think he fails to realise the extent of his appeal after a lifetime of charming the knickers off women. I, on the other hand, threw every effort into my flirting routine.

'Becker,' Shelley sings as we approach, turning away from her desk to give an obvious flash of her long, bare legs. 'Can I get you a coffee? Tea? Water?'

'I'm good,' Becker replies, coming to a stop, prompting me to do the same. I may as well not be here. Shelley is completely blanking me, and I notice, again, that she hasn't asked *me* if I'd like a drink. No, her full attention is on Becker, and it only becomes more acute when my boss places a palm on the edge of her desk and leans in towards her. She smiles demurely. I have to physically restrain myself from muscling my way between them and declaring Becker's *status* to this female. 'I need a favour,' Becker says, all low and raspy.

It not only piques Shelley's interest, it also piques mine. 'Of course,' she says, shamelessly crossing one leg over the over and leaning back. I grit my teeth and nearly crack them with the force of my bite when Becker gives a knowing, sideways smile. 'Anything for you, Becker,' she purrs.

'Any other interest in the 1965 Ferrari?'

She returns his knowing smile before turning to her computer and tapping a few buttons. 'This is breaking client confidentiality.'

'But it's for me,' Becker says quietly. Suggestively.

Oh my days, I want to poke the disgraceful philander in the eye. I'm about to step in, to take a leaf out of Becker's book, when it occurs to me that Becker is fishing for information – information that Shelley can give to him. Me staking a claim could hamper that. For fuck's sake. So, begrudgingly, I hold my tongue for a few moments while she continues to tap and glance up to Becker every now and then.

'There,' she says quietly. 'Bill Temple and Larry Stein have commission bids.'

'How much?'

'Highest is 110K.'

'Larry?' Becker questions.

'Good guess.'

'American,' he muses thoughtfully, like that's a significant point.

'Speaking of Americans,' Shelley says, scanning the screen.

Becker visibly stiffens. 'Don't say it.'

'Brent Wilson.'

'Motherfucker.' He smashes his fist down on Shelley's desk, making me jump. I don't think I need to intercept the flirting now, because Becker's mood has just taken a nosedive. He's no longer smiling coyly. Now he's practically growling at the mere mention of Brent's name. 'Block him,' Becker orders harshly.

Shelley flashes him a shocked look. 'You know I can't do that,' she protests, shaking her head to reinforce her words.

'I'll make it worth your while.'

I shoot him a look and Shelley visibly straightens up in her chair. Is he for real? Has he forgotten I'm here? '*How* will you make it worth her while?' I ask, more than pissed off.

He looks down at me, his mouth snapping shut. 'It was a figure of speech.'

'It wasn't last time,' Shelley pipes up, and my eyes are back on her in a heartbeat. She looks smug. I'm totally dumbfounded, yet I can't blame her since she doesn't know Becker's *status*.

'And what did you get last time?' I ask.

'Eleanor,' Becker pipes up, warning me. I don't care. I want to know, even if I'm pretty certain already, and I know it's going to eat me alive.

I hold my finger to my lips to halt him, then deliver a calm, 'Shhhh,' tilting my head to the side when his mouth drops open. 'Well?'

'Nothing.' Becker takes my arm, and I shrug him off, glaring at him.

'Dinner,' Shelley interjects, pulling my attention to her. She looks pleased with herself. I want to slap her. 'To start,' she adds.

The bitch. 'I'm sure your boss will appreciate this news,' I say, totally unruffled. 'Feeding Becker confidential information in return for . . .?' I can't say it. 'How sad, Shelley. You have to bargain for sex.'

Her smug look plummets as I swivel on my heels and walk gracefully, and with the utmost dignity, towards the elevator. I want to rip everything in sight to shreds. I hear Shelley's angry whispers from behind me as I push the call button and enter the lift.

'She won't say anything,' Becker snaps, dismissing Shelley's panic. In my spite, I want to march straight back to Timms's office and prove him wrong. The wanker.

'Don't count on it,' I call as the doors close. And as soon as I'm out of sight and the lift is moving, I yell, kicking the wall of the elevator before falling against it.

All of these women. This unexpected possessiveness coursing through me. It could be destructive. I need to channel it. My damn mind is racing with thoughts of how that dinner progressed. Did he give her a good fuck from behind? Spank her arse? I slap the ball of my palm into my forehead and massage the thought away before it gets the better of me. Becker can fuck right off if he thinks I'm subjecting myself to this shit every time we go out on *business*.

The doors open, and I engage my leg muscles to step out, but my foot only lifts an inch from the floor before I see him. His stance is wide, his hands in his trouser pockets, and he's standing slap-bang in the middle of the elevator opening, blocking my path. He looks solemn behind his glasses. How the heck did he make it down here so quickly?

I don't entertain him. Instead, I pass him and head for the revolving doors, ignoring the curious look from the receptionist. I'm a little surprised that Becker hasn't intercepted me, but not so surprised when I enter the turning doors and they jar to a halt. I breathe in some patience, then turn to confront him. He's in the next section of the revolving doors, maybe because he deems it safe having a sheet of glass between us. He'd be right.

His sleepy eyes behind his glasses have a soppy edge to them, and his bottom lip is protruding, so much so there's a risk of him tripping over it should he move forward. He looks sorry as he holds onto the metal handle, stopping me from pushing the door around.

'Are you mad with me?' he asks lamely.

'Not at all,' I quip on a sarcastic laugh. 'I love the fact that you've probably fucked every woman in London. Fills me with joy.'

'I haven't fucked *every* woman in London.'

'How many, then?' I have no idea why I'm asking this. I really don't want to know. Besides, I've seen the endless photographs on the internet.

His shoulders jump up on a guilty shrug. 'A few.'

'A few hundred? A few *thousand*?' I feel nauseous and jealous, the thought of another woman feeling him, touching him, seeing him naked, sending me positively insane. I thought I only had to worry about the threat of his love affair with his treasure. But seeing him in action, seeing these women fall all over themselves for him, I'm now feeling threatened for other reasons.

Arghhhhh!

'I don't know how to do this, Eleanor.' Becker dodges my question smartly, and I'm grateful. Guessing numbers is one thing. Having confirmation is another.

'And I'm not sure if I can show you,' I retort shortly, and his face drops, hurt invading it. I feel guilty, damn me. My fingers come to my temples and press into my skin, trying to push the stress away. 'Please stop flirting.'

He frowns, like that's an unreasonable request. It tells me that I was right with my assumption. It's natural for him to behave like that around women. 'You mean like you just did in Simon Timms's office?' he questions in surprise.

Yeah. I asked for that. 'I was proving a point.'

'Which was?'

I snap my mouth shut and think. I have no answer, and his raised eyebrow and expectant look tells me he's aware of that. I've been as bad as him today, shame on me. 'Two wrongs don't make a right,' I huff, taking the door handle and pushing my weight into it. It doesn't budge.

'I don't like it when you're mad with me.' Becker pushes his bottom lip out again, enhancing his sorry face.

'Pick up your lip,' I order shortly, trying to push the door again. It goes nowhere, but Becker's lip does. He juts it out even further. 'Stop it.'

His eyes droop.

'Becker, I'm being serious.'

'So am I.'

'You're being a juvenile.'

'Well, I kind of am when it comes to love.' He gives me an adorable smile. He knows what he's doing, and I can't really challenge that, because he's right. 'If I flash you my arse, will you forgive me?' he asks on a hopeful smile.

I drop my eyes on a shake of my head. 'I'll forgive you if you promise to stop with the stupid games.'

'Okay. I promise, I'm sorry. Old habits die hard, huh?'

I give him a look of utter disbelief. 'You'll die if you don't pack it in, because I'll bloody kill you.'

'Yikes, that bad th . . .' He fades off, and I glance back up to his adorably annoying face, finding he's staring past me. And he looks worried. I turn to see what's captured his attention.

And go stiff as a board.

Chapter 14

All of the blood rises to my head and reddens my face.

Alexa.

It's a good job I'm trapped behind the glass, because I can't guarantee my conduct if I wasn't. Becker's ex-screw is looking me up and down like I'm the most repulsive thing she's ever seen, her enhanced lips pursed, her blond hair in a harsh up-do. I'm suddenly moving, the glass pane behind me pushing me around, and I soon find myself within a metre of her on the pavement, nothing between us.

'Ah,' she sings, super over-the-top. I know by her tone and the derisive look on her face that the next thing she says is going to be scathing. 'It's the skivvy.' She flicks her silk scarf over her shoulder.

Be cool, Eleanor. Be cool.

'Becker prefers to call me his girlfriend these days,' I retort on a sweet smile.

She can't hide her shock, though she tries her hardest. 'Not for long. He's never been able to resist these legs wrapped around his waist.'

Kill her. No, kill her with kindness. That's what I should do. Don't rise to it. Be refined and grown up. 'Oh fuck off,' I spit, throwing my bag onto my shoulder, just as something meets my back with a thud. I jolt forward, courtesy of Becker barrelling into me. He's worried, and so he should be. I've endured enough brash women today.

'Becker.' Alexa eradicates all the spite from her voice and

smiles all sweet and innocent at my boss. No, my boyfriend. He's *my* boyfriend. 'Lovely to see you.'

'Yeah.' He takes my elbow and pushes me on. I don't protest. In fact, if I could click my fingers and magic us away, then I would. Then I wouldn't have to tolerate the daggers currently stabbing into my back as we escape, and in a stupid fit of possessiveness, I slide my hand onto his arse, for the benefit of Alexa.

'See you at Andelesea!' she sings. I'm halfway to turning around, a little confused, when I remember . . .

The gala at Countryscape. 'She's going to be there?' I blurt out, dropping his arse like it's white hot, turning my stunned face up to him. His attention is centred firmly forward, his flawless profile and perfect nose in perfect view.

'Sounds like it.' He speaks on a slight mutter, keeping up his pace.

'Great.' I don't trust Alexa. Not one little bit.

'Princess?' Becker's concerned voice snatches me from my unpleasant thoughts, and I look up at him, seeing the concern in his eyes, too. 'You okay?'

'Fine. When's the gala?' I walk on in determined strides, planning every evil thing I will do to Alexa if she so much as sniffs Becker.

'Saturday. You got my tux sorted, didn't you?' he asks, his footsteps close behind.

Shit, shit, shit. I need to get his tux dry-cleaned. 'Yes, all done.' I cringe, then proceed to mentally drop-kick myself across Bond Street. Not just because I've fucked up, but because *she* is going to be at the Andelesea Gala, and Becker's going to be in a tux.

'What are they showcasing at Andelesea, anyway?' I ask. The most famous annual gala in the art world is renowned for boasting exclusive exhibits.

'Heart of Hell.'

My steps falter. 'The gigantic ruby?'

'That's the one.'

I'm not so irritated now, more envious. I'd love to see the elusive gem that's been the talk of precious-stone experts for decades. It's been kept from public view by its discoverer and private owner, J.P. Randel, since it was unearthed in 1939. Everyone was beginning to think it was a myth. 'So it *does* exist?' I ask, keeping my pace as Becker follows me, but then I remember something in the NDA, and I skid to a stop. 'Wait, am I coming with you?' I ask the open space in front of me.

I catch sight of Becker out the corner of my eye, then he's standing before me, a thoughtful look on his face. 'Of course.'

'Oh good.' I smile brightly at him. 'That'll please Alexa.'

'Eleanor, don't let her bother you. She's a leech.'

'She's not bothering me.'

He rolls his eyes and cocks his arm out for me to take. 'I need to pick a dress for you.'

He does? 'Do I have consultation rights?' I ask, letting him lead me down the road.

He ponders my question for a few moments, then looks down at me with a conniving grin. 'I have only a few rules that you must adhere to. Other than that, I'm pretty flexible.'

'And what are the rules?' I'm wary, and I get a strange feeling that I need to be.

'Legs out and high heels.' He reels off his demands wistfully, a delighted smile on his face. He's already thought about this. Those rules came too quick and easily. So I'll be wearing a cocktail dress? I nod agreeably to myself. 'And no knickers,' he tags on the end.

'No knickers?' I blurt out, throwing him a horrified look. 'A short dress and no knickers? At Countryscape?'

'You're a clever girl, princess.' He stops and takes the tops of my arms, bringing his face close to mine. 'High heels, short dress, no knickers,' he whispers, his eyes scanning my face while he holds me in place. I'm not stupid. I know why he's insisting on me wearing a short dress and no knickers. Not only will he relish in the thought of my arse bare beneath, but he's also making allowances for a spanking session should the urge come over him. And I don't doubt it will.

'That could be awkward when I drop-kick Alexa.' I say thoughtfully, and Becker laughs loudly.

'Fucking hell, I love you.'

Warmth. God, it's the best feeling. 'I'm not going to give you any reason to spank me.'

He grins and plants a forceful kiss on my lips, sucking me further into his debasing world. 'I don't need a reason to indulge in what's mine, princess.'

'When are you going to accept it, Mr Hunt?' I ask around his kiss. 'You do not own me.'

'Keep telling yourself that.'

'I will.'

He grabs my hand, checking for traffic, before we cross the road towards the side street where Becker parked his pretty red Ferrari. 'Did you get hold of the Andy Warhol exhibition catalogue?' he asks as he opens the door and I slide in.

'They've reserved one for you. It'll be mailed this week.'

'Super.' He shuts the door and rounds the car, sliding in and switching his specs for shades before he starts the car and pulls off. I go to my phone to check my emails, seeing one has just landed from Sotheby's.

I frown. 'There's a problem with the O'Keeffe painting.'

Becker swings me an alarmed look. 'A problem?'

I scan the email, searching for more information. 'They don't say. They've asked me to call them.' I dial Sotheby's as Becker takes a corner. 'Oh, wait,' I hang up before it connects and point my phone at the sign for New Bond Street. 'We may as well stop in.'

'Good idea.' Becker takes the turn and slows in search of a parking space, and I scan the street too, looking down the side streets for any available spaces as he crawls along.

'Nothing,' I say, pointing to the entrance of Sotheby's. 'Just drop me outside and wait. It shouldn't take long.'

Becker pulls up and idles at the kerb. 'They better not have discovered it's a fake,' he says, giving me high eyebrows. 'That would be ironic, wouldn't it?'

I laugh and jump out. 'Back in a minute.' When I enter, it's busy, people criss-crossing the foyer. 'Is Frank Gardener available?' I ask when I arrive at reception. 'My name's Eleanor Cole. The Hunt Corporation.'

The man on reception dials an extension and talks briefly before hanging up. 'He won't be a minute. Please, take a seat.'

'Actually, can you tell me where the ladies are?' I'm suddenly desperate for the loo.

'Yes, just over there on the right.'

'Thanks. Will you let Frank know if I'm not back?'

'Of course.'

I hotfoot it to the ladies, taking a right as instructed, but I skid to an alarmed stop when I see someone at the end of the corridor, pushing his way through a staff door. 'Shit,' I breathe, diving back around the corner before Brent sees me, plastering my back to a wall. What the hell is he doing here? I look left and right, weighing up my options. I have only one. Hold my bladder. I can't see him. Don't *want* to see him.

I hurry back to reception and find a chair, my eyes watchful as I perch on the edge, my mind racing. *What's he doing here?* My stomach rolling, I pull up my emails, checking the transfer details with Becker's bank. 'Oh no,' I nearly die, and all thoughts of Brent Wilson disappear when I see I've entered a digit wrong. 'Fuck. Fuck, fuck, fuck.' I break out in a sweat, scrambling through my contacts for the number of Becker's personal banker.

'Miss Cole?'

I look up, finding a man before me. 'I'm sorry, can you just give me a minute?' I ask as the phone rings. 'I've just realised I entered the bank account details wrong for the transfer. I'm assuming that's what the problem is with the O'Keeffe?' Someone picks up, and I hold a finger up for Frank to wait. 'Hi, yes, it's Eleanor Cole, the Hunt Corporation. I believe there's an issue with a payment to Sotheby's.'

'Yes, we've been trying to call Mr Hunt.'

'You can speak to me.' *Please speak to me.* 'I have clearance from Mr Hunt. My name's Eleanor Cole.'

'Okay, we'll need to go through a few security questions. Can you type into your keypad the third digit of the account password?'

'Absolutely.' I stand and pace up and down as I follow his instructions and then answer all the questions fired at me, my eyes batting back and forth to the huge clock hanging on the foyer wall.

'Thank you for clearing security,' he eventually says. 'The account number provided doesn't exist.'

'That's my fault. I entered a digit incorrectly.' Bloody hell. Becker will kill me. 'Can we rectify that now? I'm at Sotheby's.'

'Of course. Do you have access to online banking?'

'I have the app.'

'Excellent. If you enter the details again, I'll make sure it goes through without delay.'

I put him on loudspeaker and click the app, but the damn thing won't load. I could kick myself. I put my hand over the phone. 'I don't suppose you have a spare computer I could use?' I ask Frank, who's waiting patiently nearby.

He smiles kindly. 'This way, Miss Cole.'

I go back to my phone. 'I'll call you back in five minutes once I'm at a computer.'

'Okay, Miss Cole.'

I hang up and follow Frank as he leads me into a private office. 'I'm so sorry about this,' I say, a little embarrassed. It's the first payment I've made for Becker and I've fucked it all up. *Idiot!*

'Don't worry. The painting is all packaged and loaded onto the van ready for delivery. I knew there would be a simple explanation. We've dealt with the Hunts for many years.' Frank motions to a chair, and I take a seat as he backs out of the room. 'Just call me if you require any assistance.'

'Thank you, Frank.' I go straight to the computer and pull up Becker's private bank as I call them back. 'Hi, yes, I'm—' I'm cut dead in my tracks when he door swings open and Becker appears.

'What's the problem?'

Damn. He must have found a parking space. I cringe as I tap in his login details. There goes my hope of fixing the problem before Becker knows I've fucked up. 'No problem,' I sing, returning my attention to my phone as Becker rounds the desk and joins me. He looks at the screen. Frowns. Gives me the eye. I can only shrug, and he sighs, catching the gist of the problem.

'For fuck's sake,' he breathes. 'People will think—' He stops talking abruptly when a security guard flies past the glass door, and both our eyes follow, both our foreheads wrinkling. 'What's going on?' Becker asks, walking to the door and looking out. I join him, hearing the commotion. Frank hurries past, and Becker stops him. 'Frank, is there a problem?'

'No,' he squeaks, carrying on his way. 'Good to see you, Mr Hunt.'

I look at Becker, getting a funny feeling.

'I have a funny feeling,' he says, reading my mind. He follows Frank, and I quickly grab my bag and follow Becker, but as I've nearly caught up with him, I remember something. *Shit!* I backtrack, dashing back to the office and deleting the digits from the login screen before catching up with Becker. The commotion has heightened, and I arrive to find Frank throwing curses left and right, turning the air in the posh auction house blue.

And Becker looks absolutely savage, staring at Frank incredulously. 'What do you mean, the O'Keefe is gone?' he asks, and I baulk. *What?*

Poor Frank looks like he's about ready to pop under the pressure. 'It was on the van, and now—'

'Goddamn it, Frank.' Becker slings his arm out and sends a pile of paperwork on a nearby table wafting into the air. 'I've been trying to acquire that painting for years, and now you're telling me the moment I buy it, it disappears?'

I stand silent, as Frank's sweats increase and Becker's rage grows. And all I can think about is Brent. The rivalry. The game of one-upmanship going on between the two men. I bite my lip, not liking the nasty feeling in my gut.

Becker takes my hand and tugs me out of the room. 'That's the last time I do business with Sotheby's,' he mutters over his shoulder, making Frank bury his head in his hands.

'Becker,' I say as I'm pulled along, but he doesn't stop, just continues, annoyed. 'Becker, Brent was here.'

He stops in a heartbeat and swings stunned eyes my way. 'What?'

'When I went to the ladies, I saw him. You don't think . . .'

His lips twist, his eyes close, and then he stalks away, giving me my answer. Oh my goodness.

Shit. The word is running on repeat in my mind. *Shit, shit, shit.*

Chapter 15

I wasn't about to ask Becker where he keeps his tux, so as soon as we were back at The Haven and he'd disappeared in his office to sulk about his stolen painting, I used his distraction to my advantage and performed a ram-raid on his apartment in a panic, flying through the wardrobe in his bedroom like my life depended on it. I eventually found it tucked away in a closet in the corner of his bedroom, lost behind a mountain of other suits. After I pulled it free, I made a hasty dash, praying that the dry-cleaner's would have it ready for Friday at the latest. I struck gold. Giles at Fosters knew exactly who I was, or who Becker was, and responded to the sweetest smile I could muster, telling me he'd have it ready tomorrow. After thanking him profusely, I made my way back to The Haven, calling Mum on my way to check if it's still convenient – since she's a social butterfly these days – for me to go home next weekend. After an excited *yes*, I hung up and made a mental note to book my train ticket.

The next day, I stroll into Becker's office to collect some files and find his granddad at his desk. Mr H looks up over his glasses, holding a broadsheet with slightly shaky hands. 'Eleanor.'

'Good afternoon, Mr H.' I wander over and take a seat opposite him, resting my phone on the desk 'Where's Becker?'

'He's taking a delivery.'

'A delivery?' He never mentioned any deliveries today, and I certainly haven't organised any.

'I don't ask.' Mr H looks down at the newspaper, shaking his head. 'In broad daylight, too,' he muses, and he turns the sheet so I can see. Not that I need to. The theft from Sotheby's has been a hot topic, as you'd expect. It turns out me screwing up the bank transfer was a blessing in disguise. 'Becker mentioned you saw Wilson there moments before the painting was discovered missing.'

'I don't trust that man.' I admit. 'Becker seems happy to move on, but Brent doesn't.' I know my man. He won't let Brent get away with turning him over like that. His ego won't allow it. Neither will his fierce need for revenge. And that's left me wondering with growing worry where that leaves us.

'Becker doesn't need much encouragement to play Wilson's game.' He huffs and tosses his paper to the side, and I glance over to where it's landed, noticing a file that's been knocked askew, dislodging a few papers from inside. I wouldn't usually take much notice, but this file is blue. All the files in The Haven are red.

The tilt of my head is discreet as I try to zoom in on the image in the bottom left-hand corner of one of the strewn sheets. It's a woman. An old woman, with jet-black hair that's cut into a very harsh, unflattering bob. The colour is equally unflattering against her pale skin, and her eyes are feline-like, a suggestion that she's indulged in a little too much surgery.

'How's your mother?' Mr H asks, pulling my attention back to him.

'She's good. She has a new . . .' I pull up when I fail to locate the right word to reference Paul, my face twisting when mental images of him brandishing a baseball bat, naked in my mum's hallway, assault me.

'Chap?' Mr H offers, sitting forward in his chair.

'I guess.' I shrug.

'You seem bothered.'

'I never imagined my mum with anyone except my father.'

Mr H nods in understanding, and I watch as his old eyes fall to the file that his newspaper's landed on. He's quick to tidy up the strewn papers, tucking them neatly back inside. 'Is she happy?' he asks, glancing back at me.

I'm not quick to answer, despite the answer being easy. My eyes are on that file, until Mr H coughs and snaps me from my staring. 'Deliriously.' I can tell by the way the old man is looking at me that he knows my mind is racing, wondering what that file is. *So what is it? And why is he trying to conceal it?*

When his eyebrows raise on a small grin, I feign casualness, reaching forward and stroking the beautiful double-pedestal desk that deserves the admiration I always give it. 'I love this desk.'

Mr H smirks. 'You recognise it?'

'Of course,' I confirm. I recognised it the moment I stepped foot in here on that fateful day when Becker Hunt became my boss. And later my lover. Or boyfriend. 'It's a replica of the Theodore Roosevelt desk.'

'It is,' Mr H says, caressing the surface with a quivering palm. 'Looks just like it, I agree. An amazing imitation.'

Now I'm studying his hand more than I am the desk. Some days his shakes are better than others, and today they are particularly bad. He shakes off his shakes, still chuckling, before it fades and silence descends. He's looking at me with a knowing smile as he slowly pushes his glasses up his nose before joining his hands and resting them on his stomach. 'That fire in your eyes is blazing, Eleanor. Nearly matches your hair.'

I feel that fire reach my cheeks and start pointlessly faffing with the hem of my dress. 'I'm happy.'

'That's very apparent.'

'I'd be happier if you and Becker made peace,' I tell him, not liking the sour expression that passes over his face at the mention of his grandson and their rift.

He looks across the super desk over his glasses. 'Shall I tell you why I want to tan that boy's arse?' he asks quietly.

'Okay,' I agree warily, unable to resist the temptation of being indulged in any information that concerns his grandson.

'Getting your hands on something that is thought lost in history gives you a rush like nothing else,' he tells me, nodding his head. The old man is speaking of the lost sculpture, the one he's forbidden his grandson to search for. The one Becker says he doesn't need to find any more.

'You sound like you're talking from experience.'

'I've found a few little things in my time.' He winks cheekily.

'But not the sculpture.'

'No.' His answer is short and clipped. Resentful. 'I gave up on that after I lost my wife. But Becker's father didn't give up after he lost Becker's mother, Lou.' He smiles, revealing a perfect set of pearly whites. They are far too flawless to be real, especially on a man in his senior years. 'And you know what happened because of that, don't you, Eleanor?'

I nod. That lost sculpture has a lot to answer for. 'You were so mad.' I state the obvious because I don't have a clue what else to say. I don't blame the old man for going off the deep end when he found out that Becker tricked Brent Wilson into buying a forgery. Lord knows what he'd do if he found out Becker sculpted it, too.

'Of course I was mad. I lost my son and his wife as a direct result of that damn sculpture. I'll take an arrow before I willingly let my Becker boy follow in their footsteps.' Sadness washes over him, and I quickly feel so very guilty for being so fascinated and curious about *Head of a Faun*. 'My beloved Becker was twenty-two when it happened.' He goes on without the need for me to press. 'Travelling the world and filling that smart head of his with a wealth of information. That boy's mind is like a sponge. Soaks up everything.' He smiles to himself, that proud edge back, before quickly slipping back to sour. 'Stupid boy is more obsessed than his father ever was.'

Is. Not *was*. 'But he said he's letting it go,' I tell him quietly, almost hesitantly. 'He told me he doesn't need to find it any more.'

Becker's granddad's smile is sympathetic. I don't like it. 'I have lost my reckless son and my innocent daughter-in-law because of a silly family competitiveness that goes back nearly a hundred years.' There's a bitterness in his tone that I just cannot comprehend. The word *reckless* is on the long list of words that I would use to describe Becker. Along with *maverick*. Both signify elements of risk. Becker takes risks. I've considered them to be calculated. Now I'm not so sure. While Becker's father was pushed to take the risks that resulted in his death, I don't think Becker needs that push. I think he takes risks without thought. Like it's inbuilt.

'Becker promised me he had both stopped looking for the sculpture and stopped provoking Wilson,' Mr H goes on. 'He did neither, so I'm mad with him. He lied to his own grandfather,' he finishes, leaving that last statement lingering. What he means and hasn't said, is that if Becker would lie to his flesh and blood, then he wouldn't think twice about lying to me.

'Right,' I murmur dejectedly, my eyes dropping to my lap.

'You know him by now, Eleanor. Everything about him. You don't need me to tell you, but I will tell you this.' Struggling forward a little, he smiles. 'Life is more precious than anything,' he almost whispers, but I hear it like a foghorn. 'I hope Becker realises that quicker than I or his father did. He has you, and I can see how fond he is of you. It fills my heart with joy. But I'm not delusional. And you shouldn't be, either. He's like a dog with a bone, and not even you can make him let go.'

I stare at the old man, absorbing everything he's told me. Life is more precious. I'm certain Becker thinks that now, but what if he won't give up on that sculpture? What if this is something I have to accept? And if I do accept it, am I prepared to watch him self-destruct? Or fail? Or end up like his father? Dead. I flinch. And what about me? Will I end up like Becker's mother? I'm flinching again. Life is more precious. I'll never forget Becker's words and the sincerity in them when he told me the tortured tale of his parents' deaths. I'm more important to him than that sculpture. That's what he told me. But I also appreciate his passion. His addiction to the thrill. And I can't lie, there are moments more regular than I will ever admit that I myself wonder. I wonder if it can be found. I wonder what Becker's face would look like if he did find it. Wonder where it is. Wonder how it would feel. My heart skips and I fight to control it. It's not worth the risk. *But the bigger the risk, the bigger the reward.* Finding *Head of a Faun* would be the ultimate reward for Becker. And him finding the peace he'll get from that would be the ultimate reward for me.

I'm not sure how long I'm lost in my thoughts, but when I finally glance up, Mr H is staring intently at the computer screen, as if he knows what I've been pondering and doesn't want to disturb me. 'What have we here, then?' he muses quietly.

'What's that?' I ask, craning my neck to try and get the screen of the computer in view.

'Just rewinding through the CCTV footage. Winston was chasing something up the corridor last night. I worry about rats.'

I grimace on a shudder, hoping I misheard him. 'Rats?'

He hums his confirmation. 'Central London, sewers, and old buildings unfortunately attract the little blighters.'

I shiver, like I could have an army of them crawling all over my skin right now. 'Ewww.'

'Goodness Goliath!' Mr H hollers, flying back in his chair like something has jumped out of the screen and slapped him. I recoil, shocked, as he starts grappling with the keyboard. 'Lord above, make it stop.' He surrenders the keyboard and covers his glasses with his palms. I'm about to go to his aid, help him out and shut down the screen, when I remember what he was looking for. I remain in my seat. Rats. My mind starts to conjure up the image of a filthy great big rodent. If he's spotted one, then I don't want to see it. Oh God, we have rats?

I'm useless in my chair while Mr H repeatedly peeks through spread fingers, groaning in anguish each time he does before snapping them shut and shaking his head. He's going to have a seizure.

The power. Cut the power. I start to search for the socket, set on wrenching the plug out so I don't have to face what's clearly a monster of a rat on the screen of the computer, but with no obvious cables leading anywhere, I drop to my knees and scramble under the desk.

'What's going on?' Mrs Potts voice makes my head lift, relieved, until it collides with the underside of the solid desk with an almighty crack.

'Ouch!' I yelp, my hand going to the top of my head and rubbing frantically as I drag myself to my knees. Mr H is still mumbling nonsensical words behind his palm, and Mrs Potts is standing at the doorway, taking in the mayhem that she's walked in on. I keep my hand on my pounding head and point to Mr H with my spare. 'He's found a rat on the CCTV footage,' I tell her, hoping she isn't as squeamish as me and will rid the screen of the horror before Becker's gramps passes out.

'A rat?' She's barrelling towards me fast, rounding the desk and thrusting her face in the screen. 'Oh I say,' she breathes, moving back. She *actually* moves away, making me wonder how big that damn rat actually is. I'm moving back to my apartment immediately.

I watch in stunned silence as she, too, slaps a palm over her eyes. Her other hand rests on Mr H's shoulder, offering support in his moment of need. 'I don't know how to work these damn fancy computers, Donald.'

Great. So now it's down to me to sort this out. I drop my head back on a moan while I summon some bravery to face the horror movie playing out on the monitor. 'For God's sake,'

I mutter, trudging across the office and rounding the desk. My eyes are half closed as I muscle past Mr H and Mrs Potts, trying to distort the images as I search for an *off* button.

Half closed, but they are also half open, and they can see the screen like my eyes have a magnifying glass held in front of them. My string of motions cut dead. As does my heartbeat. There's no rat, but what I'm looking at makes that more of a regret than a relief. 'Oh ... my ... God,' I choke over my swelling tongue. 'Oh my God!'

'Make it stop,' Mr H cries.

I can't. I want to, but I can't, no matter how loud my brain is screaming the orders to shut down the computer. I've been rendered incapable of movement. Through shock.

Because what's on the screen is certifiably shocking.

Me.

Palms spread on the wall in the corridor outside this office. Naked.

Make it stop!

With Becker smashing into the back of me like a wild wolf on speed.

And I just stare at it, mouth hanging open, eyes set to pop out of my head, while his dear old grandpa and Mrs Potts hide behind their hands next to me. There's no sound coming from the footage, but that is only a mild consolation.

Make it stop!

I fly into action and reach behind the screen, grabbing the first cable I lay my hand on and yanking it out. I could collapse to my arse in relief when the screen finally dies, leaving blackness. Though the mental images will never leave me.

The silence is agonising. My palms are resting on the desk, my eyes closed, as I try to catch a breath. I should leave – hope that this will never be mentioned or thought of ever again. It's a big hope. I'll never be able to look old Mr H or Mrs Potts in the eye again. I'm mortified. I want to open the drawer of this desk, shove my head in, and shut it repeatedly. It'll probably be less painful than the embarrassment I'm feeling right now.

'Well,' I laugh like a blundering fool. 'At least there are no rats.' I want to cry. I'd take a million rats, dog-sized rats, and let them crawl all over my naked body if I could rewrite the last five minutes of my history. But I can't. And I'm devastated.

Pushing myself up by my palms, I straighten my shoulders and clear my throat. 'Good afternoon,' I say, forcing my feet into action to take me away from this God-awful awkwardness.

I could be drunk, if my stability is anything to go by. I'm shaking with embarrassment. I wish I *was* drunk. In fact, I'm going to find some alcohol right this minute and drown my humiliation.

Shutting the office door behind me, I find the nearest wall and let my forehead meet it. Repeatedly. Nothing can redeem me. It's bad enough that they warned me against getting personally involved with Becker. They didn't like the thought. I bet they positively *hated* the sight.

Chapter 16

I drag my dejected body down the corridor, through the Grand Hall, and into the courtyard. I need fresh air. Or water so I can drown myself. The round stone fountain catches my eye as I wander across the cobbles. 'Too shallow,' I say to myself, as I rest my arse on the edge, performing my customary flinch at the soreness. I look over my shoulder into the water again, gauging the depth as my reflection shimmers up at me. I only need a few inches. It's doable.

'Hi.' Another reflection appears, one of a woman, and I swing around to find an immaculate blonde clad in an impeccable trouser suit. I look around, wondering where she's come from.

'Hello,' I say warily. 'Eleanor.' I offer, taking her hand. 'You are?'

'Emma,' she sings, but says no more, leaving me still wondering who she is and where she came from. Dropping my hand, she gestures around the courtyard. 'I've never had the privilege. He always comes to me.'

Why is she talking in riddles? 'You mean Becker?'

'Who else?' She laughs, sending her hand into the beautiful Stella McCartney handbag that's suspended from the crook of her arm. She drags out her phone and starts tapping on the keys while I stand like a plum before her, admiring her well-turned-out form. 'He's just gone to check the delivery,' she says, keeping her focus on her phone.

I'm beginning to get irritated. She's said plenty and told me nothing, except her name. 'What have you bought from him?' I ask, curious. I don't recall any mention of an Emma and I haven't seen one in the endless client files that I've encountered here at The Haven.

She laughs and drops her phone back into her bag. 'Oh, I don't buy from Becker. He buys from me.'

I frown, just as the man himself appears from the showing room across the courtyard. He looks pleased with himself. That could change when he finds out what I've just endured in his office.

'Emma.' Becker gives her a devilish grin, and she giggles, turning her full attention onto him. Why wouldn't she? He looks heavenly, as always, but he's changed out of his suit and is now in a pair of grey sweatpants and a white T-shirt that accentuates every line on his chest and stomach. Is it even possible for him to ever look like a bag of shit? A shadow on his cheek catches my eye – a grey smudge. He's been in his secret room again. What's he up to in there?

'Anything take your fancy?' Emma asks, returning his devilish grin.

'A few options.' He stuns me when he snakes his arm around my waist and pulls me into his side. Emma, surprisingly, doesn't bat an eyelid. She just smiles at me, like she's privy to something secret. I cock my head and flick my eyes between the two of them, not liking her obvious discretion. 'Invoice me for what I've taken.' Becker tells her. 'And good call, by the way.'

Emma smiles and backs towards the alleyway. 'This way?' she asks, pointing over her shoulder.

'That way,' Becker confirms. 'Thanks, Emma.'

'Anytime.' She bashes her lashes and saunters off, disappearing down the alleyway.

'Who was that?' I ask, reaching up to wipe the smudge of dirt from his face.

His eyes follow my hand to his cheek, and he holds still

until I'm done. 'Emma.' He takes my hand and leads me to the showing room.

'And who's Emma?'

'That woman you just met.'

He's being vague. 'Have you . . .' I don't know why the hell I'm asking. I'm a glutton for punishment.

'Yes.' He doesn't hesitate, astounding me.

My stomach bottoms out. Nice. I break our held hands. 'I truly relish the thought.' My quip sounds as sarcastic as I meant it to.

'About as much as I relish the thought of your ex-*boyfriend*.' The enhancement of the word *boyfriend* is piercing. And like my previous quip, meant to be. I skid to a stop, as does Becker. My face is outraged, whereas his is deadpan.

'One man, Becker,' I point out, holding a finger up in demonstration. 'Just one.' I can't bring myself to even think of all the women who have had a piece of him. It would be pointless; I'd lose count. 'You cannot compare.'

His jaw tightens. 'One is one too many.'

'Are you for real?' I ask on a laugh.

He pushes his face to mine, stopping my amusement with the flash of fire in his eyes. 'How many times have I told you? I am very real, princess. Would you rather I lie to you?' He looks angry. His audacity stokes my irritation, and I draw breath, prepared to let loose on him. But a firm palm slaps over my mouth, silencing me. 'He had your heart, Eleanor. Before you, no one has ever had mine.'

I gulp behind his hand and press my lips together, even though my chances of speaking are limited with his hand firmly wedged against my mouth.

'So yes,' he continues. 'One is one too many.'

I have no come back to that. Not a jiffy. So I reach up and take his hand, slowly pulling it down. I need to get shot of this silly possessive streak. I can't change his past, and, actually, I should be grateful that he's being so honest with me. Even if it stings. 'I'm sorry.'

'Me too.' Becker steps into me and takes my cheeks with both palms, squeezing, before raining kisses all over my face.

I sigh, letting him at me. 'What have you been up to in your secret room?' I ask quietly, aiming for a complete subject change.

'Trying to relax.' Becker answers, pulling away and finding my eyes. Trying. He obviously failed. He's been on edge since I told him who I saw at Sotheby's the other day. Has he found out anything? Surely the police would want to talk to anyone there, including me.

'The police have been in touch.'

He's a mind reader. It scares me. 'And . . .?'

'And they want to take a statement from you.'

'What about you?'

'I've told them what I know. Which isn't much.'

'Are they coming here?'

He snorts. 'Not a chance. Hell will freeze over before I let a copper inside the walls of The Haven. They're lucky I talked to them at all.'

I wince, seeing the article I found on the internet about his father's death. A mugging gone wrong. It's ridiculous. And his mother? The police weren't exactly helpful then, either. 'And what should I say to them?'

'The truth, Eleanor. Just tell them why we were there and what happened.'

Easy for him. I can't help but worry that he's not going to let this slide. Brent didn't want that painting. He knew how much Becker wanted it and that's the only reason he's acquired it. Yet I keep going back to . . . how? How does a business-man like Brent Wilson steal a bloody Georgia O'Keeffe from Sotheby's?

'Becker,' I start, but his finger covers my mouth and he delivers that sexy shush.

'I'm over it.' He moves his palms to my shoulders. 'Paula is proud of me.'

Paula? Dr Vass, his therapist? 'You're still seeing her?' Voices in my head remind me of that conversation between Becker and his granddad, the one where old Mr H demanded his grandson sought therapy instead of using me as his medicine. So he's doing both? Is that a good thing?

His expression takes on an edge of annoyance, his hand going to the back of his neck and stroking at his nape. 'Yes. She's like a dog with a fucking bone now she knows about you.'

I laugh on the inside, recalling her surprise when she learned of my trip to Countryscape with Becker. 'And what does she make of us?' I ask.

'She was quite shocked when I told her that I'm kind of attached to you.'

'Attached to me?'

'Yes, like one of my treasures.'

'Is that what *she* said?' I can see her now, analysing how Becker sees me. Like one of his prized treasures.

'Yes.'

I'm offended. 'Does that mean you'd rather burn me than let someone else have me?'

The look of disgust that invades his face is profound. He could be chewing mud. 'Pretty much, yes.'

'That's so romantic.' I laugh, bringing my palm to my forehead to smooth out the wrinkles caused by my frown.

'I never claimed to be romantic.' Becker snatches my hand from my head and starts pulling me across the courtyard towards the showing room. 'But I'm going to try.'

'You are?' This should be interesting.

'Yes. Paula has given me a few pointers.'

'You asked your therapist for relationship advice?'

'Among other things.'

'Like what?' My mind is racing.

'Like what dress you might like,' he tells me nonchalantly. *Really?* Oh God, this could be a catastrophe. Did Becker tell her that my colouring isn't exactly versatile? Did he tell her that I have a rather curvy arse? 'Why did you have me take Paula's calls those times?' I ask.

His steps stutter slightly, and I glance up to find him pouting to himself. 'I wanted her to get to know you before I declared my situation.'

'What situation?'

'You, princess.' He sighs tiredly, as if bored of the conversation. '*You* are my situation.'

'You make me sound like a burden,' I grumble, pouting.

'You kind of are.'

My slighted state just got even more slighted. That's charming. 'You're a situation for me, too, you know? Being mixed up with your boss isn't ideal. Especially one who's a con artist, forger, and has you sworn to secrecy.'

He stops us and circles my neck with his big palms, looking down at me with a slight edge of tiredness. 'Nothing about this is ideal, Eleanor. That much I've figured out.' His expression softens and he loosens his grip of my neck a little, forcing a smile. 'Just keep stumbling with me, princess, and I'll keep stumbling with you.'

'Will we ever stop stumbling?' It could get tiring, wear us both down.

Becker's forced smile transforms into a genuine, cheeky one, and he drops a chaste kiss on my forehead. 'I fucking hope not. I love stumbling with you.' He opens the door to the showing room, and music penetrates my hearing. I throw him a questioning look as Miike Snow croons 'Silvia'.

'Your therapist really gave you advice on what dress I might like?' I ask, thinking this situation will probably tell me everything I should know about Paula and her intentions. I'm suddenly feeling threatened by the woman whom I haven't met, and who sounded so sincere on the calls I had with her. Someone casting a negative light on our relationship is the last thing I need. She compared me to one of Becker's treasures. She's also a woman, so should naturally fancy Becker. She has a heartbeat and a vagina. It's a given. Forgive me, but my faith in womankind isn't the strongest it's ever been.

Becker nods slowly. 'Yes, she did.'

'And what did she say?' I ask warily.

'She said to pick what I would like to see you in.' My faith in womankind is restored again as he coaxes me into the showing room and points to the huge white wall at the back of the room where three dresses hang from hooks – the dresses he'd like to see me wearing. 'I picked these,' he declares proudly. My faith in womankind might have been restored, but my faith in Becker plummets.

My feet stutter to a stop. I'm speechless. Nearly. 'Wow.' I'm faced with some seriously racy dresses, not anything I would expect to be seen in at a posh gala at Countryscape. One is black ... and leather ... and short. The other is green, with a plunging neckline and it's even shorter than the short black number. And the blood-red one? Well, I can barely see it.

'My final decision depends on a few things,' Becker tells me, wandering slowly over to his carefully exhibited display. I keep my eyes glued to the dresses. There's a metre of white wall between each, and my eyes are jumping between them, worry plaguing me. I can't say that I'd feel comfortable in any, but something tells me that my comfort isn't high up on Becker's list of priorities.

Just like when Becker has one of his priceless treasures on display in the showing room, there is nothing else to focus on, other than these dresses. Except, of course, my filthy-minded boyfriend, but I dare not look at him now. It'll confirm how serious he is about me wearing one of these napkins. So I stare at the dresses instead, hoping that at least one will miraculously double in size.

I won't ask. I refuse to ask the question. I don't want to know. Because I'll be horrified. But I'll also be delighted. 'What does it depend on?' My inquiry sails from my mouth before I can stop it. I know what his final decision depends on. I take a risky peek at him, finding that adorable, mischievous grin. He has an apple in his hand. A big, green, shiny apple that's being casually tossed into the air and caught with ease as he stares at me. After taking a big bite of the lush green fruit, he starts to chew slowly, as he lowers and places the apple gently on the floor. I smile on the inside. He's not done with that apple.

Keeping his hazel eyes low, he prowls towards me, pulling his T-shirt up over his head. My knees are instantly weak. Will the day ever come when my knickers don't flood with desire at the sight of him? Part of me hopes not, but the sensible side of me appreciates the inconvenience it may cause.

I stiffen when I feel the heat of his body closing in, my upper body bowing, my throat drying.

Then his mouth is at my ear. 'Let's take off your dress,' he whispers, before biting my lobe and grazing my skin as he drags his teeth down my flesh. I can smell apple mixed with his clean cologne, creating that unique Becker scent. Electricity surges through me, crackling and stabbing at every sensitive part of my body, most significantly between my legs.

'I have work to do,' I murmur.

'Me too.'

I open my eyes as he takes the hem of my floral sundress and slowly, so very slowly, painfully slowly, drags it up my body, looking deeply into my eyes as he does. I don't put up a fight. As I feared, I follow his orders like a faithful dog, swallowing and lifting my arms so he can rid me of my dress. And then the underwear goes – bra, knickers, the lot – leaving me a blank canvas for Becker to play with, my nipples buzzing and hard.

After casting my underwear aside, he weaves his fingers into the hair at my nape, playing gently for a few moments before circling my naked body until he's poised behind me. Soft lips meet my shoulder, my head automatically tilting, my eyes closing. 'You smell heavenly.' He inhales deeply, sliding his hand to my front, his palm spanning my tummy. I'm tugged back. 'Taste so sweet.' His tongue trails a firm lick up the side of my throat to my ear. My hand finds his on my stomach and clenches hard, my eyes rolling in pleasure. 'Look amazing.' He grips my jaw hard until I open my eyes. 'Feel incredible.' Flexing his hand on my tummy until I release it, he slides it down my skin and delves into the wetness awaiting him. My arse flies back on a distressed cry, crashing into his groin. He hisses. 'We need to try on these dresses before I abandon our fitting and fuck you to Italy and back.' He rips his body from mine, causing physical pain. 'By the wall.' Taking my upper arm, he pulls me over to the bare wall opposite the dresses and positions me at the foot, right in the centre.

I'm aching for his touch. Aching for *him*. It takes every scrap of willpower to stay where I am, and a bit more when he abandons me and makes his way over to the dresses, his inked back being waved like a red flag. I can see him adjusting his groin as he goes.

'This one first,' he says, unhooking the black dress from the hanger and unzipping it as he wanders back to my pulsing form. No amount of deep breathing is steadying my shakes, or my thrilled heartbeat. I know what's coming, yet I have no inclination to hinder Becker's intentions. Even my backside is tensing excitedly in preparation. Whether business or pleasure, this man thrills me no end.

Making a point of keeping his eyes on my reddening face, he sinks to his knees before me and holds the dress open at my feet. I get no vocal order, just a sharp nod of his head, so I step in and pray to every resistance god to help me hold it together as Becker pulls the black leather up my body, arranging it slowly around my boobs. He then turns me to face the wall. The sound of the zipper being fastened is the only noise as he calmly pulls it up. Until my restricted lungs drain of air. The irony of this whole situation doesn't escape me. I'm panting like a dog on heat, like he could be slowly stripping me rather than dressing me.

My red locks are gathered and tied up meticulously. 'Shoulders,' he says simply, kissing one before the other. I bring my palms up to the wall before he can demand it, relaxing. It doesn't matter if I close my eyes or force them to remain open. Either way, my arse is taking whatever Becker decides to dish out.

Placing steady hands on my hips, he walks me back until I'm in position. 'It's tight,' he muses, crouching behind me and resting a fire hot fingertip on my ankle bone. 'Could be tricky getting it to where I want it to be.' That fingertip trails up the inside of my leg, past my knee to my inside thigh as he rises with it. I swallow down the scratchy dryness in my throat. 'Let's try.' Smoothing his hands down my hips, he reaches the hem of the leather and takes hold but tortures me by delaying his next move. Crazily, I'm silently pleading for him to hurry things along. His lips meet my neck and suck gently, pushing a strangled moan past my lips. 'Does my filthy princess want me to spank her?'

'Yes,' I don't hold back. My want is obvious in every breath I draw and every twitch of my buzzing body.

'Does she love me indulging in this gorgeous arse?' He bites my neck and thrusts his groin against me severely. I whimper my desperation, and he growls possessively. On a swift, brutal yank, my dress is whipped up to my waist, jolting my body as it goes, exposing my naked backside to his glimmering hazel eyes. 'Fuck . . . me,' he sighs, relinquishing all contact. My forehead meets the wall, my eyes squeezing tightly shut. 'Take your head away from the wall, princess.'

I comply immediately, knowing there's a damn good reason for his request, and then his hand meets my arse on an ear-piercing smack.

'Fuck,' I whisper, the flames instant, and so is the waterfall between my thighs. His hand goes straight between my legs, his fingers sinking into the wetness and spreading far and wide. On a frustrated shout, I ball my fists and clench my teeth, allowing the pleasure to override the sting.

'Beautiful.' His front meets my back, his arm curling around my waist and locking me to him tightly. 'Give me that mouth,' he orders, nuzzling into my cheek to encourage me. My head turns, my lips finding his in a heartbeat, my balled fists relaxing back into flat palms against the wall. I'm kissed like there's no tomorrow, ravenously, our tongues duelling, my mind bending.

Then he abruptly pulls away a little, leaving me gasping in his face. 'I like this one,' he says, husky and low, flexing his hips into my back to show me just how much. He's lead behind his sweatpants as he unzips me and lets the leather tumble to the floor. 'Step out.' I obey without hesitation, looking down to my feet. He kicks the dress to the side carelessly. His action tells me that the black number isn't an option at all. The dress is leather, therefore sticks, therefore doesn't make for a smooth transition from a covered arse to an exposed one. Becker's considered that in his dirty mind. That dress is a no.

I'm left holding myself up for a few moments while he collects option number two – the green one – and I take a risky peek over my shoulder, groaning under my breath at the sight of his magnificent back. The lines of ink are rolling as he reaches up to the hanger and removes the dress, and though it kills me to relinquish the beautiful view, I quickly face the wall when I see him start to turn. *Keep it together, Eleanor.*

He makes it to me fast, crouched behind me. 'This one looks promising.'

I lift my foot, then the other, and stiffen as he pulls it up my body, stopping to drop a sweet kiss on my stinging arse on his way. If I could see him, I know I'd find a satisfied smile on his face, and a fragment of my scrambled mind tells me to devote more time to questioning his kinky quirk. But it's soon snuffed out by the sound of his voice telling me that it's only *my* arse he feels so possessive over. Just mine. No one else's, and despite my sore bottom currently being less than grateful for this, the perverse part of me smiles on the inside.

'Arms.' Becker's soft instruction puts me back in the showing room, where today I am the piece of art on display. Releasing one at a time, I let him help feed my arms into the dress. My hands are on the wall, my back bowing as Becker draws the zipper up, skimming my skin as he does. The room begins to spin when his palms slide to my front and find my breasts. 'Hard nipples,' he whispers, flattening his palms and circling over the material-covered nubs, sending my body further into bedlam. 'There are just too many parts of you that I want to devote my time to.'

'I'm not going anywhere,' I say hoarsely, resisting the urge to release the wall and allow my hands to join his.

'No, you're not.' His hands move fast and whip up the dress, the force nearly lifting my feet from the floor. My eyes clench shut in preparation, my muscles hardening.

His palm collides with my other cheek.

Hard.

Thwack!

I grunt and jolt forward, holding onto my scream, and then his fingers are plunging into me, transforming that suppressed yelp into a moan of pleasure. Becker joins me in my groans, teasing, pumping, circling, feeling. 'On a scale of one to ten,' he murmurs, tickling my ear with his dulcet tone. 'How turned on are you right now?'

My arse is screaming, but nowhere near as loudly as the tight bud of nerves currently being worked carefully. 'Ten,' I breathe, circling my hips to increase the friction, feeling the pressure descending from my stomach. Always a ten.

He laughs lightly in my ear and removes his hand, and I whimper my devastation. 'Shhhh,' he hushes me, his fingers walking up my front to my throat. 'We're nowhere near that ten, princess.' Wrapping his palm around my neck, he applies a light pressure and guides the back of my head onto his shoulder. 'I'm enjoying this.' I bet he is. He manipulates my face to the side and attacks my mouth again, flinging my chaotic mind into blankness with the power of his lips on mine and the force of his tongue exploring my mouth. I whimper, moan, gasp for breath. I can't think of much, but I can be grateful that we only have one more dress to test in his experiment. I can keep it together for another few minutes.

Becker unzips me while maintaining our passionate kiss, frees my arms from the material, and quickly casts the dress aside. Then he pulls back, panting. I lose myself in the fiery depths of his eyes as he stares at me long and hard. 'One more,' he says quietly, and I nod, licking my lips. It wasn't a question, but I sense he is seeking my consent. One more dress means one more hard whack across my abused arse.

Becker smiles so brightly I can't help but match it as I shake my head. My wicked-minded man is in his element, and though I'm lacking one desperately needed climax, I'm in my element with him, which makes me as depraved as him. We're made for each other.

A loving kiss is pushed into my temple as he inhales, before he breaks away and goes to collect the final dress. The barely existent red one. Getting comfy in my standing position, I wait for him to return, knowing the exact moment he's behind me again. Not because I can hear anything, but because I can smell his clean scent mixed with the apple.

'This one goes over your head,' he says, prompting me to push away from the wall and reach into the air. 'Good girl.'

I smile at his praise as he slips the dress over my arms and pulls it down my body, making a point of grazing my skin as he does. My smile stretches wide. He's pulling it down into position, just to yank it back up again. Though he won't need to pull or yank far. The red dress is scarcely a dress. The sound of an approving hum is a good indication that he favours this one above the others but, again, how I look isn't top of Becker's agenda.

'Turn around,' he instructs gently, helping me on my way by holding my waist. When he comes into view, his obvious awe as he steps back rockets my confidence. I wouldn't dream of wearing a dress this short, but the look on his face is worth it alone. His eyes are drifting up and down my scantily clad body as his jaw ticks. It's a sign of him gathering strength. 'You look too fuckable for your own good.'

I smile as I take a look for myself, my eyes dropping down my front. It's super tight, but the blood-red fabric has some give, making movement easy. It's surprisingly comfortable for something that's clinging to every curve I have.

Becker looks like he's fighting off the urge to pounce on me, and just when I decide to make my move, tempt him into losing that fight, a sharp crack from outside pulls both of our attention to the door that leads into the courtyard.

'Dorothy,' Becker mutters, pacing over. My arms instinctively wrap around my body, trying in vain to conceal the minuscule dress. And the scene from Becker's office comes flooding back to me the instant I hear the rush of water from the outside tap. She's filling up her watering can. I haven't told Becker about my mortifying moment. An arse-spanking session got in the way. Oh God, help me. After torturing the old lady with a special screening of the Becker and Eleanor show, the last thing I want to do is expose her old eyes to what else we get up to in private. 'Becker—'

'Shhhh.' He puts his finger to his mouth as he pulls the door open a fraction and peeks outside. Not even the glorious sight of Becker's back can keep my eyes from scanning the floor for my floral sundress, my hands going to the hem of the red number currently gracing my body, ready to peel it off, but I'm grabbed before I can see through my plan to restore my respectable state. 'What do you think you're doing?' he asks.

My eyes are wide and wary. 'Getting dressed.'

'We're not done yet.' He whirls me around and takes me back to the wall.

He can't be serious. 'Not when Mrs Potts is outside,' I whisper-shout, glancing back to the door, checking for any signs of bolts or padlocks. There's nothing. My panic is ignored and my hands taken and placed on the wall. 'Becker, we can't.' My hips are claimed and tugged back. 'Please, not when . . . ohhhh . . .' My head drops back, the feel of expert lips dotting kisses across my neck. The fact that Mrs Potts is lurking outside is forgotten in a moment, my mind now centred on my sinful boyfriend and the sinful things he does to me.

'Feel good, princess?' he asks cockily. I nod my head for fear of yelping my pleasure, and Becker chuckles, the gorgeous sweet sound resonating deeply. When his fingers toy with the hem of the red dress, I hold my breath, waiting for the movement that will jolt me. But it doesn't happen. I look down, finding the dress still in place. What is he waiting for? 'Your arse looks amazing in this dress.' He's having a moment, admiring my backside. Then his arms fly up, taking the dress with it. Not that I feel it. My body doesn't move an inch, but the dress is now around my waist. 'And, fuck me, if it doesn't slide like silk across your skin.' An apple appears in my field of vision. 'Open.'

My eyes bug as I stare at the shiny green fruit, and I hear Mrs Potts only metres away, nothing but a single unlocked door between us. This feels so wrong, yet my mouth still drops open and Becker pushes the apple between my lips.

'Bite.'

I sink my teeth in and close my eyes. In my darkness, I hear what sounds like scratching at the door, followed swiftly by a gruff bark.

'In a minute, Winston,' Becker mutters under his breath. 'I'm nearly done.'

I tense, suddenly registering that each of my cheeks has taken a solid slap from my previous 'fittings'. So which one gets double-whammy? Both are still lightly pulsing from the aftermath of Becker's punishing palm. Given the choice, I can't say which one I'd prefer to take another blow.

Not that there's a hope of me being given the choice.

Or the time to prepare.

The flesh of my right cheek erupts into an angry inferno of flames on the loudest thwack, and it's his most brutal delivery yet. My scream is muffled by the apple in my mouth, and tears spring into my eyes. *Holy shit!* My body flies forward and begins to convulse in shock. It's too much . . . until those talented fingers find their way to my core again. Then I'm faced with the conflicting sensations of pleasure and pain. I start to sweat, feeling his lips creeping over the top of my exposed shoulders. I can't cope with the heady mixture.

Then he throws a curveball when he matches the brutal slap with another to my left cheek. This time, I grit my teeth, so hard I bite a huge chunk from the apple, sending the rest of the fruit tumbling to the floor. I spit out what I've bitten off and drink in air, set to let out an almighty bellow of shock, frustration, pain, passion. But a hand slaps over my mouth, silencing me.

Motherfucker!

I have a cursing party in my head, thumping my fists against the wall. The sting is biting, but Becker's working hard, thrusting into me wildly, finger-fucking me into a mind-numbing oblivion. My hips start meeting his circling, matching his rhythm, desperation coiling me up like a tight spring. He better hold onto me when this orgasm hits, because I'm set to go bouncing off around the room. I've lost control of everything. My body is moving instinctively, searching for the release that will settle me down. It's there. Not far away. I'm reaching for it, trying to seize it and hold on tightly, but it keeps slipping away defiantly.

'Fuck,' Becker curses on my behalf. He must sense I'm plateauing, because a second later, his mouth is at my ear. 'Keep quiet,' he rumbles, slowly removing his hand from my mouth. I savour the rush of oxygen filling my strained lungs. I can hear the faint snuffles of Winston that I conclude are him sniffing at the door, investigating the sounds, and probably the smell, too. I just hope Mrs Potts doesn't notice his inquisitiveness and comes to find out what has his attention. And I'm not hoping because I'm worried she'll cop another load of my naked body. I'm hoping because I don't think even an audience would stop me taking what I need from Becker right now.

'Please,' I whimper feebly, desperately feeling the wall like I can find what I'm looking for there.

He answers by kicking my legs apart before pulling his sweatpants down a little and guiding himself to me. The feel of him simply brushing at my entrance cools the burning ache within me. Then he rams forward and dowses it completely. There's no need to break me in. I'm saturated, which is a good job because we haven't time to mess about. Becker finds his flow immediately and charges forward repeatedly, banging into me at an epic rate. It's what I need. Full force to slam the elusive orgasm out of me. His fingers claw into my hips and yank me back onto him, my body bending to give him better leverage.

'Oh shit,' I gasp at the wall, grappling for support and not finding it.

'Come on, baby. Focus.'

'I'm trying,' I choke, feeling the blood gush into my core. I tense everything, closing my eyes as Becker continues to attack me with his powerful drives.

'Claim it, Eleanor,' he hisses, jacking me up on every thrust.

The force of my climax when it hits nearly takes me out.

'Go on, baby.' He bucks one last time and grunts, holding me against his groin as every muscle turns to mush and renders me limp and lifeless. I fall back, going dizzy, the bolts of pleasure hitting me from every direction, coming and coming and coming. I'm struggling to find my breath, relying on Becker to support me. 'I've got you,' he says calmly, his arm appearing over my shoulder, bracing against the wall as he holds me to him with his other.

My head rests back against him, and I find the strength to lift my arms and hook them over his neck. I swear, I could fall asleep standing in his arms. 'You didn't come,' I mumble drowsily, shuddering when he pulls his hips back and lets his still-solid cock slip free.

'You needed that more than I did.' His sweatpants ping back into place as he rains kisses on my damp, flustered face. He turns me in his arms and flicks eyes full of wonder down the dress that's all bunched around my waist. 'We have a winner.'

I laugh loudly, forcing Becker to quickly cover my mouth again. 'Sorry,' I mumble against his fingers.

'You will be.' Replacing his hand with his mouth, he lifts me from my feet and pins me to the wall while he devotes a few moments to lovingly kissing me back to life. 'You're quite a distraction in the workplace, Miss Cole. I might have to enforce punishments.'

I bite his lip. 'You've just spanked my arse to Italy and back. I should slap your face.'

My lip is bitten in return, a smile building on his flawless face. It surpasses sexy. He looks sinful. He *is* sinful. My half-hearted threat hasn't fazed him in the slightest. 'Lucky arse.' His throaty tone could easily get me ready for round two.

'I'll make your face glow brighter than my backside,' I counter.

'I like it when you talk dirty to me.'

'I'm not talking dirty.'

'Say "renaissance",' he whispers in my face, low and sexy. My stomach flips as he takes my wrists and thrusts my arms up the wall behind me.

'No,' I breathe.

His knee comes up and pushes into my centre, and I damn myself to hell for groaning like a sorry, desperate idiot.

'Say—'

'Never.'

'Winston!' Mrs Potts shrill scorn interrupts our back and forth, and we both whip our eyes over to the door. 'Come away from there,' she orders sternly.

'Oh fuck, here comes Mrs Trunchbull,' Becker jokes, though there's nothing to joke about, and he might agree when I've shared the news that I'm yet to share. I pull the red dress off urgently and make a grab for my floral sundress, swooping it up off the floor.

'Your granddad and Mrs Potts were checking the CCTV footage for rats earlier,' I tell him as I hurry into my dress.

Woof!

'Winston, come here!'

Becker frowns. 'I've told him, there are no rats. I have the place laced with fucking poison.' He starts to gather up the other dresses from the floor, the material of his sweatpants stretching over his taut arse. The sight makes my frantic motions falter for a split second.

Woof!

'For goodness' sake, there's nothing in there.' Mrs Potts annoyed words soon snap me back to life.

I wrestle with my dress. 'They found something a little more disturbing than rats.'

'Like what?' Becker remains bent at the waist, collecting up the black leather dress.

'Like footage on the CCTV of you screwing me like you might never have sex again.'

Becker shoots up and gawks at me. 'What?'

'In the corridor the night I left.'

Recognition lands on his face, his mouth dropping open. 'Oh fuck.'

I nod my head in agreement. 'I happened to be in your office with your gramps when he stumbled upon it. Then Mrs Potts joined us, too.'

'Oh fuck.' His arms drop to his sides, the dresses hanging.

'You must know there's a camera in the corridor.'

'I asked Percy to wipe them. He must have got side-tracked.'

'Probably because you asked him to break into my apartment with you.'

'Are you going to hold that against me forever?'

'Yes,' I retort simply, looking around and spotting a camera in the corner. 'Make sure you delete the last half hour.'

'Stupid dog.' The door flies open and Winston bolts in. 'Oh!' Mrs Potts takes in the scene, her head swinging from me to Becker a few times. 'There *is* someone in here, then.'

I don't go bright red. I don't know why. Maybe because shame is something I'm getting used to. Or maybe I'm becoming as cocky as my gorgeous boyfriend. 'Just leaving.' I bowl past Mrs Potts, abandoning Becker to face her alone as he fights his way into his T-shirt.

Chapter 17

I take it upon myself to leave work early so I can meet Lucy. I need to escape the magical world of The Haven, just to remind myself that there's a real world beyond the walls of Becker's dangerously idyllic sanctuary. Lucy doesn't know it yet, but I've packed some things and I'm getting ready at her place for our night out tonight.

I look down at my phone as I sit on the wall outside the glass building that houses TC&E Accountants where Lucy works, seeing the text from Becker that arrived a few minutes after I left. I didn't open it. I can't reply within five minutes if I don't know what it says. Now it's been thirty minutes since my phone chimed, six times longer than my allotted time, according to his NDA, and I have another message. My phone pings again. Make that another two. On a smile, I open the first message.

I miss you already. What time are you home?

Home. Is that what it is now? I scroll to the next message.

You've just breached your contract. Strike 2.

I roll my eyes insolently, moving to the next.

You're walking a very thin line, princess.

I recoil in disgust. 'I'm barely walking at all, thanks to you.'

My bum cheeks sing their agreement as I exit the screen, casting my mind back to the library, when I confessed my knowledge of the secret book and the map. Three strikes and I'm out? The map. The piece of art with a story amid the beautiful design. The missing piece. The key to Becker's mission.

I pull up Google. And I stare at the search bar, fighting the urge. This is becoming a habit. My fingers work mindlessly, typing in *'Head of a Faun'* and I scroll the results. Of course, the results are limited and tell me nothing I don't already know. *What did you expect, Eleanor? Directions to the missing piece? A diagram of where it can be found?* My shoulders slump, my mind wanders, and not for the first time, I sense the frustration Becker must feel over the mystery of the lost piece of the map and the sculpture. Where would one even begin to look for it? God, to have confirmation that Michelangelo really did destroy it himself. That would be the perfect outcome. But, also, what a travesty that would be. Old Mr Hunt's words come back to me. *Getting your hands on something that is thought lost in history gives you a rush like nothing else.* I smile. I bet.

Stop it, Eleanor!

I toss my phone into my bag and jump a little when some feet appear in my downcast vision, just a few inches from mine – feet graced with black shoes that need a good polish, the leather riddled with scuffs.

I glance up, wary, and recoil a little, taken aback by the sheer size of the man looming above me. He's as tall as he is wide, suited but scruffy, and his face is crabby, his thinning hair slicked back with too much wax. Or it could be grease. I can't be sure.

He smiles at me, and I try to force one in return but fail miserably. I must look as bewildered and cautious as I feel. 'Hello,' he says politely, his voice gruff and deep, like he smokes forty a day.

'Hi.' I find myself withdrawing, leaning back a little on the wall. I want to stand; I feel threatened sitting under his towering, overweight frame, but I'll never get to my feet without having to brush past him, and something tells me he knows that.

'Eleanor Cole?'

My worry intensifies. How does he know my name? 'You are?' I don't confirm who I am, since I have no idea who this is *and* why he's here.

'Stan Price.' He reaches into his inside pocket and pulls something out, flashing it at me. A badge. 'NCA.'

I just about manage to hold onto my heavy jaw to stop it hitting the pavement. NCA? National Crime Agency?

'You are Eleanor Cole?' he goes on, moving to the side, my eyes following him.

'Yes, is this about the stolen O'Keeffe?'

He smiles. 'No, actually. A colleague is dealing with that case.'

'Oh.' Then what on earth could this be about? Naturally, my mind goes straight to the fake sculpture, which is bad because if it doesn't thrill me, it makes me anxious. And now I'm anxious. 'So, how can I help you?' I'm at a loss where my even tone is coming from, because on the inside I'm stressed. All I can see is *Head of a Faun* and Becker with sculpting tools in his hands. And then that vision changes. Becker with handcuffs on his wrists.

'You work for the Hunt Corporation, yes?' He lowers himself next to me on the wall, never letting his eyes leave mine. I feel like he's assessing me, gauging my persona and disposition.

'Yes,' I answer short, sweet and quickly, fighting not to show a shred of my nerves. I'm so fucking nervous. 'I'm sorry, what's this about?'

Stan Price smiles. I'm not sure if it's genuine or forced. 'We're investigating some suspicious activity in the art world,' he says, and every muscle in my body stiffens, though I fight with all my might to hide it. 'I wondered if you may be able to help.' His eyebrows raise expectantly.

'You're investigating suspicious activity, but not the stolen

O'Keeffe?' My nerves are becoming more frayed by the second. Fuck, I don't know how the frigging hell to handle this. All I can see is the evil, almost amused face of *Head of a Faun*.

'Yes, like I said.'

I breathe in discreetly. 'If I can help, I will.' I give him a friendly smile, forced as shit. 'What am I helping with?' I'm pretty sure this isn't standard questioning practice, though pointing that out might make me look as guilty as I am. *Don't give him a thing!*

He smiles. 'Can you tell me if this person is familiar to you?' He reaches into his pocket and pulls something out, and I frown, looking at the photograph he presents. I can feel Price watching me closely, searching for any hint of a reaction.

'She's not familiar,' I lie, and I stun myself with how easily I do. I've seen this woman before, and I've seen her in The Haven. Not physically, but I got a brief glimpse of her picture before old Mr H repositioned his newspaper on Becker's desk to cover the blue file. Her harsh black bob on her old pale skin is unmistakable. 'Sorry I can't help.' I look up at Price, and he watches me quietly for a few moments, slowly replacing the photo in his inside pocket.

Then he smiles, but, again, I can't figure out if it's sincere or not. 'Never mind.'

'Who is she?' I ask, unable to hold back.

'Lady Winchester.'

'Lady?'

'Yes, a lady.'

'Why would you think I'd know her?'

'You work for the Hunt Corporation – the most renowned and exclusive company in the business. Let's just say that Lady Winchester likes to dabble in the trade. I just wondered if maybe you'd come across her.'

The blue file. That's all I can see now. Not red like every other file at The Haven. It was blue, standing out from the rest. Why? 'Maybe you should talk to my—' I just hold my tongue before I blurt out *boyfriend*. 'Boss,' I finish coolly. 'I haven't been at the Hunt Corporation for long.' Frighteningly, I know exactly what I'm doing. Price won't be asking Becker anything, and he has no intention to, either. That's why he's here asking *me*. He's sussing me out. Again, why? I don't know, but I'm shocking myself, giving off a cool, innocent persona, when on the inside I'm in all kinds of chaos. I've lied, and it was instinctive and natural for me to do so.

'Maybe I'll do that.' Price smiles again, this one definitely insincere.

'What are you investigating?'

'I'm not at liberty to say.' He hands me a card, and I take it. 'Should you happen to think of anything that you think might assist me in my inquiries, give me a call.'

'But I don't know what you're investigating, so how will I know if there's anything I can help with?' I'm being smart, and it's coming oh so naturally. My sinful saint is rubbing off on me.

'Your relationship with Becker Hunt ...' He fades off for effect.

'Relationship?' I question. 'He's my boss.'

Price nods slowly, eyeing me with too much interest. 'Good day, Miss Cole.' He stands and backs away slowly.

Good Lord, I just lied to the police, and I did it without any hesitation. I really am drowning in Becker's world, and, oddly, I don't feel any regret. After all, I made my decision when he turned up in Helston and brought me back. I'm in his corrupt maze, and I'm not planning on finding my way out. I love him. So I will protect him. Does he need protecting? What the hell is going on?

'Good day, Mr Pr—'

'Actually.' He stops. 'Since I have you here, what was Mr Hunt doing at Sotheby's on the day of the theft?'

While he has me? Cornered, he means. And I have every confidence that he knows exactly why Becker was at Sotheby's that day. 'Becker purchased the O'Keeffe in an auction. There was a mix up with the transaction. I was there, too.' I'm sure he also knows that. 'We were on our way from Parsonson's when I received their email. We were passing, so I stopped in to deal with it.'

'And did you?'

I frown.

'Deal with it,' he goes on.

'You mean pay for it?'

'Yes.'

'Well, no.' I laugh. 'It was discovered missing before I completed the transaction online.'

'Oh, well that was a stroke of luck.'

I regard him carefully. What is he suggesting? 'Have you spoken to Mr Wilson?'

'Brent Wilson?'

'Yes.'

'Like I said, my colleague is dealing with the case.'

'Well, perhaps you could tell your colleague to speak to Mr Wilson.' I smile and get to my feet, seeing Lucy in the distance breaching the exit of her building. *Normal. Just act normal.*

'Good day, Mr Price.' I skirt past him, and quickly head towards my friend. I register her expression and my smile falters. She looks like a colossál zit, angry, red and throbbing. Following her filthy stare, I spot a tall, leggy blonde sashaying across the street.

'Printer-room girl?' I ask, casting my eyes back to Lucy.

'Eleanor!' She snaps out of her mood and rushes over, her arms held wide open. 'What are you doing here?' She crashes into me, knocking me back a few paces. 'I thought you were picking me up in a taxi.'

'Thought I'd get ready at yours.'

Breaking away, she holds me at arm's length, looking me up and down. 'You okay?'

'I'm fine,' I say on a laugh, glimpsing over my shoulder, finding no trace of Price. But it doesn't ease me. He must have followed me here. Am I being watched?

'You sure?'

I return my attention to Lucy, slapping a huge smile on my face. 'So sure.' I link arms with her, getting us on our way, forcing myself not to scan the street for Price.

'How's Mr Magnificent?' she asks.

'He's magnificent.'

'Officially moved in?'

I frown to myself, feeling Lucy's hard, teasing stare on my profile. That's not been discussed, I'm just there. *Home.* That's what he asked. When will I be *home*? We step into the road and weave around the back of a few stationary cars. 'Are you missing me?' I ask, throwing her a sideways grin.

'Yes, actually,' she grumbles. 'How is it going?'

'I love him so much.' I blurt out of nowhere, and she pulls me to a stop, looking at me like I'm a nutter. I don't know why I felt the need to say that. Maybe my hidden stress after my encounter with Price has got me analysing exactly what the hell I'm doing.

'I know you do,' she says softly, almost sympathetically. 'But do you trust him?' It's a sensible question that any good friend would ask. Especially since we're talking about Becker Hunt – the modern-day Casanova. A man who has never been committed to anyone. Hell, a man who can't even *say* the word without developing a nervous twitch. A man who's never surrendered his heart and has never accepted another's. A man who's had more women than Ivana Trump has shoes. A man who . . .

'Yes.' My answer is sure and assertive. Others would probably think I'm fucking crazy. But I do trust him, and that reason is actually very simple. Becker trusts *me*. It's evident in all of his actions, the things he's shared, the way he looks at me. He trusts me with his secrets, but most significantly, he trusts me with his heart. It's fragile. He's given me a rare and precious gift. I'm keeping it, I'll protect it, and I'll love it like I've never loved anything before. Fiercely. Passionately. For ever. 'With my life,' I tag on the end, to wipe any element of doubt from Lucy's mind.

'Wow. Should I buy a hat?'

'Jesus, no.' I laugh nervously on behalf of Becker. If commitment makes him twitchy, I expect marriage would have him spontaneously combust.

'I can't believe a word you say. I remember quite clearly you calling Mr Magnificent, aka your new boyfriend, a tosser, a wanker, a twat—'

'He's still all of those things.' I nudge her in the side. 'And it just makes me love him more.'

'And does he love you?'

'Oh, he loves me,' I say, smiling. 'More than his treasure, which means I'm worth fucking *millions*.'

Lucy chuckles as we descend the steps of the Tube station. 'Come on. Let's get ready and drink wine. I need to get you when I can, since he's taking you away from me.'

'He's not taking me away from anything.' I say, reclaiming my arm and holding on to the handrail. That's not true. He's taking me away from my conscience and my senses.

I glance at my apartment door momentarily while Lucy finds her keys. I feel no sentimental pull towards my little home. I feel nothing. I thought perhaps my lack of missing it was simply because of all the distractions at The Haven. I was wrong. I never want to step foot in there again. I shudder as Lucy pushes her door open, and I get my phone from my bag. 'I need to call Becker,' I say, dialling as she heads straight to the bathroom.

'To check in?' she calls over her shoulder, sarcasm tinging the edges of her question. No, I'm calling to pick his brain on Price.

'So, she's alive,' he says when he answers as I drop to the couch. 'How's your arse?'

His question prompts me to wriggle a little, instantly feeling the burn. 'Sore.'

'Good.'

Lucy's head pops out from behind the door. 'What's sore?'

I wave a hand dismissively at her and return to Becker, hearing the sound of a sweet laugh from down the line. And it wasn't Becker's sweet chuckle. It was a woman's. 'Where are you?'

'At this exact moment in time?'

'Yes, at this exact moment in time,' I press, listening carefully for any more background noise.

'Well.' He coughs. 'At this exact moment in time, I have a lady's hand resting on my inside thigh.'

I'm standing fast. 'Whose hand?'

'Henrietta.'

'Who the hell is Henrietta?'

He laughs lightly. I don't know why. Let me tell him that a man has his hand on *my* inside thigh. See how he reacts. 'She's my seamstress, princess, and currently measuring my inside thigh.'

Mental images of Becker's sturdy, thick, strong thighs invade my mind. And a woman holding a tape measure there. 'I might learn how to sew.'

He laughs, a heavy, full-on burst of amusement. 'I only have thighs for you.'

'Oh, you're hilarious,' I breathe, but on the inside I'm laughing along with him. 'I hope you have your trousers on.'

'Actually, it's very hard to measure a thigh with too much material in the way.'

'Is that what she tells you?' I ask, sitting back down and relaxing a little with our playful banter.

'Thanks, Hen,' Becker says, and then I hear the sound of footsteps, followed by a closing door. 'You're jealous.' There's laughter in his tone, and definitely satisfaction.

'Yes, I am.' I openly admit, no shame or holding back. 'I want to be touching those thighs right now.'

'But you need girl time,' he reminds me, cocky as can be.

I roll my eyes to myself. 'Yes, I do.'

'Seems you also need some Becker time.'

Now I'm full-on scowling down the line. I'm not playing his game. 'I had plenty of Becker time yesterday in the showing room. And last night. And this morning.' I shift on the sofa, getting a cool, hard reminder of what Becker time entails.

'Don't pretend you wouldn't bend over for me if I was there,' he says with totally warranted confidence. 'Have a good night, princess.'

'Wait!' I blurt out. I've been so caught up in his playful banter, I've totally forgotten why I called him in the first place. 'Someone from the NCA stopped me outside Lucy's office.'

I don't like the lengthy silence that follows.

'Becker?'

'Who?' He's not happy.

'Price. Stan Price.' I give him his answer without delay. 'Showed me a picture of a woman. Asked me if I recognise her.'

'And did you?'

I recoil, glancing over to the bathroom, hearing the whoosh of Lucy's shower and her singing over the top of it. 'Yes,' I confess. 'I saw her picture in a file on your desk. Lady Winchester.' More silence. My mind races. 'But I told Price she wasn't familiar to me.'

Becker lets out an audible gush of relieved breath. 'Good girl.'

'Who is she?'

'She's a filthy rich old lady who's rumoured to be involved with a collection of forged Picassos.'

What? Oh God. 'Why do you have a file on her?'

'She bought a Ming vase from the Hunt Corporation a few years ago. Don't get any ideas. Gramps got the file out to destroy it. We can't be associated with crooked people. Bad for business.'

I gape down the line, astonished. 'Are you for real?'

'How many times do I have to tell you? I'm very real. We don't associate with carelessness. The police sniffing around isn't ideal.'

Yes, I can appreciate that, given the secret room where Becker loses himself from time-to-time and carved a fake Michelangelo. 'Just promise me you have nothing to do with the Picassos,' I beg, needing absolute clarification.

'I promise you,' he replies sincerely, and I sink into the couch, relieved.

'Why didn't Price just ask you?' I ask.

'Because he knows I'll tell him to fuck off.'

I gawk down the phone. 'Don't hold back, will you?'

'They weren't exactly helpful when Mum and Dad were killed. Why would I help them?'

I tingle from top to toe as a result of Becker's spat words, feeling resentment bubbling in my veins, my lip curling. My protectiveness stuns me. I'm so very glad I played dumb. To hell with the police. They weren't there for Becker. Why the hell should he ever cooperate for them? 'He also asked about my relationship with you,' I go on.

'And you said?'

'I told him you're my boss.'

Becker laughs hard. 'Don't you think the whole fucking world knows that we're fucking, Eleanor?'

I frown down the line. 'I didn't think of that at the time, when I was being interrogated by the *police*. And do you want to rephrase that, Hunt?'

'Sorry,' he says, a little sheepishly. 'In love. The whole world must know I'm in love with you. Better?'

I grin to myself. 'Much. So now Price knows I'm a liar.'

'Price can think what he likes, princess. I couldn't give two shits. But at least he knows he's wasting time trying to ply you for information. The Hunt Corporation has always been a private company. Let's keep it that way.'

I go quiet, once again the gravity of my position at the firm and my involvement with Becker hitting me hard. 'Okay,' I agree quietly.

He sighs. 'Get ready and go have a drink with Lucy.' His instruction is soft and comforting. 'Relax, princess. And be safe.' He hangs up after his final order, just as Lucy appears from the bathroom.

'All clear?' she asks, rubbing at her hair with a towel.

I chuck my phone on the couch and stand, ignoring her question but taking on board what Becker has instructed me to do. Relax. 'What are you wearing?'

She grins and scoops up the Topshop bag from the floor. 'Brace yourself.' She whips out . . . something.

'What's that?' I ask, tilting my head as she unfolds the garment.

'This' – she shakes the material until I'm looking at something very . . . small – 'is a playsuit.'

My eyes roam from top to bottom of the material. It doesn't take me long. 'That's tits *and* legs,' I point out. 'You *are* breaking your own rule.'

She scoffs and drapes the pink, *very* short, *very* low playsuit over the back of a chair. 'I feel like getting glammed up.'

I give the playsuit a dubious look. That's a pulling outfit, the kind of outfit a woman wears when she wants attention. 'Is everything okay with Mark?'

'Fine.' She shrugs and grabs the hairdryer, flipping her head over and turning it on. 'Can't a girl pull out all the stops once in a while?' she calls over the roar of air.

'You mean pull out her tits *and* legs?'

'Potato, patarto.'

Chapter 18

Covent Garden is a hive of activity, groups of tourists still roaming among the hardcore Londoners who have ventured out to play. Being the good friend that I am, I didn't abandon Lucy in her disgrace and instead supported her. That is why I am now skimpily clad in a short black draped dress, but my boobs are tucked safely away. My hair is piled high and messily, and my tiny black purse matches my heels. The ones that pinch like a bitch.

Lucy spots two stools at the bar and makes a beeline for them, grabbing the cocktail menu when she arrives. 'You know what I think?' she says, burying her nose in the leather-bound book with lists and lists of drinks.

'What do you think?' I ask, settling next to her and placing my tiny bulging purse on the bar.

'I think we should work our way through the mojito menu. Every flavour.' She looks up and waves a beckoning hand to the barman. 'We'll start with the blackcurrant.'

'How many are there?' I ask, craning my neck to see. Lucy turns the menu away from me. Her sly action tells me there are a lot of flavours on that menu.

'Just a few.' She points at the page and smiles sweetly at the barman. 'Two of the blackcurrant, please. And when you see our drinks an inch from the bottom, start making the strawberry.'

'Like your style.' He laughs and grabs two tall glasses as Lucy slaps the menu down and turns her stool into me. I have to admit, her tits and legs look amazing, and she's pinned up her short blond hair haphazardly. She looks lovely.

'How's Mark?' I ask again, undoing my bulging purse to retrieve my lipstick. The unfastening of the zip relieves the pressure from inside, sending all of the contents spilling out onto the bar.

'A bigger bag, perhaps?' Lucy teases, waving her oversized clutch under my nose.

'Here.' I slide my phone, keys, and purse across to her. 'Put these in that suitcase. My zip's going to break.' She laughs and takes them, tucking them neatly in her huge clutch bag. 'So, how is he?'

She shrugs nonchalantly, taking a quick peek around the bar. 'He's good.'

The barman slides two of the most elaborate-looking black-currant mojitos I've ever seen across the bar, and Lucy dives on hers, wrapping her lips around the straw and slurping loudly. 'Hmm, yum.' She ignores the bewildered look that has crawled its way onto my face, keeping herself hunched over her drink, working her way through it like it's a life saver. Or a distraction.

Reaching forward, I claim my mojito, all the while keeping suspicious eyes on my friend. 'Just good?' I ask coolly.

She's still refusing to look at me. 'Yeah, good.'

I settle back on my stool, analysing my shifty mate. I can't usually shut her up once Mark is the topic of conversation, whether she's gushing about how he's *the one*, or she's moaning about printer-room girl. Her eyes start to flick from corner to corner of the bar. She's scoping the joint. Closely. Nervously.

I'm getting more and more worried the longer I study her. It's not long before two more mojitos are sliding across the bar, and I look down to see I've worked my way through the glass mindlessly while I've been sitting here pondering what's got into my friend.

'Thanks.' I smile at the barman, swapping my glass with the fresh one. My lips haven't even made it to the straw before

Lucy has supped her way through the strawberry mojito. 'Why do I get the feeling you're looking for someone?' I throw it out there and watch as she looks at me out the corner of her eye.

'Not at all,' she mumbles before quickly holding her empty glass up to the barman.

She's lying. What's going on? Then I suddenly recall something she told me on one of our phone calls. 'Oh my God,' I breathe, taking her glass and putting it down before forcing her stool around so she has to face me. 'Tonight's the work party you're not invited to, isn't it? They're coming here.'

She hangs her head in shame. 'Might be.'

It makes sense. The playsuit, pulling out all the stops. 'What are you thinking, Lucy?' I ask, exasperated.

'I'm thinking that if I'm not here, Miss Nimble Legs will have those pins wrapped around Mark's waist quicker than you've fallen in love with Becker.' She scowls at me, and I recoil, a little offended. 'I'm not particularly happy about stooping to such levels, but she hasn't given me much choice. Have you seen it?' she asks, nodding her head like a demented puppet. 'Her fucking legs stretch to Jupiter.'

I see in my mind's eye the gorgeous woman sashaying from Lucy's office building, and Lucy's sour face as she watched those long legs strut. My friend feels inferior. She's short, and the tall leggy blonde from floor eighteen is clearly giving her an inferiority complex. 'Mark screwed her. That's all.' I'm a fucking hypocrite. I was hardly cool when we bumped into Alexa the other day.

'What do you mean?'

'I mean, maybe that's all she's good for. Long legs to wrap around a man's waist.' I wince at my stupid comment, remembering another pair of long legs that, apparently, Becker likes wrapped around him. I literally jerk my head to the side and toss the stray thought out on a wrinkled nose. He only has thighs for me.

'Eleanor!' Lucy shrieks.

'But you're a keeper, Lucy,' I rush to finish, kicking myself for using one of printer-room girl's best assets, and kicking myself harder because I put that asset around Lucy's boyfriend's waist. 'He wants *you*.' I sag on my stool. I thought my own silly little insecurities were unreasonable, but at least I'm not stalking Becker around London. 'Oh, Lucy,' I say in despair, dropping my head into my hands. 'How do you know he's going to be here?'

'I might have stumbled across a group email at work detailing the plans.' She doesn't sound in the least bit embarrassed by her confession. 'Eleanor.' She comes closer. 'Trust me, since Miss Nimble Legs found out Mark and I are dating, she's seriously raised the stakes. The flirting, the dresses at work, the coy smiles. She's like a fly around shit.'

'But he's with you,' I point out, for the hundredth time. 'Does he know how you feel?'

'God, no. I don't want him to think I'm needy.'

I give her a sardonic look, one that suggests she's deluded. Not that she notices, because she's looking over my shoulder, her eyes rooted on the door. I don't bother looking. Her round eyes clue me in on who's just walked in. And I know the moment Mark spots her, because she virtually dives into her mojito before turning the most over-the-top smile onto me and laughing loudly. At nothing. Oh, this is great.

'Lucy?' Marks voice drifts over my shoulders from behind, and I watch in astonishment as Lucy does a double take.

'Mark!' she sings, slipping down from her stool and giving him a hug. 'I didn't know you'd be here. Eleanor invited me out.'

I gulp down my stunned cough and tackle my drink before I give her away.

Mark showers my insecure friend with plenty of affection, kissing her full on the lips and then helping her back onto her stool. His actions and persona reinforce my thoughts. The leggy blonde from floor eighteen doesn't stand a chance. I just need to convince my friend of that before she blows it. Men hate needy women.

'We started in the Punch and Judy,' Mark tells Lucy, though I know she already knows that. 'But this place does a mean mojito and the music is great after nine.'

I raise my glass and smile when he registers the mojitos. 'Already found them.' I smile. 'How are you?'

'Great.' He's relaxed and cool, his beard a little shorter than the last time I saw him. 'How's the boss?' A small knowing smirk materialises. 'Or boyfriend.'

'Magnificent,' I reply, spiking a laugh from Lucy.

'You girls want a drink?'

I look to Lucy for guidance, seeing her slowly shaking her head. I don't get it, but I play along, nevertheless. 'No, I'm good.'

'Yeah, you carry on. I don't want to interrupt your night,' Lucy says, calm, cool, and completely composed. And once again, I'm gaping at her. She's killing me. I swear, the girl has a split personality. I throw her a brief look of condemnation that she completely sidesteps. Once again, her eyes are cemented somewhere else, and with Mark still hovering beside us, it can only be one other person. Looking discreetly in the direction of Lucy's fire stare, I see her. The girl from floor eighteen. She's immaculate. Polished. Perfect. I feel sick on Lucy's behalf. She's chatting in a group – work colleagues, I guess – but her attention is flicking repeatedly to Mark's back. And it hasn't escaped Lucy's notice.

Oh shit. I predict fireworks very soon. I sip my mojito, looking at Mark to gauge his take on the situation. He's just paying the barman, completely unaware of the daggers being tossed behind his back, aiming for . . . what's her name? I make a point to ask Lucy the moment the coast is clear. The whole scene is making me nervous, and I'm damning Lucy to hell for dragging me into the middle. My nerves only amplify when I see Lucy go all tense. She may as well be foaming at the mouth, and only a split second later, I find out why.

Miss Nimble Legs appears, her long, delicate fingers reaching for Mark's arm. My hands twitch, ready to grab Lucy and hold her back. Oh, she's a bold one. I can see the evil glint in her eyes. She knows exactly what she's doing. 'Mark,' she purrs, resting her hand on his arm and holding it there. 'The drinking games are starting.'

Mark looks over his shoulder, but not at her. He's looking past her, to the crowd of work friends on the other side of the bar. 'Be there in a sec, Melanie.'

That answers one question. I've also had something else cleared up irrevocably. Mark isn't in the slightest bit interested in Melanie. His dismissiveness may as well have been a slap in the face, and Melanie's sour expression tells me it hurt just as much. I hope Lucy is seeing this. I watch as Melanie slides off. Lucy's narrowed eyes follow her path. They don't even stray when Mark leans in and kisses her sweetly on the cheek. 'Why don't you come and join us?'

'No.' Her answer is mindless, her focus still firmly centred on the interloper. 'I'm good with Eleanor. Go have fun.' She turns a sweet smile onto him.

I want to smash her head on the bar. And I'm talking about my friend, not the brazen floozy who's now giggling and thrusting her chest out as Mark joins the crowd. Lucy is so blinded by hatred for that woman, she can't see what's staring her in the face. Namely, a man who isn't in the least bit interested in what Lucy is viewing as competition.

I swivel on my stool, back towards the bar, and search for the waiter. 'Two more.' I hold up my empty glass and resist the urge to order shots. I feel like I need it. It takes the waiter a few minutes to prepare our next round, and the whole time, Lucy is growling next to me.

'Stop it,' I warn.

'Stop what?'

It takes everything out of me not to fulfil my previous thought and smash her head down on the bar. She needs some sense smacking into her. 'He's not interested in her. Look.' I throw an arm out and watch as she turns her creased face towards Mark. 'She's vying for his attention and getting nowhere.' At that precise moment, Mark turns and chucks Lucy a wink and a cute smile. 'He wants to be with you, though that might change if he finds out you've been stalking him.'

'I haven't stalked him,' she argues, turning slowly on her stool and spotting the fresh mojito – this one blueberry.

'No? What would you call it, then?' I ask, fully intending on the condescending tone. She deserves it. She's being silly.

'Look at her, Eleanor,' she moans, throwing her arms in the air. 'Tall, gorgeous—'

'Easy,' I finish for her, fairly or not. But I'm basing my conclusion on what I know and what I've seen. And besides, Lucy is my friend. I have a moral obligation to be bitchy towards a woman I don't know, especially when said woman is sniffing around my friend's man. Lucy pouts as she peeks out the corner of her eye. 'He's obviously smitten with you.' I reach for her hand and squeeze it. 'Don't play her game. He's yours. Rise above it.' I ignore my mind's gentle reminder of the *fuck off* I threw in Alexa's face. Acknowledging it would make me a hypocrite.

I see Lucy mulling over my words, staring down at her glass. 'I'm in love with him,' she says quietly.

'Never!' I gasp, earning a slap on my arm. I laugh it off and relax a little, now she's stored away the invisible daggers. 'Of course you're in love with him, you fool.'

'Less of the insults,' she grumbles. 'Looks like we've both been struck by Cupid's arrow.'

Struck? I laugh.

How about stabbed?

Chapter 19

An hour later, we've made our way through the rest of the mojitos, moved onto wine, and I fear Lucy hasn't listened to a word I've said. She's got progressively more pissed, worse since she started on the wine, and her eyes are wandering again. I can't blame her. Melanie has been trying to climb Mark like a tree for the best part of the evening.

'Dance floor,' I declare, jumping down from my stool, ignoring the fact that I just stumbled forward a little. Robin S has just kicked in with 'Show Me Love', which has kicked my feet into action. I have the urge to dance. Besides, it's a perfect way to distract Lucy. 'Come on.' I grab her hand and drag her across the bar before she can protest, and I don't let go of her once we've shimmied our way onto the dance floor. I send our arms into the air and start lip syncing, drawing a needed laugh from Lucy, who swiftly joins in. We twirl, sing, throw some serious enthusiasm into it, and neither of us are focused on anything else, except each other. Which is just what's needed.

It's going well, my tactics working a treat, but my delighted smile is soon wiped from my face when something hard connects with my arse. The contact ignites the heat in my recovering cheek and sends me jolting forward on a grimace of pain. 'Shit.' I make to swing around, set on finding the offender and returning the favour to their face. But I don't make it very far. Two solid arms come around my body and lock me securely to an equally solid chest. My eyes widen, shooting to Lucy.

She's grinning. It worries me for a split second, but then the moulding of his body into mine eases me. 'Mr Magnificent!' Lucy squeals, kissing the tips of her fingers on both hands and throwing her invisible kiss over my head. I hear the sweet sound of Becker's chuckle in my ear, then his wood-and-apple scent invades my nostrils. My hands rest on his across my stomach and my head cranes back, trying to see him.

He smiles, lopsided and cute, his hair mussed and sexy and gorgeous, his eyes glimmering behind his glasses. 'You were putting on quite a show,' he muses, swaying to meet my slowed rhythm.

'I knew you were watching me.' I join him in his light banter as Lucy staggers over to the bar and scoops up more wine.

'Is she rat-arsed?' Becker asks as she flops onto her stool and draws the proverbial daggers from where she's safely stored them.

'Totally,' I confirm, turning and throwing my arms around his neck. He accepts willingly, and though I know the appearance of my Mr Magnificent has caught the attention of many women nearby, I let the looks of awe go straight over my head. Being an outsider to Lucy's situation has had clarity explode around me, making my own situation perfectly clear, even in my slightly drunken condition. All the women who I've seen as threats are nothing more than a mild inconvenience. I have this sinful bastard's heart, and I'm keeping it. 'I love you,' I declare, loud and proud, shouting over the music, hoping everyone in the bar hears me.

Becker grins wickedly and lifts me from my feet, blowing my hair from my face when a few wayward strands slip free. 'And I love you, you corrupt, drunken little witch.' He lands a forceful kiss on my lips and starts carrying me from the floor.

'Where did you come from?' I ask, once I've been placed on my stool.

'Heaven, princess.' He flips me a wink, moving back so I get his full height in view. He looks perfectly casual in a pair of worn jeans and a white T-shirt. God, I could jump his sinfully sexy self.

'Oh, that's cute.' Lucy interjects, throwing a wobbly fist into Becker's bicep. 'He's a charmer.'

'How are you, Lucy?' Becker asks, running dubious eyes up and down her half-naked frame as he tosses a couple of twenties on the bar. 'Whatever the girls are having,' he says to the barman. 'And I'll have a Haig on the rocks.'

'A-fucking-mazing,' Lucy slurs, pointing her empty in the general direction of Mark's group, who are now all huddled around a tall table doing shots. 'My boyfriend is fucking amazing, too.'

Becker looks across to where Lucy is pointing, then to me on a frown. I shake my head. It's a *tell–ya–later* look, and he catches it swiftly, handing me my wine.

'You ready to settle your bill?' the barman asks, obviously concluding that Lucy and I are well on our way to a drunken oblivion and will probably be stumbling home soon.

'How much?' Becker asks before I have the chance, going back to his pocket.

'One hundred and sixty-eight.'

'What?' Becker looks at me in shock, eyeing up the drink he's just placed in my hand, maybe considering confiscating it.

'Eight mojitos at sixteen quid a pop. Plus the wine and your Haig.' The barman slides the bill across the bar for confirmation, but Becker waves it away, throwing down a pile of notes.

'You okay?' he asks, now clearly concerned by the confirmation of how much alcohol has passed my lips.

'I'm being supportive.'

'By getting blind drunk?'

I shrug guiltily on an innocent smile. 'I'm a good friend. And I feel fine. I think all the secrets I'm keeping are burning away the alcohol.'

He rolls his eyes as his tumbler of amber liquid rises slowly to his full lips, and my rapt stare journey with it. 'Cheers,' he says, tipping the neat whisky back. 'What's going on?' Becker indicates across the bar to Mark. 'Have they had an argument?'

I'm not worried that Lucy will notice us talking about her like she isn't here. Because she isn't. Not in mind, anyway. She's gone full-force into glaring mode again. 'That leggy blonde is what's wrong.' I discreetly nod at Melanie, prompting Becker to seek her out.

'Whoa,' he blurts out, resulting in a swift jab in the shoulder from me. 'Sorry.' He smiles nervously. 'But she's hardly unnoticeable with one tit hanging out.'

'What?' I throw my eyes past Becker. 'Oh my days.' He's right. One boob has broken free from her low-cut dress and is jiggling happily while she throws a shot back. All eyes in the bar are on the girl from floor eighteen, except the men aren't staring and licking their lips, despite it being a rather attractive boob. They're looking embarrassed for her. She's clearly steaming drunk, and when she throws herself at a very horrified-looking Mark, I know immediately that Lucy's invisible daggers could, quite possibly, turn into very tangible ones. I see her leaving her stool like an eject button has been pressed. 'Stop her,' I shout, pushing Becker, who quickly cottons on and seizes the top of Lucy's arm.

'Hold your horses,' he says calmly, pulling her back. 'Mark's doing a pretty good job of fighting her off himself.'

We all look and find Mark pushing Melanie away, an offended look on his face. 'I'm cool,' Lucy snaps, yanking herself free from Becker's grip. Mark seems to be handling a steaming drunk Melanie perfectly, but she's blotto and determined, and tosses an evil scowl in Lucy's direction before she makes a beeline for him again, which confirms that she really is a nasty player. 'Oh no she didn't,' Lucy laughs coldly, and is suddenly gone from Becker's side. This time, he doesn't catch her, and

I can only watch as she flies across the bar like a rabid dog, frothing at the mouth.

'Oh God, you have to stop her.'

'For fuck's sake,' Becker grumbles, slamming his glass down and going in pursuit. I'm hot on his heels, fearing the worst. I can't blame Lucy for snapping. She's endured enough. Heck, *I've* endured enough.

Becker is fast as he swoops across the bar.

But Lucy is faster, and she's apparently in no mood to handle the situation delicately. No, she goes in like a bull in a china shop, practically ripping Melanie off Mark and tackling her to the floor. They hit the deck with ease, alcohol assisting, and start rolling around like a pair of brawling men. I reach the inside of the circle that has naturally formed around their scrapping bodies and skid to a stop. I'm so stunned by the scene playing out in front of me, I just stand, watching . . . a bit like Mark, who's next to me, his beer held limply in his hand as he gapes at the two women rolling around on the filthy floor.

'Oh, Lucy,' I sigh, my palms coming up to my cheeks in despair. For someone who always acts so cool on the outside, she's acting pretty uncool right now. She's brought the whole bloody pub to a stunned silence, which means everyone can hear every word being screamed.

'You piss-taking piece of shit!' Lucy screeches, lashing with her nails at Melanie's dress. 'Keep your filthy paws to yourself!'

'He wasn't complaining in the printer room,' Melanie retorts, grabbing onto Lucy's hair and yanking it, making my friend hiss in pain.

What I'm witnessing now is, quite literally, a cat fight, each woman hissing, thrashing claws, rolling around and kicking out their legs. It's ugly. I glance blankly up at Mark, and his eyes fall down to mine, all wide and lost. 'What the fuck?' he splutters uselessly as my friend does an amazing job of falling spectacularly from grace. Or crashing. What is she thinking? I search for Becker in the crowd, wondering where he's disappeared to. He's probably concluded that he wants no association with this, and I wouldn't blame him.

I roll up my proverbial sleeves and prepare to dive in and split them up, but just as I put one foot forward, Becker appears through the dense gathering of people. My gratitude is immense, my relief profound . . . until I notice that he's carrying something.

Something big.

And red.

'Oh . . . no,' I breathe, watching as he locks and loads . . .

A fire extinguisher.

He wouldn't?

I half close my eyes, stepping back and wincing.

He fires.

And the loudest whoosh of noise erupts, followed by an explosion of white foam.

He would.

My hand slaps over my mouth, watching in horror as Becker soaks the two crazy women, walking forward with the canister in one hand and the hose in the other, ensuring they get the full hit of white stuff. The shouting has stopped, being replaced with shocked gasps, and the two scrapping women have been replaced by two huge foam monsters, slipping around unattractively on the floor. The deafening hissing of the fire extinguisher seems to stretch on for ever, and once Becker's finally drained it, he tosses it aside and brushes his hands off. 'Sorted,' he says, completely unfazed, as he brushes down his T-shirt.

The audience – which is basically everyone in the bar – flicks astonished stares from Becker to the silenced women, back and forth. Then the doormen come crashing through and Becker takes my arm. 'Time to go.'

I'm hauled through the throngs of people, my feet working fast out of necessity rather than obedience. Becker has a determined hold of me and judging by the look on his face, I'd do well not to object.

Once we make it outside, he releases me and scans me up and down with worried eyes. 'You okay?'

Me? I shake myself to life and point aimlessly over my shoulder. 'I'm fine, but I don't think Lucy is. We need to get her.'

He stops me from going back and reaches forward to wipe something from my cheek. 'You're not going back in there.'

I hear an almighty crash from behind me, and Becker peers over my shoulder before dropping his chin to his chest and groaning. I turn, finding Lucy being hauled out by a doorman, followed closely by Melanie. And they're at it again, both fighting to free themselves from the clutches of the bouncers.

'For the love of God.' Becker's patience is wearing thin, and he starts to lead me away determinedly, but I shrug him off and step back, ignoring the aggravated expression that gets thrown my way.

'I can't just leave her here.'

'Where's her boyfriend?' he asks, scanning the crowds for Mark. 'She's his problem, not mine.'

'No, but she's *my* friend, therefore *my* problem.' Just as I say that, I hear a vicious curse, and then a loud rip. Bracing myself, I investigate the sounds, finding Melanie's exposed boob has company. The whole top part of her dress is missing, and Lucy is laughing wickedly, like some unhinged psycho woman.

'You skank!' Melanie shrieks, grappling to cover her dignity.

'You'll do well to keep your hands to yourself.' Lucy breaks free of the doorman's hold and starts to pull her non-existent playsuit into place, before pointlessly brushing her soggy hair from her face. She looks a state. Any attempts to regain any self-respect or composure will be futile.

'Is she always such a handful?' Becker asks dryly, pulling me close into his side.

I say nothing, shrugging him off and turning on my heels. I

march over to my friend to claim responsibility of her, dragging her away. She doesn't fight me, and it isn't because she's exhausted after ten minutes straight of bucking like a donkey. 'What has got into you?' I say, turning Lucy around and shaking her.

She seems to snap out of her destructive mode the moment her eyes land on mine. 'Mark,' she says, her expression panicked. 'Where is he?'

Mark appears behind Lucy, his bearded jaw tight. Long gone is the dumbfounded expression. Now he looks hacked off. 'What the hell are you playing at?' he asks shortly.

Lucy's blue eyes dull, anxiety filling them as she swings around to face him. 'She was all over you like a rash.'

'And I ignored her,' he replies calmly.

'She was goading me.' Lucy sounds desperate as she rushes to spill her excuses for her behaviour. 'I couldn't take it any more.'

Becker moves in close to me. 'We should go.'

'I'm not leaving her,' I reiterate firmly, stepping away. I need to be here for Lucy, because this isn't going to end nicely.

'Princess, your friend has just been brawling in a bar. I've just tampered with fire safety equipment. The police might be on their way, and I don't want to be—'

'Then go!' I snap. 'Don't let me inconvenience you.'

Becker's up in my face quickly, his face tight. 'You're not an inconvenience, princess, but being arrested might fucking be.'

My eyes widen. Yes, because then he would *have* to talk to the police. I fly around and find Lucy screaming bloody murder. I hurry over, arriving by their side, not that either of them notices my presence. 'Lucy, let's go.' She needs to calm down. And we need to get out of here.

'You shagged her!' Lucy screams, demented, huffing and puffing. 'In the printer room at work!'

'I've told you over and over. It meant nothing,' Mark roars, flinging his body around and stalking off. 'And we weren't even together.'

Lucy runs after him, and I follow, keen to get her home before she does any more damage, or before I hear blue sirens. 'Lucy, please, come on.' I reach to grab her arm but miss by a mile when she dives forwards and pushes Mark in the back.

'She wants you!'

He slams to a halt, as does Lucy, as do I. Then he turns slowly and breathes in deeply. His calm actions force Lucy to keep her gob shut. 'I love *you*, Lucy. She's nothing but a woman I scored with because I could. Because she was free and easy and throwing herself at me. She was a means to an end during a drought. Nothing more. How many times have I got to tell you?'

This is the point when Lucy should back down. But no. 'Tell *her* that!' she screams in his face, staggering forward on unsteady legs.

'I fucking have!' he yells, pushing her arm away. They quickly become entangled in a blur of flying arms, Lucy lashing out in her drunken stupor and Mark trying to restrain her mad arse.

Oh, Jesus, could this get any worse? Becker stalks past me and puts himself in the middle of it, his patience frayed, and Lucy's flailing limbs are soon restrained. 'I have her,' Becker says tightly, securing her back against his chest. 'Go, mate. We'll sort her.'

'Thanks.' Mark straightens himself out, looking at a heaving Lucy with a mix of annoyance and pure frustration before he hails a cab. One pulls over quickly. 'It's over, Lucy. You clearly don't trust me and I can't be in a relationship like that.' He gets in and the cab pulls away.

Becker relinquishes his hold of Lucy as soon as the cab disappears around a corner. And then the wailing starts. Big, heaving cries of despair. I'm not going to patronise her, tell her she's a twat and that she's fucked it all up. She already knows that. Taking her jerking shoulders gently, I guide her around, tenderly but hastily, as she shudders under my hold, giving

Becker a sorry shrug. He looks absolutely and completely exhausted by it all.

'I'm driving,' he says, indicating up the road. I follow his extended arm and see his flashy black 5-series a few hundred yards ahead. 'We'll drop her off on the way home.'

There are two things I note. The first, Becker said 'home' again, like The Haven is *my* home, too. Secondly, 'drop her off' implies we'll be leaving her. The first I'm thinking is best left unaddressed for now. Besides, I quite like the sound of it. The second needs addressing this minute, because I definitely don't like the sound of that. 'I'm not leaving her,' I tell him, loading my voice with determination that he shouldn't dare argue with.

But he does. 'And I'm not leaving you.' He has a quick scan of our surroundings.

'Then it looks like you're staying at Lucy's, too,' I say quietly, and I find I imitate him, looking around.

'Princess,' Becker sighs, exasperated. 'You're coming home with me.'

A sniffle and a splutter reminds me of my wreck of a friend who is still in my hold. 'I'm not leaving her,' I grate, backing up my declaration with a determined glare. She's pissed, she's been dumped, and she's emotional. 'She needs—' Something suddenly springs to mind, and I frown as I glance down and search Lucy's hands. 'Our bags,' I say, looking back at the bar. 'We left our bags in the bar.' The crowds have died down, but the doormen are keeping watch, looking rather foreboding. They'll be fine. I'll explain the problem, and I'm sure they'll oblige and let me in to collect our bags. I thrust Lucy towards Becker, a silent demand to hold onto her, and head for the bar.

'Eleanor!' he yells, and I look over my shoulder, having to hold back my laugh when I see him keeping a weeping Lucy at arm's length, a wary look on his face. 'I don't do emotional women.'

'No shit,' I mumble, taking off and leaving him to deal with her.

'Princess, get your arse back here now!'

I ignore him and arrive at the doors, smiling sweetly at the doormen. Both glare at me like I'm something on the bottom of their chunky boots. 'Go away, little woman,' the largest one grunts, linking his arms behind his back and looking straight through me. *Little woman?* If I didn't need those bags, I'd show him how little this woman is. I had nothing to do with the anarchy inside, but I guess I'm guilty by association.

I smile tightly. 'We left our bags on the bar. Would you be so kind?'

'No.'

My neck retracts, insulted, and my battle to keep hold of my temper gets a little trickier. I can hear Becker behind me yelling my name, getting more and more irate with each shout. I don't have time to fuck about.

'Oh, screw you, ape-boy.' I dip between them stealthily and leg it to the bar, hearing the delayed sound of hard strides hitting the floor behind me. I spot my purse, but Lucy's huge clutch bag is nowhere to be seen. 'Crap.' I grab mine and scan the floor.

'Hey!'

Whirling around, I clock ape-boy coming at me, his huge feet stomping angrily. 'Oh shit.' I abandon my search and dart for the fire exit, flying out of the doors like a hurricane. I take a precious moment to remove my heels, before speeding off across Covent Garden, checking over my shoulder for the doormen, finding them in hot pursuit. Jesus, for colossal beasts, they're fucking fast. I return my attention forward and power on, seeing Becker up ahead, still holding up Lucy.

His eyes go like saucers when he sees me barrelling towards him. 'Are you fucking kidding me?' he blurts out, his eyes following my sprinting form as I sail past.

'Run!' I shout, starting to laugh, the absurdity of the night suddenly hitting me like a brick.

'I'm gonna spank your arse until it fucking bleeds, Eleanor!'

'Okay!' I call, thinking my agreement might get him shifting quicker.

Taking a swift glimpse back, I see him tossing Lucy's hysterical and useless weight over his shoulder before breaking into a sprint that defies reason with a woman sprawled all over him.

I make it to Becker's BMW only a second before him, puffing and panting like a loser, whereas Becker has hardly broken a sweat. The door opens and he practically chucks Lucy into the back before throwing himself into the driver's seat. I join him quickly, falling into the passenger side and slamming the door. But Becker doesn't speed off like I expect. He's staring in his rear-view mirror, eyes narrowed somewhat. I look over my shoulder out the back window and see the two gorillas standing in the road, bent with their hands braced on their knees, but that's not what has Becker's attention. There's a car parked nearby, and once I've seen who's in the driver's seat, I shrink. Stan Price. He's watching Becker's car, and something tells me he's seen the entire crazy episode outside the bar. And me. Has he been following me all night? I don't say anything, mindful that Lucy is with us. I don't want her asking questions, so I just look at Becker and wait until he looks at me. When he does, his lips are straight, his nostrils flaring, and he shakes his head mildly as he starts the car and pulls off quickly.

'What's he doing here?' I ask quietly.

'Not now,' Becker warns, looking up to his rear-view mirror to Lucy.

Looking back, I find her still crying, her head limp and bobbing with the motions of the car. *Not now?* So what's he got to tell me? I return my attention to Becker, eyeing him suspiciously. I hope he doesn't think this is the end of it. I want answers.

'Well, that was a pleasant evening,' he says seriously, keeping his attention on the road. 'We must do it again sometime.'

Despite myself, I laugh, falling back into the seat. 'Anytime.'

He shakes his head mildly, looking across to me.

'What?' I ask.

'I'm so in love with you, princess,' he says quietly, probably to save Lucy's ears and remind me of why I'm caught up in his wild world. 'You're fucking chaos, but I love you so damn much.'

I'm chaos? He's hilarious, but I say nothing and place my hand on his thick thigh, squeezing.

'Perfect,' Lucy squawks from behind us, springing to life, telling us that Becker's attempt to be sensitive has fallen flat on its face. 'My life is over and you two are drooling all over each other. Don't mind me. I'll just curl up into a ball of despair and rot. Where's my bag?' she asks, a hive of activity breaking out in the back of Becker's car – mutters, curses and jerky movements.

I stiffen in my seat, feeling Becker looking at me. I bite my lip and face him, and he frowns, cocking me a questioning look, only briefly before returning his attention back to the road. I know what he's thinking. He's thinking I risked delaying our escape and had us chased down by London's finest cavemen in order to retrieve that bag. And I haven't got it. 'I couldn't find it,' I whisper, for what reason I don't know. I'm going to have to tell my rankled friend that sacrifices had to be made, and her bag was one of them. 'You left your bag on the bar. It was gone,' I say over my shoulder.

Lucy shoots forward, wedging herself between the two front seats. 'What?'

'Yes, what?' Becker mimics, his head turning from the road to me.

'I didn't exactly have all the time in the world to crawl around searching the floor,' I grate through clenched teeth. 'Thing One and Thing Two were quite speedy.'

'Oh, this is marvellous,' Lucy cries. 'My purse, my keys, my phone.'

Purse. Keys. Phone. Oh my God. *Stupid, stupid, stupid!* I swing around and nearly head butt Lucy. 'My phone, keys and purse were in your bag.'

She huffs her displeasure, looking up at the roof of the car. 'And *your* phone, keys, and purse.' She adds my losses to her list like it's a genuine inconvenience for her. 'Why didn't I stay at home?' she asks the ceiling.

'Because you're a paranoid twat,' I mutter moodily, throwing myself back around.

'I am not.'

'Yes, you are,' I retort childishly, waving my bag in the air, unwittingly poking her.

'Oh, so you managed to save *your* bag?'

'It was still on the bar.'

'And my make-up,' she blurts out, another loss coming to her. 'It was Chanel.'

'Nothing could sort your face out right now,' I retort. 'Not Coco, not Estée, and probably not even Photoshop.'

Lucy gasps and launches forward that little bit more, dislodging some drops of foam from her hair that spray my cheek. 'Why are you being such a heartless cow?'

'Because you're—'

'Enough!' Becker slams a fist into the steering wheel, abruptly interrupting our petty row. 'Just zip it, the pair of you.'

We do. We're not stupid. Becker's anger is palpable, rolling off of him in waves. But something tells me it's not me or Lucy who's got him rankled. What the hell is Stan Price doing following me? 'You just made me hit my car,' he yells, smacking the wheel again before putting his foot down aggressively and flinging us back in our seats. Lucy, being far forward, almost sitting on the dashboard, has a greater distance to be flung than me, resulting in a shriek of shock as she catapults back. I know better than to laugh, despite it being hilariously funny watching her squirming around on the back seat, trying to sit up.

'Super,' Becker seethes. 'So Lucy's bag containing *your* phone, keys, and purse, are somewhere in that bar, assuming someone hasn't stolen them?'

'The barman might have picked it up,' I say quietly, suddenly comprehending where he's heading with this.

'Your keys to The Haven and your purse, which I'm assuming contains your access card, are lost?' He turns a tight look onto me. 'And . . .' He takes a breather before finishing, but he doesn't need to finish. I mind read the rest. *And Stan Price is loitering around.*

I shrink in my seat. 'Or maybe the barman picked them up,' I repeat in an attempt to pacify him.

'Fucking brilliant.' He laughs coldly. 'And I'm heading towards Lucy's apartment, but she doesn't have her keys to get in?'

Oh. I hadn't thought about that little issue. My only concerns were the millions of pounds worth of Becker's treasure at The Haven, my lost key card to his sanctuary, and the fact that Stan Price has clearly been following us. But again, why? Just because of Lady Winchester? I'm becoming increasingly suspicious.

Becker looks up to the rear-view mirror. 'So what am I supposed to do with you?' he asks Lucy's reflection seriously as he takes a hard left, sending me and Lucy sailing clumsily into the side of the car.

I'm vehemently trying not to ask Becker why no keys to Lucy's apartment would be a problem, since he managed to break into mine just fine without any. But that wouldn't be smart, not even when he's in a good mood, so it definitely wouldn't be my brightest move now, when he looks like he could strangle me and bite my friend's head off.

'She'll have to come back with us,' I say calmly.

His horrified expression tells me what he thinks to that before he can vocalise it. 'No.'

'Then drop us off at a hotel.' I realise the problem. It's called

Becker's circle of trust and Lucy is not in it. 'The Stanton will do.' I chuck in his face in pure spite. There are millions of hotels in London, and I just named Brent Wilson's. I'm deplorable.

'You're pushing it, princess.'

Lucy remains quiet, aware of the sudden elevated animosity, and I look back, cringing when I realise her silence is more likely because she's looking a little green. I pray to every Greek god that she holds her nausea in check. Her eyes begin to roll. Then she slumps back in the seat.

Becker looks up to his rear-view mirror and shakes his head. 'I'm going to thrash your arse, Eleanor,' he promises quietly, spinning the wheel as he slams on the brakes, making a quick about-turn in the road. 'So, *so* fucking hard.' The tyres screech, the BMW turning smoothly, before we're racing off in the other direction.

Jesus Christ, if he ever fancies getting out of the art world, then he could head straight to Hollywood where I'm certain he'd make a killing as a stunt driver. I grab my seat and hold on. 'Looking forward to it,' I fire back impertinently, turning in my seat. I find Lucy sprawled across the back, front down, her face squished in the leather. I frown at her sorry state. 'She's passed out.'

Becker grunts, putting his foot down when a traffic light up ahead turns to amber. He whips his phone out and slams his thumbs across the screen, bringing up a map. I crane my head to see it, spotting a red blinking light in the centre. He mutters under his breath and rids the screen of the map before dialling and taking the phone to his ear. 'Percy, the CCTV footage I told you to get from the bar,' he begins, piquing my interest. 'There's a bag containing Eleanor's iPhone, her keys, and purse.'

He pauses, and I hear the muffled voice of Percy down the line. 'Oh dear.'

'Yes,' Becker chucks me a glare. 'Don't fuck about. Stan Price is keeping close company.' He hangs up and drops his phone into his lap.

The mention of Price brings back my suspicions. And since Lucy is now sparko . . . 'Stan Price can't just let himself into The Haven without a reason,' I point out.

'Stan Price has never needed a reason for anything, Eleanor. He doesn't exactly play by the rules. I'm not taking any chances. The last thing I need . . .' He tails off and looks up to the rear-view mirror again to check Lucy's still out for the count.

'Are you saying Price is corrupt?'

'He's old-school. Doesn't like all the red tape, so tends to ignore it.'

My heart thrums a little harder. 'And what does he hope to find at The Haven?'

'Who the fuck knows. All I know is some of my clients pay good money to maintain anonymity. The police sniffing around won't be good for business.'

'And what if my bag isn't in the bar?' I ask. Will he have to change all the locks?

'Don't wor . . .' Becker fades off, glimpsing at me briefly, nervously. What was that? 'I'm sure it's there.'

I sit back in my seat, studying him. Then I rewind to a few moments ago. The map on his screen. The red blinking dot. The fact that he turned up at the bar out of the blue and I never once mentioned where I would be. 'You're tracking my phone,' I blurt out, outraged.

'Good fucking job, too,' he spits in return, no guilt or embarrassment evident.

How dare he. 'You can't keep tabs on my every movement.'

'I can, I am, and I always fucking will.'

The arrogant bastard. 'I'll get my own phone,' I declare, before he can hit me with it being a work phone, so technically he can do what he likes. He might own the phone, but he doesn't own me.

'Shhhh,' Becker hushes me, and I look moodily out the corner of my eye to see him holding a finger to his lush lips. 'It's standard GPS tracking, princess.'

I scoff. 'Sure it is.' Standard my arse. I'll be taking my phone to pieces at the first opportunity. I signed up for corruption. Not being tailed.

We zoom through the lights, just as they turn red.

'Careful,' I mutter, looking out of the passenger window. 'Don't want to give the police a reason to pull you over.'

I hear him laugh under his breath. 'Careful,' he counters, reaching over and squeezing my bare knee. The skin on skin contact nearly has me bursting into flames, damn him. 'Don't want to give me reason to slap your arse silly.' Smoky eyes, hooded and filled with sinful promises, hold me still in my seat.

I've given him plenty of excuses to slap my arse silly in the past hour. What's another transgression between me and my gorgeous sinner?

Chapter 20

Becker isn't taking any chances. We don't enter The Haven via the factory units; we pull up to the kerb outside the alleyway on the street instead. Apparently, he's not risking taking the back entrance in case Lucy wakes up. I don't think he has anything to fear. She's totally sparko on the back seat.

I watch as Becker wrestles her from his car, holding my tongue to prevent me from blurting out something snarky. He's cursing and muttering under his breath. The urge to enflame his irritation is overwhelming. 'You're doing a stellar—' I physically slap my hand over my mouth to halt the flow of my condescending encouragement.

His jerky string of movements falter for a few worrying moments, and I brace myself for a barrage of abuse, but after taking a loud, calming intake of breath, he continues to wrestle my dead weight of a friend from the back seat. 'I have never, not once, let a perfect stranger into The Haven.' Once he's unbent his body and has Lucy's floppy body in a fireman's hold, he turns and hands me a security card.

I accept, my smile unstoppable. 'You let *me* in.'

One of his lovely eyes narrow on me, his lips twitching. 'Best stupid move I've ever made. You going to open this door?'

I oblige quickly and push the door open, holding it for him to pass. 'Certainly . . . sir.'

'Oh, girl, you know how to push my buttons.' He paces past me and disappears into the dark alleyway, leaving me to follow with a huge grin on my face. 'Where are you going to put her?'

The lights activate and the first thing I see is Lucy's mouth hanging open, dribbling. I grimace.

'In Winston's bed.'

'You can't do that.' I laugh, though it's tinged with nerves because I know he probably would.

'Watch me.' He marches on, determined. 'She's going to have a stinker of a headache in the morning.'

'She needs a shower,' I say as we breach the end of the alley, breaking into the courtyard. The sensors detect us and spring to life, illuminating the outside space.

'She's taken up enough of your time this evening,' Becker gripes uncharitably as he lets us into the Grand Hall. 'I want my girlfriend back.'

When I should be telling him off for being so insensitive, I find myself smiling like a prat instead. I . . . God, I just want him to gobble me up, the delicious, scandalously, handsome crook. 'At least you still have a girlfriend.' I say, wondering how Mark's doing. I'll call him in the morning.

Becker negotiates Lucy down the corridor, and I worry all over again when he stops by the kitchen door. He wouldn't? He can't. I'll never be able to pick her up out of Winston's bed.

I wait with bated breath, ready to stop him. But after a few worrying moments, he shakes his head and continues on to the end of the corridor where his granddad resides, opening the door opposite Mr H's suite. I rush past him and pull back the covers of the spare bed.

Becker lowers her to the mattress. 'My God, she stinks.'

I laugh, thinking Lucy is going to be absolutely mortified come morning. 'You'd better go before I undress her. She's got enough to be embarrassed about.'

He shakes his head in despair and backs out of the room. 'Your arse looks amazing in that dress, by the way.' He grins cheekily and pulls the door closed.

I'm smiling as I start the task of peeling Lucy's damp clothes away. It proves trickier than expected; the playsuit is like the Rubik's Cube of outfits. 'How the hell do you get out of it?' I ask myself, forcing her dead weight onto her side with effort. I find a zip, but quickly figure that even by undoing it, I've still got to get the thing over her head, and with shorts attached that's going to be pretty impossible while she's unconscious. I give up. 'I'm sorry, Lucy, but you're going to have to sleep in it.' I try to compensate by tucking her in, all cosy and warm, before leaving her snoring. I shake my head at her on a fond smile. She probably won't even remember our row in the morning.

Closing the door behind me, I follow my senses to Becker's office and spend a while staring at the depiction of Adam and Eve on the huge wooden doors. The Garden of Eden. If only I'd known when I first clapped eyes on this door. The temptation I'd be faced with, just like Eve. The irony of the wooden carving has never escaped me.

I suddenly feel a little sleepy as I push my way in and yawn, coming to a stop when I see Becker sitting on the edge of his desk with a tumbler in his hand.

'My girl's tired.' He knocks back a drink and comes to collect me, and I don't murmur a word of protest as he gathers my useless body into his arms. 'Time for bed, princess.'

My head hits his shoulder and my eyes are immediately heavy. 'Thank you for letting her stay.'

'No problem.'

'You're still in trouble.'

'For what?'

'Stalking me.'

'Get over it.'

I sleepily snort and increase my hold around his neck. 'And why is Price following me?'

'I don't think he was following you this time, princess.'

'Then why is he following you?'

'Like I've said, probably to see if I have any dealings with Lady Winchester.'

I stifle another yawn as Becker takes the steps and lets us into his apartment. 'I don't like him,' I declare. 'And if he comes poking around again, I'll drop-kick his fat arse back to his office.' He laughs as he lays me on the bed and I sink into the sheets, the scent wafting up making me even more sleepy. 'I will protect you for ever.'

'Yeah?' he asks, smiling through his kiss to my forehead.

'Yeah,' I confirm. 'He should be trembling in his scruffy boots.'

'You're crazy, woman.' Becker's hands stroking over my hair is hypnotic, and I sigh, rolling over and snuggling down, my eyes refusing to remain open.

'Must be,' I mumble sleepily. 'After all, here I am loving you.'

Chapter 21

My eyes flutter open, finding a hazy darkness and an empty space next to me in the bed. I blink and gain some focus, looking down my body to find I'm still in my dress from last night.

'Good fucking morning, princess.'

I look up and find Becker in a chair across the way, he, too, still in his clothes from last night. 'What time is it?'

'Five.'

My face bunches in disgust, and I fall back to the mattress dramatically. 'Why am I still dressed?'

I hear him approaching, and then I feel him gather me up from the sheets. 'I didn't want to wake you.'

I curl into his chest as he walks us out of the bedroom. 'Why are *you* still dressed?'

'I didn't want to disturb my time admiring you sleeping.'

'You watched me all night?' He just sat there and looked at me? Why didn't he strip us down and get into bed, give us naked cuddles?

'Yes.' He says no more, passing his bathroom and heading towards the door, and I'm soon being carried down the stairs. 'I was mulling a few things over.'

'Like what?'

'How madly in love with you I am.'

'That's because I'm a slave to your corrupt bones,' I say, frowning into his shoulder as we pass the library and the kitchen, and then we're at the double doors that lead into his grand hall. 'Where are we going?'

'I want to show you something.' Shifting me in his hold a little, he rummages through his pocket and a few seconds later, the door is open and we're inside the huge space. I'm detached gently from his body and placed on my feet.

'What are we doing in here?' I ask, wondering, worriedly, if maybe he's going to point out everything and declare its authenticity. My sleepy eyes bounce across all of the pieces. It could take a while.

'It's all real,' he says, grabbing my attention again. My cheeks flush a little when I find him smiling knowingly. If he thinks I've pulled a smash and grab on his heart, then I trump that with a breaking and entering on my mind. He can't blame me for seeking constant reassurance. He's a master forger. I'm dealing with situations and information that are wildly unbelievable.

Taking my shoulders, Becker holds them firmly and ensures he has my eyes before he goes on. 'Awake?'

'Barely,' I grumble. 'Why am I up at five o'clock?'

He smiles a bright smile, way too bright for this time. 'Stay there.' Releasing me, he wanders off across the room, weaving around the haphazardly stored pieces of art and antiques until he arrives on the far side opposite me. I follow his arse the entire way, but then he turns and I lose my view, so my eyes climb his torso to his face. 'You looking at my arse, princess?'

I don't answer. It's pointless.

He laughs under his breath, dropping his eyes to the floor as he slowly turns away from me again, revealing his wonderful asset. I swallow and imagine sinking my nails in, squeezing and following the sway as he rocks into me. I feel hot in this huge airy room. Then the bastard doubles my weakness when he takes the hem of his T-shirt and pulls it up over his head, exposing the beautiful art on his back. I have no problem deciding what to centre my attention on. His arse is a magnet for my eyes, but I can see that whenever I like – day or night, even when concealed by material. It doesn't hinder the pleasure. His tattoo, however, can only be appreciated when his back is bare. Like now. It's stunning. A masterpiece, even if it's incomplete. I cock my head as I admire it, imagining it whole. The missing piece not missing any more. The key to locate *Head of a Faun* right there on his back. 'Do you still think about it?' I ask out of the blue, my mouth out of control. He flexes his shoulders, making every muscle beneath the ink undulate scandalously. I clench my teeth, watching in awe. 'Yes,' he admits, slowly turning around, painfully slowly, his face boyish but manly, his sleepy eyes tender but hard, his soft bristle scruffy but perfect. 'Except when I'm thinking about you.' His head tilts. 'And you?'

'Hardly ever.' I will never admit my mind catches me off guard too often with wondering. But I think he knows.

He smiles. He definitely knows. 'Take your clothes off. You can leave your knickers. For now.'

The tremors of need in me are instant, savaging my body. I'm wide awake now.

I start to strip down, my line of sight never straying from his. I unzip my dress slowly and pull the material away from my body, letting it tumble to the floor at my feet, but when I think his gaze might follow its path down, he chooses to keep my eyes. My hands go to my back and unclasp my bra and my already hard nipples turn to bullets once I'm free from the pink satin. But his sparkling eyes still don't stray from mine.

I wait for instructions, but none come.

Then his hands move towards the waist of his jeans. Slowly. Torturously. I want to scream. On the inside, I am. 'Becker, please don't—'

'Shhhh.' He unleashes his sexy shush, silencing me abruptly, and I start to fidget, impatient. He smiles victoriously, cranking up the heat in the room to unbearable levels. Nimble hands work his belt leisurely, each motion – the pull of the buckle, the feed of the leather through his belt loops – undertaken to have maximum impact on my patience levels.

'Struggling?' he asks, dropping the belt to the floor. It lands with a thud as if to tease me, to emphasise the fact that I'm one step closer to naked Becker. I mildly nod and fix my eyes on the fly of his jeans. 'Me too.' He lazily unfastens the button, followed by the zip, and the red waistband of his boxers appears. Power red. It's appropriate for the moment, because he is certifiably king of my world.

His jeans are pushed down his thighs, and I blink, moistening my eyeballs before I focus on the vision of his white boxers wrapped around thick thighs that could crush me. I concentrate, like if I stare long enough and hard enough, I might be able to burn the material away. Becker ups the ante when he cups himself over his boxers, his jeans halfway down his legs.

That's it. He's provoking me, pushing me. He's gone too far. I move forward.

'Hey,' he barks, and like a robot programmed to obey his command, I stop. 'You. Will. Wait.'

'How long?' I push the question through a tight jaw.

'How long would you wait for me?' he counters calmly, dropping his hold of his arousal and bending slightly to push his jeans to his ankles. He kicks them off and takes his hands to the red waistband of his boxers. 'How long, Eleanor?' He slowly drags them down his thighs, and his impressive cock springs free proudly. 'How long would you wait for this?' His palm wraps around it possessively.

I rip my enthralled eyes away from his groin and reveal the desperation flooding them.

He sees it, even from all the way over there. *How long would I wait?* My mind's not my own right now, not functioning to its full ability, yet I sense there is more to his question than meets the eye. How long did his grandmother wait for Gramps? How long did his mother wait for his dad? While they were searching the world for that sculpture?

The truth is, I would wait, for however long it takes him to find what he's looking for. But I won't confirm that. I *mustn't* confirm that.

He widens his stance and relinquishes his hold of his erection. He looks so magnificent. Tall, powerful, defined. He's art personified. 'How quickly do you think you can make it to me?' His lips pucker, making them look even more plump and lush than usual. It distracts me for a moment.

I gauge the distance between us, seriously considering my answer and being quick about it. If I run, and I'm willing to, not long at all. 'Five seconds.'

His head nods agreeably. 'That quick?'

Is he testing me? Challenging me? 'Yes.' I'll sprint if I have to. I watch him crouch and go to the pocket of his discarded jeans, all the while looking at me. 'What are you doing?' I ask.

He finds what he's looking for and rises slowly, looking pleased with himself. He has something small in his hand, but I can't see what. He holds it up, and my curiosity gets the better of me. 'What's that?'

'Five seconds?'

'Yes.'

I catch the most roguish, boyish grin forming, just as the room falls into darkness. 'And now?' I hear him ask in the blackness. Oh, he's playing all right.

'Ten seconds,' I answer cockily, visualising the Grand Hall in my mind. I've been here long enough to know my path through the art and antiques.

I start to move forward, remembering the large Victorian table to my left, the Rembrandt to my right, and the Louis XIV chair up ahead, but the odd sound of a surge of energy halts my progression. 'What's that?' I ask, starting a futile spin on the spot, searching for the source of the noise. It's a constant whirring sound, like something is charging up. 'Becker?' My hands come up in front of me, feeling at thin air. I don't like this. The blindness, the exposure, the vulnerability. 'Becker?'

'Shhhh.' His hush invades my ears, but he's not close. No-where near. I spin again, now disorientated, unsure of what direction I should be heading in. 'Stay still, Eleanor,' he tells me firmly, and I do.

Blue light springs from every direction, and my eyes slam shut, my hands coming up to my face for extra protection. That wasn't normal light. It was bright and blue and sharp.

'Open your eyes.'

'What will I see?' I ask, nervous. Nothing Becker shows me should be a surprise any more, yet he's constantly surprising me.

'You'll see your saint, princess.'

My hands drop from my face and my eyes open without hesitation. It takes a few seconds of blinking and adjusting my sight, and then I see it.

'Oh my goodness,' I whisper.

Chapter 22

He didn't lie. Becker really is the first thing I see, still all the way across the room, but there's something else – something that I have to look *through* in order to see him. He smiles and then looks around the room himself, giving me the silent instruction I need to do the same. My hand comes to my mouth when they all register. Hundreds of them, everywhere.

Light beams.

They're not as bright any more, now that my shocked eyes have adjusted. Now they are glowing softly in the darkness. The Grand Hall is a maze of blue shards of lights, all criss-crossing, spanning one wall to the other, floor to ceiling. My mouth is slightly agape as I gaze around, slowly turning on the spot and looking up into the rafters before returning my sight to the space before me. There are only two small spaces free from lights, and I'm standing in one. Becker is in the other. I smile in wonder, remembering Mrs Potts chuckling when I questioned security in the Grand Hall.

'Are they activated?' I ask, trying to ignore his nakedness and focus on what I know will be my task.

'Only in maintenance mode. You'll hear a sharp chime if you breach a beam.' It looks impossible. There are too many of them, all randomly crossing. 'You get one spank for every sensor you activate.'

'What?' I gasp, stunned. My arse will be black and blue!

'One spank, Eleanor. Now hurry up. I'm getting impatient.'

The fucker. This is a win–win for him. If I make it to him

quickly and without error, he gets to fuck me sooner. If I make a hash of it and activate any one of these hundreds of beams, he gets to spank me silly, and *then* fuck me. My arse is still sore. I'm not up for any more thrashings this week. I just want to be violated.

'And what do I get if I make it to you without setting one off?'

'You won't.' He's egging me on, and that is the only reason I'm going to make sure I do this. I could run through those beams, set off a hundred and accept my fate, then enjoy being violated. But I want to succeed in my challenge more. Prove to him that I can do this. But . . .

I'm constantly proving myself to him, constantly running his gauntlet and coming out the other side relatively unscathed, doing him proud. When will he prove himself to me? *He has, Eleanor!* I scorn myself a little, listening to my subconscious. He's given me his heart, and that's the grandest gesture of all. Probably even more significant than him sharing his secrets with me. But still. Becker gave me his heart without even really realising. 'I want to know what I get in return,' I reiterate.

'Me,' he says quietly. 'Every wicked, corrupt, vulnerable piece of me.'

'I have you already.'

'Do you?' He smiles as I frown, my eyes narrowing in question. He has more to give? Or more to share? 'Get that sweet arse over here so I can show you.'

Is there anything more tempting than that? I eye up the glowing beams before me on an unsure smile as I tie my hair into a ponytail. There are five horizontal stretches of light to consider within my height range, each a foot or so apart. Studying the one nearest my feet, I lower to my knees as I tuck the loose strands of hair behind my ears. My palms meet the floor and I drop to my tummy, all the while assessing the height of the beam from the floor. Taking only a small intake of air so as not to expand my chest too much, I close my eyes and roll onto my back, waiting for any sound that will tell me I've breached the light. It doesn't come. I open my eyes and see the ceiling of the Grand Hall through the beams above me. I grin. I feel far too proud, and maybe a little cocky, because that's only one beam down. I have a way to go yet before I can claim my victory, *and* my prize. *What's my prize?* I look left and right, then above me, seeing I'm now closed in from every direction. I'm in the centre of four beams that form a square around me. The beam nearest the floor is lower than the one I just rolled under. I won't clear it, so I weigh up my other options. I need to step over it, while ducking the one above. 'Okay,' I whisper, carefully rising to my feet, holding my breath.

'Breathe steady.' Becker calls. 'Breathe through your moves.'

I watch the beam as I bring my knee up to my chest, angling it so I don't trigger the beam above. Keeping my arms close to my body, I dip and place my foot on the other side, straddling it.

'Clever girl,' he praises with sincere pride.

My breathing has now fallen into a calm, steady rhythm, and my muscles are no longer tense. I find I can roll under the next two beams, step over another three, and bend my body to clear two more, but when I make it over halfway, I find I can do none of those things on my next move. The beams are spaced more tightly and there's a huge dresser blocking the other way. If I try to move it, I'll trigger a sensor. There's no way past. I look from side-to-side, searching for another route. There must be one, unless Becker has purposely set me up to fail. But no. Whatever he wants to give me, he *really* wants to give me.

'There's a way, princess,' he says, distracting me from my search. He nods, affirming what he's told me. I shouldn't have looked at him standing there waiting for me, beautifully bare.

I close my eyes and fight to relocate my focus. 'How many more beams do I need to clear?'

'Just three if you go the right way,' he answers. Three. Just three? I'm over halfway and it's taken me nine moves to get here. How? I open my eyes and re-evaluate my position. I'm definitely not going forward, and if I go back, it'll take way more than three moves to make it to him. The dresser. I gaze up to the top of it, estimating it to be roughly four feet taller than me. That has to be it. It's almost impossible to determine whether there's a way forward from there, not until I reach the top, but it's my only option. There are three drawers at the bottom and shelves spanning the rest of the way up. And there is only one beam hitting the wood, halfway up to the right. I open the middle drawer and rest my foot on it, applying only a little bit of my weight, testing the stability. It's a Georgian dresser. Solid and sturdy. It must be nearly three hundred years old and has probably withstood a lot more than little old me playing Spider-Man on it. I take the sides and jiggle tentatively, happy with the lack of movement, and then push my weight off the floor, bringing my other foot up to the drawer. I spend a few moments ensuring I'm steady, before having a quick check for the beams. Then I make my next move, hauling my body up onto the first shelf. The huge dresser remains firm, keeping me safe. I'm desperate to have a quick peek to my right to find Becker, but I fight off the compulsion, realigning my concentration. My next move will put me on top of the dresser. The sense of achievement gets the better of me, and I bring my knee up, anchoring it on the top of the wood before pulling the rest of my body up.

Beep!

I gasp and freeze, mindful that I could activate the alarm again. I didn't hit the beam; I know I didn't!

'You missed the one above your head, princess.'

Keeping as still as I can, I cast my eyes up and spot the stretch of blue light just a few inches above my head. Then I look ahead and spot my way out. There are three beams in front of me, avoidable if I use the holes from various missing bricks in the wall. I smile. My instinct didn't fail me. I can smell freedom in the form of an intoxicating wood-and-apple scent, but holy fuck, this is going to take some serious body-bending to clear.

'Take your time,' Becker says softly, encouragingly. My heart is now hammering, a little in apprehension and a lot in excitement. So I practise some breathing, working hard to calm down my racing heart. I can't fail now. Just one spank. It's not none, but I can live with one.

I reach for one of the holes in the wall, but then retract my arm, figuring very quickly that my plan's not going to work. My foot. I need to get my foot into it. Shit, that looks hard. Positioning my bum on the edge of the dresser, I check below and find no beams close to the edge, so I slide my legs down the side so I'm sitting on the edge. Then I brace my hands behind me and point my toe, reaching to the wall under the beam before me. My toe skims the brick. 'Damn it,' I curse, shuffling carefully forward, constantly scanning my surroundings and position. My foot reaches and settles, and I exhale, my cheeks puffing out. My leg is extended to full length, my muscles strained like an overstretched elastic band with both hands gripping the top of the dresser. I need to be quick. I won't be able to withstand the pull for long. Looking down to where my hands rest on the edge of the wood, I anchor them firmly, then push my bum off the edge, keeping my other foot wedged into the side of the dresser, hoping it doesn't slip, before reaching with my right hand and grabbing the wall. I exhale, and I'm sure I hear Becker release air, too. I can feel him watching me, though there's not a cat in hell's chance of me looking to confirm it. Not unless I pull an *Exorcist* move and spin my head on my shoulders. I breathe out as I bend forward to dip under the beam but stop just in time to realise that my head will likely cut straight through another beam a foot in front. Glancing over my shoulder, I see the one behind is a little further away, but Lord knows how I'll bend back *that* far. Fuck, I might be nimble but I'm hardly a contortionist.

'Jesus Christ,' I breathe, beginning to sweat. I'm literally suspended between the wall and the huge piece of furniture, like a jumping jack floating in mid-air. I'm going to have to catapult myself onto the wall and hope for the best. If I can just bend enough and hold my position to move under the beam, I can use the dresser as a launch pad to spring to safety. 'If you could see me now, Dad,' I mutter to the heavens, shifting a little to root my feet into position firmly. I start bowing back, arching my spine slowly and deliberately inch by inch and circling to the side, trying to give the beam a wide berth. My teeth clench as my spine curls, vertebrae by vertebrae, folding slowly until my torso is at a right angle to my lower body and I can see behind me. I begin to shake, the strain getting too much to bear. 'Come on,' I encourage myself, feeling like my spine could snap at any moment.

The blue glowing line comes into my view. I start inching to the right, passing beneath it. I swear, if I were to stick my tongue out, I could lick the light. It's literally skimming my nose. 'Fucking hell.' I have to stop a second to reposition my hand on the wood when it slips a little. 'Shit, shit, shit,' I curse, my limbs starting to vibrate with the strength it's taking me to unbend myself. It hurts terribly, but I battle through the pain, my muscles burning. And when my foot begins to slip as well, I have no option but to propel myself and hope for the best.

I close my eyes as I take off, my foot and hand leaving the dresser and following the path of my torso, under the beam. I hear Becker gasp, and then I feel the impact. I slam into the wall and quickly open my eyes, finding the holes in the brickwork and grabbing on. 'Oh my God,' I breathe, looking down to the floor, just to make sure that I'm where I'm supposed to be while listening carefully for any accusing beeps. Nothing.

The most incredible sense of achievement bombards me.

I check the beams below me and clear them, jumping down from the wall. The ground beneath my feet feels so good. I land with my back to Becker, smiling victoriously across the hall. Then I slowly turn to find him, unable to disguise my elation or stop myself from having a thorough inspection of his naked body as I calm my breathing down. I take my time, working my way up his physique, noticing he's perspiring himself, a film of shimmering sweat coating his chest. I pass his pecs, the scruff at his neck, his throat, his chin, and finally make it to his face. The happiness shining back at me through his hazel green eyes eliminates every ache and pain. My muscles stop screaming with overstretching and start screaming with longing.

His smiling eyes are joined by lips that stretch the widest I've ever seen. '*That*,' he says sharply, grabbing my hips and pulling me into him. Our naked chests collide, the heat of our bodies mingling deliciously, 'was the sexiest thing I've ever seen in my fucking life.' He spins me around so my back slams into his chest, and I cry out, feeling his erection pushing into my bottom and his palms covering my breast, squeezing deliberately. My breathing goes to shit again, and I very nearly stop when he rests his lips on the nape of my neck. I'm hypersensitive to everything. I don't know whether it's adrenalin or what, but every touch feels like pure fire.

'I've just fallen in love with you some more,' he whispers, sucking on my flesh. 'Fuck me, Eleanor, you have no idea how incredible your body looked moving through my maze.' He pushes me forward, and I close my eyes, waiting for it as he yanks my knickers out of the way. I triggered the alarm once.

Smack!

I'm spun back on a yelp and hauled up to his body. 'How do you want me, princess? The hard fucker, or the masterful love-maker?'

My legs wrap around his naked hips and cling on tightly, my palms resting on his skin. 'You're a master at both.'

'I have more experience in one than the other.' He raises a sardonic eyebrow that goes way over my head. He might have more experience being a cold, emotionless fucker, but his new-found tenderness is pretty masterful, too.

Reaching for my hair tie, he pulls it free and my red locks tumble down my back. 'I need something to grip onto.'

I ignore his cheek and slide my hands into his mussed-up locks. 'Touché,' I quip, giving it a severe tug.

He winces on a grin before lunging forward with his mouth, crashing his lips to mine and returning my brutality. His fingers delve into my hair and fist it. I'm instantly in the game, matching the severity of his hold and kiss, plunging my tongue deep and firmly.

He stalks forward with no regard for any of the blue beams that I've just broke my back avoiding, and one alarm triggers, then another and another. 'Fuck,' Becker curses, performing an about turn and taking us back to the wall. 'We'll wake Gramps.' He dips and picks something up, and the noise dies in an instant, along with the thousands of light shards. Blackness falls for a split second before the lights kick in. And he's on me again, resuming our desperate kiss. With me still coiled around his waist, he drops to his knees, then takes me down to my back. The hardness of the floor doesn't bother me in the slightest. I wriggle beneath him, widening my spread thighs so he's nestled comfortably between them. Our hands and mouths are everywhere, grabbing and kissing hectically. I can feel the length of him, hard and hot, gliding across the heat of my clit.

'Becker,' I pant between rushed tongue strokes. 'Inside.'

'Is someone in a hurry?' His hand tickles down my side, onto my leg, and wraps around my upper thigh, tugging up.

'No more games.'

'Shhhh.'

'Don't shush me.' I'm pulling at his hair in a frenzy, trying to angle my hips just so.

He's having none of it. He lifts his lower body, getting to his knees. 'Shut the fuck up, princess.'

I scream my frustration, and he flips me over, pulling my knickers aside and giving my arse a warning smack.

'That's two,' I yell, pissed off, rolling onto my back again. 'I only activated one alarm.'

'Yes, but you're making far too much noise right now.' Sliding his arm under my lower back, he rises to standing, lifting me with him before steadying me on my feet. Then he lets go and wanders across the hall, taking long, slow strides that showcase his arse and back to their full beauty.

When he reaches the Louis XIV chair, he slowly takes a seat and spreads his legs. My eyes drop to his crotch and my tongue slips across my top lip.

'Move.' His order kicks my feet into action, but my focus remains on his cock as I make my way over to him. 'See something you want?' he asks assuredly.

'Yes.'

'I might let you lick it.' His fist wraps around the girth and slowly starts to pump. 'I might not.'

I reach him and flick my eyes up his body. His face is tight, his eyes on my breasts. I take my palms to them and cup firmly. My sensitive nipples pucker like they could be submerged in ice. 'See something *you* want?' I ask, as he continues to work himself.

'No.' He looks up at me. 'I see something I *have*.'

I half smile, lifting a brow. I relinquish my hold of my boobs and cheekily slide two fingers down the centre of my stomach, into the top of my knickers. 'And what about this?' My breath stutters when my touch finds the liquid fire between my thighs. 'Does this belong to you, Becker?'

'We've been over this, Eleanor,' he breathes tiredly. 'Stop being so stubborn and accept that I own you.' He drops his cock and reaches forward, knocking my hand away from the apex of my thighs. I inhale a feeble gust of air. Feeble because I planned on sounding shocked, but all I achieved was unadulterated craving. For him. He slips a finger into the side of my knickers and slowly draws them down my legs. 'Step out and get on your knees.' He lets the small piece of material around my thighs drop to the floor and then rests back in the chair, reclaiming his cock.

I'm knelt at his feet quicker than my dignity should allow. 'And now what, sir?' I'm selective with my words. I know what that one does to him, and a small hiss confirms it.

'Kiss it.' He holds himself firmly and thrusts his hips up a little.

I do as I'm bid, resting my hands on his thighs and leaning in. I keep my eyes on his as I lower my mouth to his cock and drop a gentle kiss on the very tip. He moans, gliding his fist up. A small bead of pre-cum appears. I can't resist. I dip and lick it up, groaning teasingly.

He pushes me away and sits forward, sacrificing his own pleasure for mine, his fingers slipping between my legs, past my trembling lips, and pushing into me unforgivingly.

'Oh God.' I'm instantly rigid, and triumph is quickly plastered all over his extraordinary face. He circles his fingers precisely, prompting me to spit out a plea for mercy.

'You want me?' he hisses.

'Yes.'

'How badly, Eleanor? How badly do you want me fucking you right now?'

'Badly.' My torso concaves sharply, my head going limp. I can't deal with this. 'Becker, please.'

He removes his fingers and my body goes limp at his feet, my shoulders slumping. 'Help me.' He takes my chin and pulls my face up, flashing a condom in my face.

I take it and rip it open quickly, discarding the empty foil packet to the side. My fingers are clumsy as I take it to the broad head of his cock.

'Steady,' he murmurs, holding himself vertical from his lap. I'm too desperate to be steady, all fingers and thumbs, and once Becker's realised that, he takes over and quickly covers himself.

With one fast move, I'm hauled onto his lap and with a sharp shift of his hips, he thunders up on a harsh bark, me on a scream. He brings me down, pushing his hands into the tops of my arms and his back into the chair. His stupidly defined chest sends me cross-eyed. If I could find my senses, I could probably find the energy to dribble at the sight, but he lifts me fast and drives back up, so fucking deep, groaning and dropping his chin lifelessly to his chest. 'Fucking hell,' he whispers hoarsely.

I swivel on his lap, grinding down as his head flies up, pleasure rife through the sweat and strain on his face.

'You feel so good,' he pants, encouraging me to circle again, transferring his hold to my hips. 'I love seeing you like this.' Our eyes lock. The intensity bouncing between us is rampant. Every one of my nerve endings is in a pickle, the spasms relentless. I grind again, loving the glints of wonder sparking from his eyes. He's letting me take control, holding back on his power and instinct to smash into me. I make sure I don't disappoint.

'Do I feel good wrapped around you, Becker?' I ask, rolling firm and deep. His cheeks puff out, his fingers clawing into the flesh of my hips. 'Tell me, you holier-than-thou-twat. Do I feel good?'

'Jesus, Eleanor,' he chokes, blinking his eyes a few times, the sensation of his cock gliding smoothly into me stirring the pressure, pushing it forward.

'Not so holier-than-thou now, are you?' I lift and push down precisely.

'Fuck!'

'Do you like me talking dirty to you?' Around I go, up and down on a slap of flesh. '*Renaissance*,' I whisper provocatively, smiling on the inside.

'Eleanor.' His eyes roll into the back of his head, the groans coming thick and fast.

I meld the flesh of his shoulders as I fall forward, my breathing stuttering slightly as a result of the change in angle. He's so deep, so thick and warm. I get my nose close to his and swivel my hips again, not just once, but twice, three times, four times, with no break in between. He starts mumbling incoherent words, which I'm sure are prayers. 'Answer my question, Becker,' I breathe in his face, driving forward and up. I have to bite back my scream when the move I instigate hits deeper, shocking me.

'How do you do this to me, princess?' His face is wet now, sweat beads trickling down his forehead. 'Tell me how.'

'You love me,' I say huskily. He's only had sex with women for nothing more than physical pleasure. Add emotion, and he's in alien territory. He's bamboozled by it. Lost but found. I rest my mouth on his and push my hands into his hair. 'I do this to you because you love me.'

'Every second of every minute of every hour of every fucking day.' He traces his fingers up my waist, my sides, my arms, until his hands are in his hair with mine. He links our fingers and crushes them together, pushing his forehead into mine. His cock is pulsing rhythmically within me, stroking my walls soothingly. He blinks slowly and breathes in calmly. 'I'm fucking besotted.'

'Infatuated,' I counter.

'Smitten,' Becker adds. 'I can't wait to make love to you every single day.'

'And good-fucking-mornings?' I ask, my voice throaty from dryness.

He grins and brings our hands to between our mouths. 'Good-fucking-mornings.' He kisses a knuckle softly. 'Good-fucking-afternoons.' And another knuckle. 'Good-fucking-evenings.' And another. 'And good-fucking-nights.' His last kiss on my hand is drawn out and harder than the others.

I'm so bloody happy. 'Can't wait,' I whisper, and he laughs, but it dries up in an instant when his sudden movement stirs him within me, catching us both off guard, reminding us that we're still connected. 'Oh.' I collapse forward, burying my face in his neck helplessly.

'Fucking oh,' Becker mimics as I feel his throat bulge from his hard swallow. 'Let me see your face.' He nudges me from my sanctuary, forcing me to comply. My forehead meets his again. 'I'm aiming for an eight.' His tone is dripping with cockiness, and he falls straight into a steady thrusting of his hips, swaying up and grinding me down controlled and leisurely. I whimper, my thighs compressing around his, my body following his fluid pace. The friction on my clitoris each time I plunge down is creating an addictive sensation that I never want to end. A ten. Always a ten. I'm caught between a full-on, shake-worthy orgasm and consistent, trembling pleasure.

My head falls back on my shoulders. 'Oh, Becker,' He's meticulous, precise . . . fucking amazing. The pleasure-induced haze he's shoved me into is heaven. I have the ability to push myself over the threshold that will see me coasting furiously towards explosion, but I have no inclination to finish just yet. He feels too good. I want to stay here forever, feeling like this. Overwhelmed. Bursting with love for my certified unlawful man. I have strong morals, but I have stronger feelings for Becker Hunt. I've never experienced feelings so intense. Feelings that change your outlook, play with your principles, and challenge your integrity. And most of all, clouds any inclination to find them. Because they would be easy to find. All of those things are built into me. They are there somewhere, but even more significant is my willingness to hide them, to not want to find them, to change my mindset completely. To make myself understand him, because I know he's not all bad. Maybe a little questionable in the ethics department, but not bad. He loves me. He's given up on something for me. He needs me more than redemption or peace. I'm his source of peace now.

'Talk to me, Eleanor,' he demands, strained and lusty. 'Tell me how you feel.' I know what he wants. Reassurance. 'Tell me,' he presses.

He's upped the stakes, increased his pace, washed my mind of everything except the sensations he's creating. He's preparing to come. I can hear it in the change of his breathing pattern.

'I'm still lost in your maze.' I roll my forehead on his, absorbing each drive. Becker Hunt is a jigsaw puzzle. I know he thought the sculpture was the missing piece that would complete him. Now he believes *I* am his missing piece. 'I'm happy lost in your labyrinth of debasement.'

'Good. That makes me feel a whole lot better about what I'm going to say next.' He pulls out of me slowly, depriving me of the gorgeous feel of him, and stands, detaching me from his front and placing me on my feet. He turns away from me and walks across to a cabinet. What's he doing? Oh no. My prize. What's he going to hit me with now? The police? Lady Winchester? Another forged treasure?

'Becker?' I ask, gulping down the strength I might need as he opens and closes the cabinet and returns to me. He negotiates my useless body to the side. And when he's happy with my placement, he drops to one knee before me.

What the bloody hell?

I study him, my eyes getting progressively wider by the second. 'What are you doing?' I ask, moving away, taking a few steps back, like distance might make the sight before me clearer, because I know I can't be seeing right. He's gazing up at me with a cheeky smile on his face, yet I can see nerves there, too.

He holds something up. A ring. A gorgeous emerald ring that deserves far more admiration than I'm giving it. I take only a quick glance at the stunning piece, just to check if I'm following, before my eyes are back on Becker. I laugh, my hand coming up to my chest and applying pressure. 'Becker, this isn't funny. Stop it.'

'Will you marry me, princess?'

I laugh harder, beginning to feel hot as I back away from his naked, kneeling form. I have to stop when the back of my thighs meet a table. 'Very funny.'

'I'm not playing, Eleanor. You've just scaled my grand hall naked. You were made for me.' He thrusts the ring at me, walking forward on his knees. 'Will you marry me?'

'The ring,' I say, moving away, scared of it, and not just because it's flawlessly beautiful. It's a whopper of an emerald, set in a thick band of precious metal.

'What about it?' Becker asks, looking down at it. 'Don't you like it?'

'Is it real?' I spit my words out quickly, my mind completely scrambled.

'Really, princess?' He looks insulted. I have no idea why when he's hit me from every direction with revelation after revelation. I'm surprised I haven't keeled over with shock after everything my poor mind has been subjected to since I met him. And now this?

'Well, I don't know.' I say on a laugh, throwing my arms above my head. 'You're a master forger. You forge shit. Expensive shit. You pass worthless shit off as priceless shit.'

'It's real,' he says tiredly. 'So will you?'

'Seriously?' I blurt out, all laughter evaporating and my shock now being demonstrated as you would expect.

'Am I speaking in a foreign language, princess? What don't you understand?'

'You,' I cry, sticking myself to the table behind me. 'You've barely figured out that you're in love with me. Now you want to marry me?'

His bottom lip juts out on a sulk.

'Pick up your lip,' I snap, my hands finding my hair and

delving into the strands. 'I don't understand. If you're worried about me telling people about the sculpture, then you shouldn't be.'

'I'm not worried about that.'

'Then why?'

'Just ...' He growls and stomps on his knees towards me. 'Just because.'

'That's not a good enough reason.'

'How about because you amaze me?' he retorts, short but soft. 'How about because when I look at you, for the first time in my fucking life I can see beyond what's obsessed me for too many years? How about because when you smile, I melt? Or when you laugh, my heart bucks? Or when we touch, I feel like I'm over-heating? How about because I feel like you were made purely to be mine? Because you're fearless. Bold. Full of spirit that I envy. Or because you love me more than I hoped anyone could? And you accept me. Everything about me. That you're loyal. Brave. Fucking beautiful. How about because you challenge me and I fucking love that? Or because when I watched you sleeping in my bed last night, the thought of you not being there crushed me. Is that enough, because I could go on, princess?'

I gulp. They're some damn good reasons.

'But it's too soon,' I say, utterly bamboozled.

'No, princess.' He shakes his head slowly. 'It's way too fuck-ing late, actually.'

I breathe in, my damn heart thumping. Look at him, there on his knees, his face so bloody hopeful. My saint. My sinner. The corrupt love of my life. Why am I questioning this?

What do I get in return?

You get every wicked, corrupt, vulnerable piece of me.

And isn't that the biggest prize? I love every deceitful, shady part of him. It's only slightly fucking with my head. For the most part, I'm plain relieved that I'm here, tangled in his web of secrets.

'Begging isn't beyond me, you know,' he says, regaining some rigidity in his arms and extending the ring towards me.

'Then beg.' My order is automatic.

And so is his smile. He rests his delicious arse on his heels and relaxes his arms by his side, studying me. 'I don't need to beg,' he says, never taking his eyes from mine. 'My corrupt wicked little witch wants this as much as I do.'

I pout, and Becker raises his eyebrows. Then he looks down at the ring and something changes in his persona. Sadness fills the air, and it confuses me. 'While you were out with Lucy last night,' he says quietly. 'I went to see Gramps in his suite.' He looks up at me, and I see the tears at the backs of his eyes. I step back. 'I told him how I felt about you. What you mean to me. How you make me feel.' He holds up the ring. 'I asked him for this. It was my grandmother's. Gramps found this emerald on one of his expeditions and had it made into this beautiful piece. When my grandmother died, Gramps gave it to my dad. He gave it to my mother.' His voice wobbles, and my lip does, too. 'The most important women in my life have worn this ring. So now it's yours.'

I swallow, trying to wrap my mind around this. But why am I wasting time doing that? 'Yes,' I choke, and he nods, extending his arm to me. I take it and let him pull me to his lap, silently accepting that I'm going in the deepest there is. I'm signing up for life.

To share his secrets and his crimes. What's happened to me? I've lied to the police, and I did it without question. At that moment, I made my decision once and for all. I've made my bed. It's time to lie in it. Literally.

He reaches for my hand and slips the gorgeous ring onto my finger before taking me to the floor, smothering me in his body, and rests his lips on mine. Wet kisses are dotted over every square inch of my skin and I smile like a loon, feeling so fucking happy in the clutches of my corrupt man.

'I wondered why you had your power boxer shorts on,' I say.

'Today was a big day.' He lifts his face from mine and stares down at me. 'I just wrapped up on the biggest deal I'm ever likely to negotiate.' He grins as he stands, lifting me from the floor and taking me back to the Louis XIV chair. He settles and positions me on his lap so I'm straddling his thighs and spreads his big palms around my waist, pulling me forward until our mouths are a hair's breadth away from each other's.

'I love you,' he whispers, angling his head and catching my lips, tickling my tongue gently with his as he slips his hands onto my bum, pulling me in further still. 'And I fucking love this arse.' He speaks into my mouth as he lifts me, his cock falling to my opening. I whimper, finding his shoulders and holding on. 'And I love the look of that ring on your finger,' he says, easing me down slowly.

He starts guiding me atop his lap, slipping in and out meticulously. 'I'm sorry for asking if your grandmother's ring is fake.' I feel terrible.

'You're forgiven.'

'And thank you for fixing things with your granddad.'

'Thank you for reminding me that life's too short.'

I find my stride in an instant, my desire still coating my inner walls, making him glide effortlessly within me. Every drive makes me shiver, the intensity of the moment making my head spin in the best possible way. Breaking our kiss, he drops his head back against the chair, his lips parted. And he stares at me, his eyes lazy and hooded as his hands on my hips guide me up and down, slowly, languidly, our breathing drenching the air around us. It doesn't take long for the slippery friction to push me over the edge. My hands brace into his shoulders, my mouth dropping and taking his gently.

'You're there.'

I nod, not wanting to lose the contact of our tongues, continuing with the tender circling. I sigh, and I go on for ever with the peaceful sound as I'm submerged in pleasure like no other, letting my low hum draw out until my lungs have deflated and I'm limp on his lap.

'Oh yeah.' Becker gently signals his own climax with vibrating hips, holding me down so he's immersed snuggly within me. He circles deeply and deliciously, wheedling every modicum of pleasure from us both, moulding my arse cheeks. We're heaving. We're sweating. We're both clinging onto each other. And we're sharing the gentlest of kisses, our tongues lapping lazily as we ride our climaxes.

'Good fucking morning,' I say huskily, smiling when I feel his lips stretch beneath mine.

He slows our kiss to a progressive stop and rains soft pecks from one side of my mouth to the other. Then he pulls away and spends some quiet time brushing some wayward strands of hair from my damp face. I sit quietly on his lap and watch him concentrate on his task, wondering what's going through that corrupt mind of his. A few months ago, I would have made an educated guess that he would be thinking of all the delicious ways in which he could violate me. Now, I'm not so sure.

So I ask. 'Tell me what's on your mind.' I reach forward and trace the edge of his nipple, continuing to watch him.

'I'm thinking,' he says, his gaze flicking from my mouth to my eyes again and again. 'I'm thinking I'm the luckiest man alive. I must be. I've found a woman who I trust not to hand my arse to the police on a plate.'

His face is the epitome of happiness. I can't help but match it. I grab his cheeks and smother him in kisses. I want to sleep with him every night, wake up with him every morning, have good-fucking-anything's every day. Nothing could make me doubt what we have.

His hands cup my bottom and he stands, pushing me up over his shoulder so I have the stunning vision of his naked butt and his tattoo to feast on while he carries me from the Grand Hall.

I wanted all of his secrets.

All of *him*.

Now, I truly do.

I rest my hand over the map, positioning the emerald of the ring right in the centre of the missing piece. 'Stop it,' Becker says over his shoulder. 'Stop it right now.'

I retract my hand and furiously try to stop my mind getting carried away. But, oh, how beautiful his tattoo is, and I can't stop myself from wishing it was complete. 'You could find the missing piece of the map. Doesn't mean to say you have to find the sculpture.'

'You know that's ridiculous.'

'I know,' I sigh. 'What would you do with it if you ever did find it?'

'Does it matter, because I'm never going to find it?'

'Just curious,' I say quietly as he carries my up the stone stairs. Never find it because he won't look, or never find it because it can't be found?

'Don't be curious, Eleanor. It's dangerous for both of us.'

I snap my mouth shut and close my eyes, denying myself the sight of the map. It spikes way too much intrigue. And I now appreciate the danger.

So why can't I stop thinking about it?

Chapter 23

When I wake a few hours later and find him missing from the bed, I jump up and rush to the bathroom, and once I'm showered and have plaited my wet hair over my shoulder, I pull on a cerise pink shirt dress and tan ankle boots before heading to Becker's office. Light hits my ring as I descend the stone staircase, and I smile down at the whopper of an emerald on my finger. It's truly breathtakingly beautiful. Like the man who put it there.

My admiring is interrupted by the sound of my best friend's dramatic howl, and I stutter to a stop on the stairs. Then I hear Becker curse.

Lucy.

I hurry to the kitchen and push through the door, and the first thing I see is Winston, collapsed in his bed looking royally pissed off. Then I find Lucy slumped over the table, still in her daring pink playsuit. Her head is in her hands, and Becker is leaning against the worktop in a pair of grey jersey shorts, arms folded over his bare chest. His hair is a wild sexy mess, his glasses in place. Beyond my awe, I find space to be worried. Because although I can't see Lucy's face, it's obvious that she's distraught, and Becker looks less than sympathetic.

I glare at him and mouth, *what have you said?*

He shrugs. 'I just gave her a recap on last night.'

I jump when Lucy lets out a hysterical wail, flinging her head back. She exposes a face that should be kept from public view until it's washed. Bits of sticky hair are protruding haphazardly from her head, some stuck to her face, her eye make-up is smudged over most of her cheeks, and her red lipstick is all over her chin. She looks horrific.

'Oh my God,' she cries. 'I'm such a—'

'Twat?' I suggest softly. This girl caused more stress in one night than most women can in their entire life.

'That's a bit harsh, Miss Cole,' Becker pipes up, flipping me a wink. He's got a nerve. I know he mentally called her harsher things last night.

'Yeah,' Lucy joins in, clearly thinking she has backup. She hasn't.

'He was being sarcastic.'

'Oh.'

'Who says?' Becker does an amazing job of looking insulted. 'We've all done something stupid when we're in love.' His sturdy shoulders jump up, his bottom lip juts out, and I give him an epic eyeroll.

'Who said I'm in love?' Lucy throws Becker a filthy look. 'Eleanor's the one who's fallen.'

His bark of laughter makes Lucy jump. His reaction is warranted. Stupid girl. 'Give me a break, woman.' He turns away from us and pulls the fridge open, exposing his back to the room, and, subsequently, to Lucy. I watch on a smile when her jaw goes slack, her eyes roaming the beauty of his tattoo. 'I hate to break it to you,' Becker goes on, grabbing something from the shelf before closing the fridge and turning back to face us. He has an apple in his hand. The forbidden fruit for the forbidden man. 'But even *I* can see what's going on here.' He takes a huge bite from the flesh and chews slowly, holding it up in an indication that he hasn't finished. I lose my ability to stand on steady legs, so hurry across to the table and take a seat next to Lucy, intrigued by what he's going to say. He swallows, and I swear I hear Lucy hold back a cough. 'And I'm a novice at all this love shit.' He nods and takes his apple back to his lush lips.

'You don't do too bad,' I tell him, watching as the fruit pauses at his mouth.

He grins behind it. 'Thank you, princess.' He rips another chuck away and proceeds to chew with his grin still fixed firmly on his beautiful face, looking rather proud of himself.

I look at Lucy when I feel her arm brush against mine, finding her fidgeting in her chair. 'Magnificent,' I whisper, knocking her with my elbow.

She gives me an exasperated look, shaking her head.

'Trust me,' Becker says around his chews, and we both look across to him – me cool, Lucy still fidgeting. I'm used to his lethal naked presence by now . . . kind of. Not really. But Lucy definitely isn't. She's purposely darting her eyes all over the kitchen to avoid looking at him. Becker points his apple at her. 'I've run faster and farther from women who've acted less crazy than you.'

'I was drunk,' she grunts while I grin from ear-to-ear.

'They all say that,' Becker says around his laugh.

'Thanks.' My friend rests her arms on the table and lets her head fall into them with a thud.

'Welcome,' Becker chirps, chest puffing out on a smile that tells me he thinks he's done good. I've just fallen in love with him all over again. My insensitive, clueless, crooked sinner is giving my best friend advice on relationships. Albeit crap advice.

'Be quiet now,' Lucy says, sitting up and trying to comb through her knotted mane with her fingers.

'Why?' Becker asks, hurt. 'I'm just getting started.'

'Because I might fall in love with you, too.'

I laugh loudly, receiving a surprised look from Becker and a sideways grin from Lucy. It takes Becker a few seconds to catch up. Then he shakes his head in dismay and throws his apple across the kitchen. It lands in the bin with accuracy. 'So,' he says, squaring confident shoulders as he moseys over, peeking down at his bare feet casually. I narrow cautious eyes on him, and when he arrives at the table, both Lucy and I follow his cool face down as he bends, resting his elbows on the table before us. 'My princess told you that she's in love with me?'

I roll my eyes. This is old news to him, the bumptious idiot.

'Am I sharing something new?' Lucy asks.

'No.' Leaning in, he takes his glasses off and slips an arm between his teeth, chewing thoughtfully. 'But I can tell *you* something new.'

He can? Like what?

'What's that?' Lucy asks.

'Yes, what's that?' I mimic, and he grins mischievously.

'Your best mate will soon be my wife.' He nods his approval to his own declaration and takes my hand, thrusting the gigantic emerald under Lucy's nose. Oh, the bastard.

Her stunned eyes drop to it, then swing to me. 'What?'

I smile, nervous as shit, damning Becker to hell. I should be the one to tell my best friend, not him. 'I haven't had the chance to mention it.'

'Oh my fucking God,' she blurts out, seizing my hand from Becker and having a good inspection of my ring. 'Is it real?'

I snort, forcing back my laugh, and Becker huffs his disgust as he pushes himself up from the table on stupidly taut arms. He leans over to the worktop nearby and collects something before throwing it on the table before us. My eyes follow its path and expand in surprise when I register what it is. Lucy's bag. He got it back? 'I have your phone, purse and keys in my office, princess,' he tells me before turning and striding out, leaving Lucy still gawping at my ring and me gazing at the map on his back. 'You can go home now, Lucy,' he calls over his shoulder. 'I want my fiancée back.'

'She was my friend before she was your fiancée,' she shouts, getting all possessive as she drops my hand.

Becker stops, his hand poised on the kitchen door

handle. 'Do you give her good-fucking-mornings, -afternoons, -evenings, and -nights?'

'What?' Lucy throws me an inquisitive look, which I refuse to acknowledge, before returning her attention to my cheeky, bold man.

'Trust me, you don't.' The door closes and Lucy swings to face me, catching the grin on my face. 'He's a magnificent cock, that's what he is. I can't believe you're marrying him. What the hell, Eleanor?'

I shrug. 'I love him.'

She shakes her head in wonder. 'But it's so soon.'

I can't possibly be defensive. It's very soon, but . . . 'I guess when you know, you know.'

'And you know?'

'Oh, trust me, I know.' I know *everything*.

She seems to take a deep breath. 'Then I'm happy for you.'

'Thank you.' For the first time, I wonder what my mother will make of this. I'll tell her when I go home. I need to be face-to-face. Or should I call her?

I point to Lucy's bag. 'You should call Mark.'

She cringes. 'Would *you* want to speak to me if you were Mark?'

I stand and brush myself down. 'If I loved you, then yes.' I head towards the door.

'Hey, Eleanor,' Lucy calls, pulling me to a stop. I turn, prompting her to go on. 'Is it me, or did Becker make an uncanny amount of threats to spank your arse last night?'

'Um . . .' Fuck, what do I say to that? Yes? Yes, he has a fetish for slapping my arse stupid? God, I hope that's all she heard. 'You must have been dreaming.' I turn quickly . . . and walk right into Mrs Potts.

'Morning,' she says.

'Morning,' I sing, moving to the side to let her into the kitchen. But she doesn't shift, so I sweep my arm out in gesture for her, polite as can be. She hums thoughtfully, looking down at my hand. My left hand. Oh boy. I wait for her to speak, fidgeting nervously. She eventually lifts her eyes to mine. Smiling eyes. She knows. Gramps must have told her. She winks, happy, wobbling past me, clocking Lucy at the kitchen table. 'And who have we here?'

'This is my friend.' I rush to enlighten her. 'Lucy. She got locked out last night so Becker said she could stay here.'

Mrs Potts raises her nose in the air, eyeing Lucy, who has wilted under the old dragon's glare. 'You look like you've been in a scrap with a tank of gloop. Would you like breakfast? Tea?'

'I'm gagging for a cuppa.'

Her phone rings, and Lucy's face drops.

'Answer,' I prompt.

'What should I say?' she asks, glancing down at her bag. I see every muscle in her tiny frame tense.

'He's calling, which means he wants to talk.'

'Right.' She dives on her bag like it might run away if she doesn't seize it quickly, and after grappling clumsily for a few seconds, she pulls out her phone. Then stares at the screen, her face twisting. 'It's my mum.' She stabs at the reject button and tosses it down. 'I can't be doing with her now.'

'Rather uncharitable of you, dear.' Mrs Potts says scornfully, and I look across to find her lips pursed in disapproval.

'She'll just nag me about going home to see them.'

'And why don't you?'

'Because I'll be forced to muck out at five in the morning. I've been in London for over two months and I can still smell horse shit embedded in my skin.' She raises her arm to her nose and sniffs on a grimace.

'Oh, you lived in the country? How lovely.' Mrs Potts wobbles over with her tray of teacups. 'I lived in the countryside when I was a girl. Where do you come from, dear?'

I open the door again and make my exit, leaving Lucy and Mrs Potts chatting. The smooth fabric of my knickers rubs my tender arse as I wander the corridor to Becker's office. But I still smile.

Pushing my way in, I find him with his phone at his ear. He looks frustrated, his fingers slipping under his glasses and rubbing into his sockets. 'I'll pay whatever they want, just don't let that car go to auction.'

My jaw tightens when I quickly get the gist of the conversation. The vintage Ferrari that he wants and which Brent Wilson also wants. Becker's potent aggravation tells me the call isn't going well.

'There are strings you can pull, Simon. You just won't.'

I hear Simon Timms's insulted gasp from over here and watch as Becker removes his fingers, revealing rolling eyes. Brent getting that car will put him in a bad, *bad* mood.

'It wouldn't be the first time a lot is pulled at the eleventh hour. I'll double my offer.' He shifts in his chair, making the coiled muscles of his bare chest ripple sinfully. I quickly look away. He won't appreciate my admiration right now. 'Is this because I didn't pull strings for you on *Head of a Faun*?' Becker questions with a slight curl of his lip. 'Are you holding a childish grudge, Simon?' He narrows his eyes on his desk, listening. 'Fine. Doesn't look like I have a choice but to bid. I'll be there.' He slams the phone down aggressively and throws his arms into the air. 'Dickhead.' Anger sizzles in the air around us. He isn't happy.

'Okay?' I ask stupidly, taking a seat.

'Super.' He quickly dials someone else and takes his phone to his ear again. 'Percy, back to Plan B,' he says simply, before hanging up. 'Why do people insist on making things complicated?' He looks at me like I should know exactly what he's talking about. 'I haven't got time for this.'

I throw him a blank look, hoping he'll catch it and

enlighten me. He doesn't. He scribbles something down on a pad, and I find my neck craning in an attempt to catch what he's writing.

'What's Plan B?' I ask, too curious.

'Plan B is the plan that will guarantee I get the car.'

'And Plan A isn't?'

'Always have a backup. That's the first rule in this world. How's Lucy?'

I rest back in my chair. 'Chatting with Mrs Potts.'

He looks past me, seeming to fall into a bit of a trance. He's here, but he's not here, something clearly playing on his mind.

'Becker?' I ask. He's distracted. 'Everything all right?'

'It will be.' He gets up from his chair and rounds his desk, my eyes following him suspiciously until he's looming over me, his chest in my face. I force myself to disregard it and find his eyes in an attempt to decipher him. He's crowding me, and his vacant expression has been replaced with a mild grin. 'What are you doing today?'

I shrug. 'I have plenty on my list of things to do. Anything you want to add?'

'I have a meeting with the Countess of Finsbury at three,' he tells me. 'She wants to see the Rembrandt.'

'Ooh, the countess. Sounds important.'

'She is. Get the showing room ready.' He moves in and slams his lips on mine. 'I'm going to buy myself a car.' Biting my bottom lip, he pulls away slowly, dragging my flesh through his teeth. 'I'll be back for three. If I'm running late, you'll have to start without me and make small talk.'

'What small talk can I make with a countess?'

'She's fond of me. I'm sure you'll find some common ground.'

'What?' I blurt out, horrified. Fond of him? I'll be the last person she'll want to make small talk with. 'How fond?'

The widening of his smile tells me, and I breathe out my exasperation.

'Fine. I just won't mention who I am beyond my professional title, else she might not buy the painting.'

He winks cheekily and slides his hand into my hair, giving it a little possessive yank. 'Do you drive?'

'Yes,' I answer quickly, but avoid mentioning that I've not been behind a wheel since I left home.

'Good. You can borrow a car to take Lucy home. Any except the Ferrari, and I'm taking Gloria.'

'You trust me with one of your cars?'

He looks regretful all of a sudden. And a little worried. 'Why, are you a bad driver?'

His expression, coupled with a sudden comprehension of something, makes me worry, too. Namely, Becker's hi-tech garage. 'My driving is perfect. It's your fancy garage that concerns me.'

'You'll be fine. Just line the wing mirrors up with the hydraulic bars at the front.' He dismisses my concern in a heartbeat.

'The key cabinet,' I point out hastily. 'It opens with eye recognition. *Your* eye.'

'The override code is 72468232537.' He reels the number off, making my eyes widen further with each digit he says.

'Say what now?'

'I'll text it to you. Make sure you delete it once you've memorised it.' He hands me my phone, keys and purse. 'It's a good job I was tracking your phone, huh?'

'Remove it,' I say, looking up at him. 'Now.' I thrust my mobile towards him, my face serious.

'I'll do it when I'm back, I promise. I'm already late.' He slams his lips on mine. 'See you later, princess.' He saunters out, tensing and flexing his back muscles as he goes.

I scowl, and once I've had my fill of his tattoo, my eyes automatically drop to his butt. His butt is safer. It doesn't make my mind go to dangerous places, only filthy places. 'Good luck at the auction,' I say quietly.

'I don't need luck. Trust me. And stop looking at my arse,' he tosses over his shoulder.

'It's my arse now,' I throw back.

Chapter 24

I found Lucy still looking bedraggled in the kitchen, having been caught up in conversation with Mrs Potts.

It's only when we're on our way to the garage and I finally open Becker's text that I'm reminded of something that perhaps should have occurred to me before bringing Lucy down here. The message contains the code, as Becker promised, but it also has a note tagged on the end.

72468232537. Don't take Lucy into the garage. Have her wait on the street for you and drive round. She isn't in my circle of trust x

'Shit,' I curse, coming to a halt.

Lucy walks into me, knocking me forward. 'What's up?'

'Nothing.' I turn her back around and usher her down the corridor. 'We need to go this way.'

'This place is like a fucking maze,' she grumbles, letting me guide her back through. I laugh my agreement and let us into the Grand Hall, taking the lead so I can weave her through all of the stock. 'Eww, it stinks in here.'

I look over my shoulder and find her pinching her nose. 'That smell is thousands of years' worth of history.'

'Looks like a load of junk to me.'

I shake my head in dismay. 'This way,' I call, hiding my secret smile when I clock the huge cabinet that I scaled this morning in order to reach my target and devour him. Then I look down at my ring finger, my smile widening. I'm getting married. And I'm marrying a con artist. Or ex-con artist. Whatever. He's corrupt, which basically means I am now, too.

'Now *this* is pretty,' Lucy declares as I let us into the courtyard. 'This I could work with.'

'Come on,' I push, jogging across the cobbles.

'Where are we going?'

'Down here.' I indicate the alleyway as I breach the opening.

'Are you serious?' she asks, with every scrap of caution she should. I remember my reaction to the dark hole the first time I found myself in it. 'I can't see a fucking thing.'

I reach back and feel for her hand, finding it on the brick wall.

'Argghhhhhh!' She screams and retracts. 'What is that?'

'It's me, you idiot,' I laugh. 'Give me your hand.'

'It's creepy.'

I tug her on, knowing the exact moment the lights will activate. 'There,' I say, dropping her hand and pressing the button that'll release the door at the end. I look back to find her palms over her eyes. 'Follow the alley to the end and let yourself out onto the street. I'll drive round and get you.' I dash off, back down the alley towards the courtyard.

'What?' she screeches, the contained sound piercing my eardrums. 'Eleanor!'

'The lights will go off soon. Hurry up!' I leave her behind, hearing constant echoed curses and yelps.

I'm out of breath by the time I've made it back to the garage. Hurrying over to the key cabinet, I open Becker's message and start tapping in the override code, my hits of the keys slowing when I begin to fathom the significance of the long string of numbers. On the final digit, the door releases, but rather than rushing to open it and grab some keys, I study the keypad instead, mentally going through the sequence of numbers in my head again. Except this time I don't need to look at the message that Becker sent me. I simply spell something out across the keys.

SAINT BECKER

I smile at the cupboard as I slip my phone into my bag, opening the door. I'm immediately torn. Keys. Loads of keys, and I don't know which ones to take. 'You'll do.' I reach in and grab the set for the Audi.

Shutting the cupboard, I head for the silver RS7, pressing a button on the fob. The lights blink, the locks release, and I jump in and get comfy in the sport seat, looking for the adjustor, my hands feeling around the front before locating a button on the side. I begin to inch closer to the wheel. 'Perfect,' I declare, starting the engine. I swear, the thing purrs beautifully, and my bunched fists come to my mouth, my teeth sinking into my knuckles. I'm nervous and excited all at once. I can feel the power humming beneath me already, and I haven't even moved yet. I need to take it easy. I bet this thing goes like shit off a shovel. Pulling the sun visor down, I locate the familiar white button and press it, then watch as a section of the ceiling starts to lower before me. I slot the gearstick into drive and feel to my side for the handbrake ... and find nothing. So I glance down. No sign of a handbrake. 'Where are you?' I mutter, looking around the car for anything resembling one. I growl my frustration and grab my phone, dialling Becker.

He answers on a hushed whisper. 'You've not scratched one of my cars, have you?'

'I can't scratch it if I can't drive it. Where's the handbrake?' I ask impatiently as the hydraulic lift comes to rest on the garage floor.

'What car are you in?'

'The Audi.'

'Good choice, princess. There's a little lever by the gearstick with a red light. Press it.'

I click my phone to loud speaker, dropping it to my lap before releasing the handbrake and gripping the steering wheel with both hands. Then I lightly apply some pressure to the accelerator.

And fly forward.

'Fuck.' I slam the brakes on and come to a screeching halt, the front wheels on the ramp. 'Whoa,' I breathe, pushing myself back in my seat, my arms braced against the steering wheel.

'What did you do?' Becker sounds panicked. 'Take it easy.'

'I am.'

'Tease the pedal, princess. Don't slam your foot down.'

'I didn't slam my foot down.'

'Eleanor, I haven't got time to give you a driving lesson. I'm trying to buy myself a new fucking car.'

'I don't need a driving lesson,' I spit indignantly, teasing my foot on the pedal and inching forwards carefully. 'I can drive perfectly well, thank you.' I sound haughty. I shouldn't be. The second I finish speaking, the ear-splitting sound of scratching metal fills the garage. My ears practically bleed, and though I know I need to be braking, I can't. My foot has seized up, making the shrill noise carry on forever. It's cutting right through me, my face screwing up in dread.

'Eleanor!' Becker yells, shocking the muscles in my foot to life. I slam on the brakes and come to an abrupt halt. After I've calmed my rushed breathing, I press the button for the window and stick my head out the second the gap is big enough.

Oh fuck.

'Eleanor?'

'Yes?' I squeak, trying to sound totally normal, like I'm not staring in horror at a jagged scratch down the side of one of Becker's precious cars.

'What was that?'

'Nothing.' I disconnect the call and release a barrage of expletives. 'Fucking hell.' I reverse and straighten up, ignoring the further raw sound of a matching scratch. 'Stupid garage. Why can't you have a normal one, you holier-than-thou twat?' I jolt to a halt when the wing mirrors are lined up, then jab the white button aggressively as I take my foot from the pedal and listen as the lift comes to life, the hydraulic bars shifting and starting to carry me up to the opening in the ceiling. 'He's going to go—' I stop jabbering to myself when I notice the hydraulic bars beginning to move off-line from the wing mirrors, and I frown, looking back. 'Oh fuck,' I whisper when I realise it's not the bars moving. It's the car. 'Oh my God.' I panic, slamming my foot down on the brake. 'Shit!' I'm not in position any more, which means the back of the Audi is probably going to be sliced off at any moment. I should never have agreed to this. I whack the car into gear and try my hardest to be gentle on the accelerator, which is hard when you're working under pressure. I only need to move forwards a couple of feet. Just a couple. I watch the wing mirrors like a hawk, and just when they are a foot or so away from being lined up again, another deafening sound penetrates the air, except this time it's metal on concrete. The lift judders a little, but still continues on its journey, scraping up the back of the car as it goes. I sag in my seat, exhausted after my trauma as the derelict factory comes into view. He needn't think I'm going through that again when I get back. I'll park it up here and Becker can get it down himself, and if he wants anything left of his car, then he won't complain about it.

I pull my belt on, drive forwards when the doors open, and quickly make my way round to pick up Lucy. Her face offers a little light relief when she scowls at me after I've pulled up at the kerb. 'I've been standing out here freezing for ten minutes,' she complains, dropping into the seat. 'Don't ever abandon me in that scary alley again.'

'It's not scary.' I pull out into the traffic and fiddle with the controls on the wheel, flicking through the radio stations.

She brushes at her hair. 'I feel like I've had a family of spiders move in.'

I laugh, feeling Lucy's eyes on me, and I look to find her studying me. 'What?'

'I can't believe you're marrying him.'

'I know. You've already told me.'

'How do you think your mum will take the news?'

'Better than you.'

'I just don't want you to get hurt. Do you really know him?'

'Trust me, Lucy,' I reply quietly. 'I know him.'

I reach for the radio, flick it on, and CamelPhat & Cristoph's 'Breathe' comes over the speakers. I crank the volume up and start to sing along as I jig in my seat, and Lucy quickly joins me, singing at the top of her voice. I laugh, all scratches and a potentially pissed-off fiancé forgotten . . . for now.

Chapter 25

For some strange reason, I feel all reminiscent when we pull up outside our building. I don't know why, since I've shivered with dread each time I've been here lately. I see me and Lucy leaving together, whether on a night out or on our way to work. Either way, we're laughing together each time.

'I'll walk up with you,' I tell her, unclipping my belt. 'I should collect a few things while I'm here.' There's no way I'll get all of my belongings in this car, and I'm unsure as to what I should take, anyway. I've furnished my tiny apartment, but I doubt Becker will welcome all of the paraphernalia at The Haven. Should I sell it? Or just leave it in there? I have over nine months to serve on my tenancy. Which reminds me; I should get the paperwork and call the letting agent to hand in my notice. Or should I? What if things don't work out between Becker and me? I'll be daft to leave myself with nowhere to live. My head starts to spin as I eject myself from the Audi, cringing when I see the full extent of the damage I've done. I'll keep my apartment on. He might kick me out after he sees what I've done to his car.

After Lucy has let us into our building, I go ahead, taking the stairs and rounding the corner, but I come to an abrupt halt when I find someone loitering outside our apartments.

Lucy walks into me. 'Jesus, Eleanor, what's with you today?' She huffs her way past me, but soon pulls up, too. 'Mark.'

He offers a small smile. Lucy has frozen in front of me, and I can see and feel her anxiety. I want to jab my friend in the back to shock her back to life, to prompt her to get on with the apology she owes Mark, but Mark speaks up before I have the chance.

'You're a stupid cow, Lucy,' he says quietly, stepping forwards. He looks a little untidy in some old jeans and a T-shirt. It's a far cry from his usually well-turned-out self, and it's also an indication that coming here to sort things out was more important than grooming and dressing well this morning. He sighs and shakes his head. 'But I love you, you loopy cow.'

My heart melts, and I hear a whimper emanate from Lucy, her body relaxing. 'I'm sorry,' she wails, throwing her arms into the air before letting them fall like bricks to her side. 'I'm an idiot. I didn't want to lose you to that leggy thing. I didn't know what to do.'

'Come here.' He opens his arms and she more or less sprints into them. 'You stink,' he says with little concern, squeezing her to him.

'I need a shower.'

'No shit.' He pries her away and messes with her tangled locks on a frown. 'I'll help you.'

I start to inch towards my apartment door, set on leaving them to their happy reunion.

'How long have you been waiting?' Lucy asks.

'Not long. Becker gave me the head's up that Eleanor was bringing you home.'

'He did?' Lucy asks, surprised.

'He did?' I mimic, swinging around. I'm about to question how he got Mark's number, but then I remember . . . he had Lucy's bag retrieved from the bar. I'm not stupid enough to wonder how he'd get Mark's number. That man's capabilities frighten me. A measly telephone number in a locked phone isn't going to give him much of a headache, especially with his whizz kid Percy on hand.

'Yeah,' Mark confirms, smiling at me. 'He's invited us out

with you. Some posh gala thing at a countryside mansion. You know, he's actually a nice bloke.'

Some posh gala thing? At a countryside mansion? 'I'm sorry, what?' He must have his wires crossed. Andelesea?

Mark looks down at Lucy, who's gazing up at him dreamily. 'But he said *you* have to be good.'

'I'll be on my best behaviour,' Lucy vows, giving me an enthusiastic smile. 'We'll celebrate!'

'Celebrate what?' Mark asks, looking down at his excitable girlfriend.

'Becker proposed to Eleanor, and she said yes.'

'No shit?' Mark swings a stunned look to me. 'Congratulations.' He comes over and hugs me. I'm a little shocked, but I embrace him nevertheless, pleased he seems genuinely happy for me.

'Thanks.'

'A double date,' Lucy sings. 'Yay!'

I laugh as Mark frees me, trying to morph my face into excitement rather than confusion. I'm struggling. I slip my key in the lock and let myself into my apartment. Then I call Becker. It rings and rings, and eventually goes to voicemail. 'Call me,' I demand, before hanging up and looking around. That reminiscent feeling has gone. Cold chills spring onto my skin as I zoom around my apartment, gathering as much as I can into my arms and making a hasty exit.

Negotiating the mountain of things in my grip, I rest my chin on the top of the pile and raise my knee to semi-free a hand. It takes some serious manoeuvring, but I eventually manage to unlatch the door and use my foot to hook it open. I pass through and let it slam behind me, shuddering and shaking off the creeps. Then I make my way down the stairs, peeking to the side and taking the steps carefully.

When I reach the lobby door, I have to wedge my belongings against the wall, pushing myself into it in order to free a hand.

The cold air from outside eventually hits me. And so does a voice. 'Here, let me help you.' The familiar tone sucks all of the strength out of my arms, and my mountain of belongings crashes to the floor.

I stare like a dumbstruck fool at Becker's arch-enemy. 'Brent.' I blink repeatedly, hoping he's a hallucination that will disappear if I moisten my dry eyes. He doesn't. He's standing before me, larger than life. 'What are you doing here?' I ask, dipping to collect my things from the floor. Anger. It's bubbling deep in my tummy, and I hate the fact that there are nerves mixing up with it. This is the son of the man who Becker thinks is responsible for his parents' deaths. My nerves are warranted. He's also on my list of suspects who could have broken into my apartment. Plus he's still playing games with Becker, goading him, making it impossible for us to move on. And he's here now. What is he doing here now?

'I happened to be in the area,' Brent answers, bending and helping me.

My teeth grind. Sure he was. Did he happen to be in the area the night my apartment was broken into? And I know he was in the area when the O'Keeffe was stolen. I stand when my arms are full and push past him, hurrying to the Audi.

As I reach the car, I realise the keys are in my bag and I haven't a hope of getting them out without freeing my hands. 'Shit,' I curse under my breath, releasing the pile of clothes and letting them scatter at my feet. I find the keys and press the unlock button, but the boot doesn't shift when I try to lift it. I growl to myself, ignoring the dent surrounded by scuff marks on the shiny silver paintwork of Becker's Audi. 'Open,' I mumble, feeling my panic run away with me. I need to be cool. Not show him he unnerves me.

'Are you moving out?' he asks from behind me, his interest clear.

I blank him and proceed to stab at every button on the key

fob, pleading with every Greek god for help. The boot finally pops open, and I waste no time scooping my things from the ground and shoving them in messily. I want to physically itch myself.

My clumsy string of movements halts when a hand appears by my side, a familiar pair of knickers hanging from a finger. 'You missed these.'

I snatch them from him, too worried to be embarrassed, and throw them in with the rest of my clothes. 'Why aren't you at the auction house?' The question slips, my nerves getting the better of me. *Think, Eleanor!* What's wrong with me? I handled the copper perfectly, but this man here shoots down my stability with one look. I've just volunteered the fact that I know Brent's bidding on the 1965 Ferrari that Becker wants, and since Becker sourced that information on the sly from Simon Timms's secretary, I'm guessing Brent was purposely keeping his intention to buy it under wraps. Or will he steal the car once Becker has bought it?

He homes in on my slip-up like a wolf. 'Well, since I'm not at the auction house and someone is working on my behalf, neither you nor he could know of my intention to buy the Ferrari. So who did Hunt fuck to get that information?' The question pierces my itchy skin like a hot poker.

'I guessed.' I slam the boot shut and head for the driver's door. 'Since your life's ambition is to try and get the upper hand.'

'Try?' Brent muses. 'It didn't take much trying. In fact, I just took a call to congratulate me.'

My heart sinks. He got the car? Something tells me Becker wasn't as gracious in defeat today as he was when Brent won the fake sculpture. Shit, he's going to be in a foul mood. 'Why are you here, Brent?'

'Well, I heard you've been talking to Stan Price. Throwing accusations around.' He strolls casually to the other side of the Audi and stares across the roof at me.

I'm blank for a moment. He looks pissed off, understandably, I guess. 'There were no accusations. I merely advised Price that I saw you at Sotheby's that day. Because I did.'

He smiles. It's salacious. 'I thought, working for Hunt and all, you would've learned how to keep it zipped.'

'I have no loyalty to you, Brent.' Go. I should just leave. 'Why are you here? Why are you doing this?'

'Because this is what Hunt and I do, Eleanor,' he answers simply, knocking me back a bit.

'Not any more.' My retort isn't nearly as curt as I wanted it to be, more a breathy gasp. My nerves are frayed. 'Becker's done with this game you're playing.' It seems ludicrous to describe this madness as a game. Lives have been lost. Crimes committed.

'You believe that?'

'Yes.' I open the car door, eager to escape. 'He wants no part of it, and neither do I.'

'But you are a part of the game, Eleanor. Like it or not. And you're a surprisingly appealing pawn to win.'

I bristle, pausing by the door. 'You've got the sculpture, you got the painting, you don't get me, too.'

He shakes his head on a little laugh. 'He really does have you fooled, doesn't he? But, for the record, I'd trade the sculpture for you. I'd even throw in my new Ferrari. The one Hunt was so desperate to add to his collection.'

I laugh lightly in disbelief. He's amassing all of these things, all things that Becker wants, and he thinks he can trade them all in? For me? And worse still, I sense he thinks that Becker would take his offer. 'You can't buy me,' I snipe.

'Anything can be bought, Eleanor.'

'Not me,' I affirm with grit. Besides, Brent may have the car Becker wanted, but he doesn't have the sculpture. Not that he knows that. 'Brent, do yourself a favour and stay away from me.'

'Or what?'

I take a moment to consider my *or what*. 'Or you're going to push Becker too far, and, trust me, you really do not want that.' I jump in the Audi and race off down the road, my heart thumping wildly in my chest. Because I get the feeling that Brent is doing exactly that. Pushing Becker to get the reaction. To keep the game up.

Chapter 26

After driving back to The Haven, stupidly recklessly, taking all of my frustration out on my fellow drivers, I leave the car in the factory unit and walk around to the front, my unease settling with every step I take into Becker's sanctuary.

When I break into the courtyard, I stop for a moment and breathe the last piece of air I need to bring me back down to calm.

'Is it frogspawn?'

I look across to the fountain where Mrs Potts is hunched over the water with old Mr H, her nose wrinkled.

'Don't be daft, Dorothy.' Becker's grandfather pokes at the surface of the water with his posh walking stick. 'Frogs wouldn't take up residence in a fountain, and where would they come from, anyway?'

'They might have flown here.'

'Flying frogs?' His old face crinkles in disbelief.

'You can get flying frogs,' she protests on a shrug.

'They don't fly, Dorothy. They glide, and you won't find any in central London.'

She raises an indignant nose. 'Then what do you suppose it is?'

'Some kind of algae, I expect.'

I laugh as I watch the old pair. Yes, I'm back in my sanctuary, and it's such a relief. 'Afternoon,' I call, and they both swing around.

'Eleanor.' Old Mr H leans on his stick for support. He's

smiling brightly, his old hazel eyes flashing with sparks of true happiness, so much so, I have to blink to protect my eyes from the brightness. I cast my eyes over to Mrs Potts and notice she has a fond smile gracing her lips, too. They both look significantly peaceful. Accepting.

'So let's see it, then,' the old man says, hobbling towards me.

He reaches for my hand, and I remain still and quiet while he gazes down at the ring. I'm blushing, too. I can't help it, and I look across to Mrs Potts to see her palm resting on her bosom, tears in her eyes. 'It looks beautiful on you,' old Mr H whispers wistfully.

I smile lightly. 'I'm so happy you and Becker have sorted out your differences.'

'Me too,' he admits. 'And if someone would have said to me two months ago that my wayward grandson would be asking my permission to put this ring on a lady's finger, I think I would have keeled over.' He reaches for my cheek and gives it an affectionate rub. 'I'm glad that lady is you. I'm so proud of him, Eleanor, despite some of the stunts he's pulled. Despite him misleading me. He's a passionate, devoted man, and you've enhanced that.'

He needs to stop or I might cry.

'That ring is precious,' Mrs Potts pipes up. 'It's a symbol of how precious you are to Becker boy.'

I blink my eyes, stepping back when Mr H finally relinquishes his hold of me. 'I'm a bit overwhelmed,' I admit.

Both smile at me knowingly. 'I found that emerald in Cambodia,' Mr H says. 'It was 1952. I set it in that band when I proposed to my Mags.'

'Worth three million!' Mrs Potts chimes, and I baulk at them, my hand naturally covering the precious gem. Just wrap my hand in cotton wool, why don't you? Three million?

'Good God,' I breathe.

'Welcome to the family, dear,' Mrs Potts says, coming over and throwing her arms around me. Her big bosom pushes into me, her squeeze fierce and so meaningful.

'I'm glad I'm here,' I admit, cuddling her equally as hard. My God, how did I get so lucky?

'Enough of that.' Mr H pulls us apart on a laugh. 'Eleanor has work to do.'

I straighten, avoiding their eyes so they can't see the happy tears threatening to escape. 'Do you know where Becker is?' I ask, starting towards the Grand Hall, wiping at my eyes discreetly.

'He's not back yet.'

He's not? But it's nearly three. 'Okay, I'll get—' I'm interrupted mid-sentence when my phone rings, and I look down to see Mum's calling. It reminds me that I still need to book my train tickets for my visit home. God, I can't wait to see her face when I tell her. 'I'll be getting on.' I hold up my phone as I carry on my way. 'Hey, Mum.'

'Hi, sweetheart.' She sounds as cheerful as she always does these days. I can't help but smile, my happiness for her drowning out the sadness that it's not my father who's making her happy. 'I'm making plans for when you come home.'

I hurry to Becker's office as I listen to the intricate schedule of activities that she has planned. I'd love to tell her my news now, but I really want to do it face to face. See her reaction, because I just know she's going to be beside herself with joy. 'All sounds great, Mum,' I say, smiling, loving how upbeat she sounds. 'Listen, I have to go. I have a countess coming to see a Rembrandt. I need to prepare.'

'A Rembrandt?' she squeals, delighted. 'Good Lord. What would your father make of this super career you're carving out?'

I swallow down my laugh. He'd turn in his grave, that's what he'd do.

'I'm so proud of you, sweetheart.'

'Thanks, Mum.' I land in Becker's office and shut the door behind me. 'I really need to go.'

'Okay, darling. I'll call you next week.'

I hang up and spend a few moments marvelling and appreciating how bright she sounded. 'Tickets,' I say, quickly pulling up Google on my phone. I order a return ticket for the week after next and send it to the printer, rushing to the double pedestal masterpiece desk. The printer doesn't kick in, but the screen on the printer is telling me to load a new ink cartridge. Fabulous. Ink. Where does he keep the ink? I drop into the chair and grab the brass pull of the left-hand top drawer and tug, but it doesn't shift. It's locked. 'Damn,' I mutter, trying the remaining three drawers in quick succession before moving to the other pedestal and working my way down the four drawers on that side. All locked. I growl under my breath, my eyes flitting around his office. It'll have to wait. I need to get the showing room prepared. It's nearly 3p.m. 'Where are you, Hunt?' I say to myself, getting up. My phone rings, and I glance down at the screen to see the estate agent calling. 'Hello,' I say as I make my way around Becker's desk.

'Miss Cole, Edwin Smith from Smith and Partners here.'

'Hi, Edwin. I don't mean to be rude, but I'm late for a meeting. Can I call you back?'

'This shouldn't take long. I have good news for you. We have an offer on the shop.'

I come to an abrupt stop. My heart suddenly aches a little. 'That's great.' I don't sound very happy at all.

'Full asking price, too. They're cash buyers, so it will be a very quick and easy transaction. I assume you'll be accepting it?'

I swallow and nod, the ache intensifying. This is it. The last scrap of my dad's legacy will be gone. It's bittersweet. Mum will be relieved of the financial burden, but I'll be burdened with more guilt. I clear my throat. 'Of course.'

'Excellent. If you could let me know the name of your

solicitor, I'll get the deal memo drawn up. I'll need the spare sets of keys, too, ready for handover.'

Keys. Goddamn it, the keys. 'I'll get it sorted, Edwin.'

We say our goodbyes and I stare down at my phone. Just do it. Get it out of the way. I pull up David's number and dial. He answers almost immediately. 'Elle?'

'I didn't get my keys back for Dad's store.' I get straight to the point. 'The agent just called me. It's sold, so they'll need all the keys ready for completion. Would you mind dropping them into the agent on the high street when you're passing?'

He's silent for a second. 'Sure.'

'Thank you.'

'Listen, Elle, about that night in the pub . . .'

'Let's not, David,' I say, heading for the door. No rehashing today. Or *any* day.

'I just wanted to apologise, that's all. I was out of line.'

I slow to a stop again. That's big of him to admit. 'Okay.'

'And for everything, actually. I'm sorry for everything.'

I smile at thin air before me. He might be sorry, but I can't be. His betrayal led me to somewhere special. And now . . . closure. 'That means a lot, thank you. Listen, I really must go. Thanks for the keys thing.'

'No problem.'

I hang up and exhale, but my relaxed body soon tenses up again when my mobile sings. Becker. God, I bet he's seething after losing the car to Brent. I get on my way, mindful I still need to get the showing room ready, and hurry to the Grand Hall as I connect the call. 'Hi,' I squeak, my neck shrinking into my shoulders, waiting for his fury.

'Hey, princess.' He surprises me with his upbeat greeting. He sounds far too chirpy for someone who has just lost to their nemesis. 'I have a new woman in my life.'

'What?' I cough, coming to a stop in front of the Rembrandt. I know what that means . . . I think. A woman like Gloria?

'We'll need to make room in the garage,' he goes on. 'I can't decide whether to get rid of the Merc or the Audi to make room for her.'

I should refrain from advising him that his quandary of which car he should get rid of has technically already been decided. He'll see for himself when he pulls up into the factory unit. I shrink a little, but then straighten back up when the puzzle starts to click slowly together: Brent's smugness; Becker's chirpiness. It's familiar. Clarity smacks me in the face like a boulder. *I don't need luck. Trust me.* Oh good Greek god. He promised me no more secrets. He promised! I want to be mistaken but judging by Brent's smug news earlier and Becker's happy mood right now, plus the fact that I know Becker will be out for payback after the O'Keeffe theft, there can be no other explanation. Becker sounds as cheerful as he did when we left Countryscape that time, when he'd just turned Brent over for fifty-fucking-million.

I feel my way to the chair – the one that Becker fucked me on after he proposed to me this morning with a three-million-quid emerald – and collapse into it. My hand rests on my stomach to hold it, my tummy spinning. How does he think he'll get away with this one? I don't even know what he's done or how he's done it, but I'm going to bloody well find out. Just not yet. I want to look into his corrupt eyes when I hit him with my suspicions. Plus, he doesn't know that I have cause to be suspicious, or where the cause for suspicion has come from. He doesn't know that I've encountered Brent today, and I'm thinking he shouldn't.

'Eleanor?' Becker says. 'Are you there?'

'Congratulations,' I shriek, startling myself. I can't be sure, but I think the sound of a bang could be Becker dropping his phone, probably as a result of being startled too.

There're a few seconds of muffled noises down the line before he's back. 'Thanks,' he says, obvious wariness lacing his tone.

'Welcome.' I clamp my teeth together and smile nervously at the Rembrandt. 'The countess will be here soon. I need to get the painting over to the showing room.'

'You've not done it yet?'

'No, I . . .' My words tail off when I remember why I'm running behind. I must not tell Becker that I bumped into Brent. Or that I've spoken to my ex. Not right now. Maybe never. 'I took a call from the estate agent dealing with my father's shop. There's been an offer, and I've accepted.' My mind is reeling, wondering what Becker's done and how the hell he's done it.

'That's great. You must be relieved.'

'Yeah,' I reply quietly. Great. Is it? And how the heck has he got a new woman?

'Have you seen Gramps today?' He cuts into my tatty mind with his question, and I'm grateful, because my brain is beginning to hurt.

'Three million quid, Becker.'

'Oh, I didn't tell you that bit?'

He knows damn well he didn't, a bit like he neglected to mention that he planned on turning over Brent again. Wasn't fifty million enough self-satisfaction? 'No, you didn't.'

He chuckles, light and sweet. 'Don't worry, it's insured. But don't lose it, eh?'

Air inflates my cheeks. 'I have work to do. I'll see you soon.' I'll grill him about the car when I can look him straight in his shady face.

'Actually,' he says. 'Something just came up. I have to stop by in Clapham. Can you take care of the countess yourself?'

Clapham? What's in Clapham? I narrow an eye, suspicious. 'Sure,' I say slowly. 'Where will I find the papers in case she wants to see them?'

'In the file in the library. See you soon, princess.'

I hang up and tap my foot, trying to figure out what's gone down. I know how much Becker wanted that car. How's he pulled this off?' 'What have you been up to, Saint Becker?' I ask thin air, as I try to think. My brain begins to ache again. I haven't got time for this, and something tells me I need it. As well as some aspirin to soothe my thumping head. I go to the library to fetch the paperwork before collecting the painting and weaving my way through the maze of Becker's other treasures with the utmost care, peeking over the top of it as I go.

I reach the showing room and lay it gently on the floor, tuck the file in the corner, before grabbing the only easel in the room and positioning it near the back wall, perfectly centred, so when you enter the room, it's the first thing you see. My next job is stripping down all of the protective coverings, so I start to pick and feel for an edge to peel at.

'We have visitors.'

I look over my shoulder and find Mrs Potts's peeking around the door. 'Two minutes.'

She nods and backs out of the room, leaving me to continue carefully peeling away the coverings. The painting in all of its glory is revealed, and it literally takes my breath away. 'Wow, you're so pretty,' I muse, my eyes skating over the oil on panel. The frame is now perfect, and the painting looks so much brighter in the flesh, polished and almost new.

A shrill laugh distracts me from my admiring, reminding me that I haven't got time to sit here gazing at the magnificent piece of art. I jump up and place the painting on the easel, making sure it's dead centre and secure before gently releasing it and tentatively pulling my hands away.

'Ready, dear?' Mrs Potts is back.

I give a sharp nod, feeling unreasonably nervous, and hold up the protective sheeting with a questioning face. Mrs Potts puts her hand out, and I rush over to give her the rubbish. 'Thank you,' I say, brushing down my dress and moving back a few steps.

'Good afternoon.'

The greeting makes my head snap up and my back snap into shape. The accent told me what I would be faced with before I got a chance to look, so I don't know why I'm surprised when I find a woman in fur. It's everywhere, in the form of a hat on her head, a stole over her shoulders, the cuffs of her suede gloves, and the trim of her leather riding boots. She's tight-jawed and looking me up and down.

'Where's Becker?' she asks, sniffing back her obvious disappointment to find me here instead.

I need to nail this. Grin and bear it. So I do. I slap a ridiculous smile on my face. 'He's tied up.' I didn't mean to say that.

She looks at me, her painted on eyebrows forming high arches. 'Tied up, you say?'

She's imagining that. Becker tied up. She must be sixty. A looker, even if she has a stick up her arse. 'You'll be dealing with me today.' I sweep out my arm, gesturing to the painting. '*Petronella Buys, Wife of Philips Lucasz.*' Just talk about the painting. I can do that. 'Are you familiar with Rembrandt, madam?' I ask, smiling at the painting fondly.

'Of course.' She sniffs, unimpressed and maybe a little insulted. I keep my smile in place as she wanders into the room, cocking her head from side-to-side, studying the painting. 'It's not as spectacular in the flesh as I anticipated,' she says, and I only just swallow down my surprise before it leaps from my mouth. It's fucking stunning, the ignorant cow. I already didn't like her. Now I positively loathe her. I watch her scanning the art, her lips twisting. 'What do you think, sweetie?'

Sweetie? I frown. That's a bit familiar. 'Well, I think it's beaut—' I choke to a stop when someone appears in the doorway of the showing room.

'I think it's average, Auntie.' Alexa nails me in place with a look that could turn steel to ashes as she sashays into the room. Oh ... good ... Greek ... god. My eyes follow her every step, my scowl rivalling hers. It takes every teeny tiny piece of my self-control, but I manage to stay on this side of the room, as oppose to throwing myself across it and wiping that smug smirk from her face.

Auntie? Oh my days. 'Excuse me for a moment.' I rip my death glare away from Alexa and dart out of the room, leaving the countess and her niece – her fucking *niece* – in the showing room alone. I'm guessing this is not part of the showing protocol, and Becker won't be best pleased if he finds out I've left his treasure unattended, but this is an emergency. I can't be trusted in that room with that woman.

I dial him and look through the door, seeing the countess and Alexa standing in front of the painting.

'Princess.' He still sounds chirpy. Not for long.

I swing around, hunching over a little, like making myself smaller will reduce the risk of being heard by them. 'Don't *princess* me. The countess has brought a relative along.'

'Oh.'

'Oh?' What does he mean, *oh?*

'I feared she might.'

I gasp. *The bastard.* 'You knowingly put me in this position?'

'It's a massive sale, princess. If you can pull this off, you can pull anything off.' Is he testing me again? 'Anyway, she's less likely to pounce on you than she is me.'

'Which one?' I ask, checking over my shoulder. 'Auntie or niece?' They're still looking at the splendid painting.

'Both.'

I cringe and force myself to ask the question that keeps molesting my mind. 'Becker, tell me you haven't . . . with . . .'

'I haven't, though she's tried plenty.'

I grimace, looking up to the heavens. I bet she has, and I bet she scared Becker to death. It's quite a feat. 'You wanker.'

'Now, now, princess. Let's not get personal.'

'Fuck you, Hunt. You knew damn well Alexa would be here.'

'Sell the painting, Eleanor. Not a penny under thirty million. Make me proud.' He hangs up, and I close my eyes, calling on all of my willpower. Sell the painting. Just sell that painting for a cool thirty million and kick her out of here. Just not literally. Escort her out. Or better still, call Mrs Potts to show her the way, because putting myself in a dark alleyway with that woman could be fatal.

My head drops back in mental exhaustion at the thought of being professional and courteous. Never a dull *fucking* moment. The phrase 'the things you do for love' is being tested to the limit here. 'You're a bastard, Becker Hunt.' But I'll show him.

Filling my lungs with plenty of air, I whisper encouraging words to myself as I wander back into the showing room. Both women turn to me when they hear my steps, and both sets of eyes narrow to evil slits as they follow my path to the foot of the painting.

I remember Becker's approach to showing a piece. He stood back silently and let the work speak for itself, let the client silently study it, but the atmosphere is too heavy to do that. Plus, I expect the only thing in this room they'll study is me. So I adopt a different approach. 'Oil on panel,' I begin, searching deep and shifting everything I know about Rembrandt and this painting to the front of my mind. 'Amazingly preserved, and I think you'll agree it's stunning in the flesh.' I ghost a finger delicately over the frame. 'Dated 1635, and until now its whereabouts was unknown.'

'And where was it?' The countess asks, throwing a spanner in my works. That's the only thing I don't know, damn it.

I smile tightly, ignoring Alexa's amused smile. 'Lost in history,' I reply coolly and finally.

'The paperwork? Certification?'

'All present,' I say, glancing over to the file in the corner. I take a few steps back, giving them space, and also because being too close to Alexa is giving me hives. 'I believe Mr Hunt sent the papers to the National.' *What am I doing?* 'I'll ensure you have access to them once they've been returned.'

Her head whips to mine. 'The National?'

I smile on the inside. 'The National Gallery,' I confirm, for no other reason than relishing in making her hear it again. 'They have the companion portrait of Philips Lucasz. They're keen to have the two pieces back together.'

Urgency springs into her eyes. 'Price?' she demands.

I join my hands in front of me, remaining calm and collected. 'Thirty-five.' I reel off my price confidently, keeping a perfectly straight face, even when her eyes slightly widen. She wants this painting, and not even the National will stop her.

'Thirty,' she counters, slipping some glasses on and leaning towards the painting, her eyes travelling across the oils slowly.

'Thirty-five, Lady Finsbury,' I affirm, glancing at Alexa. She's silent, watching me in action. I expect she knows fuck all about art, which begs the question why she's here. Becker. Becker is why she's here, and she can't hide her disappointment that he's not. My lips tip into a satisfied smile.

'Thirty-two,' the countess counters.

'The price is thirty-five, Lady Finsbury.'

'Fine,' she barks, striding towards me. 'I want to see the paperwork. In person.' She looks me up and down, and I take it all. I know what's coming next. 'And I want Becker to show me it.'

Of course she does. 'I'm sure that won't be a problem.' I'm being sickly sweet and it's killing me, but I've done my job. *More* than my job.

'Very well.' She arranges her fur stole over her shoulders and wanders out, and I catch Mrs Potts through the glass looking busy, but she still manages to chuck me a reassuring smile. I smile right back, satisfied and proud for maintaining my professionalism, despite dealing with two very tricky customers.

But my smile soon falls away when my skin becomes irritated

again, and I turn and find Alexa giving me evils. 'My aunt wants to deal with Becker in future, not his skivvy.' She saunters past me, slipping her oversized sunglasses on, and my body turns slowly to follow, my lip curling in contempt.

'I'll put forward your request when I see him in bed tonight.' She stops, turning to face me.

'Pillow talk,' I go on, seeing her stiffening before my eyes when I give a casual flash of my ring. I take the few steps that bring me close to her, then lean up on my tiptoes so I can speak into her ear, forcing myself to tolerate our closeness. 'He loves it when I talk dirty to him.' I carry on past her. 'Mrs Potts will show you out.'

'Certainly will, dear,' she confirms, looking at me like a proud grandmother. It's all I can do not to skip my way to the kitchen. I need a cup of tea and some time to reflect. Thirty-five million! I can't wait to share the news with Becker.

I'll tell him that I've trashed his Audi later.

Chapter 27

Winston is circling around his dog bowl like a nutter when I walk into the kitchen, and Mr H is trying to calm him down so he can get some food into it. 'Sit,' the old man shouts, shooing the burly beast away. 'For the love of Apollo, will you sit down.'

Woof!

Winston's nose is twitching crazily, his tail spinning like a propeller. 'All right, all right.' Mr H gives up trying to force an excitable Winston into obedience and empties a healthy helping of dog biscuits into his bowl. He dives in, the sounds of grunts and gulps drowning out Mr H's mumbled moans as he struggles back to vertical, using the worktop and his walking stick for help. 'Greedy guts.'

Winston, oblivious to the disapproval of his table manners, hoovers up the contents of his bowl in a few gluttonous gobbles, before proceeding to cough all over the place.

'See, indigestion.'

I laugh, attracting old Mr H's attention, as I wander over to the fridge. 'Sold for a cool thirty-five million,' I say casually, pulling the door open. I spot an apple and help myself, smiling as I sink my teeth in and turn to face Becker's granddad. He's grinning like I've never seen him grin before.

'Quite a handful, the countess, isn't she?' He hobbles over to the kitchen table and takes a seat.

A bark of sardonic laughter erupts from my mouth, forcing me to slap my hand over it to stop some apple shooting out. I nod in agreement as I chew and swallow. 'If by that you mean rude, disrespectful, and plain awful, then I'm inclined to agree.'

'And you had the pleasure of her niece, too.' He rests his walking stick against the side of the table, looking at me over his glasses, his chin nearly meeting the collar of his shirt. 'Bet that made your day.'

My face twists in disdain as I make my way over to him, taking a seat opposite. Winston is at my feet immediately, sitting and searching for some attention. I reach down and give his ear a scratch. 'She wants Becker. She hates me.'

He chuckles. 'Get used to it, Eleanor. She won't be the only one who'll hate you.'

I shrug off his comment. He's not telling me anything that I don't already know.

'How's your mother?' he asks.

'She's ...' I pause, wondering what word to use. Happy? Thriving? Reborn? 'Amazing,' I answer, because she is.

'And what did she have to say about the news of your engagement?'

'I've not told her yet,' I tell him, making the old man's grey eyebrows jump up in surprise. 'I want to tell her face-to-face. I'm going home to see her soon.'

'You should have her come to London. We can celebrate.'

'I've already purchased my ticket home. Maybe another time. She's never been to London before.'

'Never been to the capital?' He looks sympathetic, and I appreciate why. Everyone should experience the grandeur of London at least once. And if they're anything like me, they'll never want to leave.

'Never,' I confirm. 'Dad wasn't much of an adventurer.'

He smiles fondly. 'You were rather attached to your dad, weren't you?'

'Literally.' I smile. 'He liked having me nearby. I used to watch him working on old junk while I dreamed of selling a

Rembrandt to a snooty countess for a cool thirty-five mill.' My smile stretches when he grabs his tummy and throws his head back on a laugh.

'Bet he would be very proud of you, my girl.'

My smile falters a little. I think shocked might be more apt. Forged sculptures, a con-artist boss, a secret map, the police. 'Maybe,' I murmur. 'He always told me that the high-end world of antiques wasn't worth the bother. Obviously, I don't agree. I love it here, as you know.' I smile and the old man returns it. 'But it's not much fun being interrogated by the pol—' I catch my tongue.

Mr H's old face frowns, and he pushes his glasses up his nose. 'The police? Did they find out who broke into your apartment?'

'Um . . .' I stall, my brain engaging. Becker told me his gramps was the one to get Lady Winchester's file out so it could be destroyed, so he must know the police are investigating her. Right? 'A policeman approached me when I was meeting my friend outside her office. He asked a few questions about Lady Winchester.'

He sits back, surprised. 'Price? Stan Price?'

'That's the one,' I confirm, 'I didn't like him.'

'Then you have a good sense of character,' he says on a sardonic laugh. 'I'm sorry about that, my darling. You shouldn't have to deal with such nonsense.'

'It's fine,' I assure him, brushing off his concern. 'I honestly didn't know what I should say.'

'Don't tell them anything, whether you know or not. He was far from helpful when we needed him after Lou's car accident.'

'It was Price who dealt with Becker's mum's death?' This is news to me. When Becker said the police were less than helpful, I didn't think he meant Price in particular.

'He hardly dealt with it, rather he dismissed it. All the nonsense that's happened since Lou was killed might not have happened had he done his job.' His words resonate deeply, and he shakes his head, as if trying to shake away all of the memories that plague him.

'Do you really think the Wilsons are responsible?' I ask. We're talking murder here. Not stealing or conning, but killing.

'We have the proof, Eleanor.'

'So why didn't the police do something?'

'Because Stan Price is in Wilson's pocket.'

'What?'

'Wilson has dirt on Price, that much I've figured out. I just don't know what.' His eyes drop a little to the table and he smiles a small smile. 'I'd love to know where Becker's hiding that map so I could destroy it and put my mind at rest.'

I wince, feeling all kinds of guilty. I know where that map is, not that it will make much difference. 'But it's plastered all over his back,' I remind him.

'True.' He sighs. 'It's quite something, don't you think?'

'Beautiful,' I agree. 'The detail is just incredible, the equator, the compass.' I still find my head shaking in wonder every time I think about it or see it. And I know I can't stop my mind racing with thoughts of where the heck the missing piece could be. And as I look at Mr H, I wonder ... does he still battle his curiosity? I'd love to ask, but he looks a bit vacant. The air needs clearing of the sadness it's suddenly laced with after the mention of Becker's parents. 'I'm so looking forward to the Andelesea Gala.'

That soon grabs his attention. 'Becker's taking you?'

'Yes, and they're showcasing the Heart of Hell.' My eyes must be glimmering as spectacularly as that ruby. 'I can't tell you how excited I am to see that precious stone, Mr H. Did you know the discovery of that gem was rumoured to be a myth? Just a publicity stunt?' I don't know why I'm saying this. Of course he knows.

'I did, dear.' He smiles fondly at me. 'I hope you enjoy it.'

He reaches for his paper, knocking his stick where it's resting against the table. 'Damn it.' It hits the floor, and I'm quick to dip and collect it up for him. 'I'll get it,' he assures me, leaning down.

'Mr H, leave it,' I scold him, sure I can hear his bones cracking as he tries to bend.

'I've got it, Eleanor.' His feeling fingers brush the stick.

'Really, Mr H, let someone help you.' I swipe the stick up, astounded by his stubbornness, before setting my half-eaten apple on the table and quickly getting to my feet to help him sit up. 'You shouldn't be straining like that.' I get him comfy and go to place the stick against the table, feeling the gold topper rattling in my grasp. 'I think this is loose,' I say, just as the knob comes off in my hand. *Shit.* I quickly start to screw it back on, startling when the old man's hand shoots out fast to claim his stick.

'I'll sort it, dear.' He makes quick work of tightening the gold knob, offering me a mild smile as I retract my hands.

I laugh, though I can't deny it's wary. 'You hiding something in there?' The old man moves fast. Sometimes.

Mr H belly laughs. 'Would you mind making me a nice cup of—' He's interrupted when the door to the kitchen flies open, and I look to find Mrs Potts brushing off her hands, like she's just taken care of some unpleasant business.

And I remember. She has.

'Tea?' I finish for the old man as I wander over to the kettle. 'Everything okay?' I ask Mrs Potts, visions popping into my mind of her dragging the countess and Alexa down the alleyway by their ears.

'It is now *they've* gone. Nasty, snotty-nose riff-raff.' She slams the door behind her and puffs out her bosom. 'Needn't think they're better than any of us,' she rants on, marching over to the stove and yanking the oven open. The delicious smell in the kitchen intensifies. 'I nearly ripped some dahlias from my flower beds and stuffed them down her posh neck to shut her up.'

I snigger as I flip the tap and fill the pot. 'Waste of dahlias.'

She laughs her agreement as she pokes at her pastry before setting it aside and turning, wiping her hands on a tea towel. Her smile fades quickly and, wondering why, I follow her worried eyes and find old Mr H looking pale. I drop the kettle and fly across the kitchen, Mrs Potts following me.

'Mr H?' I say, my hand rubbing his shoulder as I assess his condition. His eyes have glazed over, his light grey hair darkening with sweat. He looks vacant. He's also shaking terribly, worse than I've ever known.

'Donald?' Mrs Potts speaks loudly, barging me out of the way. I don't protest, willingly letting her get to him. 'Donald, look at me.'

He doesn't, and though none of the symptoms are fading, Mrs Potts's concern doesn't increase. She seems quite calm, like she's done this time and again. 'Is he okay?'

'Just a funny turn, dear.' She pushes her arm through his and encourages him to stand, which he does with more effort than usual. 'Come on, let's get you lying down.'

It's the first time since I've known Becker's grandfather that he hasn't complained about being bossed about or physically assisted. He looks washed out, drained of colour. I don't like seeing him like this. I rush to open the kitchen door, holding it while they hobble through together. 'I'll call Becker.'

'No need to worry him, dear.'

Mr H jerks and loses his grip of his stick again, and it clatters to the floor at my feet. 'I've got it,' I say, bending to retrieve it. The gold knob rolls a few feet, and I reach for it, trying to screw it back on for him again.

'Leave it,' the old man wheezes, and I glance up at him, confused, finding him staring at me. His eyes. They look haunted, and I slowly pass his stick over. Taking it, he shakes his head and lets Mrs Potts continue guiding him out of the kitchen.

My brow is wrinkled, my lip being nibbled harshly. He was fine. And then . . . not.

A sad whimper has me glancing down to find Winston looking as sad as he sounds. 'He'll be okay, boy,' I say, aware that I'm saying this more for my reassurance than Winston's. 'I promise.' He sticks to the side of my leg as I wander over to the table to collect my bag. I'm doubting Mrs Potts's insistence not to call Becker. Or maybe she's right. He'll only panic, speed home, and risk getting himself into an accident.

I look down and find Winston still at my feet. 'Fancy a walk?' I ask him, and he looks up at me with droopy eyes. 'Come on. We could both use some fresh air.' I still have the unpleasant lingering aftermath of Alexa pinching at my skin.

Chapter 28

An hour roaming the park really didn't do me any favours. Open space and a lack of company left a massive void to worry about old Mr H. I called Lucy in an attempt to take my mind off the old man who I've become so fond of, and it worked to a certain extent. She's all loved up, seeming far more settled after the explosions last night. She didn't mention the girl from floor eighteen once.

When I've settled Winston in his bed, I go in search of Mrs Potts to find out how Mr H is. I poke my nose around every door, not finding a soul in any of the rooms, leaving me concluding that she's still in his suite with him. It only increases my worry, but not wanting to knock and disturb them, I reluctantly make my way back to the showing room to start packing away the Rembrandt, anything to keep me busy instead of hanging around worrying.

I'm surprised when I wander in and find Becker there, carefully wrapping the painting. His shirt-covered back holds my attention for a few moments, my mind picturing the map beneath the layer of his clothing. No matter how much old Mr H wants that map gone from their lives, it's never going to happen.

'You're back,' I say from the doorway.

'I'm back,' he replies softly, finishing packaging the painting and lifting it from the easel. 'I've just seen Gramps.'

'Dorothy said not to call you and cause undue worry.' Do we need to worry? Taking the easel, I carry it to the corner of the room and put it in its rightful place. 'How is he?'

'He was very sleepy. I left him to rest.'

I relax, relieved. 'I'm glad. He had me worried.'

'Yeah, me too. He'll be fine.' He exhales, sounding tired. Worn down. Worried? 'Now, let's talk about the Audi.'

My arms turn to stone, braced against the sides of the easel. Fuck. I forgot about that. 'I sold the painting,' I blurt out, whirling around. He's glaring at me, arms crossed over his chest. 'Thirty-five million,' I declare proudly. 'Not thirty, but thirty-*five* million.' Becker's head cocks to the side a little, amused. 'I told her the National wanted it. She bit my hand off.' His face remains unimpressed, and it begins to rile me. He threw me in the deep end and forced me to tread water alone. And I did bloody well, too. 'You could at least look pleased,' I snap petulantly. 'And since you seem so keen to talk about cars, let's . . .' I only just manage to rein myself in before I clue him in on my suspicions about the vintage Ferrari. I keep forgetting that Becker doesn't know about my encounter with Brent. And he mustn't. It'll only anger him and encourage him to continue with these crazy games.

'Let's what?' He takes a threatening step towards me.

'Nothing.' I evade his eyes.

'Princess . . .' he extends my pet name, sounding guarded. 'Let's *what?*'

'Nothing.' I laugh, aiming for nonchalance, but I only achieve guilt. I'm still not looking at him, and I dare not, either. 'I have a pile of paperwork to get through.' I thumb over my shoulder and back away. 'Must get on.' I turn and hurry away, wondering at what point he might share his recent rip-off, if he will at all. I might have it all wrong. After all, he promised me no more secrets. But Brent has told me that he's got the car; Becker's also told me he has a new woman in his life. So, who has the fucking car?

I hear Becker's phone ring as I make my escape, thankful

that he's distracted from chasing me down and pressing me. For now, anyway. I don't know how to handle this. 'Called to gloat?' Becker asks when he's answered, rather than your customary *hello* or *hey* or *afternoon*. There's also a ton of menace behind the question. I hear him curse, and I risk a peek over my shoulder, seeing him stabbing at the screen of his phone with his thumb. He's cut the call. He looks mad. Why? I don't know, and by the look on his face, I don't want to. I turn and hurry out. 'Stop where you are, princess.'

I stutter to a halt and freeze, like he could have pressed a pause button on me. I don't like the authority in his command. Neither do I like the fact that I'm apprehensive, rather than my usual lusty self when he throws orders at me. Then my brain seems to jump-start.

Called to gloat?

Oh . . . no . . .

I shrink like a blooming flower that's had burning hot water poured over it. There's only one person who Becker would ask that question, and in my haste to escape, I didn't think about it quickly enough. I would have run faster had my brain engaged sooner.

'Something to tell me?' he asks, his voice brittle with annoyance. I close my eyes when I sense him coming closer, until he's pushed up against my back and breathing in my ear.

I shake my head into his cheek, keeping my mouth shut. I don't know why I'm denying it. That was Brent on the phone, and he's kindly filled Becker in on our little meeting outside my apartment. Which means Becker's obviously assumed – rightly – that Brent's told me that *he* won the car. So why is he being so reproachful? He's the one in the wrong, not me.

'Why didn't you tell me Brent Wilson was sniffing around your apartment?' he asks, his hips pushing into my back, a calculating move that could work for him. Grind me down with his sinful expertise. Make me mindless and desperate and willing to throw myself into a fire if he will only indulge me.

I breathe in. 'Why would I when I know you'd get angry?'

'I'm not angry,' he whispers hoarsely. 'You smell like apple.'

My teeth sink into my lip as I fight off the want he's un-earthing. He's mad but playing it cool, and it occurs to me that he's not mad that Brent Wilson has dropped him in it, but because Brent ignored Becker's demand to stay away from me. But we need to get back to the matter at hand. 'Have *you* got something to tell *me*?' I counter.

'Yes, I have.' He slips an arm around my waist and captures me, hauling me back. 'Today, I ripped off Brent Wilson for over a hundred million.' He finishes his calm announcement with a light kiss to my ear.

I exhale from relief. At least, I think it's relief. Because I'm not overthinking. My imagination isn't running away with me. But is Becker telling me because he's been caught red-handed? He doesn't sound proud or pleased or smug. He sounds almost indifferent. It's just another score for Becker against Brent, but I'm beginning to wonder where the gratification can be found if Brent isn't aware that he's been wronged. Where's the satis-faction in that? But I should have expected this the moment the O'Keeffe went missing. Becker was never going to let that lie. But where does it end?

Becker lifts me a little and attaches his lips to my neck. The apprehension has vanished and the familiar want and lust is back full-force. He's feeling uneasy, knowing Brent has been sniffing around again, trying to turn me against him. He doesn't need to worry. I'm his and, apparently, no amount of crimes will change that. Will he ever pull a stunt that will be morally too much for me to handle? My compassion for Becker's history is helping me empathise and accept his crimes. And now I understand that his need to keep the upper hand over Brent will be fierce since he vowed to abandon the search for the lost sculpture. Becker needs to get his revenge one way or another.

This is one way – ripping off Brent repeatedly – and Brent's not helping matters by countering his attacks. The other is resuming the search and finding *Head of a Faun*, and after what I've learned about his parents' deaths, I should never allow that. Never. So I'm compromising. I'd rather keep Becker and accept that he's going to con Brent for the rest of our lives together rather than lose him to a myth. 'How?' I ask.

'The original has been switched with a pukka replica.'

I remain calm. He blows my mind in more ways than one. Carving sculptures, switching cars. 'Is that what you've been up to all day?'

'Yes.'

'So Brent's paid millions for a replica?'

'Yes.'

'Where's the original?'

He spins me around and grabs my cheeks, grinning. 'In our garage.'

I scowl at him. 'You promised me no more games.'

'He only wanted it because I wanted it, princess. And now he thinks he has it.'

I can't argue with the truth. Damn Brent for goading Becker. 'He's bound to find out.'

'How?'

'I don't know. Maybe when he sells it.'

He rolls his eyes. I don't know why. It's a perfectly reasonable worry. 'He'll never sell anything that he knows I want. That's his satisfaction. Mine is looking at that car in my garage every day knowing he *thinks* he has it.' He winks cheekily, and I shake my head, done for the day. That's self-satisfaction at its best.

'Am I to assume that your granddad can't know about this?' I ask flatly. His look of worry gives me my answer, and I sigh heavily. 'I can't believe I've let you drag me into your corrupt world.'

His finger meets my lips. 'You love my corrupt world.' He

gives my arse a solid squeeze. 'I'll show you just how corrupt I am in bed tonight.' Replacing his finger with hard lips, he kisses me passionately, deeply, and meaningfully, swallowing me up until he eventually slows to a stop and nips my lip playfully. 'Thirty-five million, eh?'

'It makes me feel better about the three million on my finger.'

He laughs and kisses my head as he leads us back into the showing room and collects the painting with his spare hand. 'How awful was she?'

'Which one?'

'Alexa.' He spits out her name like a bad taste.

'Very awful. She insists her aunt only wants to deal with you in future, not your skivvy.'

'I bet she does. Anyway, let's get back to your other accomplishment today.' He looks down at my frowning face as I sprint through my day. Other accomplishment? 'My mangled Audi.' His lips straighten. 'It was quite a welcome-home surprise when I pulled up in the factory.'

'Ah.' I raise a finger, my indication that I'm about to give him a perfectly reasonable explanation for trashing his car. 'I knew you'd be bringing a new woman home, so I wanted to make space in your garage.'

He laughs loudly, making me feel so much better. 'You'll be punished.'

'How?' Why I'm asking is beyond me. We all know what my punishment will be.

'You'll wash Gloria in your underwear every Sunday for a year,' he declares, smiling in approval. I'm surprised. No arse-slapping? 'And I'll spank your arse occasionally while I watch,' he adds, glimpsing down at me.

'You're a dirty-minded arse.'

'And soon to be your dirty-minded husband.' He collects my left hand and kisses his grandmother's ring, and for reasons beyond me, everything weighing my mind down lifts.

I settle into his side. 'Do you really think your gramps will be okay?'

'He's a tough old boot.' We enter the Grand Hall, and Becker props the painting up in the corner before reclaiming me and getting us on our way again. 'Happens now and then.'

'We were only chatting,' I explain, letting Becker lead us into the kitchen. He releases me and heads to the fridge like a homing pigeon in search of his apples. 'It was all very sudden. One minute we were talking and the next he was all white and shaky. And you should get him a new walking stick.' I hate to think what would happen if the knob came off while he was using it. He could take a tumble.

Becker turns around from the fridge with an apple halfway to his mouth. 'Why? He's rather attached to that one.'

'There's a piece loose.' I wander over to the kettle I abandoned earlier and take it to the stove. 'I tried to fix it, but the stubborn old boot insisted it was okay.' I notice Mrs Potts has left the oven on, so I quickly turn off the dial and then face Becker. I find him staring at the floor, quiet and still.

'Becker?'

He snaps out of his trance and gives me round eyes. 'Tell me what was said.'

I withdraw, shaking my head a little. 'What about?'

'His stick.'

'His stick?'

He throws his apple aside and stalks over to me, taking the tops of my arms. 'Yes, the stick. Tell me.'

I pull myself free, backing away, seriously disliking his disposition. 'What's gotten into you?'

He sighs, dragging in a calming breath. 'I'm sorry. But, please, try to remember what was said.' He comes close and pulls me in for a hug, stroking the back of my head comfortingly.

I close my eyes and rack my brain, quickly finding what I'm looking for, and what Becker really wants, though I'm totally perplexed as to why. 'He knocked it over and was prepared to break a bone rather than let me pick it up for him.'

'And there's a piece loose?'

'Yes. The gold knob on the end.' Seriously, it's not that big of a deal. 'Is it a priceless family heirloom or something?' He seems quite upset at the notion of a broken walking stick.

Becker stills against me for a few moments before pulling away, looking at me vacantly. He's thinking, but I haven't the foggiest idea what about. I can only stand here, becoming increasingly impatient as I wait for enlightenment. I'm about to repeat my previous question, when his eyes spring up to mine, wide and questioning.

'Becker?' I say warily, watching as he starts to march doggedly around the room.

He halts and presses the balls of his hands into his forehead, his back rolling from his deep breaths. 'I can't believe I haven't realised before.'

'What?' I'm getting mad now, wanting information faster than Becker is willing to give it.

He strides out of the kitchen and I'm in hot pursuit before I've asked myself where he's going.

Following him down the corridor, I note the tension making his back muscles protrude beneath his shirt, and his hand goes through his hair more than once, ruffling up his brown waves. He's on a mission, and I haven't got a clue what that mission is. He passes the library, the staircase to his quarters, his office, and eventually reaches his granddad's suite.

He takes the handle and pushes his way into the room. I fear the worst. Old Mr H wasn't in a good way. A confrontation with Becker – whatever Becker's reason – could cause undue stress. I need to stop him. I hurry forward and catch Becker's arm, trying to pull him back, but I get shaken off. I peek past him and see Mr H lying in his bed, Mrs Potts sitting next to him in an old fashioned, high-backed winged armchair. She looks up at us hovering at the doorway.

'How is he?' Becker whispers, surprising me. Everything suggested he was ready to go on a rant.

'Resting,' Mrs Potts frowns, and I see the question in her eyes. It's probably matching mine. 'Best to leave him,' she says diplomatically, like she senses Becker has plans to do otherwise.

He ignores her and wanders quietly to his bedside. 'Gramps,' Becker says quietly.

Mrs Potts is up from her chair quickly, circling the bed. 'Becker boy, I think it's best we let him rest.' I admire her valour, but nothing is getting Becker out of this room until he's done whatever he needs to do . . . which is what?

He places a hand over his granddad's frail, wrinkled one, and rubs a little. 'Gramps, don't pretend to be asleep.'

'He's not pretending, Becker.' Mrs Potts swats his hand away, but he shrugs her off, determined, and moves in closer to his granddad, whose eyes are lightly closed, his breathing steady.

'Gramps, I'm not going until you open your eyes.'

'Becker boy, what's gotten into you?' Mrs Potts starts trying to pull him away, and for reasons unbeknown to me, I hurry over and take her arm, nodding at her reassuringly when she turns shocked eyes onto me.

Becker thanks me by reaching back and taking my arm, squeezing gently. The small gesture nearly breaks my heart. Whatever he's doing, I have every faith that it's necessary. That he's confident he's not putting his granddad in any danger.

Becker releases my arm and leans down, getting his face close to old Mr H's. 'Tell me, Gramps. Tell me why you had a funny turn.'

I hold my breath, and Mrs Potts looks at me, clearly confused.

My heart nearly stops when Mr H's eyelids start to flutter. He's not asleep. He can hear every word. His eyes open, revealing glassy orbs that zoom straight in on his grandson. I hold my breath, and I can tell by the rise of Becker's shoulders that he's holding his, too.

'Fine,' the old man rasps, staring into Becker's eyes. 'I'll tell you, Becker boy.'

I find myself backing up, wary of the old man's haunted eyes.

His nostrils flare.

He flicks his eyes to me.

And he takes a deep breath before he speaks.

'Your wife-to-be just found the missing piece of the map.'

Chapter 29

Life stands still for a minute, my pulse whooshing in my ears.

Becker recoils, and Mrs Potts staggers back, taking me with her. I'm in no position to catch her, leaving her scrambling for a nearby cabinet for support.

'What?' Becker asks on a whisper, pure wonder in his question. Mr H struggles to nod as he looks away, like he can't face the evident fascination sparking from his grandson.

I'm held rapt by what's unfolding before me, unable to voice my shock. I haven't found anything. What's he talking about? I haven't a bloody clue where the missing part of the map is.

I hear Mrs Potts catch a breath. 'Well, I'll be damned,' she whispers.

Becker approaches his grandfather, who looks older and frailer than I've seen him before. 'Your walking stick.'

Mr H refuses to look at Becker, and my gaze shifts quickly, back and forth between the men, mesmerised by what I'm hearing. The stick? My mind is in a tangle, struggling to keep up. I reach for Mrs Potts, who takes my arm to steady me, moving in quickly when I wobble from the rush of blood to my head. Becker catches my stagger and rushes over to relieve Mrs Potts. 'I don't know where it is,' I blabber mindlessly. This is absurd.

'No,' Mr H grunts. 'You don't know, not technically, but you've unwittingly found it.'

I blink back the fog from my glazed eyes and find Becker staring at his granddad, shocked, confused ... excited. 'You've had it all this time? How could you?'

'Why would I encourage you, Becker boy? After everything? Your mother, gone. Your father, gone.' He's getting distressed again, and I fold on the inside, especially now I know how Gramps and Becker lost their family. 'I live with that guilt every damn day. I should have destroyed that blasted map when I had the chance. All of it.'

I hold my breath. I'll always worry that Becker won't be able to let it go of his need to find that sculpture. That he won't be able to resist the temptation. He can say he's capable of walking away until he's blue in the face, but I don't know if I can believe him. Especially if he knows where the sculpture can be found. The ultimate vengeance would be finding it, something his grandfather and father failed to do. This is personal. Becker wants peace. He can rip Brent Wilson off day after day for the rest of his life, but that's a consolation prize. His only true peace will come from fulfilling his life's ambition. What he sees as his calling. Which is finding the sculpture and avenging his parents' deaths. Finding what he's been searching for.

Frighteningly, in this moment of madness, I realise that now. And I positively hate myself for being curious and intrigued by the story. I hate that I've wondered if and where the sculpture can be found. I hate that I've got a thrill each time I've thought about it. And I hate that I've slowly and silently come to understand Becker's obsession. But now, the potential of really losing him to that myth is all too real. Because the map can be completed.

'When your father posted the map back to you,' the old man says, 'I intercepted it.' He gives Becker cautious eyes. 'I knew he'd found the missing piece, and I didn't want you to have it.'

'So you took it?' Becker asks on a choke of air.

'So I took it,' his grandfather confirms.

'All this time you know I've been searching for it, and you had it?'

'You weren't supposed to be searching for it,' Gramps bellows, his back lifting off the bed with the effort. 'You promised me you wouldn't.'

'Where's your stick?' Becker starts scanning the room, as do I, searching for the old man's walking aid. It's been here at The Haven the whole time. The missing piece of the map has been right under Becker's nose, hidden in his grandfather's walking stick. But it isn't under his nose now. Now, old Mr H's trusty walking stick is nowhere to be seen.

'Don't tell him.' My demand comes out of nowhere, and Becker shoots a shocked look my way.

'What?' Becker asks, his eyes widening by the second.

My mind instantly straightening out, the gravity of my situation hitting me hard, I say what I mean. 'I don't want you to know where it is.'

'Eleanor—'

'No,' I warn, feeling my jaw tightening. 'No, Becker.'

'I need to know,' he grates, realisation replacing his shock – realisation that I'll fight him on this. I'll fight him with everything I have. I've accepted so much, but not this. No way. There's a reason his grandfather has kept the missing piece of the map from Becker, and I'm with him. All the thrill, all the excitement, it's gone. I will not stand back and watch him follow in his father's footsteps.

'No,' I repeat.

'It doesn't mean I want to find the sculpture.' He's lying. I know he's lying.

'Medusa, give me strength!' Old Mr H yells. 'You expect me to believe that passion and urge in you goes away just like that? That need for vengeance deep, deep inside you, boy, will never be gone, no matter how hard you try, and no matter how much time you dedicate to our *business*. Having a woman on your arm hasn't quenched your thirst for adventure. It hasn't chased away the thrill of danger, so don't you dare try to convince me otherwise.'

I drift off into my own world, wondering if the deep-seated urge Becker's fighting will ever go away. The adventurer and daredevil are inbuilt into the Hunt men. It's part of their DNA. Maybe it will be a constant battle and worry. Maybe those desires in him will fade over time. Who knows? Nothing is certain.

'I love her,' Becker says as he looks at me, his eyes glazed and confused. 'I love her more than the sculpture, Gramps. I'm more obsessed with her than I am about finding that lump of marble.' His jaw is going wild, ticking madly. 'I just need to know for my own sanity. To put it to rest.'

Old Mr Hunt huffs disbelievingly. I can't help feeling insulted, yet the reasonable side of me points out that he has every reason not to believe Becker. And it has me wondering . . . did the old man confess the whereabouts of the missing piece as a test? To see if Becker would choose me or the sculpture? The thought stings. I was completely unaware that I'd found the missing piece. Mr H could have easily passed off his funny turn as something else. Or could he? Becker knew immediately there was something amiss. Seems my saint is a little more on the ball than I am. But then again, he's a Hunt man. They're exceptional at so much, including sleuthing. 'So you won't look for it any more?' Mr H asks outright, his expression daring Becker to lie.

'No.' Becker shakes his head adamantly.

Old Mr H glances over to me, and I shake my head mildly, silently begging him not to tell Becker where his stick is, or what he knows is on that missing piece of the map.

'There are some numbers,' he starts quietly.

'No,' I shout.

But the old man ignores me, a million apologies in his eyes. 'A code,' he goes on, and I close my eyes, trying to hide from the wonder that I know will be on Becker's face.

'Why did you keep it, Gramps? Why didn't you destroy it?'

The old man's lips purse, though he doesn't speak.

So Becker goes on. 'Because you couldn't let it go, either, could you? You kept that piece as a private trophy.'

The old man sinks into the bed on a heavy sigh. 'My stick is in the wall.'

Becker gasps his shock, and I close my eyes again, so tightly, maybe to escape the crazy I'm faced with. Now what? I can't let him go off and hunt for that sculpture. I can't risk losing him. This is beyond my ability to handle.

The torrid tale of his parents plays on repeat in my head as I open my eyes and look at Becker. He's in a trance, and I can see his mind spinning, plotting and planning. He's already looking for that damn sculpture again. 'No, Becker,' I warn.

He stares up at me blankly, giving me nothing. So I take his arms by his biceps and dig my nails in. 'Do you hear me?' I grate, my temper getting the better of me. I can't help it. My panic is escalating with each second he remains quiet, knowing he's thinking too much. 'Do you hear me?' I shout, crashing my fists into his shoulders viciously. I'm not letting him do this. Not to us, and especially not to himself. 'Tell me you hear me.'

'Vengeance for my parents, Eleanor,' he says calmly.

I start shaking my head fast, tears springing into my eyes. I knew it. I knew he didn't mean it when he told his granddad that he was through. No more searching. No more obsessive need to hunt down what may not even be there to find. He never had any intention of giving up. He's incapable of it. 'No.' I say quietly.

The seriousness in his hazel eyes terrifies me. 'Yes,' he replies.

'I'll leave you.' This threat is all I have, and I beg it's enough. The tears break and tumble down my cheeks as I frantically search my mind for more words to throw in his face in my desperate attempt to discourage him. 'I'm guaranteed, Becker. A life with me is guaranteed. There's no guarantee you'll find what you're looking for.' My words become broken and my body starts to jerk as he watches me falling apart. 'You've lost too much already. Please don't risk us,' I sob. 'Please don't make me live without you.'

His vacant beauty just stares at me as silence descends, and reality hits me. I can't live my life in fear of losing him. I drop my gaze as I toy with the ring on my finger, swallowing down the lump of despair in my throat. What's more important to him? It's a stupid question – one I wished I'd never asked myself. Because the answer hurts.

'Eleanor?'

I look up, finding Becker watching me, his eyes wide and wary. I stare right back, my mind a muddle of confusion. Then I slip the ring from my finger and hold it out to him. Becker shakes his head, stepping back, refusing to accept it. So I place it on the sideboard.

Then I turn and walk out. I can't feel my legs. I can't feel a thing, aside from the awful ache in my heart. I'm not enough for him at all. I'm not his priority, and of every mad thing I've accepted, I can't accept not being number one to him.

'Eleanor,' Becker shouts, coming after me. 'Eleanor, no, wait.' He grabs my arms, and I swing around violently, wrenching myself free.

'No,' I grate, and he recoils, his face falling.

I back away slowly and leave him feeling lost, refusing to look at anything as I wander aimlessly through the corridors of The Haven. I refuse to slip into the kitchen and say goodbye to Winston. I refuse to admire any of Becker's treasures as I enter the Grand Hall.

And I refuse to cry.

I've sacrificed my integrity and morals for Becker Hunt. I gave him everything. My trust, my devotion, my heart. My all. And he can't even give up one thing for me.

'Eleanor?' Old Mr Hunt's frail voice hits me from behind, and I stutter to a stop. Like an omen, I'm within licking distance of the chair where Becker proposed to me. 'Dear girl, just hold your horses for a moment.'

I clench my eyes shut, silently begging him not to make this any harder than it already is. 'I've accepted so much, Mr H,' I say, hating that I can't control the distress in my voice. 'I can't accept this.'

'Accept what?'

I turn and look at the old frail man, astonished. He needs to ask? 'You know as well as me that he'll go looking for that sculpture. I can't hang around worrying if he'll come back to me. I can't do that.'

'You're a part of this family now, Eleanor. Don't leave us.'

I weep despairingly, letting him pull me into his arms and hug me. The old man's big frail body feels warm and strong against my hopeless form.

'You are enough for him,' he whispers quietly. 'I have to believe him. I saw it in his eyes just now when you left. I saw it in the reflection of his tears when he promised me he would let it go. I heard the devastation in his voice when he cried on my shoulder, darling girl. I couldn't let you walk away. I had to do something.' His arms rub at my back soothingly while I sob into his chest, my shoulders jerking uncontrollably. 'Please, Eleanor. Stay. My boy has found something to live for besides his treasure. Don't take that away from him.'

I'm useless in his arms, crying like a baby. But past my uncontrollable emotion, I manage to wonder if there's a small selfish reason for old Mr H making such a heartfelt plea. I wonder if he fears that if Becker no longer has me, there will be *nothing* to stop him from resuming the mercy mission that he's so adamant he can walk away from. I can't be certain, and it's something I wouldn't insult Mr H by asking. He has every reason to have that fear after losing his son and daughter-in-law. Which begs the question why he's told Becker. He didn't have to. Or did he? Maybe he needs peace, too.

'Gramps?' Becker's soft calling of his granddad is thick with distress, and old Mr H releases me, wiping my eyes before I can reach to do it myself. He smiles down at me and nods, eyes full of encouragement. I can't speak through the huge lump in my throat, so I nod in return. Then he turns and wanders away, stopping briefly by his grandson and kissing him gently on his forehead.

Once we are alone, I find myself diverting my eyes everywhere, unable to look at Becker, my mind a riot of silent confusion. I see a chair nearby and move towards it, but stutter to stop before I make it there. I can't sit on that chair. Not after he proposed to me there. I change direction, heading to the dresser to lean on, but, again, I don't make it. I see myself climbing the side of it. Everywhere. Reminders. I close my eyes and keep my back to him. I don't know what to do. All I can hear are old Mr H's pleading words, and all I can see is Becker's torment. And that damn sculpture.

'You're all I need, Eleanor.' His words bring me back into the room, his voice rough with emotion.

My heart skips a few beats, and I swallow harshly, turning to seek him out, needing to see him. He's standing at least ten metres away, looking lost and hopeless among his treasure, his angel eyes glazed with tears.

'Watching you walk away just then is one of the most painful things I've ever faced,' he whispers, his gaze sinking into me, heavy with a thousand emotions. 'I never lose, Eleanor. I've made sure of it since I lost my parents. Then I met you . . . and I lost my heart.' His voice quivers, and I battle with the water pooling in my eyes. He steps forward, hesitant. 'Please don't leave me,' he begs. 'I can live without that sculpture, but I could never live without you.'

'Stop.' I sniffle, struggling to see him though my hampered vision. 'Just stop.'

His lip trembles as he holds his arms out to me. 'Don't make me be without you. I had a moment of weakness, that's all. The revelation caught me off guard, gave me a lapse in focus.'

My hands come up to my face, hiding from Becker as my despair continues to pour out of me. I feel strong arms tentatively circle my shoulders, and he hauls me into his chest, embracing me with the power of a thousand men. 'I only need you.'

His nose sinks into my neck. I can feel the wetness of his tears on my skin, my arms coming up to his back and feeling gently as he holds me like the world might end if he lets go.

He cuddles me until my sobs finally abate and my tears stop streaming. Breaking gently away from me, he threads his fingers through mine and toys with them quietly for a few moments. Then he starts walking backwards, his angel eyes lifting to mine in silent hope. My feet begin to move, following his steps. I put up no resistance.

He remains silent the whole way to his private space, and as soon as the door closes behind us, he slowly and quietly starts stripping me down. I stand before him, fascinated by the concentration on his face as he carefully removes all of my clothes. His eyes roam over my skin as he carries out his task, but they never meet mine. So I continue to watch him, starting to understand what he's doing. He wants to show me how he feels, eliminate any doubt that has crept into my mind, and he thinks this is the best way to do it.

My bra is removed thoughtfully, his fingers brushing my skin here and there. Each time he touches me, I hold my breath, and he smiles mildly to himself, feeling my struggle to remain still while he undresses me. Dropping to one knee, he draws my knickers down, and I step out of them, before he takes each foot in turn and lifts it slightly from the ground so he can remove my shoes. When I'm totally bare before him, he feels around me and cups my arse, then reaches forward with his lips and rests them on the sensitive flesh to the side of my pubic bone. My hands come up fast and find his shoulders, my body bending at the hips on a lumpy swallow. I take one hand to his hair and comb through his ruffled waves, as my other feels his rough cheek.

He rises before me, smoothly and slowly, not once taking his eyes off mine. 'Your love is mine.' He swoops in and tackles my mouth, firm but slow, walking me back and caging me in against the door. I fall into his pace, match his passion, and wrap my arms tightly around his shoulders. 'Mine to cherish,' he mumbles past my lips. 'Mine to protect, to worship, to admire.'

'I'm not a piece of your treasure.'

'Oh, baby, you really are.' I swallow his words and hope they find my soul and brand themselves there. 'I'm never freeing you from my maze, Eleanor Cole.' He physically fights with himself to disconnect us, then reaches for his shirt buttons and starts undoing them one by one, purposely slowly. Inch by inch, his chest is slowly revealed, and my eyes flick to his, aware that's he's watching me admiring his perfection. 'Yours,' he says simply, rolling his shoulders and shrugging off his shirt. It gets tossed aside, and then his hands move to his trousers, unfastening them slowly, making a meal of his task, knowing I'm desperate to have our naked skin touching. The sound of his zip coming down is deafening in the silent room. The sexual tension is crippling.

All of the moisture in my mouth has evaporated. Becker smiles and pushes his trousers and boxers down his legs together, revealing his thick, sturdy thighs. I breathe out shakily as he kicks off his remaining clothes, and then he reaches forward and clamps my wrist in his hold, yanking me into his chest. Our bodies collide, soft curves on cut muscle, and my forehead meets his shoulder, my breath ricocheting back into my face. There's a need rooting itself inside of me, one that demands I physically attach myself to him, because I don't quite feel complete when we're not connected. It's beautiful and unhealthy at the same time. The more I learn about him, the stronger I feel.

'Naked cuddles.' His gravelly tone tickles my ear, and I flex my neck and roll my shoulder, trying to contain my hot shivers. Hooking one arm around his neck, I let him lift me from my feet and carry me to the bed where I'm laid down gently, and then he crawls up me on his knees and spreads himself all over me. And I realise. He really does just want a naked cuddle. To feel close. To hold me and reflect on what's just happened. To make sure we're okay.

And then I also realise . . .

I want that, too.

He hugs me tightly all night, like he's scared I'll disappear should he give me space to move. Neither of us breathe a word, though the silence is riddled with our thoughts. They are screaming, demanding to be shared. Yet we keep them to ourselves. I can tell when he's trying to clear his racing mind because he increases his already tight hold, trying to squeeze away the crazy in his head.

Me? I just accept the various levels of constriction, trapped beneath him, while trying to process everything, as well as deliberate and worry about what might be whirling around in Becker's head. I know what he said to his grandfather – all of the convincing words about letting go of his desire to find the sculpture. But what Becker said and what he is actually thinking are two entirely different things. I saw the excitement that he tried to conceal when his gramps told him what I'd unwittingly discovered. But just because the map can be completed, it doesn't mean the sculpture can be found. I can't lose Becker. Not to a woman, and most definitely not to a myth.

My hands resting on his back strokes and feels across the ink. I can almost feel the edges of the map swelling, like they're raised and pulsing.

Like they're coming to life.

Chapter 30

By morning, Becker is still like a second skin on me, and I'm guessing I've had only a few hours' sleep. I drifted in and out of consciousness all night. Each time I found myself dosing off, Becker squeezed me that little bit harder, telling me that sleep wasn't close for him and his mind was still racing.

'I'm sorry.' He breaks into my sleepiness with his raspy apology in my ear, snuggling deeper into me. The heat he's kicking off is both comforting and stifling.

'For what?'

'For being a twat. For making you feel so desperate that you walked away from me.'

I smile, holding him to me. My head has been in some pretty strange places throughout the night. Scary places. Worrying places. *But I'm enough for him.* It's what I've told myself repeatedly. Yet I know Becker will still get his vengeance, just in a different way. He'll continue to rip off Brent Wilson. It's like his own private satisfaction, since he can't have the gratification and recognition of finding the missing treasure. I can't help but feel happy to let him have that.

'Thank you,' he says above me, stroking my hair on a sigh. He lifts a little, his hands taking mine to above my head. 'Thank you for loving me when I didn't want you to,' he says, searching my eyes. 'Thank you for staying when I tried to force you away. Thank you for making me hurt so badly when you left me.' He winces, like he's remembering that feeling. I hope he is. 'And thank you for knowing me better than I know myself,' he finishes softly, sinking his face into my neck. 'My search is over, because I've found what I need.'

I close my eyes, and we lay there for an age, wrapped in each other's naked embrace, both of us quiet, until Becker starts to chuckle, knocking me out of my daydream as he emerges from his hiding place in my neck. 'What?' I ask, as I gaze up at him.

He puts his finger to his lip. 'Shhhh . . .' he hushes. 'Listen.'

My ears prick up and my eyes dart, listening carefully. It's silent. I'm just about to question him again, but then I hear something. Becker's smile stretches, and I search the room, confused. The wet-sounding snort comes again, and Becker starts to unravel our tangled limbs. He gets up and wanders casually out of the bedroom area to the door of his apartment. My eyes are presented with their usual predicament when Becker's naked and with his back to me, but it's his tattoo that gets my attention today. It's glowing at me, as if reminding me of its presence and how it came to be there, but I zoom in on the small empty space in the centre that's been the bane of Becker's life, shaking my head at the thought of Mr H keeping it from his grandson all this time. Becker could find the sculpture now, if it's there to be found. Can it be found?

Eleanor!

My returned curiosity starts to play games with me. It's caught me off guard. So has the flutter of excitement that's just sprung into my tummy – excitement that I fight with everything I have to push away. Oh my God, what is wrong with me? It's like there's a little devil on my shoulder, one that's trying to tempt me into stupidity. *Go away!*

I quickly shake myself back into the real world, watching as Becker opens the door and immediately stands back. I don't have time to cover myself with the sheets. Winston bolts across the space and launches his stocky body onto the bed.

'Whoa!' I fall to my back and accept his attack, his tongue all over my face, his paws trampling over my naked body.

'Winston,' I laugh, trying to fight the burly beast off. 'Winston, get off me!'

I hear Becker laughing as he returns and joins us on the bed, pulling at Winston's collar. 'Come on, get down.'

But the bulldog is having none of it, and I recoil, as does Becker, when he growls and bares his teeth.

'Hey,' Becker warns, keeping his distance. 'Get off the bed.'

Woof!

'Don't shout at me,' Becker bellows back.

Woof!

'No!'

Woof!

'Forget it.' Becker bravely swoops in and grabs Winston's collar, then proceeds to wrestle him from the bed, while I sit up against the headboard, smiling my amusement. Winston puts up a good fight. He clearly hasn't learned who's boss, but he's quickly revealed that he's all bark and no bite. 'Didn't think so,' Becker grunts smugly, guiding him away from the bed. 'Now, sit.'

Winston looks to me, like he's searching for some guidance as to whether he should obey his owner. It cracks me up. 'Sit, boy,' I say, laughing, and he immediately does, making Becker bark his annoyance.

'You listen to me, you daft dog. Stay.' Becker's bare feet thump the floor as he makes his way back to the bed, constantly checking behind him to make sure his wayward pet is staying put. I bite my lip, watching Winston follow Becker's every pace with his droopy eyes, a definite curl of his jowly lip. And I stay still as Becker gets on the bed and inches towards me, keeping a close eye on his dog, worried that he might spring into psychotic mode at any moment. He takes my arm, and Winston lets out a low grumble.

'What are you doing?' I ask, putting up a little resistance when Becker tugs me towards him, still watching his dog.

'He needs to learn who you belong to.'

I pull back. 'Becker, this—'

'Jesus, princess, don't fight me. He'll think I'm attacking you.'

I stop struggling and allow Becker to pull me onto his lap, all under Winston's close observation. 'He looks pissed off,' I say, following Becker's slow approach as he blindly negotiates my legs around his waist, turning me into him so I'm straddling his lap. I lose my sight of Winston. I'm not cool with that at all, not when he's so . . . volatile.

Once Becker has me where he wants me, I glance over my shoulder and find Winston hasn't moved a muscle. 'Mine,' Becker declares crisply, skating his palms to my bum and squeezing. 'All of it, boy. Get used to it.'

Woof!

'Share?' He questions. 'No, I don't think so.'

Woof!

'I'll let you cuddle her,' he goes on, and I smile, totally endeared by the conversation he's having with his dog. 'But you will remember who she belongs to.'

Winston whimpers dejectedly, as if completely understanding what Becker is saying.

'You want a cuddle now?' he asks, and Winston releases another whimper, this one pleading. 'Come on then.' Becker pats the mattress next to us, and it takes Winston no time at all to catapult his heavy body up onto the bed. We jolt as a result of his landing, and I laugh, feeling his wet tongue attack my back.

'Hey,' Becker scolds sharply. 'I said you could cuddle her. I said nothing about kissing.'

I release Becker's shoulders and give Winston some fuss, scratching at his ears until he caves under the pleasure and collapses to his side beside us. 'You're so cute,' I coo.

'But not as cute as me, eh?'

Chuckling, I take my spare hand to Becker's head and muss up his hair before scratching behind his ear. 'Not as cute as you,'

I confirm, bringing the sweetest smile to his handsome face.

'I adore you, woman.' He hauls me forward and demonstrates how much, cuddling me fiercely. 'I fucking adore you.'

I smile into his shoulder, returning his clinch. 'Super,' I breathe, something catching my eye – something glimmering from Winston's collar. 'What's that?'

I sit up and reach forward, turning Winston's collar on his neck until Becker's mother's ring sparkles up at me.

Becker laughs and unfastens the buckle. 'Who put that there, boy?' he asks, but Winston just looks up through droopy eyes. I'm sure if dogs could shrug, he would. Becker fingers the ring for a few moments, lost in thought. Then he looks at me as he holds it out. 'Can I?' he asks nervously.

I say nothing, just nod and hold out my hand, letting him slide his grandmother's emerald ring back onto my finger.

Where it should be.

Chapter 31

It's the day of the annual Andelesea Gala. Things have been quiet around The Haven the past couple of days, the atmosphere heavy, and I've lost myself in work in an attempt to hide from it, despite it being Saturday. Gramps is on his feet, but Mrs Potts is keeping close by his side. His walking stick, however, isn't. One can only assume it's still hidden in the wall, and I've had to force myself to stop thinking about whether Becker knows where that hiding place is. The old man is quietly pensive. Ghosts are clearly back to haunt him. And Becker.

I've spent the past few hours in Becker's apartment, slowly getting ready. The winning dress is like a second skin, and the shoes comfier than the height of the heel would suggest. I glance down and smile at the nude Choos.

'Fuck . . . me . . .' A stunned voice hits me from behind, and I whirl around, finding Becker adorned in a black tuxedo, looking like he might have just fallen from Heaven. Good lord, he looks unfathomably handsome. And angelic. My Saint Sinner.

My fiancé.

He looks just about as perfect as perfect is possible. Gorgeous. The fact that his bow tie is simply hanging around his neck only adds to his already ridiculous sex appeal. Jesus, I could eat him alive.

Just like that time in the revolving door, he stands, stance wide, hands in his pockets, and accepts the close scrutiny that he's under. His good looks are dangerous on the best of days.

Tonight, in that tux, he's lethal. I won't be able to take my eyes off him all night.

Lifting my delighted gaze, I find his face. He still has his scruff, and his hair is a roughed-up mess atop his beautiful head. And his glasses . . .

I sigh happily and fall into a daze, mentally undressing him as I reach up and put my earring in. 'You look edible,' I confess, no holding back. My fiancé is plain fucking magnificent.

He says nothing and moseys over, his face straight, his eyes running up and down the blood-red dress. When he reaches me, I finish putting my earring in and let my arms fall to my side, returning the favour and standing quietly while he drinks me in. 'Are you attached to this dress?' he asks seriously, reaching forward and drawing a light line from my hip up to my breast.

I clamp my lips together to stop any tell-tale signs of want escaping.

'Princess?'

'Yes.' I push my answer out with some determined effort.

'Well, later it will be coming off quicker than abra-fucking-cadabra.'

I smile, fond memories of our first time together bombarding me. 'I look forward to it.'

He grins and reaches for my hand, taking a comfy grip. 'Ready?'

'You sure this isn't too much?' I indicate down my dress. 'Won't they all be in gowns?'

'You are not *they*. That's one of the reasons why I love you.' He points to my dress. 'This is you, and it is most definitely me, too.'

'Because you can access my arse.'

'Precisely. The fact you look like a savage beauty only makes it all the sweeter.' He whirls me around, and my back hits his chest with force. I gasp – part in shock, part in anticipation. His strong forearm rests on my belly and constricts, forcing me to him. Then his lips are at my ear. I can feel his mood pressed into my bottom. 'I feel it's only right that I tell you what I plan on doing to you later.' His palm meets the outside of my inner-thigh and starts a torturous climb up, making my whole body begins to pulse.

'What are you going to do?' My voice is jagged, broken by a craving that I'm unable to control. It's standard when his hands are all over me. When he's whispering in my ear. When he's simply close by.

'I'm going to fuck you.' He makes no bones about it, his hand reaching my knickers and cupping me possessively over the material. My arse pushes into his groin in a futile attempt to escape his touch. 'So fucking hard, you'll be seeing stars, princess.' He slips a finger past the seam of my knickers and releases a hot stream of air into my ear. 'Jesus, you're drenched.'

I sigh, eyes closed, body rolling.

He enters me slowly, deliberately, and circles his fingers expertly. I cry out, and he thrusts his groin into me. 'Who owns you, Eleanor?'

'No one,' I gasp, flexing my hips to meet his rotations.

He bites down on my ear, and I can feel him smiling against me. Then his fingers are gone, and it's all I can do not to scream my devastation. The hem of my dress is lifted quickly and a clean, precise palm collides with my arse.

'Fucking hell, Becker.' I jolt forward, and he catches me, twirling me around.

'I thought we agreed no knickers?' He dips and slowly drags them down my legs as I narrow my eyes on him.

'I don't remember agreeing.'

'Are you protesting?'

'Yes. It'll be . . . chilly.'

'On the contrary, it'll be very hot.' He grins as I lift each foot in turn and he casts them aside. Bloody hell, I must remember not to bend, sit, crouch.

He pulls my hem down, satisfied. 'Let's go.' He takes my hand and leads on, leaving me no option but to bury the craving he's triggered.

'Did you see your granddad?' I ask, brushing my hair from my face and patting at my damp cheeks.

'Yes.'

'And how is he?'

'Quiet.'

I glance up at Becker, seeing him focused forward, not a hint of his thoughts evident. I'm not sure whether to be worried or relieved by this. The showdown over the map has unsettled . . . everything.

When we arrive at my apartment block to pick up Lucy and Mark, I can't help but stare up at my window, lost in thought. I came to London a single woman and planned on keeping it that way. This apartment was my new home. In less than three months, I'm engaged and this place isn't my home any more. It's burning my brain trying to figure out how my life has turned around so quickly, and how I've lost my conscience, morals and sanity along the way. 'Still no idea on who broke into my apartment?'

Becker, too, looks up at the window. 'Whoever it was covered their tracks very well. Someone was looking for something.'

'Like what?'

He shrugs. 'Inside information on the Hunt Corporation, I guess. Everyone knows getting into The Haven is impossible.'

'I'm just glad they can't break into my mind.'

'People will try. Never forget that.'

I inwardly laugh. As if I could. 'It's got to be Wilson, hasn't it?'

'I would have guessed that, yes. But he's not smart enough to cover his tracks. He's sloppy.'

'Not smart enough? He stole an O'Keeffe in broad daylight.'

Becker looks at me out the corner of his eye, humming his agreement, as Lucy and Mark hop in, all excited. Our conversation is brought to an abrupt halt. 'Evening,' Lucy sings, getting comfy in the back.

I turn in my seat, finding my friend dressed in a lovely pink cocktail dress, with thin straps and a high neckline. 'Went for legs tonight, then?'

She glances down on a smile. 'I googled Andelesea. I'm guessing tits *and* legs wouldn't go down well. Though judging by the length of that red number, I shouldn't have worried.'

Becker laughs as I reach for my dress and wriggle it down my thighs.

'I wouldn't have complained,' Mark pipes in, grinning. He looks dapper in a black tux, too, though his bow tie is fastened neatly, and he's shaved, unlike Becker. He's also styled his hair, unlike Becker.

'You both look great,' I say, turning back in my seat as Becker slams the car into gear and shoots off down the road.

He looks up at the rear-view mirror. 'Are you going to behave tonight?' he asks Lucy.

'Hand on my heart.' She grins, and I turn into Becker.

'Are you?' I ask.

He chucks me a roguish smile. 'Why, princess. I'm a saint.'

Chapter 32

The huge elaborate mansion set in the middle of nowhere has the same effect on me it did the last time I was here, except it seems more foreboding in the dark, all lit up by floodlights. I shiver and peek up at all of the cherubs keeping watch as we roll slowly up the gravel driveway.

After a few noises of awe from the back passengers, we all get out, and Mark and Lucy gaze around in wonder. 'Wow,' Lucy breathes. 'This is some posh shit.'

I roll my eyes and accept Becker's hand, and he leads us up the endless steps, Lucy and Mark following. When we breach the grand entrance hall of Countryscape, I feel a very different atmosphere to the last time we were here. It's bursting at the seams with toffee-nosed aristocracy, all draped in ball gowns and tuxedos, sipping from cut-crystal champagne glasses. A woman in the corner is strumming a giant harp, providing soft, rhythmic music, and a waiter is hovering on the threshold of the doors, a tray resting on one palm, his spare arm folded neatly behind his back. I take a glass when he offers the tray, but Becker ignores him, strolling straight through the crowds. I check behind me for Lucy and Mark. Both have helped themselves to a glass of champagne, both gawping around the mansion with wonder in their eyes. I flick my head in indication for them to follow, stalling when Becker is intercepted by an old woman. Her royal blue gown is elaborate but stunning and her multi-coloured beaded purse a total colour-clash, but actually quite quirky. She looks familiar. Her harsh black bob, her feline features that suggest way too much sur—

I physically recoil. Oh my Lord, it's Lady Winchester!

'Becker.' Her eyes light up like diamonds.

'Lady Winchester.' Becker confirms my fear and slaps a smile on his face, greeting her politely. He takes her hand and kisses each of her taut cheeks. 'You look as ravishing as ever.'

She chuckles and gives him a playful knock of his arm. 'Nonsense. I look like my face has been run over by a bus.'

Lucy squawks loudly, nearly spraying the old lady with her champagne, and I give her a jab in the side with my elbow. 'Sorry,' she blurts.

'Don't be, lovely.' Lady Winchester brushes Lucy's rude gesture aside with ease. 'My endeavour to retain my youth has backfired on me.' She points to her chin, which I notice now is particularly hooked. 'My cheeks are stuffed with sacks of liquid, and I've had more stitches in my face than it would take to sew a leg on.'

Lucy and Mark laugh loudly, while I study Becker, trying to read the situation and his persona. He looks entirely comfortable.

'So, who are these fine young people?' she asks him, waving a bent finger at us.

Forced into pleasantries, Becker makes the introductions. 'This is Mark, Lucy, and Eleanor.' He waves a hand casually to each of us as he pulls his mobile from his inside pocket and frowns down at the screen. 'Excuse me a moment, Lady Winchester.' He strides off, answering the call, without another word or a second look at me, so he can't see my stunned expression. Who's that, and where is he going?

Lady Winchester gives all of us the once over with her sparkling eyes. 'Into threesomes?'

It's me coughing over my champagne this time. Did I hear her right?

'Don't look so shocked, kids,' she says off-hand. 'I might look like a train wreck, but I've still got the moves.' She winks, and Lucy and Mark fall apart, along with Lady Winchester, while I stare at her, shocked. 'Come, let me lavish you with tales of London in the sixties. I was a sex siren.' She beckons them into her personal space, and both of them go, fascinated.

I take their distraction as an opportunity to hunt down Becker, taking off in the direction in which he headed, and I soon find myself in the huge room where the auction was held, but instead of the rows and rows of chairs facing a rostrum, there are now round tables edged with chairs that have huge black silk bows fastened to the back. Each table is covered in blood-red organza, with black orchids arranged elaborately in tall glass vases, and the tableware – plates, bowls and napkins— are all black. Black and red. It's harsh but forgiving. It's sexy but tasteful. It's miles away from the originality of the mansion, but very much in keeping with the Heart of Hell, the giant ruby that's being showcased this evening. People are milling around, some already seated. I spot Becker at the bar.

'Haig,' he mutters to the barman as I join him. 'On the rocks.'

I place my glass down beside him. 'That woman. It's *the* Lady Winchester, isn't it? The one from the file at The Haven.'

'Yes,' he answers shortly, keeping his attention away from me. It's no wonder Becker made a sharp exit from her company. I'll be sure to steer clear of her for the rest of the evening. We can't be associated with people under investigation for forged art. Because, of course, my Becker is as straight-laced as they come.

The barman hands Becker his drink, and it's knocked back in one. He slams his glass down and holds onto it, his fingers white from his harsh grip. I eye him, seeing his breathing increasing, like he's getting more and more worked up. Something's not right. Who called him? What did they say?

'Tell me what's going on,' I demand, feeling a bit fretful.

'Why don't *you* tell *me*?' He looks at me, pure disdain

tarnishing his angel eyes. His lips twist, and he leans in as he reaches into his inside pocket. 'Why are you making calls to your ex?'

His question is a bolt out of the blue, and I am less than prepared for it. Fuck. 'It's not what you think. I was simp—' I stop abruptly. Wait a minute. 'How do you even know?'

He looks at me out the corner of his eye, and realisation slams into me.

'You've got my bloody phone bugged, haven't you?' I'm flummoxed. 'That was Percy on the phone giving you details of my recent calls.' What the fuck is he playing at?

'If you don't get the message across,' Becker ignores my accusation, his tone menacing, 'then I'm not opposed to doing it myself. I doubt I'll be as diplomatic as you.'

'What's that supposed to mean?'

'Do you still think of him?'

'Seriously?' I blurt, outraged. 'No, I don't.' What's the matter with him? 'I asked him to return the keys for my father's shop. That's all. I didn't think it was worth mentioning it because—'

'Because what?'

'This!' I snap, boring holes into Becker's profile with an angry gaze as he stares ahead. 'But it seems I didn't need to mention it, since you're fucking spying on me.'

'I'm not spying. I'm—'

'Do you trust me?' I ask calmly, though on the inside I'm raging. After everything he's put me through?

'I trust you. It's everyone else I don't trust.' He shoves his glass away. 'I haven't got time for this.' Taking the fresh glass being handed to him by the barman, he knocks back another Haig and slams his empty down.

'You haven't got time for this? You mean *us*?' I ask, prickling with irritation. 'Nice to know you're invested. Maybe I haven't got time to wrap my head around the *shit* you keep landing on me,' I seethe. 'I'm not hanging around to be accused of whatever your paranoid brain conjures up. Have a good night, Hunt.' I storm off, needing to get out of here before I swing at him. He hasn't got time for *this*? What, now or ever?

The arsehole.

Making my way from the room, I resist the urge to go back and slap his face. Then I wish I had, because someone else has just caught my eye. Someone I fucking hate. My hackles shoot up. I swallow down my growl of anger, my eyes drilling into Alexa's back as I force myself to continue on my way. My feet have become heavy, telling me that leaving Becker here would be a stupid move with her loitering around. Those long, skinny legs look poised and ready to wrap around a waist at any moment.

I bump into a chair, knocking it into the table. 'Shit,' I curse, ignoring all of the disapproving looks being thrown at me. 'Sorry.' I don't rush to put the chair back, and instead stumble my way towards the door, now set on finding the ladies and composing myself. I'm not leaving here with that floozy on the prowl.

My heels hit the mosaic tiles of the entrance hall, and I dip and weave through the scattered crowds, apologising constantly for bumping into people as I go.

Then I'm suddenly not moving any more. I yelp when something grabs my wrist and yanks me to a stop, nearly pulling my shoulder out of its socket, and before I register who, what and how, I'm being guided back through the crowds. Becker's unique smell invades my nose, his arm coiled around my waist. 'Get off me,' I spit, wriggling to free myself.

'Shut the fuck up, princess.'

'Go to hell.' My feet are barely touching the ground as he moves with conviction, looking straight ahead and ignoring all of the curious looks coming our way.

He heads to the right, taking us through a ballroom that has an orchestra set up in the corner, and then down a corridor. I'm pushed into the room, and the door slams loudly. I take a quick glimpse around to see where he's taken me. There's a fireplace, large and elaborate with stone carvings, and huge armchairs scattered here and there. It's a smoking room.

He points a finger in my face, snarling. 'There's not one thing in this world that pisses me off more than you.'

He's got a nerve. I've done nothing wrong. 'Back at ya, Hunt.' My eyes, damn my eyes, automatically drop to his crotch. I suck my lip between my teeth when I see he's solid. Because he finds himself hard, even when he's mad with me. I look up through my lashes at him, to the poised, het-up beast of a man before me.

Who's loaded to the eyeballs with craving.

He releases a strangled growl, and the next second, he lunges at me, tackling my body and virtually throwing me at the wall. My mouth is taken greedily, hard and forceful, and I accept it all, bringing my leg up, curling my thigh around his waist. But he pushes it down aggressively, biting on my lip. My protest gets no further than my throat before I'm spun around, pushed front-forward into the wall, meeting it with force. I feel his hand meet the back of my thigh, and I clench my eyes shut, knowing what's coming. He wrenches the hem of my dress up.

Smack!

I scream, a mixture of pain and delight, before he flings me back around and grabs me behind my thighs, hauling me up to his body. One hand holds me in place against the wall while his other makes quick work of freeing himself from the confines of his trousers.

Then on a carnal roar, he levels himself up and smashes into me, jerking me up the wall. The shock invasion has me slamming my head back, clawing at the material of his tuxedo at his shoulders.

Holding still, he pants into my neck, giving me a few needed moments to meld around his solid cock. 'Start breathing, princess,' he orders, slowly slipping free.

His command reminds me that I'm holding my breath, and I let it sail out, beginning to shake in his hold. I stare up at the ceiling, bracing myself for him. This is going to be hard. He reeks power, is leaking with a need to possess me. And then it happens. His first forceful slam into me. I find his neck to muffle my scream, not resisting the need to bite down onto his shoulder through his suit. He doesn't hold back, ignoring any pain I might be causing from my vicious bite. He repeatedly and forcefully plunges deeply, thrusting me up the wall on low grunts, hitting me harshly each and every time.

'Becker,' I yell, detecting the first sign of release on the horizon.

'Me too,' he confirms, increasing his pace to an almost unbearable level. There's no time between each of his drives to recover. The pain is constant, but so is the pleasure. His face remains submerged in my neck as he drives us to ultimate rapture. We're both just clinging onto each other, grappling, clumsy and chaotic.

My build up is gradual, almost annoyingly slow, but when it finally hits, it literally takes me out. 'Shit,' I choke into Becker's shoulder, solidifying in his hold as surges of pleasure rip through my body like an epic tornado. 'Jesus,' I breathe.

'Yeah,' he whispers, jacking me up the wall and joining me in my spiralling ecstasy, his cock swelling and pulsing, compressing against my internal walls.

I feel deliciously full and sated, still tingling, still constricting around him as I peel my eyes open and push my lips into his wet neck, sucking gently. But my contented attention is interrupted when something across the room catches my eye.

Alexa.

She's standing in the doorway, holding the handle. Watching us. I hold her eyes for an age, relishing in the desolation she's trying to hide, before slowly turning my attention back to Becker. I nuzzle into his cheek until he turns his face and lets me at his mouth. And I kiss him, slowly, lovingly and like he belongs to me. Because he does.

'I love you,' I mumble between rotations of my soft, swirling tongue, nibbling my way up his cheek.

'I love you more,' he breathes, and I smile sickly, letting him ravish me for a few, precious seconds. And when I look back to the door, Alexa is gone.

Becker exhales, releasing me and pushing my legs gently from his waist. I keep myself propped against the wall, pulling my dress down while he fastens himself quietly, thinking. When he's done, he looks up at me and catches my chin in his fingers, holding my face in place.

'For the record, there's nothing in this world I'm more invested in than you.' He lets his gaze plummet to the ground at his feet, and my muscles relax as I watch him thinking. 'I just worry about things. Like what if you suddenly realise that you can't handle me? My life, my ways, my need to make your arse sore because I love the thought of it burning from my touch.' He drags in air, wincing.

Just listen to him. Sure, but so unsure. I move forward, reaching for the waistband of his trousers and slipping my fingers past. I use it as leverage and pull him towards me, and our torsos meet. So do our lips. They just touch, but the sense of belonging doesn't feel any less potent than when we're eating each other alive.

'I want to tell you something,' he whispers.

My body locks up, instinctively going into protective mode. What else could there be? 'What?' I murmur reluctantly.

'I want to tell you about the moment I realised I was in love with you,' he says against my lips. I've withdrawn in surprise before I can stop myself, finding Becker smiling shyly, his whole body tense now, too. 'When you ran away from me, after you found out it was me who was in your ap—'

I raise a hand quickly, halting him, telling him silently that an elaboration on that particular time isn't necessary. He nods his understanding. 'I stood in the middle of the road in fucking agony. I tried to tell myself that the freezing cold was hurting me, but then I realised that I was hurting so much more than anything physical could inflict.' My heart melts, but I don't interrupt his flow. 'I knew I loved you at that point. It had to be love, because I know it's the only thing in this world that hurts so badly. When I lost my mum and dad, the pain paralysed me.' He clenches his eyes shut for a split second, his head tilting back. 'Jesus, Eleanor, I never wanted to feel like that again, and when you ran away, I did. And I realised, unlike my parents' death, it was my fault. I was inflicting the pain on myself.'

I move into him quickly and circle his waist, hugging him tightly. 'Stop it.' I order, feeling his arms come around me and cling on desperately. 'Just . . . stop.'

'No, you need to know, because I feel like I'm going fucking mad.'

'You're not going mad,' I placate him, doubting myself. I must be going mad, too. The things I know, the things I've accepted. I've surprised myself. No. Surprised is the wrong word. Shocked. I've shocked myself.

'I must be, Eleanor,' Becker says. 'I can't focus on much except you, and that's not wholly a good thing.'

'Why?' I try my best not to sound affronted. I can't focus on much either, but I've seen it as a good thing. Something so powerful, it helps accept all the other shit.

'Because I might get myself into trouble.'

This makes me smile. 'I feel the same,' I offer, hoping he appreciates that. Keeping my claws to myself is proving harder and harder.

Becker forces me away and holds me by my arms, gazing down at me. 'Are you going to stay now?' He pushes out his bottom lip cheekily.

'Pick up your lip. I'll stay.' He doesn't need to know that I spotted Alexa and changed my mind.

'Super.'

He takes my hand and leads on, and when we breach the entrance of the main room, I spy Lucy and Mark seated at a table, both laughing like drains.

Becker swings into gracious action, giving Mark a slap on the shoulder and Lucy a kiss on the cheek. He helps me to my seat next to Lucy before taking the one on the other side of Mark.

'You okay?' Lucy stops a waiter as he passes and grabs a glass of champagne, thrusting it at me. I'm eternally grateful. Accepting keenly, I savour the taste as I glance around, feeling an icy glare stabbing at my back, and though it's obvious *who* it's coming from, I can't see where *who* is hiding.

I sigh, rolling my shoulders as I lean back, but relaxing when I'm constantly on the lookout for Alexa isn't easy. She's made it clear what her game is. I'm mentally kitting myself out in body armour as I sit here stewing, set for battle. I peek around the room again.

'Who are you looking for?' Lucy asks, coming in closer, leaving the boys behind her chatting and laughing.

'Alexa.'

'Who's Alexa?'

'My equivalent of your printer-room girl. Except bitchier. And more conniving.'

'Oh,' she breathes, taking a glimpse round the room. 'Hey, is that her?'

'I don't know. I can't look.'

'Well, she's spitting nails this way, so I guess it is. Blonde, perfect legs.'

'That's her.'

'What is it with perfect fucking legs?' Lucy asks. 'I hate her.'

'Who is she with?'

'Mature woman. Red gown with fur.'

'That's the countess. Her aunt. Also a fan of Becker's.'

'Nice.' Lucy knocks my knee, turning into the table, and I join her, pushing back thoughts of Alexa and what game she's playing. 'It's a bit swanky, isn't it?' She lifts her glass and swishes her champagne, looking around.

'Yes, some seriously posh shit,' I quip, and she chuckles. 'Do you feel out of place?' I ask, hoping it's a big fat *yes*. I feel *really* out of place. I could do with a friend to join me there.

'Nah.' She downs her drink and moans her pleasure. 'These aristocratic humpty-dumpty pillocks don't intimidate me. Money can't buy you happiness, Eleanor. Under all of these couture dresses and precious gems are a bunch of unfulfilled miserable bitches.' She grins. 'I wish I had gone for tits *and* legs.'

I laugh loudly and chink my glass with her empty. I'm so glad she's here keeping me grounded.

Chapter 33

Dinner is pleasant. We share a table with some people who Becker knows through business – more hoity-toity old farts – and chat enthusiastically about the trade. After we eat, Mark and Lucy excuse themselves to go explore Countryscape, and Becker shifts across to Lucy's chair. I watch him lower to the seat, smiling when I notice his bow tie is uneven, one side hanging longer than the other. I reach over and straighten it up for him.

Taking my hands from his neck, he brings them to his lap and brushes thoughtfully over my skin with his thumbs.

'This isn't you,' I say quietly, shuffling my chair in to get closer to him. 'All of the snobbish people, the noses in the air, the showiness. It's not you.'

He smiles down at my hands, and then slowly lifts his gaze to mine. His hazel orbs are shining so brightly past the lenses of his glasses. 'You've called me a holier-than-thou twat plenty of times, princess.' He brings my hands to his mouth and kisses them tenderly. 'But I'll never be holier than thou.'

'You're becoming quite the romantic, Saint Becker.'

'Shhhh,' he hushes me, his lips full and kissable. 'Don't tell anyone.' Leaning in, he nips at my cheek before encouraging me to stand. 'We need to make pleasantries with someone,' he says, leading me from the table.

'Who?' I don't like the sorry look he points at me. Not at all.

'She's been trying to collar me all evening.'

I look up and see the dreaded countess but note just as

quickly that Alexa is nowhere in sight. It's a mild consolation. 'Oh no,' I grumble.

'She's bought the Rembrandt for thirty-five million. A few gracious words are a small price.'

'Yes, exactly. She's bought it. Job done.'

'The money isn't in the bank yet.'

I could do with an iron to smooth out the creases on my screwed-up face. Her smile is getting wider and wider as we get closer and closer, and my hand is constricting harder and harder around Becker's.

'Becker, darling.' She throws her arms out, beckoning him into her embrace, and I slap on an over-the-top smile, squeezing Becker's hand tighter when he flexes his fingers to release me. He casts a questioning look at me and virtually yanks himself free.

'Lady Finsbury,' he says, presenting his cheek for her to kiss. 'Very good to see you.'

'And you.' She holds him by the biceps. I want to immediately disinfect him. 'I missed you.' She puckers her lips, showing a hint of a coy smile.

'I left you in capable hands.' He gently breaks away from her. 'I know Eleanor looked after you.' Reaching back, he grabs my wrist and pulls me forwards, as if calling for reinforcements. I should make him deal with her unbearable snooty arse alone. She's positively unbearable. My face is going to split if I have to uphold this ridiculously stretched smile any longer.

The countess gives me the once over with eyes full of contempt. 'I hear no one's hands are as capable as yours, Becker.'

My stomach twists violently, my mind begging me to run before I make a spectacle of myself. God help me before I shred her. 'Pleasure to see you again, Lady Finsbury.'

She sniffs, obviously disagreeing, and looks back to Becker. Her smile returns immediately. 'Have you seen Alexa? She's looking radiant this evening.'

I lock my lips tightly shut and mentally plead for Becker to remove me from this god-awful situation. Alexa didn't look so radiant when I caught her watching Becker fuck me against the wall. The thought brings a secret smile to my face.

'I'll be sure to say hello,' Becker assures her, and I prod him in the arm discreetly. He looks to me, showing hints of a knowing smile. 'I'll leave you ladies to talk for a few moments.'

What?

He backs away, either oblivious to my panicked eyes or just plain ignoring them. I fear it's the latter. 'Excuse me.' He flashes his phone at me and turns, striding across the room and disappearing into the crowd. *The fucker.* And who the hell is calling him now?

'So, Alexa tells me you're Becker's . . .' The countess hums to herself for a few moments, purposely waiting for me to give her my attention. Stupidly, I do. She has a cunning glint in her eyes. 'Skivvy,' she finishes.

'Lovely talking to you,' I blurt out, sounding as insincere as I intended. I spin and make off before I lose control of my forced courtesy. I'm going to kill him.

I hear the old bat call to me as I flee, but I don't care how rude I appear. I'm not hanging around to be insulted – not by her, not by her niece, not by anyone. I shake off the lingering unpleasant presence of the countess, shuddering as I make my way through the tables. Quite pathetically, I'm playing out a scene in my head, one where I'm telling her exactly what I think of her, no holding back. My language is vulgar . . . but I keep it contained in my mind. I have to remember: the money isn't in the bank yet.

Breaking free of the huge room, I come to an abrupt stop when it occurs to me that Becker gave me no hint where he would be. I scan the gatherings of people before me, reaching up on tiptoes to try and spot him. My search turns up no results, so I head over to the hall that leads to the smoking room, hearing the orchestra playing a dramatic version of 'Cry Me a River'. I smile when I see Mark and Lucy on the dance floor.

'May I have this dance?' A palm rests on my bare arm, and my body instantly tightens as my eyes drop to the hand and stares. 'Please?'

I slowly turn. 'Brent.' I inhale his name on a contained panicked gasp, my eyes darting past him. If anything was to pull Becker from wherever he's hiding, this man would be it. Where is he?

'Lost someone?' he asks, following the direction of my searching eyes.

'No.' I force the trepidation from my tone as I step away, disconnecting his hand from my arm. I think I've done well in my endeavour to appear cool . . . until he gives me a telling smirk. Victorious.

'Tell me.' He steps forward but hesitates when I instinctively move away. I should *not* be displaying any apprehension. 'Because I'm so very curious,' he muses.

I don't like where this conversation is heading. 'What?' My feet take me back with no instruction, and I run a quick scan of the area again, searching for Becker. Again nothing. *Damn it, where is he?*

Brent arches an amused eyebrow. He's getting a sick thrill out of my discomfort. 'Did you play any part in ripping me off with the fake Michelangelo?'

My heart, my lungs, my kidneys – every internal organ, in fact – drops into my heels. *Oh . . . fuck . . .*

I want to believe I misheard him, but the anger that's looming behind his clear eyes tells me I heard him just fine. I've lost the ability to function, resulting in me standing before him looking as guilty as I am, while my mind becomes more knotted with each second that I'm regarded with suspicious eyes. 'You can't prove it,' I whisper, my heart working its way back up from my shoes, bypassing my chest, and settling in my throat.

A flash of surprise flies across his face. 'So I need to prove it?'

Shit...

Oh...shit...

My eyes are wide, my body still. I can't control any of my evident shock.

'Good God,' Brent laughs, his disbelief evident. 'He really does have you wrapped around his finger.'

I nail my mouth shut. *Fuck!*

Brent continues to watch me wilt under the pressure, seeming highly entertained. 'I only had Alexa's word. Seems now I have yours, too.'

I'm in all kinds of panic, but amid it, I manage to wonder how the hell Alexa knows. 'Did you break into my apartment?' I'm on the offensive. That's it now. All the stops have been pulled out. I know Becker said he's not smart enough, but this man stole an O'Keeffe, for Christ's sake. So what makes Becker so sure?

Brent's head lowers slightly, making his Roman nose seem longer, and the light catches the grey flecks in his hair, making them shine. 'You can't prove it,' he whispers, making my lungs shrink.

'Why?' I breathe, fighting my vibrating nerves.

'Becker has never been so possessive over a woman,' he says tactically, reminding me of my fiancé's Lothario ways. 'I'm playing his game, Eleanor.'

'There is no game,' I impulsively fire in return.

'There's always a game.' He swoops in, surprising me, and wraps an arm around my waist, pulling me into his chest. Before I can muster any fight, we're on the dance floor, locked together, my feet following Brent's. 'And it's tradition for me to play along,' he whispers in my ear.

'Get off me, Brent.'

'Tell me what you know,' he demands quietly. 'How did he pull it off?'

'I don't know anything,' I grind, stiff as a board against him, moving without thinking, aware of the people around us. My attempts to break away from him are futile. 'Let me go,' I grate, placing my palms on his shoulders and pushing into him. I only manage to separate us a few inches before I'm forced back.

Brent rests his square jaw on the side of my head, getting too comfortable. My eyes frantically search for Becker again. 'You won't find him.' He twirls us round on a fake, happy laugh. 'I believe he and Alexa have unfinished business.'

That's it. I throw everything I have into getting him away from me, not caring any more if it attracts attention. 'Get your filthy hands off of me.'

He releases me, a sick smile on his face, and my hands twitch at my sides, desperate to slap him. I back away, trying to control the shakes that I've developed, the swirl of emotion – the anger, the uncertainty, the fear – all mixing up in my hollow torso, making me feel so very unstable. 'Remember, Eleanor,' he reaches up and pats the shoulder of his tux. 'I'm always a shoulder to cry on when he's got what he's wanted from you and casts you aside. Because he will.'

'No, he won't.'

Brent looks at me like he feels sorry for me, and it's all I can do not to scream that he's wrong. 'You'll come to your senses, I'm sure.'

My teeth clamp down together, grinding as I lift my hand, revealing my ring. Brent's eyes bug. 'Yes, he really does have me wrapped around his finger.' I gaze down at Becker's grandmother's emerald for a few moments, giving Brent time to absorb it, too. Then I return my eyes to his stunned expression and wait for him to look at me. When he does, I smile curtly. 'My senses have never left me, Mr Wilson. That's why I'm with Becker and not with you.' I spin and make off. My only aim now is to find Becker, and I know exactly where I'm going before my brain registers my route. It's the only quiet place in

Countryscape that I've encountered since I've been here. The place where she watched Becker fuck me against the wall.

The smoking room.

I hurry through the crowds and find myself at the door, not recalling any part of my journey here. My mind is being blitzed by my worries. It was him. He was in my apartment, and I need to find Becker to tell him.

Taking the handle of the door, I push my way in, my heart racing.

And freeze.

She's in her underwear, pulling at Becker's jacket, her hands and mouth everywhere. I want to scream, make my presence known, but everything has ceased functioning. Except my eyes. And they're being tortured by the sight before me, her mouth on Becker's, their bodies a mess of tangled limbs and frantic ...

Fighting?

'Get the fuck off of me, you crazy cow,' Becker seethes.

Alexa stumbles back on her heels from the force of his shove, grabbing a nearby table to steady herself. But she quickly regains her composure and goes at him again, her hands trying to cup his face. 'Don't try to fight it, Becker.' Her signature purr is replaced with desperation. 'We were so good together.'

He fights her off. 'Get over yourself, Alexa. What part of "I'm a taken man" don't you understand?'

The moment she realises she's fighting a losing battle is obvious because her shoulders roll and her chin raises. 'Thirty-five million,' she sniffs, simple as that.

Is she bribing him? My laugh comes out on a tiny exhale on air, but however quiet the sound, it still makes my presence known. Alexa and Becker both swing towards me – Becker looking horrified, Alexa looking like she could charge me down at any moment. Quite frankly, I feel vulnerable and, annoyingly, like an intruder.

'Oh, it's the skivvy,' she snickers, looking at me like I could be something that Winston evacuated from his arse. Yes, it riles me beyond comprehension, but her sudden defensiveness holds me intrigued. I want to know what comes next. More scathing words? More looks of contempt? Standing on the sideline unnoticed, my mind on the drag, trying to process what I was seeing, was the best thing that could have happened. My delayed response to what I was faced with moments ago means I got the full show, including the spectacular ending. Yet my satisfaction at witnessing Becker reject her so harshly aside, I'm still mad with him for deserting me with the countess, which resulted in me having to endure an awful confrontation with Brent. The fact that I've pretty much dropped Becker in it by confirming Brent's suspicions about the fake sculpture isn't featuring in my tatty mind right now.

Dangerous fury roots itself deep and starts a tormenting swirl in my gut. I should unleash it. But instead I do the safest thing for all of us. I turn and walk out.

'Whoa!' Becker has me prisoner in his arms before I make it five paces.

'You're an idiot!' I spit, losing my reason and flipping out in his arms, having a vain wriggle.

'Yeah, yeah,' he breathes, carting me back into the smoking room. 'Tell me something I don't know.' I'm plonked on my feet before he strides over to Alexa, calm as can be, snatches up her clothes, and then takes her arm. 'Out.'

'You can't tell me what to do,' she protests, stumbling alongside him. 'Thirty-five million!'

Becker more or less tosses her out the door, followed by her clothes, and slams it shut behind her. 'Fucking hassle,' he grunts, striding over to the huge fireplace as he rifles through his pocket. He takes something out and faffs for a few moments, before bringing something to his lips. I catch his profile . . .

With a cigarette hanging out of his mouth.

What?

He smokes? Once again, I'm rendered incapable of speech. I can only watch as he lights up and pulls the longest drag, his head tilting back, lengthening his stubbled throat. Then the smoke comes billowing out along with a groan of pleasure. 'Fuck, that's good.'

'You smoke?' I ask, and my question knocks him out of his euphoria and has him looking down at the white stick sitting lightly between his fingers. 'Not for years.' He frowns on a cute pout.

'Then why now?'

'Stress,' he declares, taking another pull.

I rush over and snatch it from his fingers, stubbing it out in a nearby ashtray. 'It doesn't suit you.'

He collapses into a chair and rests his head back. He really does look stressed. 'For fuck's sake,' he says to the ceiling, reaching under his glasses and rubbing at his eyes.

I march over and put myself in front of him. 'What the hell was that all about?' I point to the door, where I expect Alexa is pulling on her clothes beyond.

'A hassle. That's what. I needed somewhere quiet to make a call. She followed me.'

I laugh sardonically. I'm pissed off with him, but I'm also realistic. His hassle isn't nearly as big as mine. 'I've had a bit of a hassle myself.'

He raises a worried eyebrow. 'Like what?'

'Like Brent.'

'Wilson,' Becker growls. 'He's here?'

'Yes, he's here.'

'What did he want?' His lip twitches, threatening to break into a snarl.

I'm suddenly too scared to tell Becker, for then I have to tell him that Brent got what he wanted. Namely, confirmation of Alexa's claim. But it takes two seconds flat to weigh up my options . . . because I really only have one. Tell. 'He knows the sculpture is a fake.'

Becker's eyes bug. 'How?'

'I don't know.' *Because I told him!* 'He mentioned something about Alexa telling him.'

'Again, how?'

'Do I look like a fucking psychic?'

He ignores my sarcasm and falls into thought, looking past me. He has plenty to think about, that's for sure.

'It was definitely him who broke into my apartment.'

'He told you?' He looks surprised. No . . . he looks angry.

We're interrupted when the door swings open and Alexa presents herself, now fully dressed. 'You've just lost thirty-five million,' she taunts, landing me with a cold look.

Becker's up from his chair like lightning, marching towards her, and Alexa steps back, wary. He gets right up in her face. 'You been telling Wilson stories, Alexa?'

'Don't try to deny it.' She raises her chin. If it wasn't for the minuscule slice of doubt in her tone, she'd appear totally composed and confident. Her body language is screaming supremacy, but that quiver in her voice floors her false façade. 'I heard you,' she goes on, looking between us. 'After the auction in the entrance hall.'

Flashbacks of the occasion she's referring to blitz my mind – the moment when Becker, looking confusingly happy after losing in the bidding war, told me Brent had bought a fake. She was there? Listening? *Oh dear God!* But I'm mindful that although she knows the sculpture is fake, she doesn't know who sculpted it. And she mustn't. Becker having secret knowledge of a suspected forgery and not voicing it would be seriously frowned upon in the antiquing and art world. She knows that, and it's why she's here. But anyone knowing he crafted that forgery would cause a scandal of colossal proportions, would have him thrown in jail. It would ruin Becker, as well as accelerate the feud between him and Brent. That can't happen. They're already vying for each other's blood.

Flicking a glance across to Becker, I can tell he's on the same wavelength as me. She knows something, but she doesn't know everything.

'What's your game, Alexa?' I ask. 'What do you want? Becker in return for your silence?'

'He'll get bored of you soon enough,' she sniffs, 'Do you honestly think he'll settle for a skivvy when he can have this?' She indicates her long, lithe body.

'You . . .' I move forward threateningly, set on ripping her head off her shoulders.

But Becker catches me before my claws make it to her. 'Easy.'

'She's asking for it!' I shout, pushing him off me.

'Eleanor,' Becker yells, losing his patience. 'Nothing she can say will make any difference.' He grabs my hand and yanks it up, pointing to my ring. 'No difference, Eleanor.'

I snap my mouth shut, reading his thoughts as he raises his eyebrows, warning me to leave it there. I look at Alexa, seeing her displaying all the signs of shock I would expect. If she didn't get the message after watching Becker screw me blind, then she has now.

'I'll tell—'

'Tell who, Alexa?' Becker snaps impatiently. 'You knew about the fake, too. And just like me, you said fuck all. That makes you just as guilty as me.'

Her eyes widen, the reality hitting home. 'But you bid on it. Pushed the price up.'

Becker smiles, bright and happy. 'Why, Alexa,' he croons sweetly. 'That's because I thought it was real.' His expression straightens into a deadly serious one, as horror washes over Alexa's. 'I'm a respected dealer. Wouldn't dream of condoning a fake. You are nothing more than a scorned ex-lover looking for revenge.' Becker squeezes my hand, almost too tightly. 'Come on, princess. Let's get out of here. I'm beginning to itch.'

'Excuse me?' Alexa cries, outraged.

Flexing his fingers to get a good, solid hold of me, he leads me out, purposely taking a wide berth around Alexa in a further silent insult. 'Well, that was interesting,' he muses as we stride down the corridor, peeking down at me. 'I feel like I need fumigating.'

I manage to laugh past my easing rage. 'I think you've just lost thirty-five million.'

'Better than losing you,' he replies simply, giving my hand a squeeze.

That's sweet. So sweet. I'm costing this man a fortune. But . . .

'Aren't you worried?' I ask. 'About Brent knowing?'

'No. He'd never share his acquisition of a fake and lose face. His ego's far too big. But I can guarantee that he'll be hell-bent on getting revenge.' He looks down at me. 'And he knows my one and only weakness now.' Becker smiles mildly, though it's tinged with worry. 'I can also guarantee that he'll be hell-bent on finding the real *Head of a Faun*.'

'So he can replace the fake?' I ask.

'And then no one will ever need to know the dickhead paid fifty million for a forgery.'

Becker stares forward as we wander away from the smoking room, and I can virtually see his mind racing. He's right. Brent will now be going all out to find the real *Head of a Faun*.

And I wonder . . .

Does this change Becker's resolute vow to abandon his mission to find it himself?

Chapter 34

Becker glances down at his antique Rolex as we arrive in the grand entrance hall of Countryscape. 'Time to show you the Heart of Hell.'

'Sounds ominous.' I shudder as we pass through the crowds, and as soon as we enter the gallery, I note firstly how busy the walls are – papered in detailed print with gold-gilded framed portraits at every turn. The edges of the room are lined in roll-back day couches, all with carved wooden legs, all uphol-stered in garish velvets, and a mammoth rug covers virtually the whole floor space, leaving only a slither of the original wooden planks exposed around the circumference of the room.

And in the centre of the rug, flanked by two mean-looking security guards, is a glass cabinet containing the Heart of Hell. Even from the other side of the room I can see the shards of light reflecting off the glass from the precious gem, and despite there being scores of people scattered around admiring the ruby, it's quiet, just a light buzz of chit-chat.

Once Becker has led me to the front of the crowds and I catch my first peek, my breath is robbed from me. 'Oh my God,' I breathe, feeling like I'm immediately falling under its spell.

'Quite something, isn't it?'

'It's beautiful.' I can see now where its name comes from. The fiery splinters of red lights hitting the surrounding glass are breath-taking. I'm unable to rip my eyes away.

Becker's front meets my back, his mouth coming close to my ear. 'You're giving that beautiful red stone a run for its money.'

I smile, spotting a man on the other side of the cabinet, looking at the gem, as awestruck as everyone else in the room. 'Who is he?'

'He's the curator of PGS.'

Of course. The Precious Gem Society. I shake my head, my enchanted gaze falling back to the ruby.

'Listen.' Becker reaches around me and takes my chin lightly, lifting my head to look at the curator, like he can sense my struggle to snap out of my trance. 'It's very interesting.'

The curator coughs, making his intention to begin known, then waits patiently for complete silence. 'Good evening, ladies and gentlemen,' he begins, nodding politely to us all. 'And what a wonderful evening it is for us very lucky people.' He swoops a hand out to the cabinet, and every head in the room follows it, a Mexican wave of turns. 'The Heart of Hell, named by its discoverer, J.P. Randel, when he discovered it in Burma, June 1939. Until now, that is all we've known of the elusive gem. J.P. Randel kept it in his private collection for eighty years, wickedly denying us the pleasure of just a mere peek.' He laughs, as does the rest of the audience. 'Which begged the question whether the gem existed at all. There have been tales from his trip companions, as well as some cagey replies from experts in the precious-stone community, but nothing concrete – no sight, no picture, no word. Until now.' The crowd give a light round of applause, welcoming the gem, before quieting down and letting the curator go on. '543.6 carats, raw, rough and unset. The Heart of Hell not only gets its name because of the fire-red beauty and heart-like shape, but because J.P. claimed to have dug so deep, he swore he was only a few more shovels away from the devil himself.'

I listen, fascinated. I've never been so rapt by something.

'There's a waiter. Would you like a drink, princess?' Becker whispers, not even the beauty of *him* pulling my attention from the sparkling gem. I nod, hearing him laugh under his breath a little, amused by my mesmerised state. 'Don't move.' I feel him break away from my body, resulting in a slight shift of position so I can stand on my own two feet.

'How much is it worth?' A lady opposite me asks, a coy smile on her face.

The curator laughs, like he fully expected the question. 'Lady Seagrave,' he begins, polite and smiley. 'It is impossible to set a value on such a treasure.'

'*Everything* has a value,' she argues playfully, increasing the curator's amusement.

'Its rarity and beauty, not forgetting its story, makes it more desirable, and the more desirable, the more demand there is for it. And we all know that more demand spikes even *more* demand.' There are many huffs of agreement. 'This essentially makes it impossible to value.'

'I'll give you ten million,' Lady Seagrave shouts, spiking laughter in the room.

'Fifteen!' A tall man to her side declares.

The curator clenches his belly in amusement. 'And there we have it.'

I smile and flick my eyes past him when something catches my eye.

And my stomach instantly twists.

Brent smiles cunningly, all kinds of smugness evident on his face, and I quickly look away, rooting my gaze on the precious stone. But I can't hear the words of the curator any more. All I can hear is my pulse pounding in my ears.

I look over my shoulder, searching for Becker. I spot him lifting two glasses of champagne off a waiter's tray. My racing hearts calms, relieved to know he's close by.

Then the room plunges into darkness.

I gasp, blinking repeatedly, momentarily panicked that there's something wrong with my eyesight, but then the shrill gasps of my fellow observers assure me otherwise.

'Darn power cut,' someone says. 'Did the Masons pay the electricity bill?'

Panicked shrieks are replaced with laughter.

'Someone get the emergency generators going.'

I force myself to remain still, preventing the risk of bumping into anything or anyone, but it doesn't stop people from bumping into me. 'Ouch,' I hiss when a heel of a stiletto stabs the top of my foot. People scuffle and curse around me, knocking into me, hindering my attempts to remain still until they sort out the generators. 'For God's sake,' I mutter, shaking off a hand that grabs me for support.

'You're coming with me.' Brent's voice is close, and it flattens my plan to remain calm. His cold hand turns my blood to ice, and he starts pulling me from the room. 'Don't fight with me,' he says, increasing his grip. 'I don't want you to get hurt.'

My panic flares. It's dark. No one can see me, most importantly Becker. I'll be taken with no evidence of where or by who. 'Let go of me,' I yell, digging my heels in, making it as difficult as possible for him to move me. I just need to hold on until we have light again. Yet Brent is strong and no matter how hard I try, I can't stop him. So I yell some more, but my desperate cries don't even dent the noise around me. My stomach has worked its way up to my mouth, and I start to claw at his hand on my arm, fighting and struggling, but my feet continue to stumble forward, my shoulders being barged as I'm hauled through the darkness. All I can hear are Becker's suspicions of the Wilsons' involvement in his parents' deaths. All I can see is Brent's face when understanding of my deep involvement in Becker's world descended on him. My breathing becomes short and fast as panic truly grips me.

What's he going to do? Where is he taking me?

'You motherfucker.' Becker's voice penetrates my eardrums, followed by the cutting smash of glass shattering at my feet. I'm suddenly yanked from Brent's hold and shoved precisely and delicately aside, and then I hear a roar of anger, followed by the harsh sound of a fist meeting a face.

I jump back as the lights spring on and flood the room with a bright glare, and once my vision has cleared, I find Brent on the floor holding his jaw and Becker looming over him, shaking his fist. I expect Becker to join him on the ground and beat him to a pulp at any moment; he looks spun up with anger, but instead, surprisingly, he grabs my hand and pulls me through the crowds urgently.

Shouting erupts from behind, and I look back on a frown to see a bottleneck of panicked people at the entrance of the showing room. The lights are on. Why the sudden increase of panic and noise?

I see Lucy emerge from the ballroom looking alarmed and Mark looking confused by the pandemonium. He spots me being urgently guided away. 'Wait up!' he calls, taking Lucy's hand and pulling her along behind him. I can't wait up; Becker is determinedly pulling me through Countryscape, so I wave my arm for them to follow us instead. I catch Brent struggling up from the floor. His eyes land on mine and hold as he brushes his tux down, his grey hair in disarray as he glares at us. And for the first time, I see violence on his face. He looks positively . . . murderous.

Good God.

I return my focus forward, frightened by the intent in his eyes. 'Becker, slow down,' I pant, my feet working faster than is safe in my heels. Just like the other time I've been to Countryscape, I'm running scared. Becker takes the stairs two at a time, peeking over his shoulder every now and then to check I'm there. Or check I'm upright. I get the feeling his urgency might have something to do with his fear of seriously damaging Brent should we stick around. I can only commend his control, because if I were to hedge my bets, I would have put my life on Becker beating him black and blue. Brent got off lightly.

Once we land at the bottom of the stone stairs, Becker skids to a stop on the gravel and whirls around to face me. His hands rest on my shoulders, his eyes run a quick check of my face before dropping down my body, and his expression twists with worry. 'Are you okay?' he asks, genuine anxiety lacing his tone.

'I'm fine.' I find myself assuring him when I'm not fine at all. I feel better now Becker has me, but my mind keeps returning to the rampant thoughts bombarding my mind when Brent was trying to remove me from Countryscape. Where the hell was he going to take me? What was he going to do?

Becker wastes no time getting us on our way again, and as soon as we reach his car, he opens the door and tries to push me down into the seat. 'Lucy and Mark,' I remind him, trying to spot my friends. 'We can't just leave them.'

Becker looks back, just as they appear out of the doors of Countryscape. He turns back towards me. 'What happened?' he asks, reaching up to take off his glasses and rubbing at his eyes before opening them.

'I don't know,' I admit. 'One minute I was happily listening to the story behind the Heart of Hell, and the next minute the lights went out and someone grabbed me.'

Becker's nostrils flare dangerously, and he glances to the side when we're joined by Mark and Lucy. 'What's going on?' Lucy asks.

'Nothing,' Becker and I both answer in unison.

'Get in,' Becker says, opening the back door. 'We'll be two secs.' He pulls me away from the car, putting distance between us and my friends. His anger has faded, but his concern is all too evident. 'You sure you're okay?'

'Yes,' I assure him, seeing the stress and worry on his face. 'Why did he do that? What was he planning on doing, kidnapping me and demanding a one-hundred-and-fifty-million-pound ransom?' I joke, laughing, trying to ease Becker up a bit. But I stop the moment I realise he isn't joining me in my amusement.

'Why aren't you laughing?' It's a rhetorical question. I know why, and it scares the shit out of me. The Hunt Legacy isn't a story any more. It's my reality. 'You don't think he'd—'

'He's his father's son.' The regret pouring from Becker makes me worry for different reasons – reasons other than Brent using me against Becker in some way. I can see clear as day what Becker is thinking. He's thinking how he regrets putting me at risk, for bringing me into his world.

'Don't you say it,' I warn, stepping back, reading his mind too clearly. 'Don't you dare, Becker Hunt.'

'This is why I'm better off alone, Eleanor.'

'Shhhh!' I slam my finger over my lips, my sexy shush not so sexy, more psychotic. I'm shaking my head, too, giving myself a headache. 'No,' I affirm.

His eyes drop to the gravel, and his head goes limp, his chin hitting his chest. 'Fucking hell,' he curses quietly. Then his arm comes out and he points to the car, keeping his eyes down. 'Get in.'

I do as I'm told immediately, afraid to push his buttons. I'm not stupid. As I slip into the car and get comfortable, I reluctantly accept that Brent isn't going to let go. And I accept that despite grasping the gravity of it all, I've underestimated Becker's enemy. How could I have been so stupid?

I get the feeling that the war has only just begun.

Chapter 35

Back at The Haven after dropping Lucy and Mark home, the need for safety and security is once again dominating me as Becker collects me from the car. 'I need to check on Gramps,' he says, turning a kiss onto my forehead. 'See you upstairs?'

'I'll be in the kitchen,' I tell him. 'I need some water.'

'Okay.' He heads for his granddad's suite and I make my way to the kitchen.

As soon as I open the door, I'm ambushed by a very excitable Winston. 'You should be asleep,' I say, indulging his demand for attention for a few moments before throwing my purse onto the worktop and making my way to the fridge to get some water. But Winston's high-pitched whine pulls me to a stop, and I glance back to see him circling by the kitchen door. 'You need a wee?' I ask, as he continues chasing his tail. Desperately, by the looks of things. I kick my shoes off and rush for the door, hearing my phone ringing as I do. 'Damn.' I divert quickly and grab it from my purse, before I make my way to the courtyard, seeing Lucy's number on the screen. 'Hey,' I say as I weave through the Grand Hall.

'Eleanor', Lucy says, sounding urgent.

'Everything okay?' I carry on my way when Winston starts with the circling again. Pushing the doors into the courtyard open, I'm immediately hit with the cold night-time air. I shiver and Winston bolts past my legs, his nose hitting the floor in search of a suitable place to pee. I perch on the side of the fountain as I watch him cock his leg, his body visibly shaking as he relieves himself.

'Yeah, fine. We thought we'd catch a bit of TV before hitting the sack,' she says, and I frown for two reasons. One, because Winston is still peeing like a cart horse, and two, because Lucy can't have called me just to tell me that.

'Right . . .'The word streams out over a few seconds.

'And what do we see?'

Is that a genuine question? 'I don't know, what do you see?'

'The fucking ruby!'

'Oh,' I laugh. 'So it made the news?'

'Because it's been fucking stolen.'

I'm on my feet in a heartbeat 'What?'

'Stolen, Eleanor.'

My mind just officially exploded, scattering flashbacks of my evening everywhere – the blackout, the ruby, the chaos as Becker hauled me out of Countryscape. 'And it's on the news?'

'Yes! We were there on the night of a heist that's going to go down in fucking history.' Lucy sounds almost star-struck, while I'm just . . . struck.

'Wow.'

'Wow? Is that all you've got to say?' She sighs. 'Fine, Mark and I will be excited alone. Speak later.'

The line goes dead, and I remain unmoving, my phone suspended at my ear, as my mind goes into overdrive. 'Stolen?' I ask myself, seeing the two big fellows flanking the cabinet, plus all the cameras dotted around Countryscape. It would be impossible. I start laughing at the absurdity, then I sharply stop. Stolen. I begin to circle on the spot as my phone drops slowly to my side, my eyes taking in the perfection of Becker's sanctuary. The pure, peaceful place that's now my home. The place that harbours so many secrets. I should be tracking Becker down and sharing this mammoth news. I should be running to find him. But something is telling me that this won't be news to him. Something too loud to ignore. And this time, I know it can't be Brent.

My muscles come to life and lead me out of the courtyard, Winston hot on my heels. I'm on a mission and though my body seems perfectly set on where it's heading, my head isn't quite keeping up. My thoughts are a mish-mash of . . . all kinds of wild things. Unbelievable things.

Weaving through the stock of the Grand Hall, I let myself into the main hub of The Haven and I'm at the library a few seconds later. Winston goes to make himself comfortable on one of the chesterfield couches, and I go straight to the book-shelf that's been a source of fascination since I discovered the secret compartment.

I reach between the shelves, I feel, I find, and I pull. Then I stand back and wait for the compartment to reveal itself.

The clicking of some mechanisms, the slow creaking of wood shifting, the extended time it takes . . .

It's like a scene from a movie, one of those pinnacle moments when everyone is holding their breath, when everyone knows something monumental is about to be revealed. I don't realise that I'm holding mine until my lungs start screaming. 'Oh . . . my . . . God . . .' I wheeze, my hands coming up to my face and covering my mouth, almost as if I'm preparing to hold back the gasp of shock that I think might be coming.

Everything is functioning of its own accord, on autopilot, and I'm just going with it, not resisting, not fighting, just accepting that I am on the cusp of an immense discovery. It scares me, and, infuriatingly, it thrills me. It's got me swallowing repeated-ly and trying so very hard to steady my trembling body.

Breathing in through my nose, I step forward and reach into the darkness, taking hold of the leather book as I release my stored air calmly. I'm not feeling calm. I'm feeling all kinds of scrambled. I pull the leather-bound book from the darkest depths of the bookshelf and stare at it for a few moments. Then

I open it up. I finger the edges of the map poking out at the back for a few moments, but that isn't what I'm here to see. I turn the first page. And I see everything that I saw before, the very first time I clapped eyes on this book. I see Picasso's *Harlequin Head*, I see the Fabergé egg, and I see the Stradivarius violin.

I don't know why I'm only realising it now – maybe because it's so unbelievably far-fetched, or maybe it's simply because what I am currently thinking is way past my comprehension – but all of these things – the violin, the Fabergé egg, the Picasso . . .

They are all presumed lost to history.

Or stolen.

My hands start to shake, the book shaking with it, as I flick through a few more pages, until I find what I knew I would. A file. The one from Becker's desk that was unfamiliar to me. Because it was blue, and every file at The Haven is red. The file wasn't destroyed. It was hidden.

I open it up, breathing through my anticipation, and there, bold as the woman herself in the flesh, is Lady Winchester, smiling up at me.

And next to her, as bold as my red hair, is a photograph of the Heart of Hell.

The book starts to vibrate in my hands, and I let it fall to the floor before it can burn me. 'Oh my God.' The lump in my throat swells, making my words of shock sound broken and desperate.

'Hey, princess.'

My head snaps up, finding Becker standing by the door, his jacket off, the top button of his shirt undone, and his bow tie hanging freely. His words were quiet and passive. They were wary.

I gulp down my shock and try to unravel the crazy in my head, my eyes flitting all over the library floor. 'How did you find me in the dark at Countryscape?' I ask, the questions steaming forward, needing to be answered. I look up at him, finding him expressionless. 'How did you land Brent with a tidy crack to the jaw in the pitch black?'

'I was wearing night-vision glasses,' Becker says quietly.

'Oh, Jesus.' I stagger back and grab the edge of the bookshelf, my mind swimming, my eyes closing, like I can hide from my reality. I can't look at him. I can't look at the man I'm hopelessly in love with and try to unravel all the shit polluting my mind. I've dealt with a lot. I've questioned my morals. I've questioned Becker's, too. But how much is too much? Again, where the fucking hell does it stop?

Crime, in so many forms. Deception, fraud, vandalism, aiding and abetting, conspiracy, theft, actual bodily harm . . .

I'm going to be on the Most Wanted list. I'm going to be thrown into jail for life. My mum is going to wonder where I've disappeared to. I could never tell her. I couldn't divulge the shit that surrounds my life now. But I won't have a choice, will I? Because it will be headline fucking news. Dad was right. All of this – the beauty, the history, the money – it's all more hassle than it's worth.

Yes, it's all more hassle than it's worth. But what about Becker? Is he more hassle than he's worth? He promised no more secrets. And this is a fucking huge one. Oddly and quite crazily, that's what hurts most.

I look up at him. Even my eyes are trembling, making my vision judder and Becker appear blurry. 'Where is the ruby?' I ask.

His face is still impassive, his eyes clear behind his glasses. I get nothing – no words or evidence of his mood. He takes a step forward, and then relaxes in his standing pose, watching me, obviously endeavouring to ascertain my frame of mind, his eyes never faltering as he pulls a hand from his pocket and reaches towards me.

At first, I'm slightly baffled by his actions, wondering what he's doing. But then my eyes fall to his hand and his palm opens up.

And I'm blinded by shards of bright red light.

'Oh my God,' I whisper, my palm coming up slowly and covering my mouth. The Heart of Hell stares up at me, and my fucked-up, corrupt world stops spinning.

Just like it did when it was held protected by the glass cabinet, it holds me under a spell, and my mind blanks. The spell is strong, would probably give the one Becker has me under a run for its money. Now the gem is raw, though. There's nothing keeping it contained, no glass protecting it. Or protecting *me*. There's only air between us – me and that priceless *stolen* ruby. The power of its visual appeal is beyond description. The power of its presence is heart-stopping. It shares many of those qualities with Becker. It's the precious stone equivalent to my Saint Sinner.

'How?' I murmur, ripping my eyes away from it to find him.

He clenches his teeth, keeping the gem held out to me. 'Abra-fucking-cadabra, princess.'

An unexpected tear trickles down my cheek, catching me off guard, and I rush to wipe it away, annoyed for allowing my emotions to get the better of me. I'm crying. I don't know why I'm crying. My mind is a big fat muddle of *I-don't-know-whats*. I stand before the love of my life, a stolen priceless gem resting neatly in his palm, and stare. I just stare at it, my ability to do anything else abandoning me. He's a thief, too? Is this one revelation too far?

'Brent didn't steal the O'Keeffe, did he?' I ask, facing him.

He shakes his head.

I need to breathe. I need air. Forcing my sensibility to take over, I make to escape, needing space to process it all.

'Eleanor,' Becker calls, reaching to grab my arm.

I dodge his hand and skirt past him, making a beeline for the door. I can't let him touch me. 'Just leave me.'

'Where are you going?'

'To think.' I'm honest. I need to think really *really* hard.

'Wait.' He catches me as I reach the door, holding my hand on the handle. The inevitable happens. My body answers to him, lighting up, but my mind is fervently telling me to control it. To be sensible. To be wise and smart and vigilant. Just one of those things will do!

'I need you to give me some space.' I spell it out, forcing stability into my tone when all I want to do is crumble to the floor. I can't show my weakness. The lights going out at Countryscape was part of his plan. But Brent trying to abduct me wasn't.

This is why I'm better off alone.

'I'm in love with you, Eleanor,' he vows tightly, reluctantly releasing my hand. He says nothing more, because he doesn't need to. Those words aren't that complicated. They're simple, albeit smothered by complexity.

'I know you do,' I say quietly. 'But you can't seem to stop yourself from hiding your wicked truths from me.' I breathe strength into my dying legs and open the door, walking away from him. I follow my feet down the corridor, up the stone steps, until I find myself in his room, overlooking the Grand Hall.

And there I stand forever, staring down at the impressive space, being reminded of so many things. It's all flooding into my mind – the first time I was here, the time I scaled the furniture, where Becker proposed, the endless times I've weaved through the treasure. I stare at the giant emerald decorating my finger. It doesn't seem so big now. Then the revelations charge forward. Becker the deceiver. Becker the liar. Becker the conman. Becker the intruder. Becker the forger. Becker the thief. It's all so very far-fetched. But it's all so very true. I feel like I've been served the biggest dose of reality, and all I have to do is swallow it. Accept it. Becker the thief is just one more sinful thing to add to his list of sinful things. My sinful Saint Becker. The man I can't help but love.

Reaching up to my head, I rest the pads of my fingers on my forehead, perplexed by the fading ache. I'm suddenly calm. I'm suddenly thinking straight. I have no rose-tinted glasses on, and I'm not naïve. I'm sound-minded and resolute, and I'm asking myself the question Becker asked me one time – the time I discovered his secret room and the fact that he was quite a nifty sculptor.

Do I love him any less?

No. The answer is no.

And now I'm questioning if there is anything Becker Hunt can do that will be one step too far. I've requested space, a moment to think, but I'm under no illusion that I'll be going anywhere after I've thought. I'm simply trying to wrap my mind around another smack to my ethics from left field.

If I have any ethics left. I'm as depraved as Becker is. He's corrupted me in the worst way ... and in the best way, too.

I turn blindly and walk towards one of the couches, settling on the edge. I stare across the room to the glass wall. I'm truly frightened by how much I love him and what I would do for him. I've known all along that I'm in deep. But right now, deep seems to be bottomless. Becker's world is my world now. I should disregard the peace that engulfs me. I should try to find my conscience and my integrity. Yet I can't.

A slight movement catches my attention, and I glance up, finding Becker at the doorway. 'Just checking you hadn't split.' He looks sheepish as he backs away. 'I'll leave you now.'

'No, you won't,' I reply surely, getting to my feet. 'You're going to give me answers.'

'Okay,' he agrees on a mild nod. 'Anything.'

'Does anyone know what you do?' I ask, raising my chin in a show of strength.

'Depends what you're referring to.'

I give him an impatient look, and he smiles nervously. 'I'm referring to you stealing things, Becker. Priceless things.'

'No.'

'Well, that's not true, is it? Lady Winchester knows.'

'No, she doesn't.'

'You stole the gem for her, and she doesn't know who she's dealing with?'

He shakes his head. 'I'm elusive, princess.'

'Then how do people get hold of you? How do they know who to ask to steal the priceless object of their desire?'

'They don't. I get hold of them.'

I frown, not understanding him. 'So you're psychic, too, are you? Is that how you know they want something?'

He smiles at my sarcasm. 'There's not a lot I don't know in this world, princess. You know that. I know what people want and I know how to get it for them.'

I laugh nervously, every one of my fingertips meeting my forehead. That headache I was missing has arrived. I was giving myself too much credit. This is suddenly way beyond my ability to wrap my mind around. 'What about your granddad? How have you kept this from him?'

'Oh,' he chuckles, and then he shrugs. 'When you asked if anyone else knows what I do, I thought you meant in general. I didn't think you meant family.'

I gawp at him. 'Gramps knows?'

'Of course he knows. Where do you think I get my talents from?'

My head recoils on my neck, remembering that file on Becker's desk. His granddad tried to conceal it from me. 'Gramps?' This gets crazier. So the old man throws a wobbly when he finds out that his grandson has conned a man, but it's perfectly cool for him to perform a heist of epic proportions?

'And my dad,' he adds quietly.

'Shit.' He comes from a long line of gentleman thieves? 'What about Mrs Potts?'

He gives me an adorable smile. 'Can you see her lock and loading a zip wire or abseiling down the Empire State Building?'

His sarcastic question goes way over my head. 'You really did skydive off the Burj Khalifa, didn't you?' I laughed when he joked about it, just after he performed an expert roll across the bonnet of Gloria. Now it seems frighteningly possible.

'Who exhibits a Fabergé egg at the top of the Burj Khalifa?' he asks, completely exasperated.

'God, I literally have no fucks left to fire.' My eyes drop, and I stare at the floor. I've gone into shock. 'Mrs Potts?' I ask again.

'That sweet old lady is the original Miss Moneypenny, princess.'

My legs lose some stability, and my arse drops to his couch on a gasp. 'I thought the Hunt Corporation was a legit company.' My voice is getting higher, and I look up at him, revealing my confusion, my shock, my disbelief. Then my hands go into my hair and hold my head, expecting it to explode at any moment.

'It is.' He inches closer to me, and I give no sign of it being a problem. No sign that I'm going to rebuff him. In fact, I could do with some help rubbing away this headache. 'We cater for both, princess. Always have.' He reaches me and crouches before me, taking my hands from my head, holding them as he scans my stunned face. 'Not that anyone knows except us, of course. There are people who buy legit, there are people who do not. If it's not for sale and someone wants it, I get it for them.'

'Who are you?' I ask, laughing nervously. 'Robin Hood? Steal from the rich and give to the poor?'

I'm hit with a half-smile. 'No, princess.' He reaches up and kisses the tip of my nose. 'I steal from the rich and sell to the richer.'

I blow out my disbelief. There's no shame or signs of a conscience. Does he have one?

'Jesus,' I go all floppy, my brain hurting. He knew I had found his secret hiding place, yet he didn't remove the leather-bound book. He actually added to it, putting the blue file in there, too. He wanted me to know this. He wanted me to find out. Then why didn't he just tell me? I frown to myself. Yes, because I can imagine that cropping up in general conversation. *Oh, princess, by the way, I'm a gentleman thief.*

'The other treasures in the folder.' I look at him, crouched before me. He looks like the world has been lifted from his shoulders. He looks relieved. I'm happy for him. For Christ's sake. 'You stole them all?'

'I can't take the credit for all of it. Dad and Gramps contributed, too.'

My eyes widen. 'Fuck ... me,' I breathe out my stunned words.

'Oh, good. You've found some more fucks.' Becker rises and gives me a light tug, pulling me up and positioning me in front of him, my back to his chest, his arms curled around my waist, his chin on my shoulder. He walks us to the glass wall and stops at the foot, like he wants to remind me of the beauty we're immersed in. Releasing me, he leaves my wobbly form to hold itself up and admire the view.

'Look down there, Eleanor,' he orders softly. 'Take it all in, and then look at me.'

I follow his instruction, despite being unsure of his point, taking in the treasure. It doesn't take me long. Besides, everything down there is imprinted on my mind, branded there. A bit like Becker. Since the moment I stepped foot in this place, I was placed under a spell. I felt like an enchanted child discovering excitement and adventure. I craved it, willed it on, begged for it to lure me in and blow my mind. Then I met Becker Hunt, and I found myself following a similar pattern. I wanted him. As much, if not more, than I wanted to be immersed in The Haven and its spectacular history. Everything he had, everything he wanted to throw at me, I willed it all on. I wanted him. Now I have him. Every part, every secret, every lie, every tiny piece – the good, the bad, the ugly, and the illegal.

'Are you okay?' Becker breaks into my hectic thoughts.

'Yes.' I frown, my lips pouting. I'm not going anywhere. That I just have to accept. I look up at him, seeing peace and calm glowing back at me.

He smiles. 'This is my legacy, princess. It's written for me. My father, my grandfather, my great-grandfather. It's inbuilt. It's my destiny. It's who I am, and I so want to share it with you.'

My skin prickles with tiny stabs of love, fierce loyalty and . . . exhilaration.

'All or nothing, baby.'

My teeth grit, like my mind is forbidding me to say it. But nothing isn't an option. Being without him isn't an option. My God, what's happened to me? 'All.' I nod as I speak, in case the forbidden word doesn't make it past my clenched teeth.

'All?' he asks, taking my hand and feeling my ring.

'All,' I confirm again, watching as his lips slowly stretch into a bright smile, his eyes glimmering madly behind his glasses in wonder.

'Come here, my beautiful corrupt little witch.'

I don't waste a moment. I dive into my shady, criminal of a fiancé's arms. 'Tell me that's it. Tell me there's no more for me to find out about you.'

'I do drug-running in my spare time.'

'Not funny.' I nudge him, and he laughs, forcing himself free from my vice hold.

'I'm so lucky to have found you,' he whispers, grabbing my cheeks. 'So fucking lucky.'

I smile mildly through my squeezed cheeks, and he mirrors it, searching my eyes before hauling me into him for a cuddle. 'I didn't get to tell you earlier.'

'Tell me what?' I ask, settling into him.

'You needn't have the keys to your dad's store delivered to the agent.'

My forehead bunches. 'But they'll—'

'I bought it.'

I dive out of his arms. 'What?'

'I bought your dad's store.' The corner of his mouth twitches. 'I know it's hurting you, the thought of saying goodbye to it, and I know your mum needs the money.' He shrugs. 'Everyone wins.'

I stare at him. Just stare at him. Cash buyer. Paying full asking price. Can move quickly. 'I . . .' I can't believe he's done this for me. I don't know what to say.

'Anything, Eleanor,' he whispers. 'Absolutely anything.'

Oh God. I move into him fast, sliding my arms around his shoulders, hugging him fiercely. 'Thanks for not stealing it from me,' I say mindlessly, and he laughs. But the sound of a heavy thud brings our moment to an abrupt halt, Becker freezing with me still in his arms. He looks towards the door.

'What was that?' I ask as he pulls cautiously away and looks down to the Grand Hall.

'I don't know.' He paces to the door, wariness leaking from his body like a broken dam. He takes the handle and opens, but his movements are measured and thoughtful, like he's trying to be quiet.

'What do you—'

'Shhhh.' His shush is harsh and edged with anger, and his wary persona starts soaking into me, getting me worked up. I want to know what he's thinking but I fear asking – not only because I'll be cut short again, but because I'm worried about the answer. He's wound up, stressed and hyper alert.

'Winston?' I have to put his name out there, maybe just to remind Becker that his burly pet is roaming The Haven and the sound was likely him.

Becker shakes his head, poo-pooing my reasonable

explanation. Then the barking starts, like Winston himself is answering my question. 'Shit,' Becker curses, the sound of his dog going spare not seeming to rush him along. Instead, it makes him more cautious as he takes the stairs. 'Wait there,' he tells me, not looking back to check if I'm listening. I laugh sarcastically to myself. No way. I follow on my tiptoes, wincing each time Winston yaps. If there were intruders, surely Winston would have scared them off? What am I thinking? There's not a chance anyone could get into The Haven.

Becker creeps down the stone steps, never checking to see if I've done as I'm told, but he does reach into a hidden nook and pull something free. A cricket bat? Or . . . a weapon. I'm certain that if I was to touch him, I'd have a sharp shock. He looks super-charged with energy, hyped up on anger. The sound of Winston barking rings on, and Becker follows it, edging down the corridor close to the wall before pushing the door to his office open cautiously with the bat, looking past it. When he carefully breaches the threshold, I know something is terribly wrong the moment the cricket bat lands on the floor with a crack.

'God, no.' Becker rockets forward, leaving me to catch the door before it slams in my face. I see him throw himself to the floor, and in a numb haze of unknowing, I step forward.

Then I see the cause of his distress.

Old Mr H is lying front down on the carpet by the bookcase to the secret room, the disguised door is open, and Winston is circling and barking by his side.

My hands come up to my face, cupping my cheeks, and my mind goes blank on me. There are a million instructions charging at me, but my muscles refuse to act on them. All I seem to be able to do is stare, feeling numb and useless while Becker shouts angrily at his unconscious grandfather.

'Wake up, you old fool,' he yells, but he doesn't touch him or nudge him. He's just kneeling at his grandfather's side, his eyes darting up and down his body, like he's looking for any sign of life, too scared to touch him. 'Gramps!' When his demands go unanswered, Becker collapses to his arse and his hands delve into his hair, his face pure dread. 'Please,' he murmurs, his bottom lip quivering.

The sight of him, so utterly distressed, kicks life into my frozen form. I rush over, dropping to my knees on the other side of old Mr H, my ear falling to his mouth to listen for any trace of breath. I don't like his pasty, almost grey complexion, nor the nasty cut on his forehead. I take his wrist and feel for a pulse. A few seconds gives me something, and adrenalin soaks my veins and clears my mind. 'Phone,' I demand, holding my hand out to Becker, but he's zoned out, just staring at his lifeless gramps. 'Becker!' I yell.

His eyes flip up. They're glazed with shock. They're haunted. We both know the reason Mr H is lying unconscious on the floor. He found Becker's secret room. He knows Becker crafted the fake that Brent bought.

'Give me your phone.'

He reaches into his pocket mindlessly and hands it to me. 'Will he be okay?' His words are emotionless and sharp. He's shutting down.

I can't answer that. I dial 999. 'Ambulance,' I say calmly.

Chapter 36

I've been sitting here for so long, I'm seizing up and bedsores could be developing. The smell of antibacterial solution is now embedded into my nose, and I've drunk so much coffee my mouth is furry. I feel grubby, tired and emotionally drained.

The ambulance arrived within ten minutes and it took just a further two minutes for old Mr H's condition to be diagnosed. Heart attack. We all know the shock of his discovery triggered it. I can't bear to think how guilty Becker is feeling. Another member of the Hunt family could be lost to that stupid fucking sculpture.

Aspirin was administered, an ECG undertaken, and he was stabilised before being transferred to hospital. The whole time Becker stood like a zombie in the corner of his office, answering the paramedic's questions with one-word answers while he watched them work on his grandfather. He's completely shook up.

After a brief stop in A & E to stitch the nasty cut on his forehead and an X-ray to ensure no bones were broken in his fall, Becker's granddad was transferred to the high-dependency unit.

The old boy, usually so buoyant, if a little immobile, looks deathly pasty atop the white sheets of the bed. Becker has been mute all night, sitting as close to his gramps as the medical machinery will allow, his hand holding his grandfather's old wrinkled one gently. He's dozed off now and then, for a few minutes at a time, and has accepted the coffee I've kept supplying. All I can do is be here. He might not be able to speak to me, but I'm here, tucked away in the corner in an uncomfortable high-backed chair. The seat feels rubbery. The heat on the ward is stifling. We're both still dressed from last night, Becker in his trousers and shirt, and me in my dress, though my feet are now graced in flip-flops. Mrs Potts has been here throughout the night, too, which was definitely a good thing. She answered all of the questions from the doctors and seemed perfectly together while Becker remained in a state of shock and grief by his grandfather's bedside.

After dropping a light kiss on Becker's forehead and squeezing his shoulder, Mrs Potts came to me and smiled down at my exhausted form. I just about managed to return her smile as she reached for my left hand and homed straight in on my ring, and when she dipped and cuddled me, she spoke to me more with the might of her hug than she ever could have with words. Then she left for The Haven, telling me that Donald's suite should be cleaned, ready for his return, and Winston would need a walk.

That was around dawn. Now I don't know what time it is, and though I'm desperate for a shower and some sleep, I don't plan on going anywhere until Becker is ready. He still hasn't spoken, and I'm not about to push him.

My heavy eyes give up on me and slowly close, the muscles behind hurting as they fight in vain to keep open.

'Eleanor.'

I bolt upright in my chair and blink back the blur, finding Becker kneeling in front of me. He looks like death warmed up, his hair in disarray, his eyes pale behind his glasses, his skin sallow. 'Let's go stretch our legs.'

I look past him to find Mr H still unconscious, his body in the exact same position as it has been since he was admitted. Nodding, I allow Becker to pull me up from the chair, feeling weak with tiredness. Tucking me into his side, he walks us slowly away, heading for the main corridor. We're both utterly knackered, holding each other up, my arm wrapped around his waist. 'You okay?' I ask, just for the sake of it. Neither of us are okay.

'Super,' he croaks, his voice sounding sore and grainy.

I just manage enough energy to constrict him in my hold. 'He'll be fine,' I say, not because I feel like I should try to make him feel better, but because I truly believe the old man will be. 'This isn't your fault.' I look up and see him strain a smile. 'Was he okay when you checked up on him?'

'I found him wandering down the corridor towards my office. Said he couldn't sleep and was fetching his paper. I didn't think anything of it.'

'Did he know about that room?'

'Of course. It was his before it was my dad's, and before it was mine. But it's kind of an unwritten rule with the Hunt men. No one ventures into the secret room if they're not heading up the Corporation.' He laughs a little. 'It's like a crown if you're the Hunt man in power. A crown no one else can touch.'

'You weren't to know he'd break the unwritten rule.'

He sighs as we reach the cafe, and Becker homes straight in on the fruit bowl, rootling through, determined. I watch him scowling as he searches for his favourite fruit, eventually picking out an apple and holding it up. 'No juice spots,' he grumbles, casting it aside and taking another one. He inspects it thoroughly and growls his disapproval.

'How about this one?' I ask, digging one from the bottom. It looks perfectly green, and it has juice spots. I hold it out to him.

Becker takes it and gives it a quick inspection before tossing it aside. 'Too soft,' he spits. 'For fuck's sake.'

I smile my sympathy and turn, leaving Becker to sulk, set on getting another coffee. I find Mrs Potts directly behind me holding out the biggest, juiciest apple. Becker gasps his gratitude and reaches over my shoulder to snatch it from her palm. The crunch and the moan of pleasure are a welcome sound, and

I smile at Mrs Potts, Becker's gratification serving like an energy boost to my tired bones. I make to turn so my eyes can soak up the pleasure of him eating his favourite thing in the world, but something hovering past Mrs Potts catches my attention and holds it, and I blink, thinking maybe I'm hallucinating.

'Mum?' I say, frown lines making my forehead heavy.

'Darling!' She lunges forward and catches me in a fierce hug.

'Found her banging on the entrance door of The Haven.' Mrs Potts speaks up, tutting as she starts rummaging through her enormous carpet bag.

'It was meant to be a surprise,' Mum says in my ear. 'A happy surprise but Mrs Potts told me about Becker's granddad. I'm so sorry.' She breaks away from me and gives me eyes full of sympathy, before turning them onto Becker.

I see Paul hovering awkwardly in the background, and I offer a small smile, exhaustion zapping the energy I thought I'd found.

'Mrs Cole,' Becker says through a mouthful of apple, not prepared to rush his medicine of choice, not even for my mother.

Mum dives at him, nearly causing him to choke. 'I'm sure he'll be fine,' she tells him firmly as he smiles over her shoulder at me, curling his arm around her waist.

'Yeah, he's a tough old boot,' Becker says quietly.

'There's a waiting room down the hall,' I motion behind me. 'Shall we?'

'Yes, let's.' Mum signals for Paul to join us, and we all start to wander back to Mr H's ward. Her face. It's my kind of medicine, and I put my arm around her shoulder, cuddling into her side.

'I'm glad you're here, Mum,' I say, and she reaches up to pat my hand, hushing me soothingly. I never once thought she'd venture out of Helston to come see me in the big city. Where are they staying? How long are they here? What are their plans?

'Everything will be okay, I'm sure.' She stops and gives my cheek a fond stroke, and I smile through my tiredness.

'I hope so.'

'It will,' Becker affirms, dropping a kiss on my cheek, his eyes showing the first hint of a sparkle since we discovered Gramps in his office. 'Mrs Cole.' He offers an arm, and Mum accepts on a delighted smile, letting him lead on.

I follow behind Becker and Mum, watching as she chats, luring Becker in and even spiking a few laughs from him. My appreciation for her surprise visit grows. She'll be a welcome source of comfort and support through this crappy time.

'How are you, Eleanor?' Paul asks, and I look up, straining a smile.

'Tired,' I admit as he falls into stride next to me.

'I couldn't stop her,' he says, nodding towards my mother's back. 'I tried to convince her to call ahead, but she was adamant that she wanted to surprise you.'

'She's certainly done that.' I laugh, just as we reach Mr H's room and a shrill shriek from my mother rings through the corridor. The sharp sound makes my feet stutter to a shocked stop.

Mum has whirled around and is gawking at me, her eyes wide and bright, and Becker is nibbling on the core of his apple, smiling behind it. She swings back to him quickly, kissing a cheek. 'With my sincerest blessing,' she says, hugging him fiercely before returning her attention to me. 'Oh, Eleanor,' she sings, running forward and taking my hands.

I'm lost. 'What?' I ask, gauging Becker's face again. He's still smiling. It's a beautiful, welcome sight, even if I haven't the foggiest idea why he's looking so pleased with himself.

'A wedding?' She throws her arms around me. 'This is so exciting.'

Oh. More guilt grabs me. I want to be excited with her, but I'm just too bloody knackered at the moment. 'Thanks, Mum.'

'Oh, we have to plan.' She holds me at arm's length, her mind spinning into overdrive. I can literally see the ideas whirling around in her excited eyes. 'Just as soon as Becker's grandfather is better, we must plan.'

Paul steps forward and shakes Becker's hand, firmly and manly. 'Congratulations. You're a very lucky man.'

'Cheers. She's quite lucky herself.' Becker tosses me a little wink, and Paul laughs.

'Oh, this is so wonderful,' Mum gushes, turning her excitement onto Becker. He aims, fires, and his apple core lands neatly in a nearby bin. 'Get that grandfather of yours better so we can *really* celebrate.'

'I plan to,' Becker declares, sounding determined.

'Come on.' Paul takes Mum's arm. 'Let's leave them in peace for now. We have plenty of things to see. We'll catch up with them once they're home and have sorted out Becker's grandfather.'

Mum pouts but relents easily, and I give her a hug. 'I'll call you as soon as I leave here,' I tell her. 'We'll sort out where you're staying.'

'Oh, don't worry about us. Paul's treated us to a few nights at The Haymarket.'

She's being spoilt, and I'm truly happy for her. I smile my thanks at Paul, who shrugs his big shoulders awkwardly.

A nurse appears. 'Your grandfather just came around, Mr Hunt. He's asking for you.'

I see Becker's whole body relax with relief and feel mine go with it. 'Thank God,' he breathes, turning a relieved smile onto my mother. 'I'll see you later, Mrs Cole.' He backs into his granddad's room. 'We'll do dinner.'

'Okay,' Mum agrees, allowing Paul to claim her and lead her away. 'Love you, darling.' Her face. God, I read every word she's not saying. How happy she is. How proud.

'Love you too,' I mouth, waving as they round a corner.

As soon as they're gone, I hurry to Mr H's room, keen to see the old man awake. On entering, I find Mrs Potts in the chair that I recently vacated and Becker by his granddad's bedside, holding his hand. Old Mr H looks drained, but his open eyes are a sight to behold. It's all I can do not to sprint over and throw myself at him, yet after a few seconds of holding myself back, I lose my battle and decide he'd appreciate a hug. But as I lift my foot to go over, I freeze, someone catching my attention – another person in the room, standing in the corner. Someone big and imposing, his shoes still in need of a polish.

All the blood in my veins turns to ice.

Price. Stan Price. What the hell is he doing here?

Mrs Potts and Becker don't look particularly perturbed by his presence. Neither does old Mr H. And he has quite a presence. A serious one. He eyes me suspiciously for a few, uncomfortable seconds before he nods to Mrs Potts courteously and respectfully. She nods back, her lips tight, her eyes watchful. Then he turns to Becker and reaches into his inside pocket, producing something and showing it to him. I know immediately it must me the photograph of Lady Winchester. Oh God, is he going to ask Becker who that woman is? What will he say? Will he deny it? Good Lord, Price has been following us. What if he followed us to Countryscape? What if he saw us chatting with Lady Winchester? *Becker stole the fucking ruby for her!*

I see Becker's chest expand through his deep breath, and he slowly moves away from his grandfather's bedside.

'Price,' he says, his face grave. 'It's been too long.'

I look to Mrs Potts, but she gives me nothing, her eyes rooted on Becker.

'Becker Hunt,' Price counters, ignoring Becker's sarcasm as he steps forward. 'I'm arresting you on suspicion of the theft of The Heart of Hell.'

I stagger back, feeling my throat close up.

'You do not have to say anything, however it may harm your defence if you do not mention when questioned something which you later rely on in court. Anything you do say may be given in evidence.'

The ground disappears from beneath my feet, and I feel an arm coil around my waist. I look to find Mrs Potts by my side, her face serious. I cough on a despairing cry, finding Becker again. His face is straight, accepting, and he's looking at me, his eyes clear.

'No,' I sob, shaking my head, a few tears escaping as I tremble in Mrs Potts's arms. Becker holds me in place with his serious stare, his head shaking, his jaw tight. He's telling me to keep it together, and I haven't got the first idea how.

Price produces a set of cuffs, and Becker starts to turn away from him, his angel eyes remaining on mine until he has no choice but to break the contact. His granddad looks up at him and nods, short and sharp, and I go limp in Mrs Potts's hold. No one's breathing a word. Becker's cooperating and looks prepared to go silently and willingly. So why the cuffs? I want to scream my devastation and throw myself in front of him to protect him, but Mrs Potts has a firm hold of me, like she knows I'm a flight risk.

Price makes quick work of securing Becker's hands behind his back, before taking his elbow and starting to lead him from the room. Becker looks straight ahead, his chin high, his body tall and strong. The urge to cry out, to dive on him as he passes and tell him I love him, that I always will, nearly gets the better of me.

But I don't need to. He forces Price to a stop when he reaches me, and he looks into my watery eyes and smiles. He fucking smiles, and I have no idea why. They're going to lock him away forever! The only time I'll ever see him will be behind bars. He'll be dressed from head to toe in prison clothes. He'll never be able to violate me in the most delicious ways imaginable again. I'll never be able to touch him. To have naked cuddles. He won't ever be able to slap my arse. I realise some of these thoughts are mindless and inappropriate, but I'm spiralling quickly into meltdown. *What will I do without him?*

He studies me for a moment, holding me still with those lazy eyes, resisting the pull of Price when he tries to tug him on. 'I'm in love with you.' He nods as he speaks, reinforcing his words, and I whimper, the tears pouring down my cheeks as Price pulls him away from me.

'No,' I sob, reaching for him, feeling Mrs Potts holding me back as Becker casts a look over his shoulder.

His face is serious and beautiful, his eyes bright and sure behind his glasses. 'Don't find your way out of my maze just yet, princess,' he orders, his voice steady and strong. 'We're not done.' He disappears out of the door, and I crumble in Mrs Potts's arms, sobbing like I've never sobbed before.

Chapter 37

The ripe, green apple sitting on the huge replica of the Theodore Roosevelt double pedestal desk looks virtuous. Harmless. It looks deliciously temping and mouth-watering. It's holding my attention like a hawk would watch a rabbit as it circles the open sky above. I can't take my eyes off it. I don't *want* to take my eyes off it. For then I will have to return to the desolation that's kept me prisoner in its wicked grip these past twenty-four hours. Staring at this apple, simple as it seems, crazy as it is, has been my only few minutes of respite from the cold harshness of my outlandish reality since Becker was cuffed and escorted from the hospital. My eyes are nailed to the shiny, almost sparkling skin. I haven't blinked and my mind is doing a remarkable job of blanking out my overactive imagination.

Overactive? No. Every dreaded, awful thought that's plagued me in the past twenty-four hours has been completely warranted. There's nothing dramatic or over-the-top about a single one of my fears. My imagination isn't running away with me. I'm not being irrational. I'm not imagining the sick feeling deep in my tummy. My anxiety isn't groundless.

My heart is quickly ricocheting off my breastbone again, a light sheen of sweat forming, my breathing stuttering. I force my lips to pucker in an attempt to limit the air that's billowing from my mouth too quickly, hoping to regain a safe level of breathing before I go dizzy. My plan has the opposite effect, and I literally feel every drop of blood drain from my head, sending me light-headed. I'm hyperventilating.

'Shit,' I push myself away from Becker's desk in the chair and throw my head between my knees. The breeze that gusts past my forehead tells me I only just missed the edge of the wood in my haste. I'm momentarily disappointed. Knocking myself out seems like my best option right now. Maybe I'll wake up in twenty-five years' time when Becker is released from prison and my life can resume.

I stare down at my bare feet. My bright-red toenails seem dull. Everything around me seems dull. My life is dull.

Because he's not here.

My bottom lip begins to tremble as another wave of tears stream forward. Fighting them back requires strength that I just do not have, so I let them defeat me and watch as drop after drop of my tattered emotions plummets to the carpet by my bare feet, creating only the tiniest of splashes before the thick fibres swallow them up. My shoulders begin to jerk, and I remain slumped, bent over in Becker's office chair, waiting for this episode of grief to pass. I feel small and useless. Pathetic and weak. *I don't do weak and pathetic.*

I take my shaky hands to my cheeks and brush the streams of tears away, but no sooner have I dried my face, another waterfall replaces it.

The apple.

Sniffling and wiping my nose, I shoot up and search out the perfect fruit. Just focus on the apple. I swallow, my eyes narrowing and homing in on the green skin, my gaze so concentrated I wouldn't be surprised if the apple shot off the desk. I hear the clean crunch of a perfect set of white teeth biting into the flesh, the rip as a sinful mouth pulls it away, the wet motions of it being seductively chewed and swallowed. I begin to see all of these things, too, and my eyes close, welcoming the distraction.

There he is. In my mind's eye, bare-chested and indulging in his most favourite thing. He won't have free access to any apples in prison, and if he does, they won't be bright green, they won't have juice spots, and they'll probably have no crunch. He'll never survive.

The thought makes me mad, and my fist comes down on the desk hard, the shock travelling up my arm.

'Eleanor, whatever are you doing?'

My lids spring open and find Mrs Potts holding the office door open, her eyes wide with alarm. She's not shown a scrap of emotion since she watched Becker being carted away by the police, has barely even spoken about it. I've had no one to share my burden with.

I blink through my blurred vision as I brush away some strands of my hair that have stuck to my damp cheeks.

'Come on, dear,' she says sharply, marching over to the desk. 'We'll be having none of that nonsense.' She pulls me to my feet and forces me to face her, and I fall apart all over again, shaking in her grasp. She's made of stone. She must be. Roughly wiping at my cheeks while I snivel and sob before her, she rolls her eyes. 'Now you listen here, young lady.' She gives me a tight face, but her harshness doesn't lessen the emotion overtaking me. I'm a wreck. 'You will pull yourself together and be the woman he fell in love with.' She cocks an eyebrow and purses her lips, saying more with that look. 'Now then.' She nods her approval to her own words and takes a quick peek at my pathetic form. Becker's T-shirt is drowning me, but the smell is so comforting. 'Look at the state of you.'

I say nothing. I have nothing *to* say. I wouldn't get any words past the lump of grief blocking my throat, anyway.

She pulls at the material of the T-shirt and takes in my bare legs. 'Have you showered?'

I nod pitifully.

'Maybe so, but I know for a fact that you've not eaten.'

'I'm not hungry,' I murmur flatly, the thought of food making me come over all queasy. And panicky. Becker won't have free access to his apples. He needs his apples. 'Oh God, I need to get him out!' I turn and make for the door, my earlier silent claim, the one where I told myself I'm not being irrational, being flattened with every step I take. I'm being totally irrational now.

'What are you gonna do, dig him out?'

My bare feet skid to a stop, and I whirl around, offended and annoyed by her snarky quip. I should feel none of those things. I should be laughing, but I can't do that either, because there is nothing funny about that suggestion, no matter how much humour the old lady wove into those words. Because in my wild reality, I wouldn't be at all surprised if Becker found a way to do exactly that. The man's capabilities have floored me at every turn. Unreasonable and unrealistic as it may sound, I can't help but hope that he's a mile underground, tunnelling his way out of a cell and is going to pop up out of the ground at any moment.

I look at the office floor.

I've officially lost the plot.

'Give me strength.' Mrs Potts sighs, wobbling over, as if she knows exactly what has been running through my mind. She grabs my left hand and holds it up between us, giving us both a close-up of the gigantic emerald ring that Becker put on my finger. I start sobbing again, seeing his face when he asked me to marry him, the awe and devotion, the nerves and shyness. 'When you came to work here, Eleanor, Becker boy had no idea what he was doing. We were flummoxed when he started to let you in so deeply, let you delve beneath the legitimate side of our business here. He willed you on. We could see that.' She pulls up and waits for me to give her my tear-filled eyes. 'He wanted you to discover everything there was to discover about him, about us, about the Hunt Corporation.' Her lips purse as she waits for me to absorb what she's trying to tell me. I know exactly what. 'He didn't know what he was doing, of that I'm certain, but when he put this ring on your finger, he knew exactly what he was doing. He was letting you into something far more precious than this old rickety building and the secrets it holds. He was letting you into his heart. You're a strong young woman, dear girl. That's why he loves you. Because he believes you are strong enough to see everything there is to see and, most importantly, deal with it. And on top of all that, still love him.'

My lip wobbles.

'His talent is a legacy, dear. A historical legacy that I hope never dies, because it's *that* special. It's *that* important. The Hunt Corporation is a legitimate company.' She nods her head sharply, agreeing to her own affirmation. 'It's respected, valued and profitable. But it's not as thrilling as—'

'Stealing,' I cut in, before the crazy old lady can finish.

Mrs Potts isn't fazed. 'Legitimate business doesn't feed the need of the adventurous Hunt men.' She grins wickedly, stunning me. She's brainwashed. Has to be. People have lost their lives in the name of excitement. I'm about to point this out when she holds up a finger, keeping me quiet, as if fully expecting my argument. 'I'm not talking about the sculpture, Eleanor. It's there to be found, not stolen. If it exists at all. But that's a quest that needs to be buried along with the tragedies it's brought on the Hunt family. It's cursed.' Her eyes sink into me seriously. 'What I'm talking about is the frightening ability that our boy has inherited,' she goes on with a little squeeze of my hand, ensuring she has my attention. 'His grandfather was good. His father was great. But Becker boy . . .' Mrs Potts trails off, as if she's trying to locate the right words to pin on my unlawful love. I have a million to offer her. 'Becker boy is the master,' she declares. 'He will be back, you mark my words. This is simply a mild inconvenience, trust me. There's not a cat in hell's chance Becker Hunt can be caught. He's too clever. Way too smart. Too determined. You should know that by now, Eleanor. Where's your faith in him?'

I close my eyes to hold back my tears, reminding myself that every day I've spent with Becker brought a surprise, whether it was a shocking revelation in the form of his shady activities, or an equally shocking revelation in the form of his devotion or trust. I found I adored him that little bit more every hour. And I know those feelings were returned. I had faith then. I need it now more than ever.

Don't find your way out of my maze just yet, princess. We're not done.

I swallow down that infuriating ball of emotion and try to pull myself together. 'I just want him back,' I murmur, the ache inside of me intensifying to the point it's becoming unbearable. I don't know how much longer I can go on like this. There's work to be done but finding my focus to do it is impossible.

Mrs Potts hauls me into her embrace and hugs me tightly, patting my back soothingly. 'I know, dear. We all do.'

'Why hasn't he called?' There's been no word, no breaking story of an arrest in connection with the stolen ruby. Surely it's newsworthy. Surely Becker would know I'd be out of my mind and at least get in touch.

'I'm sure there's a perfectly good reason.'

'Like?'

The long stretch of silence soon tells me that she has no answer. It doesn't help. The unknown is petrifying. 'Call your mother and Lucy. Both are wondering what's going on.'

'Have you told them?' God, how am I going to explain this?

Mrs Potts looks me straight in the eye. 'There's nothing to tell, dear.'

Chapter 38

I know it's a bad habit and I shouldn't be encouraging it, but having Winston curled up on Becker's bed is comforting. Hearing his deep, rumbling snore goes some way towards drowning out my racing mind, though it unreasonably riles me that Winston can find sleep so easily.

After checking in with Mum, assuring her everything is fine and listening to her babble on about the wonders of London, I call Lucy. 'Mark's asked me to move in with him!' she screeches down the phone, and for the first time in what feels like days, I smile.

'I'm happy for you.'

'I'm happy for me, too! Hey, did Becker find anything out about the stolen ruby?' she asks, and I tense. 'You know, since he's in that game.'

'What game?'

'The art and antiques game,' she goes on, and I roll my eyes at myself. 'I bet that's caused a shit storm of gargantuan proportions. How embarrassing.'

'Slightly,' I quip, and she laughs.

'How is Becker, by the way?'

Locked up. 'Busy,' I say, a little high-pitched.

'We should do dinner. The four of us. When are you guys free?'

Free. 'Let you know?'

'Sure. Call me tomorrow. Gotta go. I have my notice to hand in on my poky flat.' She chuckles and hangs up.

I drop my phone to my bed and stare up at the ceiling, but I don't see the smooth painted plaster that's there. I see raw bricks. The comfortable mattress doesn't feel squidgy. It feels solid, and the duck down quilt feels rough and itchy. I shiver, my skin prickling with chills in the warm safety of Becker's luxurious bed.

Lost.

I'm lost, like a piece of treasure waiting to be found, and I plan on going nowhere until he *does* find me. Will he find me? Come back to me? I roll over and bury my face in his pillow, curling into a ball, the pain of his absence excruciating. *Find me.*

'Eleanor.'

I blink, thinking, listening. Dreaming?

'Princess.'

I sit bolt upright in bed, my eyes shooting towards the sound of his voice, my mind telling me not to get too excited. That I might be hearing things. That I might be skipping further down the road to crazy. Then I hear the loud, familiar crunch of his teeth sinking into an apple.

He chews, he swallows, and he sighs. 'Shit, that's good.'

'Oh God!' I'm off the bed like a rocket, charging across the room, and my body collides with his harshly, knocking the wind out of us both, but I don't care. I wrap myself around him tightly and cling on.

He laughs and holds me under my arse, carrying me to the bed. 'Let go.'

'No,' I snap, squeezing harder.

'I'm going nowhere, princess.'

'I don't care. It doesn't stop someone from trying to take you.'

He wrestles with me for a few seconds, forcing my claw-like grip from his neck and pushing me down to the bed. 'Sit,' he orders, crouching down and throwing a look over my shoulder. 'What's Winston doing in bed?'

I look back and see the pooch curled into a ball. 'I was lonely,' I tell him, just as Winston lets out a snorty snore.

'He's clearly missed me,' Becker mutters.

'What happened?' I ask, returning my attention to Becker. 'What did they say? What will they do? What did *you* say?'

His finger comes to his lips. 'Shhhh,' he hushes me and smiles, like it's humorous. It's not. I've been going certifiably crazy. Why's he so cool? 'Price had nothing, Eleanor. But I have something on him.'

I withdraw. Price is in Brent's pocket. 'What?'

'Percy hacked Price's offshore account.'

My hand goes over my mouth. 'No.'

He nods his head. 'Price has been taking backhanders from Wilson for years. He's as bent as they come. I always knew it, but couldn't prove it.'

My face must display the outrage I feel. 'And he really had nothing on you anyway?'

'Nothing,' he confirms on a cheeky grin. 'Except for my attendance at Countryscape.'

'Becker,' I drop my voice, an instinctive move, despite it being silly. We're in The Haven. No one will hear me. I get closer to his face, nearly nose-to-nose. His smile is firmly in place, his amusement obvious, 'But you *did* steal it,' I point out stupidly. 'How can they have nothing?'

'I told you, princess. I'm a fucking genius.' He plants a smacker of a kiss on my dazed face, and I'm suddenly positively *desperate* to ask him how he pulled off a heist of such epic proportions. 'Don't ask.' Becker halts my question before I can ask it, and my lip pushes out on a slighted pout. He laughs. 'And pick up your lip.'

'Tell me,' I press, giving him puppy dog eyes. 'Please?'

'No.'

'Becker, come on.'

'You're too curious.'

'That's your fault. Tell me how.'

'No. That's one thing you'll never get from me. If you don't know, you can't be forced to tell.'

'But I know you stole it,' I remind him.

'No, you don't.' His eyebrow jumps up, and I snap my mouth shut. 'Do you?'

'I know nothing.' I give him a nervous smile, trying desperately to display my coolness.

'Good girl.' He rises, my sight following him until he's standing over me. Taking my hands, he pulls me to my feet.

'Where's the ruby?' I ask. I can't help it. I do bloody know, and I'm so bloody curious.

'With its new owner.'

'Lady Winchester?'

'Correct.' He starts unbuttoning his shirt.

'How does she have it?' I ask, lending him a hand and starting on the bottom ones. 'You've been locked up for over twenty-four hours.' Looking up at him, I see a wave of hesitancy travel across his face, and his fingers definitely falter for a split second.

'You know I have my ways.' Shrugging out of his shirt, he drops it to the bed and makes his way to the bathroom, ignoring the frown his answer has spiked. He might have his ways but being in two places at once isn't one of them. And then . . .

I gasp, though I make sure it's not loud enough for Becker to hear. Percy. I bet Becker's little whizz kid played a part in this. I'm pressing my lips together so hard, they're starting to go numb. I watch his back, the map rolling as his arms lift, stretching.

'Percy.' I put his name out there, and Becker stops at the bathroom door and looks back at me.

'Shhhh.' He smiles. 'I need a shower.' He disappears past the glass bricks. 'Go say hello to Gramps.'

His instruction grabs my attention immediately. 'He's here?'

'I went straight to the hospital to collect him.'

'Did you talk?' I ask, nervous on Becker's behalf. Mr H knows now that his grandson crafted that fake sculpture. I can only imagine the wrath Becker has faced.

'Yes, we talked.'

'And how was he?'

'Before or after he cuffed me around the head with his walking stick?'

I sigh on a dramatic roll of my eyes. 'Very funny.'

'He was more than fine, princess. He's in my office.' The shower turns on, and I dash to the bathroom, just so I can look at him some more. Just so I know he's here. I find him under the spray, his eyes closed, his face pointed up, water raining down on his rough face. I breathe out, resting my forehead on the glass as I watch him. His movements are fluid, slow but fluid, and I'm completely and utterly mesmerised by him.

'Want some popcorn?' he asks, not opening his eyes.

I smile and rest my palm on the glass, keeping quiet, just admiring him.

'Come give me a kiss, Eleanor.' His demand is hoarse, his voice pure sex. He opens his eyes, his corrupt, lazy gaze staring me down. 'Now.'

I step into the shower and brace myself for his claim, sighing rather than yelping when I'm grabbed and pinned to the tile wall. He pulls the wet T-shirt off me and tosses it aside, and heavy, wet lashes veil his eyes as he gazes at me, his face hovering close to mine. 'I love you.'

'I never forgot that.' My fingers weave through his wet hair. 'Brent Wilson won't be pleased.'

'Wilson has got it coming.' He slams his lips to mine and pushes me up the wall with the force of his kiss, his tongue exploring my mouth hungrily. 'He makes his moves too fast. Misjudges too often. Looks at the smaller picture rather than the bigger one.' He bites my lip and pulls back, sliding his hands to my bum and cupping the cheeks possessively. 'He's a desperate man, Eleanor.'

'Weren't you even a little worried when Price arrested you?'

He shakes his head a little but says nothing.

'Why?'

'Because I'm a fucking legend and Wilson is not.'

'You're cocky.'

'I'm Becker Hunt.' He grins and takes my lips again. 'And soon, you will be Eleanor Hunt.' Growling a little, he pulls away and turns me, slapping my arse. 'Go see Gramps before I bend you over and fuck you to the Vatican and back.' I pout and he smirks as he takes the shampoo down from the shelf. 'And then get ready for an all-nighter.'

Heat. So much heat. All night. Him all over me all night long.

I grab a towel and dry myself off before throwing on some clothes and making my way to Becker's office, Winston on my heels. I can't deny the relief I'm feeling. Becker's home, the police have nothing on him, he's set Price straight, old Mr H is okay, and he's still talking to Becker. All the anxiety that was keeping me awake for the past day has drained away, making way to tiredness. I'm going to sleep for a week. Right after our all-nighter.

Pushing my way into Becker's office, I find the old boy sitting at the huge desk, his face buried in a broadsheet. He looks over the top, his glasses resting on the end of his nose. 'Here she is.'

'Hey,' I shut the door behind me and go join him, taking one of the leather chairs opposite. 'You should be in bed,' I admonish him. He looks surprisingly well, despite the few stitches on his forehead.

'Don't you start,' he huffs, folding the paper neatly and placing it to the side. 'I've had Dorothy in my ear all morning.'

'You had a heart attack, Mr H. And a nasty blow to your head.'

He waves a hand flippantly. 'How are you, lovely?'

'Me?' I question on a small laugh. 'I'm fine.' Couldn't be better, in fact.

'You've had quite the enlightenment.' The old man's lip quirks at the corner.

'Oh, you mean the fact that I've recently found out that my fiancé comes from a long line of gentleman thieves?' I match his mild grin.

'You've taken it very well.'

'Loving is accepting,' I say simply, because it really is that simple.

'The thirst for adventure.' Old Mr Hunt says, smiling across the desk at me. 'It never dies, you know. I still miss it.'

I nod my understanding, wondering if the old man is trying to tell me indirectly that I shouldn't expect Becker to give it up for me. 'Did your Mags worry about you?' I ask, suddenly a little apprehensive. I've been so busy worrying, and now feeling relieved, I've not considered the fact that I might have a life with Becker, but it will be a life of constant fretting.

Old Mr H chuckles a little. 'All the time,' he says. I'm not sure if his confirmation is a consolation or not. 'But she married me knowing what made me tick. She knew the deal.'

'Are you telling me I shouldn't ask Becker to give it up?'

He smiles. 'I'm not telling you *not* to ask him.'

'But you're telling me not to expect him to?'

'I guess so.'

Goddamn me, part of me, the compassionate part, desperately wants him to find that sculpture. Another part, the sensible part, is too scared he won't come back. What is Becker thinking? What is he planning? Is he even planning? I hum, thinking Becker and I need to have a serious conversation. And I need to seriously consider what my limits are. What I can accept. What I can't.

Mr H's old, frail hand comes to rest on the solid wood of the double pedestal desk and slowly strokes it from side-to-side. 'You recognised this the moment you saw it, didn't you?'

My eyes drop to the dark surface on a smile. 'Of course.' We've been over this before. 'It's a stunning copy of the original Theodore Roosevelt.'

'You're almost right.'

My gaze shoots up. I'm almost right? No, I *am* right. 'It's identi . . .' My words fade to nothing, and he smiles. The penny drops, and my eyes get progressively wider by the second as his hint explodes in my head. 'It's the real desk?' I blurt, sticking myself to the back of my chair, putting distance between me and the double pedestal beauty. Like, stupidly, if I touch it I might implicate myself. How ridiculous. Because I've not implicated myself enough in all things Hunt related?

'That it is,' he confirms. 'Beautiful, don't you think?'

My mouth drops open and my eyes drop back to the desk. 'Then what's in the Oval Office of the White House?'

'A stunning replica.'

'Oh my days,' I breathe. 'How?'

Old Mr Hunt rests his hands on his stomach and sits back in his captain's chair, his smile firmly in place. 'I was in America in 1945. It was a total coincidence.' He grins, and I shake my head in wonder. Yeah, I bet. 'This little beauty was being kept in storage.' He taps the top.

'After the Oval Office fire on Christmas Eve 1929,' I add, knowing the story well.

'That's right. Despite it being undamaged, Herbert Hoover used another desk that was donated by a furniture maker, and this poor thing got forgotten about.' He shakes his head and sighs. 'A travesty.'

'So you decided to steal it?'

'I was quite a handy crafter of wood.'

'As opposed to Becker's sculpting skills?'

He laughs. 'Exactly.'

'So you crafted a replica and . . .'

'And I got myself a job at the haulage firm that was hired to transport the desk from storage back to the White House in 1945.'

I laugh. I can't help it. The Hunt family are really quite something. 'So Harry Truman and all of the succeeding presidents and vice presidents have been running America from a desk that *you* made?'

'Sounds unbelievable, doesn't it?' He winks, and I'm laughing all over again. Actually, no. It doesn't any more. Nothing I learn about this family shocks me like it should. I'm immune to shock. 'Here, let me show you something.' He beckons me over to his side of the desk as he pulls open the middle drawer. I wander round, still smiling. The spirit in the old man as he shares one of his many tales is a pleasure to see. It's infectious. I come to a stop beside him and watch as he lifts all of the papers from the drawer. 'You know of the tradition, don't you?'

'The tradition?'

'Yes, the tradition that Harry Truman started at the end of his term in office.' He dumps all the papers on the desk and looks up at me.

'He signed the inside of the middle drawer,' I tell him.

'That's right.' He pushes himself back from the desk and indicates for me to look.

I move in and peek around all corners of the drawer. 'There's nothing here.'

'Of course there isn't.' He chuckles. 'I pinched this desk in 1945.'

'And Truman started the tradition in 1951.' I swing my disbelieving eyes to Mr H. 'When he got voted out of office.'

'Yes, which means . . .'

'Every US president since then has signed your forged work,' I finish quietly on a mild shake of my bewildered head, looking up at his delighted face.

'Ironic, don't you think?'

'Unbelievable.' Absolutely unbelievable.

'And even more ironic is the fact that I, too, signed the desk before I switched it. Though in a slightly more discreet place. So it's in fact *me* who started the tradition.'

'Why would you sign it?'

He shrugs. 'We Hunt men have terrible egos, Eleanor. You should know that by now.' He reaches up and clucks my cheek on a wink, just as the door opens and Becker walks in on us chuckling together.

He looks fresh, suited and booted, and his hair still wet. Oh boy, my man is a show-stopper. Becker frowns as he cleans his glasses before slipping them on. 'All right?'

'Your gramps just told me the tale of this sturdy desk.' I pat the top on a cheeky smile, and Becker rolls his eyes as he wanders over, dropping a kiss on my cheek.

'That's his favourite story. Just humour him. It won't be the first time he bores you with it.'

'Cheeky sod!' Old Mr H laughs, pushing himself up from his chair with too much effort. 'You might have skydived off the Burj Khalifa, but you didn't wander the corridors of the White House.'

Becker is over in a shot, helping him, and the old man doesn't argue. 'Careful.'

'I'll be scaling the side of a skyscraper again soon,' he quips, turning to his grandson and giving him a sharp nod, staring into his eyes and taking his cheeks in his palms, getting his face close to Becker's. 'God's speed, and all that nonsense.'

I could melt when Becker takes his grandfather in a fierce hug, holding onto him tightly as the old man pats at his back affectionately. It's the first time I've seen them embrace like this, and the comfort it gives me surpasses heart-warming. 'I love you, Gramps,' Becker says quietly, kissing the old man's head.

Emotion creeps up on me and wedges itself in my throat, my lips pressing together as I stand quietly to the side and let them have their moment.

'Good lad,' Mr H says, instigating their separation and getting on his way, raising a waving hand in the air as he goes. The door closes and I look to Becker, seeing him staring across his office, his face expressionless for a few moments before he glances across to me.

'Come here,' he orders quietly, opening his arms.

I walk straight into his body and let him hug me, getting a hint of how tightly he held his dear old gramps. 'I'm so glad you're home,' I mumble into his chest, letting a happy warmth penetrate me bone deep.

'Me too,' he whispers, sighing. 'I have somewhere I need to be.' He detaches me from his body and homes in on my questioning face. 'Therapy,' he answers on a smile. 'And I think it will be my last session.'

'It will?' I ask, surprised, though on the inside I'm all kinds of happy about that.

'It definitely will.' Dropping a gentle kiss on my forehead, he breathes in and lets all the air stream out slowly. 'I love you.'

'I love you, too, my sinful saint.' I feel his lips stretch into a smile across my skin before he pulls me away and finds my happy eyes. He stares at me for the longest time, combing through my red hair with his fingers. Then he swallows and plants one last kiss on my lips. 'See you later.' He strides out, but slows at the door, looking back at me. 'Never stop looking at my arse, princess.'

'Never,' I reply.

He flips me an endearing wink and leaves.

Chapter 39

After Becker left for his session with Dr Vass, I made a point of finding some work to do. It wasn't difficult after I took a call from Bonhams who put me onto a lord in Devonshire who was interested in the Rembrandt that the countess bought and then decided, conveniently, that she had nowhere to hang it. I checked in with Lucy, who was still on cloud nine, before calling Mum, who was at the top of the London Eye. She was so damn excited when I suggested dinner tomorrow night.

After answering a few emails, I start to finish off some filing when Mrs Potts shoves her head around the door. The smell of something delicious wafts into the room. 'I've made Mr H a roast chicken dinner for lunch, dear. Come, there's plenty to go around.'

My tummy growls its excitement. 'On my way,' I confirm, dropping the files to the table. My appetite is back with a vengeance. 'Is Becker back yet?'

'Not yet, dear. Come along.'

The phone rings from behind me, pulling my hasty pace to a stop. 'I'd better get that,' I say. 'I have a bite on the Rembrandt.'

'Okay, dear. I'll finish serving.' She lets the door close, and I answer the phone. 'The Hunt Corporation.'

'Eleanor?'

I recognise Becker's therapist's voice immediately. 'Hi Paula. How are you?'

'I'm good, you?'

'Couldn't be better,' I answer, but she probably knows this

already after her session with Becker.

'Good to hear. Is the cheeky maverick there? I have a question about a piece of art I want to buy through an online merchant, but his mobile's going straight to voicemail.'

My back straightens. 'He left hours ago to come see you.' I don't like the quickening of my pulse, nor the fact that my eyes have automatically drifted across the room to the bookshelf with the hidden compartment.

'But we don't have an . . .' She drifts off, obviously realising that she's dropped Becker in it. 'Oh dear.'

I hang up without so much as a goodbye, my pulse now pounding. But I don't try to call Becker to find out where the hell he is. Instead, I dash across the library and reach beneath the shelf, feeling for the catch that'll get the secret compartment open. My fumbling fingers hamper my urgency, my curses coming thick and fast. Eventually, the bottom section releases and I waste no time reaching in and feeling for the leather-bound file. Pulling it out, I stare down at the embossed elephants for a few tense seconds before I pull the fastener and flip the book open, going straight to the back where I know the map to be. My pounding pulse ignites the moment I reach the last page and find what I feared I would.

'You bastard,' I whisper, staring down at the empty page. No map. Nothing. I don't bother flicking through the remaining pages. It'll be a waste of precious time. With my heart in my mouth, I zoom out of the library and race to the kitchen, falling through the door clumsily. Old Mr H and Mrs Potts look up at me from the table, both quite alarmed by my abrupt entrance.

I catch a breath and hit them with my discovery. 'He's gone,' I blurt out, holding up the book. 'His therapist just called to speak to him about something she wants to buy. He told me he was seeing her today, but she's not seen him and the map's gone.' My panic is rising, the book shaking in my hands. 'He's gone to find the sculpture!'

Both of them stare at me, with not a hint of panic on their faces. 'Oh dear,' Mrs Potts says calmly, lowering the spoonful of carrots she's holding over Mr H's plate.

'Oh dear?' I mimic, recoiling. Just *oh dear*? That's it? 'Aren't you wor—' A flashback hits me – one from Becker's office this morning. 'God's speed,' I whisper, swinging my panicked face to Becker's grandfather. Visions. Visions of him hugging Becker bombard my mind. The look he gave his grandson, the hug they shared. 'You knew?' I sound accusing, but I simply cannot help it. 'You knew what he was going to do.'

Becker's grandfather's old shoulders drop with his eyes. 'I knew,' he confirms.

'How could you?' I fall back against the closed door. What's changed? The old man has constantly expressed his demand for Becker to drop it. To quit with the search.

Gramps gets up from the table, prompting Mrs Potts to rush and assist. She holds onto his arm as he approaches me slowly. My glazed eyes meet his, my shakes getting the better of me. 'Eleanor, dear, the moment I stepped into his secret room and saw that sketch of *Head of a Faun*, when I realised Becker forged that treasure, I knew he will never move on until he puts that ghost to rest. That sculpture is a ghost, dear girl. Becker boy needs to find peace, and that damn lost treasure is the only thing that'll give him peace.'

'But it might not even be there to be found,' I point out desperately. 'He could be putting himself at risk for nothing. Brent Wilson knows he has a fake. He knows Becker pushed the price up and forced him into buying it. Don't you think he'll be tailing Becker's arse?'

He smiles. He actually smiles, and it's beyond me why. This is awful. 'Let it be,' he placates me softly. 'Let him do his thing. Let him find it and come home to us.'

'He told me that I'm more important.' My voice begins to quiver.

'I've no doubt you are, Eleanor. No doubt at all. But do you want to sleep with him every night and know his dreams are invaded by that sculpture? Because they will be, dear girl. Hades have mercy, I still dream of the damn thing myself.'

I withdraw, stunned by his confession. 'You hate that sculpture,' I mumble pathetically.

'I hate that our obsession has hurt my family. It's the cause of all the heartache, and now I feel like it's the only thing to cure it. He can't move on until he finds it, Eleanor. Which means you can't either.'

I look down at his hand, where his stick has always been glued to him until recently. It's back in his grasp, but I would put my money on the fact that it's missing something. 'You've given him your piece of the map, haven't you?'

'X marks the spot, dear girl.'

'And where's the spot? Where has he gone?' I'm less scared now, more pissed off. The control I wanted is gone. I wanted to talk to him about this. I wanted us to agree on things, share things. He's taken it all out of my control.

He smiles. 'Rome.'

'Rome?' I blurt. 'But Becker spent years there.'

'As did I. But the Pantheon was never on my hit list, nor his father's, and nor Becker's.'

'The Pantheon?' I blink my surprise, wondering why on earth it would be hidden there. There's no connection with Michelangelo. None at all.

'Yes, the Pantheon. Beats me too, but that's exactly where the code points to.'

'The code?'

'Yes, those damn numbers had me scratching my head for years.'

'And Becker cracked it?'

'Of course he cracked it. Within fifteen bleedin' minutes. The boy's a genius.'

I'm a genius. 'And what if it isn't there?' I ask. God, what if it isn't *anywhere*? I'll have to live in fear for the rest of my life. I'll panic every time Becker leaves The Haven.

'I have a feeling in my bones, Eleanor.' He winks.

'So I have to just hang around and wait for word from him? A call to tell me he's alive?'

'Welcome to the Hunt family, dear girl.' He turns and ambles back to the table, cool and calm as can be, while I remain by the door, stunned. 'Come eat,' he calls, settling down and letting Mrs Potts finish loading his plate.

'I'm suddenly not hungry,' I reply quietly, opening the door. 'I think I need a lie down.'

The old pair smile mildly, both nodding their understanding, as I let myself out of the kitchen. I stand in the corridor for an age, wondering what on earth I'm going to do with myself. What if he doesn't call? What if . . .

There are so many *what ifs*, none of which I like. This is going to be torturous. Just wait here, my mind dreaming up all kinds of things? I can't.

I rush back to the library and replace the leather bound book in the secret compartment and then take myself up to Becker's apartment. And my hands are in his wardrobe as soon as I make it to his bedroom. And a small suitcase is on the bed soon after that. And my clothes are being stuffed inside a few seconds later.

I'm on my way out the door with my packed case and my passport before my brain has told me what the plan is. Wait for word? Wait here worrying to death whether he's safe? Whether he's alive? I don't think so.

And, actually, if that damn sculpture is there to be found, I want to see my man's face when he lays his hands on it. I want to see the exhilaration. I want to feel his peace. It's not just him now, it's us, and after everything I've been through to get to now, I feel like I deserve to experience the climax and know that it's the end of his mission. I need to know that we can get on with our lives without the mystery of that godforsaken sculpture hanging around our necks.

So God's speed to me, too.

Chapter 40

I stare at my reflection in the mirror of the ladies' bathroom at Fiumicino Airport, taking in my new appearance while I chew my lip. I'm wearing a wig – a black, glossy one that's poker straight to my shoulders with a fringe. I haven't had a fringe since I was six, and my pasty complexion definitely doesn't carry jet black very well. But I don't look like me. My red hair is like a beacon, would be noticed a mile off. Over the top? Not at all. Brent Wilson could be tailing Becker. I can't risk being seen, especially after his attempt to remove me from Countryscape.

On a deep breath, I have another quick faff with my new hairstyle before slipping on some shades. 'Perfect,' I say to my reflection, then I grab my case and head for the taxi rank.

I've always wanted to visit Rome – always been desperate to indulge in the ancient city and visit all the places that I've read about. But as the taxi takes me through the streets that I've longed to lose myself in, my focus is set firmly on the disposable phone that I bought at Heathrow as I programme in Becker's number. I'm not stupid. He has my phone tracked and bugged, and I know Percy the whizz kid will give Becker the heads-up on my whereabouts. Or Mrs Potts and Gramps will have raised the alarm when they realise I'm missing. Becker would have found out I was on my way to the airport before I made it there, and I know he would have me stopped from boarding the flight one way or another. I'm taking no chances.

It's still light, though dusk is falling, and I know Becker will be waiting for darkness before he hits the ancient church. We rumble down a cobbled side street, and the taxi rolls to a stop, the driver looking at me in the rear-view mirror. '*La strada finisce qui. Bisogna camminare il resto.*'

My eyebrows pinch once he's finished firing his jumble of foreign words at me. 'I'm sorry, I don't speak Italian.'

'The road. It finish,' he tells me abruptly. 'You walk now.'

'Oh.' I dive into my purse and pull out some euros. 'Is it far?'

He holds up two fingers and takes the cash. 'Two minute.'

'Thank you.' I get out of the cab, tugging my small case behind me. The air is quite close, the streets busy with tourists. Wandering down the pedestrian zone, my case bumping behind me, I want to glance up and around me to admire the old buildings that are closing me in on the narrow street, but my attention remains trained on the path before me, my concentration acute. Now I'm here, a few nerves are tickling, giving me a moment to pause to consider for the first time what Becker might say when he discovers that I've followed him. I hear a lot of swearing in my mind. And I see an angry face. I'll take his wrath. There's not much he can do about it now. It seems he's contaminated me with his thrill-seeking ways. He can deal with it.

The street narrows further for a few hundred yards, and once I've bumped my way through the crowds, it opens up onto a square. My pace slows until I eventually grind to a stop, and my head drops back, my mouth open. The sight takes my breath away. 'Oh my days,' I whisper to myself, staring at the ancient building, which looks like it could have grown up from the ground. Goose bumps pitter-patter across the exposed skin of my arms, my hands reaching up to my shades and pulling them off. I've never seen anything like it. It's beautiful but eerie, the exterior magnificent but almost gloomy. It's a beast of a building, standing proud and powerfully, dominating the piazza, looking almost too big for the space. The small buildings surrounding it look like dolls' houses, tiny and dainty, and the people wandering around look like mere specks of dust in the shadow of the Pantheon. It's the most powerful atmosphere I've ever experienced, the history that's seeping from the stone of the structure tangible. I'm rendered paralysed by it.

'Oh,' I yelp as something collides with my back and I jolt forward abruptly, being snapped from my trance.

'*Scusa!*' A man takes my arm to steady me. '*Mi dispiace, non ti ho visto.*'

I let him ensure my stability before I reach up to my head, making sure my wig isn't sliding down my face. 'Excuse me,' I say, for what reason I don't know. *He* bumped into *me*.

'Ah, English.' He smiles, and I nod, gathering myself as he releases me. 'Please, I'm sorry. It is quite busy.' He indicates around us, where crowds of people are all taking pictures or just standing staring up at the beautiful landmark. 'You are a tourist?'

'I'm here on business,' I say on impulse, backing away from him.

He tips his hat and passes me. 'Good day.'

'Good day,' I reply, wandering further into the square, look-ing around at all the cafes with tables and chairs spilling onto the piazza. I find an empty seat at one of them and settle down, taking the time after I've ordered a coffee to go over my plan. It's quite simple. I'm going to call him and tell him that I'm here. That's it. But before I face Becker's fury, I decide to have a few quiet moments to myself, sipping my coffee and absorbing the sight before me. And maybe to build up some courage. *Lord, Dad, I bet you're spinning in your grave.*

I drag it out for far longer than I planned, but the company of the Pantheon is beyond spectacular, and not only that, my mind is racing with where on earth Becker will start with his search. The building is colossal. He could be here for months, turn the place upside down and inside-out, and still not find it. If it's even here to be found.

I sit, relaxed and thinking, until the sun has disappeared

beyond the buildings surrounding the old church and a shadow creeps across the square, making it seem more foreboding. More eerie. It's getting late. I need to call him. Face the music.

I ask for the bill and reach into my bag to retrieve my purse, but after a good few seconds of feeling around, I can't lay my hands on it. Cursing, I pull my bag up onto my lap and practically stick my face inside. I frown. No purse. 'Oh no,' I gasp, my mind giving me a replay of the scene earlier when a man, quite literally, knocked me out of my trance. 'He stole my purse,' I say to my bag, looking up and around, my eyes darting as if I might find the dirty little crook. I can't believe I've been pick-pocketed. My whole body slumps into my chair. What am I going to do? I have no money, no cards. 'Shit,' I spit, looking over my shoulder to the cafe as I weigh up my options. It takes just a few seconds to figure out that I don't have many. Well, just one, actually. Run. But just as I'm coming to terms with yet another crime I'm about to add to my ever-growing list of wrongs, something catches my attention and holds it.

My heart has a little clatter in my chest. It's no wonder when he's looking so fucking delicious, his body reclined, his ankle resting on his knee, his Ray-Ban shades in place. He's a couple of tables in front to the left of me, practically within spitting distance.

My breath audibly hitches, and all worries of the anger I'll be faced with when he finds out I'm in Rome disappears at the mere sight of him.

I smile to myself, having a careful scan of his suit-adorned physique. His stare is set firmly on the ominous building before us, his fingers drumming the table by the espresso that the waiter has just placed down, and I can literally see his mind racing.

I clear my throat and get to my feet, taking the four paces that get me to the side of his table. 'Hello,' I say, looking down at him.

'I'm taken,' he mutters, not allowing his line of sight to falter as he reaches for his coffee.

His declaration brings the biggest smile to my face. 'Well, that's a shame.' I sigh, feigning disappointment. 'I've been a naughty girl and need my arse spanking.'

His coffee pauses halfway to his mouth and his face slowly turns up to me. I grin, and Becker gapes, lifting up his shades to reveal wide, shocked, hazel eyes. 'What the fuck?' he coughs, dropping his cup to the table and shooting up from his chair. 'Eleanor?'

'Hi!'

'Sweet mother of fucking God.' He grabs my arm and yanks me down to a seat, looking around nervously. I can't stop myself. I dive forward and smash my lips to his, and he doesn't fight me off. I don't know what's come over me. Relief? I hear him groan, feeling his tongue lapping gently across mine, before he growls and forces me back into my chair. Reaching down to his groin, he rearranges himself on a few shifts of his body before landing me with the filthiest glare. 'Explain, princess,' he orders threateningly. 'Now.'

All of the nerves I was feeling disintegrate under his death glare. He has a cheek. '*You* explain, you sly bastard,' I retort sharply, making sure he knows I mean business. I don't know why I've been so worried. It's *him* who should be fretting after the stunt he's pulled. It's *him* who should be worried about the wrath *he* will face. '"*I need you more than I need the trea-sure.*"' I parrot his words in a pathetically condescending tone. 'Yeah, right.' Leaning forward in my chair, I drill holes in him with my pissed-off glare. 'Don't think you can get away with leaving me in London while you play daredevil, Hunt. All or nothing.'

His jaw twitches, and then he pushes forward and gets right up close to my face. 'Get up,' he orders, and I slowly rise, never letting my angry eyes waver from his. His hand goes into his pocket and pulls out a note. It reminds me of my little predicament.

'Oh.' I smile sweetly. 'Would you mind?' I hand him my bill, and he frowns at me. 'Lost my purse.'

'You lost your purse?' he asks, eyebrow hitched in question. My face flames bright red, no matter how hard I try to stop it. He laughs. 'You got pick-pocketed, didn't you?'

'No.' I pull off outraged incredibly well, considering I'm faking it.

'I don't fucking believe it,' he mutters, rolling his eyes. 'My wife-to-be got conned. This is the worst day ever.' He tosses down another note before taking my arm and leading me across the square, constantly peeking around. He isn't speaking, his anger palpable, and it's refuelled my nerves. I knew he wouldn't be happy, but . . . yikes.

Pulling me down an alleyway, he stops, swings me around, and pushes me front forward into a wall. I yelp, knowing what he has planned. I don't fight. I may as well just get my punishment out of the way. Then I'll rip him to shreds.

My dress is yanked up, my knickers shoved to the side, and his palm comes down on a punishing, belter of a smack. 'Fuck, Becker!' I'm being spun back around in the blink of an eye and thrust up against the wall.

He gets his angry face up close again. 'I'm fucking furious, Eleanor,' he whispers menacingly, threading his fingers through my black, glossy bob. 'And if *this* isn't a wig, I'm going to spank you until your hair has grown back and returned to its natural colour.'

'It's a wig,' I murmur, watching as he visibly deflates in relief.

'What the fuck are you doing here?' he hisses. 'And where's your phone?'

'I left it at The Haven. Do you think I'm stupid, Hunt? I know your little whizz kid will be keeping tabs on my movements.'

'I should have had a fucking chip put under your skin.'

My lips twist in annoyance. 'You fucking lied to me, you scoundrel.'

A wave of realisation travels across his face, one that suggests he's comprehended just how pissed off I am. Good. Because I'm really pissed off. He won't turn this around on me. No way. 'I . . .' he begins. 'It's . . . I . . .' He stammers all over his words, getting more and more worked up and redder in the face. 'I prefer you with red hair!'

I snort and push him off me. 'Yeah, well, I prefer you in London with me, but you're not fucking there, are you?'

He breathes in deeply and squeezes his eyes shut, pinching the bridge of his nose. 'It'll drive me insane for the rest of my life if I don't follow this, princess.'

'I know,' I reply simply, making his eyes snap open. I pull my bag onto my shoulder and straighten myself out. I spent the entire flight coming to terms with that. 'So let's see if it's there, and then we can get on with our lives together.'

His neck retracts on his shoulders. 'What?'

'Let's find some treasure, Hunt.' I push past him, my small case bouncing across the cobbles as I drag it along. 'Where are you staying?'

He doesn't answer, forcing me to stop and seek him out. He looks a bit dazed.

'Well?' I ask.

He shakes himself back to life. 'Well, what?'

'Hotel. Where are you staying?'

'Across the square.'

'Are you going to show me?' I cock my head in question, and the hollows of Becker's cheeks begin to pulse.

Slowly, he flexes his head from side-to-side, rolling his shoulders. Then he strides over and snatches my case from my hold, virtually ripping my arm off in the process. 'It doesn't look like I have a fucking choice, does it?'

'No, it doesn't.' I sniff, watching as he stomps off down the alleyway, hauling my small case behind him.

'Move that arse, princess,' he spits, and I grin, starting to totter along behind him. 'Why the fuck are you wearing a wig?'

'Isn't that obvious?'

'It's fucking ridiculous.'

'I wouldn't be wearing one if you hadn't done a disappearing act,' I retort indignantly as we breach the end of the alley and emerge onto the square. The sun has completely fallen away, and now the Pantheon is glowing, the surrounding area lit by the bustling cafes.

'This way,' he mutters, striding off. I tail him, noting he's looking around vigilantly. It makes me wonder if he suspects Brent Wilson is loitering somewhere, but I think better than to ask. He might swing for me.

He leads me to a small boutique hotel just off the square, and after the tiny elevator has carried us to the top floor, he exits first, leaving me to follow on behind. Letting us into the last room at the end of the long corridor, he throws my case down on the bed and goes straight to the window, throwing it open and pushing the shutters back. I breathe in my surprise when the Pantheon comes into view over a few dilapidated rooftops, almost close enough to reach out the window and touch. 'Wow.' I close the door and wander over, joining Becker. He seems thoughtful as he stares across the tops of the buildings, his stance relaxed. I'm desperate to know what his plan is, what he's thinking, or whether he's figured out exactly where he's going to look. The building is a monster of a structure. 'Where will you start?'

He jumps next to me a little, startled back into the hotel room from wherever he was. He turns and paces towards the bathroom, pulling his jacket off as he goes. 'You shouldn't have come, Eleanor.'

I take myself to the bed and sit on the edge. 'I'm not going to sit at home worrying about you.'

His head peeks around the door, his fingers working the buttons of his shirt. 'How did you know where I am?'

'Dr Vass. She called The Haven after she couldn't reach you on your mobile.' My eyes narrow. 'And I checked your secret hiding place. No map. And then I found Gramps and Mrs Potts, and they didn't look in the least bit surprised when I told them it was gone. Seems I'm the only one who *didn't* know.'

Rather than coming back at me, he just scowls, his glasses dropping down his nose a tad. I scowl right back, daring him to argue with me. He must appreciate my anger because he huffs and goes back into the bathroom without a word. I hear the shower kick in and get up, grabbing my wash bag and making my way to him. I see his naked back disappear behind the shower curtain as I enter.

'I want you to promise me something,' I say assertively, dumping my cosmetics on the sink.

'What?'

I don't like not being able to see his face, so I reach forward and yank the curtain across. His fingers are in his hair working up a lather. 'This is it. After tonight, no more. If it isn't there, you let it go.' I lose all the anger from my face and give him pleading eyes. I can't go on like this. The constant wonder, the constant worry. It'll kill me.

Becker's eyes bore holes into mine, his fingers still on his head. Then he deflates and sighs. 'I promise, princess.'

My body shrinks in relief. 'Thank you.'

He offers a tiny smile. An understanding smile. I return it and go to the sink to brush my teeth. 'So what's the plan?' I ask.

'The plan?'

'Yes, you must have a plan. What time are we heading out?'

'We?'

'I guess we should wait until it's dark.' I take my toothbrush to my mouth and start scrubbing. 'What should I wear?' I garble.

'What should you wear?' he mimics, shutting off the shower

and grabbing a towel. 'Something comfortable.'

I spit and rinse. 'Right.'

'Be ready in twenty minutes.' He passes me, his hard body glistening wet. My hold of my toothbrush tightens, and I clench my teeth, my brain reminding me that he's working. I mustn't distract him.

I hurry through to the bedroom and rummage through my case for something suitable to wear, feeling a strange whirling in my tummy. Nerves, I think. Or is it excitement? I start to breathe deeply to keep my heartbeat steady. I don't want to display any signs of anxiousness to Becker. He'll refuse to take me. But I don't feel anxious. My hands falter as I pull on a roll-neck jumper, my mind assessing my frame of mind. Yes, my heart is thumping a little, and my stomach is twisting, but I don't feel apprehensive.

It really is excitement. I shake my head in wonder, grabbing my jeans from the bed, but something catches my eye. Becker's bag. Or something *in* his bag. *What the hell?* I inch forward, my eyes jumping from his back at the window to his bag on the bed. And I frown, reaching forward and plucking out the item of my interest and staring at it for a few moments. Then I cast my suspicious eyes across the room to Becker's back.

He moves, and I quickly stuff my find in the pocket of my jeans.

I'm taking no chances. Covering all my bases.

I'm ignoring the guilt creeping up on me for doubting him. But if I've learned anything during my time in Becker's corrupt world, it's to be prepared. It's crazy. I'm never prepared for him. But this time . . .?

'Okay?' he asks, looking back at me.

'Great.' I smile and make my way over as he returns his attention to the desk before him. He's dressed now, wearing some old worn jeans, his brown leather boots and a black T-shirt, and he's leaning over the desk by the window, hands braced on the sides. He looking down at the map, which is spread across the wood. I approach him quietly and stare down at the old piece of paper. It's not just his part of the map, though. The missing piece that Mr H had hidden in his walking stick all this time is resting where it should be, filling the hole that's been present for years. It's glowing, like it's happy to have been reunited with the rest of the map. And a handwritten note is set to the side. The deciphered code. 'How did you figure it out?' I ask.

Becker breathes out heavily. 'These numbers here on the missing piece.' He runs his delicate finger across the ancient paper. 'Gramps thought it was a code. It isn't.'

'Then what?'

'Coordinates, but they've been manipulated to look like a complex code. This map isn't as old as I thought.'

'How old did you think it was?'

'Older than seventeenth century when coordinates were invented,' he muses, his finger stopping over Rome. 'There are eight columns on the face of the porch of the Pantheon, and if I've calculated it correctly, these coordinates indicate between the fourth and fifth columns, about six metres back.'

My astonishment is obvious in my small draw of breath. 'That's quite accurate.'

'Almost too accurate,' he muses, straightening. 'But I guess I'll find out soon enough if it's a dead end.' He glances across to me. 'Ready?'

That feeling inside of me – the one I've concluded was excitement – has just soared. I nod and he smiles, taking my hand and pulling me into his chest. I could shout my happiness. He's not mad with me any more. Cupping my cheeks, he flicks a frown up to my wig before he brings our mouths together, and all of the lust I've managed to keep at bay steams forward. 'I'm still mad with you,' he breathes, sealing our lips and kissing me softly as he takes my jeans from my hand and tosses them on the bed.

I don't reply, rounding his shoulders with my arms. That was the most unconvincing *I'm mad with you* that I've ever heard. He lets out a deep growl, rolling his tongue, exploring my mouth carefully as he walks me back.

'We can spare a few minutes,' he says, taking me down to the bed and smothering me. 'Just a few minutes.'

I grin to myself, accepting and delighted, feeling him taking my arms and pushing them to the headboard. 'Hmm,' I hum, lacing my fingers with his and squeezing. His kiss is deep and soft, his body heavy atop of mine. It feels so good. So right. As ever, I'm lost in my corrupt fiancé and his corrupt world.

'Sorry, princess.' He lifts and I hear the clanging of metal, my wrists suddenly trapped above my head.

'What?' I look up and see a pair of handcuffs securing me to the bed. 'No!' I wriggle and the metal cuts into my wrists harshly. 'Becker!' I feel the mattress move and shoot my eyes down to find him standing at the foot of the bed. 'What are you doing?' I shout incredulously.

'Leaving you here where I know you're safe, that's what.' He stalks across the room and hauls up a backpack from the floor, grabbing the map.

'Becker, you can't.' I wrestle with my restraints, flipping and twisting on the mattress.

'I fucking can,' he says on a laugh, throwing the bag over his shoulder and making his way over to me. 'Did you really think I'd take you with me?'

'Yes!' I shout. 'This isn't fair!'

He reaches for my hair and pulls off my wig, tossing it on the chair in the corner on a disgusted look. 'That's better.'

'Becker.'

'I love you.'

'Fuck off!'

He smiles at me, his look, annoyingly, rampant with love. 'I'll be back before you know it.' He stalks to the door and swings it open, looking over his shoulder at me. 'And just so you know, I'm going to spank you stupid when I'm back.' The door slams and he's gone.

'Becker!' I hiss and spit all over the bed, throwing my body up violently for a few long, pointless minutes until I'm out of breath and my muscles ache. 'You bastard!' I scream. My anger is potent, my body buzzing with fury as I lay on the bed, restrained, with only my wild imagination to keep me company. I hate him. Hate him! I take a few moments to calm myself down. Now I don't feel guilty for doubting him. My instinct didn't let me down.

I start inching my body down the bed as far as I can and gripping my jeans between my feet. I have to virtually bend my body in two to get them above my head, but I manage. It takes some serious patience and time, but I eventually position my pocket by my hand. And, with a smug smile, I pull out the little silver key that I found in his bag.

Fuck you, Becker Hunt.

Chapter 41

It seems that was the easy part. I'm not sure how long I've been here wrestling on the bed to get the right angle. A few minutes? A few hours? Every tiny noise I hear beyond the door has my heart beating faster as I hiss in pain, the metal of the cuffs cutting into my flesh. What if Brent's in Rome? What if he finds Becker? My thoughts are spiralling, my anger fast converting into worry. What if I never see him again? Annoying tears of frustration start to pinch the backs of my eyes, hindering my task. It's getting the better of me.

I try to force my strung muscles to relax, my neck aching terribly, straining to see what I'm doing. 'Goddamn it,' I yell, stretching that little bit more, my muscles screaming. But then a noise from outside freezes me, and I hear a lock click. My eyes land on the door just as it moves a fraction, pushed open a little way. Oh, thank God. My veins drain of apprehension. He's back.

Yet when the door opens the rest of the way, I find I'm not looking at Becker at all. 'Brent?' I gasp.

He stands at the threshold of the room, looking at me shackled to the bed, his face a picture of perplexity. 'Eleanor?' he questions, taking in my cuffed hands.

Fuck. What now? My mind starts to sprint, but it doesn't give me a clue of what to say. What I do know, though, is that he can't make me talk. I won't say a thing. And I've quickly looped into the fact that if Brent is here, he isn't tailing Becker's arse.

'Where's Becker?' he asks, approaching the bed.

I slam my head back down to the pillow defiantly. 'Fuck off, Brent.'

He chuckles, and it's cold. 'Your sass. I love it.'

I want to close my eyes, but that would be stupid. I need to keep my eye on him. Jesus Christ, I'm helpless.

'Where is he?'

I find myself laughing. It's as sarcastic as a laugh can be. I refuse to let him see me scared. 'Call yourself a treasure hunter?' I goad, landing him with a wicked smile. 'You're here, and Becker . . . is not.'

'Don't test me, Eleanor.'

'Why? You gonna kill me, too?'

His hand comes up and feels my hair, and it takes everything I have not to cower or flinch. Everything not to vomit. I have no idea where my valour is coming from, but I'm just letting it flow, my hatred for this man unstoppable. 'Get your filthy hands off me.'

He sighs, releasing my hair, and reaches into the inside pocket of his suit jacket. 'I did warn you,' he says, pulling out his phone as I hide my frown. He presents me with his screen, and there is a photograph of Becker. Kissing a woman. A woman with glossy, straight black hair to her shoulders. 'He met her on the piazza for coffee earlier.'

My round eyes remain fixed on the picture, my mind a jumble. I try to encourage some tears of despair to come. *Holy fucking shit, where's that wig?* I peek up to the chair in the corner where Becker threw it, seeing it hanging off the arm.

'I knew he'd hurt you, Eleanor. I did try to tell you.' He stands and tucks his phone away. 'He's always been a womaniser. You owe him nothing. Now, where is he?'

I blink repeatedly, plotting my next move while Brent smiles down at me, like he's just divulged the world's biggest secret. He looks smug. Satisfied. I want to smash his stupid face in.

How long can I keep him here? I conclude very quickly that it won't be for long.

I rest my head back down and look at the ceiling.

'Where is he?'

I remain quiet, not blessing him with my eyes.

'Eleanor.' His tone is warning, and I completely ignore it. Then there's silence for a few moments, and I hear him sigh, the mattress dipping. I have absolutely no idea what happens next. I'm moving without thinking, my knee coming up and cracking Brent in the nose. 'Fuck!' he chokes, flying back with his palm over his face, blood spurting out the sides. I look up, praying for a miracle, wrestling with my shaky hands. 'Come on,' I whisper, seeing the tip of the key a mere millimetre away from the lock. I growl, having a quick check on Brent, finding him slumped on the floor looking a bit dazed. He looks up at me. And a veil of evil falls. Shit. I return my attention to the headboard and pull harder on the cuffs, hissing, seeing a trickle of blood roll down my forearm.

The key slips into the hole, and one last twist of my wrist releases the lock. I gasp, feeling the blood rush back into my arms.

'You little—'

My leg shoots out, my foot connecting with Brent's jaw, and he yelps, flopping to the bed. I grab his arm, yanking it to the bedframe, my fingers working fast, adrenalin pumping.

I cuff him to the bed.

'Fuck!' he yells.

I jump up quickly and brush my hair out of my face, my pulse racing. When I find his outraged eyes, I step back, a little dazed, a lot scared. How the hell did I manage that?

'Eleanor!' he barks, bucking off the bed, his body twisting as he hisses from the friction of the metal on his wrists. 'He can't be trusted. I've just proved that, you stupid woman.'

I grab my jeans and yank them on before shoving my feet in

my trainers and claiming the wig from the chair. Brent's face straightens momentarily while his mind plays catch-up. Then his eyes bug. 'You?'

I throw it at him. 'You're the criminal, Wilson. You're the deceitful one who can't be trusted.' I make my way to the door. 'Get comfortable. You could be there a while,' I say, yanking the door open and slamming it behind me with brute force. I run like the wind out of the hotel.

The streets are quiet now, and a quick glance at my watch tells me why. It's 2a.m. I look up to the dark sky. It's started to rain, fat drops of water hitting me hard, as I sprint towards the Pantheon, adrenalin pumping. When I reach the Piazza della Rotonda, I skid to a stop, staring straight at the mammoth marble columns that line the porch. It's dark, it's quiet, and it's *so* eerie. The glow from a few street lanterns illuminate the square a little, but the porch beyond the pillars of the ancient temple is cloaked in complete darkness.

The rain starts to come down harder, seeping into the threads of my sweater, my hair now sticking to my face. Shuddering, I tentatively walk forward, rounding the fountain, listening carefully, my eyes darting. There's a constant, distant tapping sound that's getting louder the closer I creep towards the church. But I can't see a damn thing.

Then the tapping suddenly stops, and so do my steps. I'm as still as possible as I listen carefully, apprehension creeping up my legs into my torso. I start to tremble, my eyes darting. 'Bec—' My breath is stolen from me, a hand slapped over my mouth as I'm grabbed and hauled across the piazza.

'You're seriously pushing my fucking buttons, princess,' he hisses in my ear, squeezing me to his body. Dumping me on my feet when he's carried me onto the porch of the Pantheon, he grabs the tops of my arms and shakes me a little. 'How the fuck did you get free?'

My vision clears and centres on his vexed expression. If I

thought I'd seen mad, I was wrong. He looks borderline psy-chotic. But I'm not exactly pleased as punch myself. I square up to him, bold and full of fire. 'I took the key to the cuffs out of your bag.' I push into his shoulder. 'Don't think you can play me, Hunt.' I present him with my wrists, showing him the angry, red welts. 'This princess is determined.'

His eyes widen at the sight. 'Eleanor, I'm—'

'Shut up and do what you've got to do before Brent joins the party.'

'What? Brent's here? Where?'

'He's taken my position on the bed.' I don't mean to sound proud, but I kind of am.

His neck retracts on his shoulders. 'Come again?'

'He came to the hotel.'

His eyes are getting progressively wider. 'What?'

'He came to the hotel. Obviously looking for you, but he found me instead. Handcuffed to the fucking bed.'

His wide eyes are now worried. 'Oh Jesus.' He moves in, running worried hands all over my face and neck, scanning for signs of damage.

'I'm fine.' I shrug him off. 'No thanks to you.'

He visibly relaxes but the anger returns. If we weren't in such a hurry, I'd challenge him. 'We'll be discussing this later.' My hand is taken, and I'm pulled further under the porch of the Pantheon.

'Yes, we will,' I agree, sounding as threatening as I meant. He should be worried.

Becker brings us to a stop more-or-less bang in the centre of the porch, and I see a few slabs already broken out and replaced. 'Stay there and don't breathe a word,' he orders, dropping to his knees and collecting a hammer and chisel. He starts meticu-lously tapping away, being super careful as he does, and I watch, fascinated, as he gently brushes away the dirt he's unearthing from the joints surrounding the stone.

'Why don't you just smash your way through?' I ask, thinking time isn't on his side.

'Because, Eleanor,' he pauses and glances up at me with tired, impatient eyes. 'This is the fucking Pantheon. It's been standing here for thousands of years. I already feel guilty for tampering with something so fucking ancient. Now shut up.'

I scowl to myself, slighted, and do as I'm bid, keeping quiet while he works his way around the circumference of the stone until all of the joint has been broken away. Casting aside his tools, he stands and collects a crow bar, wedging it beneath one side and standing on the end. It doesn't budge. 'Motherfucker,' he puffs, applying constant, jarring thrusts of the bar until I definitely spot a slight movement. I gasp, but keep my shout of encouragement contained, watching as he continues to coax the slab free.

'It's coming,' I whisper. 'Just keep pushing.'

Stilling, Becker slowly turns a look on to me that suggests I should zip it. Immediately.

'Sorry.' I step back and return my attention to the stone as Becker stands on the end of the bar again, pushing all of his weight into it. The slab slowly creeps up at one end, and my hands shoot to my mouth to contain my rush of excited breath.

'Get that hammer,' Becker puffs. 'And wedge it under.'

I do as I'm told, glad to help, sliding the hammer under the slab just in time. Becker's boot slips off the bar and the slab drops onto the hammer. He wipes his forehead with the back of his hand and drops to his haunches, slipping his fingers under the stone and heaving it up. 'Should have lifted more fucking weights,' he says, grunting his way through his task.

'You can do it,' I encourage him, the gap between the ground and the top of the slab growing. 'Just a bit more and flip it.'

'Shut up, Eleanor,' he grates, straightening his legs until he's standing. Then on an almighty roar, he tosses the slab up and it crashes to the ground. And it breaks clean in two.

'Oopsie,' I blurt, moving back a little to give Becker room.

'Fuck,' he curses, kicking a foot out in temper and booting his hammer across the porch.

'Well, your careful and considerate chipping away of the joints were a complete waste of valuable time,' I say as I stare at the broken slab, feeling his fire glare on me. I peek up and smile sweetly. 'What now?'

'Now I dig.' He takes a small spade and pushes it into the sandy bedding, shovelling out the dirt and casting it aside into a small, tidy mound.

Dig? How far down? We could be here for months. 'Can I help?'

'Yes,' he grunts.

'How?'

'Shut up.'

I chuck him a disgruntled look and resign myself to doing exactly that while Becker digs for what seems like forever. The mound of dirt is getting higher, and the rain is getting harder, pounding the piazza beyond the porch. My hope is dying with each shovel of dirt Becker tosses to the side, yet I won't be the one to ask at what point he gives up. Jesus, he's been looking for this damn sculpture for years. Something tells me that he won't give up until he reaches Australia. He's already had four slabs up. There are dozens more.

I study him quietly, seeing clearly that he's getting more and more frustrated with each plunge of the shovel into the ground, sweat pouring from his perfect brow. 'Damn it,' he spits, throwing the shovel into the pit aggressively. It bounces off something, creating a loud clatter, and we both audibly gasp. I look at Becker, and Becker looks at me.

'A stone?' I ask, not wanting to let my hopes get too high.

'It's a big fucking stone.' He drops to his stomach and plunges both hands into the hole, stretching, starting to move the dirt with his hands. I wait with bated breath, beginning to shake with a mixture of apprehension and excitement as I crane my neck to see into the pit.

'Is that a rag?' I ask, seeing a piece of cloth poking up in the corner.

Becker moves his hands towards it and starts shifting the dirt from around the area. Glancing up at me, he grins. 'Could be a dead body.'

'Don't.' I shiver, wondering how many bones there could be beneath this ancient church. 'Pull it,' I tell him, my impatience and uneasiness growing.

'Don't you think I'm trying? It's wrapped around something.' His head goes into the hole, grunts coming thick and fast. 'Something hard.'

'The sculpture?'

'I don't know. Fucking hell,' he breathes, heaving upward on a strained growl, fighting with whatever he's found. All of a sudden, Becker is on his knees, and then he's flying back, whatever he's fighting with dislodging. He falls to his arse, a bundle of tatty material landing on his lap.

I scramble to my feet and rush to him. 'Are you okay?'

'Super.' He starts to push the heavy bundle from his thighs, and it lands on the slabs with a thud. He winces. 'Shit.'

I laugh, probably inappropriately. I'm putting it down to nerves. 'Could you imagine after years of searching and you go and break it?'

Tired eyes climb my body to my face, and I force an awkward smile. 'No, I can't,' he mutters, getting to his knees and starting to unravel the material. I hold my breath. Is this it? Is it the long-lost sculpture? All the time and pain, and this moment could be the difference between our lives moving forward, Becker at peace, or our lives stuck in limbo, Becker constantly wondering and searching. I'm not stupid. He might have promised me that if this turns out to be a dead end he'll let it go, but I don't trust his promise. He'll never let this go.

I start to pray to all the Greek gods.

Becker's crowding the heap, his shoulders high, indicating his own held breath as he carefully peels back the material with tentative hands. 'Well would you look at that,' he whispers, sitting back and revealing what he's found.

'Oh my God.' I slowly move in closer, mesmerised by what I'm faced with. Dirt is tarnishing the surface, embedded in the crevices of the face, but there's no denying what we're looking at. I turn my stunned stare onto Becker's profile, and he slowly turns his onto mine. And we just stare at each other, neither of us able to talk, leaving an eerie quiet lingering, the rain a distant thump in the background. This is it. It's over. His search is finally over.

Becker reaches for my hand and takes it, standing and pulling me to my feet. And we stand over our discovery, staring down at it for a long, *long* time, absorbing it, taking it in, coming to terms with this colossal moment. I smile, feeling years' worth of wonder and anxiety literally draining out of the man holding my hand. It's palpable.

'It looks *nothing* like the fake you crafted,' I say mindlessly as I stare at the sculpture. Yes, it's ugly like the fake Becker forged, but definitely not evil-looking.

'I know.'

'So what now?'

'I don't know what to do,' Becker admits, still just staring. 'All these years, and now I have it, and I don't even know how I'm feeling.'

'Relieved?' I prompt, because that's how I'm feeling. So damn relieved.

'Maybe.' He looks up to the ceiling, as do I. 'I've got it, Dad.' he says quietly, squeezing my hand. 'I found it for you and Mum.'

My eyes sting from quick-building tears, and I move into Becker's side, hugging his arm. 'He'll be so proud of you.'

Becker looks down at me, a little vacant. 'I wish I could see his face,' he admits. 'I wish I could give it to him.'

'He'll be watching.' I smile and reach up to kiss his cheek. 'Wherever he is, he'll be watching.' I discreetly brush away the tear that escapes my right eye. But amid my sadness, I'm so happy I followed him to Rome so I could share this with him. And now, I know he's glad I'm here.

Bang!

We both jump from our moment, and before I can grasp what that noise was or what's going on, I'm shoved violently aside, and I lose my grip of Becker's arm. The ground grows closer to my face, my eyes closing and my hands coming up to break my fall. I hit the deck hard, but I still hear the sound of Becker crashing to the concrete too, followed by a crack of lightning.

'Fuck.' His yell is breathy, strained, and I spin around, ignoring the searing pain that's cutting through my shoulder. A rumble of thunder practically makes the ground shake, and another flash of lightning illuminates the sky and shines light on the horrid scene before me.

Becker's on his back, grappling with some hands around his neck. 'No!' I scream, seeing Brent holding him down by a thick metal chain across his throat.

'Stay away, Eleanor,' Becker coughs over his urgent words, his legs kicking out as he gasps for air and fights Brent's hold.

Oh my God, he's going to kill him! I'm up from the floor like lightning, not prepared to leave him when he's pinned down, helpless. I throw myself on Brent's back, ripping at his hair, clawing like a madwoman, anything to hamper him.

'Eleanor!' Becker yells, just as an elbow comes up and cracks me clean on the cheekbone. Stars jump into my vision, my head instantly spinning. My poor body receives another punishing clout, the air knocked from my lungs. But I force myself up again, adrenalin taking over.

Brent's momentary release of the chain to crack me one gives Becker the break he needs, and he moves fast, flipping his body over and getting Brent under him. He grabs the nearby hammer and raises it in the air. 'You twisted fuck!' he bellows, holding Brent down by the neck with one hand and brandishing the hammer with his other. 'You sick, crazy fucker. For a fucking sculpture? You'd kill for a fucking sculpture?'

'You're the one waving the fucking hammer in my face, Hunt.'

Becker throws the hammer aside, draws back his fist, and throws it into Brent's face on a roar. I wince at the chilling sound of a nose breaking. 'It fucking ends here!' Another accurate punch lands on Brent's nose, and this time blood splatters everywhere. Becker looks like the crazy one. He's lost his rag, and he doesn't look like he'll find it anytime soon. It gets to the point that I can't distinguish between the lightning bolts and the connections of Becker's fist to Brent's face.

Becker's arms pull back once more, and I jump up, running to him, unable to bear any more. 'Becker, stop.' I grab his arm to halt it sailing forward into Brent's face again. My Becker is many things, but I won't let him add murderer to his list. 'Enough!'

His body heaves and rolls, while Brent looks up at him with big, fearful eyes. He comprehends Becker's rage. He's pushed him over the edge, the one he's been balancing on for so many years. 'Okay,' Brent says, watching Becker cautiously. 'It finishes here. Enough damage has been done.'

'Your father killed my parents, Wilson. There's nothing I can do to get payback. Not even killing you would make me feel better.'

Brent breathes in deeply, fixing Becker with sure eyes. 'My father wasn't a murderer, Hunt. You know that. They were accidents.'

'And your father was involved!' Becker lifts Brent and

smashes him down on the concrete. 'Your family will never take anything from me again, do you understand? It's done!'

'Done,' Brent agrees, obviously panicked. 'It's done.'

'You don't get the sculpture,' Becker tells him on a snarl.

'You win,' Brent relents.

'I always fucking win.'

Brent lets out an amused puff of laughter, maybe tinged with a hint of nervousness, too. 'I'm too old for this shit.'

Relief floods me as I watch Becker's grip peel slowly away from Brent's neck, his exhausted body lifting equally as slowly, his eyes never leaving his nemesis. 'I never want to look at you again, Wilson. You won't walk away next time, I swear.'

'The feeling's mutual, Hunt.' Brent struggles up, sniffing and wiping at his nose as he looks across to me. 'He really has corrupted you, hasn't he?'

I find my way to Becker and curl into his side, not needing to voice my reply. I know where my loyalty lies. As well as my heart. 'Get out of here, Wilson.' Becker mutters, turning into me and wrapping his arms around my shoulders.

'Tell me how you switched the Ferrari at Sotheby's.' Brent asks, backing away from us. 'And stole the painting? Just give me that.'

I look up at Becker as he turns his face to Brent, smiling. 'Talent is something you're born with, Wilson. You can't learn it. I'm a fucking genius. *You* are not.'

Brent chuckles on a shake of his head. 'You're an egomaniac, that's what you are.'

'Fuck off.' Becker returns his attention to me, scanning me inch by inch. 'You okay?'

I nod. 'I'm fine.'

'It's over, princess.' He kisses my nose, my chin, my cheek. 'Now it's just about me and you.'

I smile, so damn happy, and reach up on my tippy-toes to get my chin on his shoulder, squeezing him to death. 'We'd better fill in that hole.'

'Nah. I like leaving something behind for people to scratch their heads over.'

I laugh lightly. He's such a maverick. 'I love—' I spot Brent swooping in quickly a few paces behind, and it takes me a few delayed seconds to register what he's doing. 'The sculpture!' I push Becker away, my legs taking on a mind of their own and breaking out into a sprint towards Brent, who now has the bundle tucked neatly under his arm as he turns, a wicked glint in his eyes.

No! God, no! I'm about to go maniac on Brent's arse, willing to throw myself into the middle of the war to stop him escaping with that sculpture. Jesus, we'll be at square one again. Becker won't have the peace he needs. Our lives will be on hold, and my worry constant, because I know for sure that Becker won't rest until he gets it back.

My legs must be a blur of movement. I'm running so fast, my objective simple. Tackle him to the ground. Hinder his escape. Do anything to stop him getting away with *Head of a Faun*.

I take the steps down to the piazza, watching my feet as I go, and just when I'm about to take off across the square in pursuit of him, my shoulder jars, nearly being yanked from the socket. 'Ow!' I yelp, turning my frantic, flushed face back. I find Becker with a firm grip around my wrist. He isn't showing any signs of urgency. No panic. Nothing. In fact, he looks as calm as can be. 'He's got the sculpture.' I throw my arm out and point to Brent's back, which is getting further and further away. 'Becker, do something.'

'Let him take it,' he says quietly.

I swing back to face him. 'What?' Has he lost his mind?

'I don't want it.'

'You don't want it?' I parrot like an idiot. 'What do you mean, *you don't want it?*'

He shrugs, and my head swings back and forth between my crackpot fiancé and Brent, who's halfway across the square with our sculpture. *Our* sculpture! 'It's cursed, princess.'

'Cursed?' I abandon Brent's back and find Becker. He's so calm. Accepting. 'Becker, you've searched your whole life for it. And Gramps. And your dad.'

He smiles. 'And now I've found it.'

'What?' My brain turns to mush.

Becker looks past me, his eyes shining bright, and I turn to follow his direction of sight. Brent has slowed to a stop across the square, looking at us a bit perplexed as he gets pelted by the heavy rain. He's wondering why the hell Becker isn't running him down. 'What's the deal, Hunt?' he calls, sounding wary.

'I won,' Becker shouts, slipping his hands into his pockets. 'I found it.'

Brent smiles, small and unsure, looking down at the sculpture in his arms. 'Are you serious?'

'Never been more serious in my life, Wilson.' Becker confirms. 'It's fucking ugly, anyway.'

I gawp at him like the crazy person that he is. 'Becker?' I question, feeling like I should slap him and knock him from his insanity.

'You can look at it every day, Wilson, and know that it was *me* who found it. Becker Hunt. Best fucking treasure hunter in the world.' He smiles cunningly. 'Congratulations, you prick. I hope you see my face every time you admire it.'

Brent shakes his head mildly. 'You can buy it for one hundred and fifty million,' he calls, holding up the bundle in his hands. 'It should about cover the Ferrari and the fake.'

Becker laughs, deep and satisfied. 'Nah. I'd rather keep the car.' His arm slips around my shoulders and pulls me in, his lips dropping a kiss on my wet hair. 'And the girl.'

Brent Wilson backs away, his head shaking in wonder. 'You crazy arsehole.'

'Maybe,' Becker counters, holding up my hand. 'But that lump of stone can't make me feel as good as she can.'

Brent laughs in disbelief. 'Have a good life, Hunt.' He turns and jogs away, looking back every now and then, obviously worried Becker is going to change his mind and chase him down. But my saint remains by my side, watching as what he's searched for his entire life disappears in the hands of the person he hates most in the world. I'm dumbfounded.

'I fucking will,' Becker breathes, looking down at my bewildered face.

'That's it?' I ask.

'That's it.'

'But . . . how . . . why . . .' I trip and stagger all over my words, scepticism rampant. 'But I don't want him to have it,' I whine, feeling more disappointed than relieved that this horrid saga is all over. Then something comes to me, and I jump back, holding Becker in place with mistrusting eyes. 'It is done, right?' I ask. 'Promise me this isn't just another chapter in the story, because if you think I'm going to sit by and worry about you plotting a heist on Wilson to get it back, then you have another think coming, Hunt.'

He laughs hard, throwing his head back. 'I'm done, princess. I promise.'

I snort my thoughts on that. 'You've promised before.'

His face straightens in an instant and he takes my hand, dipping and kissing his grandmother's ring. 'On my parents' honour, Eleanor. I will never see Wilson ever again. Come here, my gorgeous, corrupt little witch.' He opens his arms and I dive into them, letting him carry me across the piazza. The rain hammers down, soaking us to the bone, not that Becker seems in the least bit fazed. He puts me on my feet when we reach the fountain and takes my hands.

'So what do we do now?' I ask.

'Now, we dance.' He circles my shoulders with his arms and

starts turning us slowly, and I smile, bemused. He wants to dance?

Our feet shift lazily, our bodies stuck together, as we rock gently in the pouring rain. 'Shall we go get married?' Becker asks quietly, holding the back of my head, pushing me into his shoulder so I can't escape his clinch.

'Okay,' I agree easily, turning my face into his neck and smiling against his skin, hoping he feels it.

'Super.' He breaks away from me and tucks me into his side, starting to walk us as casual as can be out of the square. 'We'll have babies, too,' he says quietly. 'Two or three. And maybe we should get a girlfriend for Winston.'

I peek up at my gorgeous saint, seeing a peace so strong it's visible. He's soft against me, not one muscle tense, and his face is serene, making him even more handsome. 'Okay,' I agree again, and he peeks down at me, pulling his rain-splashed glasses away from his face so I can see directly into his beautiful eyes.

'Ready to do life with me, princess?' He scoops me up and cradles me in his arms, and I smile, resting my head on his shoulder, as he carries me across the piazza.

'I'm never ready for you, Hunt.'

Epilogue

Three years later
Becker

From the moment I set my eyes on Eleanor Cole, she triggered a confusing bombardment of feelings – both emotional and physical. It was a mystery to me for some time, and, honestly, it drove me to depths of insanity that I'd never experienced before. Not even during my epic quest to find *Head of a Faun*. I never gave fate much thought before she bowled into my life. My mind was trained on one thing. The sculpture. Two things if you include the women. I was prepared to give up both for her. Turns out I only had to give up the latter. The former, ironically, Eleanor found for me. The madness of it all makes me smile to this day, and I know it will for the rest of my life.

Peace. She found that for me, too. I've never felt more settled. I've never had so much purpose filling me. She taught me more than she'll ever know. I was meant to find Eleanor. My quest took me all over the world, to some truly beautiful places, but the place Eleanor has taken me to will never be rivalled. She's taken me to the most beautiful place of all. She's taken me into her heart. All of my quirks, my obsessions, and all of my faults. And most surprisingly of all, she understands them. She understands the need in me that'll never die. She accepts it.

So, yes, she is my Fate. I'm disregarding the teeny-tiny fact that Eleanor getting the job at my company was because I manipulated the entire process. When Dorothy told me about a girl the agency had on their books – a girl from out of town with no formal qualifications or experience working in the art world – I laughed. But then I read her CV, and I was instantly drawn in by her obvious passion for all things old. I needed to know who this woman was. So I found out all there was to know about Eleanor Cole. Then I found *her*. I watched her in the library, lost in endless books. I watched her roam the rooms of endless museums. I knew Dorothy needed the help, but I didn't trust anyone in the art world to work for me. This woman, though, was unknown in the industry. She hadn't worked in it, experienced it, seen the rivalry. She was perfect for the position, but I knew Parsonson's would snap her up in an instant, especially if Simon Timms was heading up the interview process, the slimy piece of shit. Eleanor Cole wasn't just notably knowledgeable, but beautiful, too. And sassy. And sexy. And intelligent. And passionate. And don't get me started on that arse of hers. Yes, I knew she would be good for Dorothy, but I can't deny I was also thinking with my dick.

But I really wasn't prepared for her, and I soon realised I was out of my depth. I'd been foolish, underestimating what I was truly getting myself into. She was like a super-charged energy that shocked life into my stone heart. The fire in her eyes each time I provoked her, watching her battle to fight off the surges of desire when we argued, it was all so fucking addictive. She made me lose focus. She made me think outside of my usual box.

Now and then, clarity spontaneously shocked me back to reality, and I'd find reason for a split second, find the strength to push her away and refocus on what mattered. Except I missed our chemistry-fuelled clashes the moment I put distance between us, and the conflict began to send me wild. So I'd find a way to coax her back, and the vicious circle of lust and madness would start all over again.

The urgency to find what needed to be found took a back

seat. I'd discovered something else that stole my attention. It was something that motivated me, but it was also something that scared the god-loving shit out of me. I felt something for her, and it wasn't just a hard dick. Feelings stirred deep inside of me, the most confusing feeling being jealousy. I'd never been possessive – only over my treasure. No woman had made me question what I wanted. I'd take or leave any one of them at the drop of a hat and find a replacement just as fast. The thought of any other man so much as breathing on her had unearthed a rage in me like nothing I'd felt before. It frightened me. And I could see that it frightened her. Enough to keep her away? Because she knew deep down that I would break her heart? No. She stuck me out. I cursed her for it, and I adored her for it. She took everything I threw at her. My corrupt little witch.

And here we are now . . .

The grin on my face as she walks down the aisle actually hurts my cheeks. I don't think I've ever smiled so hard. She's a vision in a simple strapless satin gown, her face naturally flawless, and her red hair glowing and tumbling over her bare shoulders. This should have happened over a year ago, but, you see, something came up.

It was quite unexpected, a bit like Eleanor was.

I look past her, my eyes homing in like a radar on my boy. He's toddling down the aisle in a mini tux, his big, round eyes beaming. My smile stretches wider when he spots me at the end of the aisle. His hand pulls away from Lucy's, and his chubby arms lift excitedly, his little legs picking up a pace. With Eleanor being led by my slow gramps, it doesn't take much speed for George to overtake them. I drop to my haunches as he staggers towards me, catching him just before he takes a tumble. 'Hey up, boy.' I laugh, lifting him into my arms and smothering his chuckling, chubby cheeks with wet kisses.

'Dadadadada!' His frantic palms smack my face repeatedly,

knocking my glasses askew and spiking a roar of badly contained chuckles from the congregation.

Eleanor's mother rushes forward to claim him, but when I try to pass him over, he shouts his protest and throws his little wilful arms around my neck. 'I've got him,' I say, transferring him into my right arm so I can welcome Eleanor into my other. She releases Gramps's hand, kisses him tenderly on the cheek, and then walks straight into my free arm, burying her face into my shoulder. I swear, there's not one thing in the world that could feel as good as this – my boy and my woman snuggling into me. I press my lips into her temple and breathe her into me. 'Give me a twirl,' I order gently, forcing her away from me. She smiles that knowing smile and performs a slow spin on the spot, giving me a peek of one of my favourite assets. I blow out air on a whistle, drinking in the exquisite sight of her arse being hugged by satin. 'Super,' I whisper to myself.

She curtseys and takes my hand, turning us to face the priest, and the holy man instantly eyes George in my hold, but a quick nod tells him to get on with things. I have an arse dying for my attention.

'Welcome,' he chants, a Bible resting across his palm. 'To the union of Eleanor and Becker.'

We stand together, our son in my arms, while the priest conducts the ceremony. Eleanor constantly squeezes my hand, and I constantly flick my gaze to hers, reminding myself that this is all so very real. Me, Becker Hunt, father and husband. They're the craziest things of all the things to happen. And the best. The most exciting, the most satisfying. I've found my treasure.

'For better, for worse,' I breathe, repeating the priest's words, keeping my eyes fixed on hers. 'For richer, for poorer, in sickness and in health.' I pause, fighting to keep the lump in my throat from hampering my vows. I'm feeling a little overwhelmed. 'Until death do us part.' I swallow, grateful to George when he reaches for my forehead and rubs his hand vigorously across my brow. Because now I don't need to wipe the sheen of sweat away.

'Are you breaking out in a nervous sweat, Hunt?' Eleanor asks quietly, smiling up at me.

'It's hot in here.' I brush off her observation before she clings on and teases me with it for the rest of our lives together.

'You have declared your consent before the Church,' the priest declares. 'May the Lord in his goodness strengthen your consent and fill you both with his blessings.'

'And treasure,' Eleanor adds, and I grin.

'Amen.'

'Amen,' the crowd repeat, and before I get the heads-up from the priest, I'm swooping in to claim my prize, kissing the ever-loving, gorgeous life out of her while George smacks us both on the head and she laughs into my mouth.

'Um . . . you may kiss your bride,' I hear the priest say over the ear-piercing clapping of the congregation. I only break away when I need to shift a wriggling George in my arms and, placing him on his little feet, I take Eleanor's hand in one, George's in my other, and walk the loves of my life out of the church.

'Ta-dah!' I sing, and George giggles relentlessly as I magic a shiny silver coin from behind his ear. He claps his hands in order for me to carry on, so I straighten him up on my lap and rest back on the couch, pulling my bow tie from around my neck and casting it aside. I show him the coin lying flat in my palm and he quietens down, his little, intrigued eyes studying it closely. I close my hand into a fist. 'Tap,' I tell him, and he smacks my hand on a shout. Then I open it up, revealing an empty palm.

'Ta-dah!' he shouts, bouncing up and down so vigorously I have to catch him quickly before he leaps from my lap. I laugh and haul him into my chest, and his little hands rest on my cheeks, his forehead meeting mine.

'You're gonna be a genius like your daddy,' I tell him, nipping at his nose. 'But no funny business. Be a good genius, you got it? I don't want to face the wrath of your mother.'

'No, you don't.'

I look up and see Eleanor by the door, still graced in her gown, a warning arch to her eyebrow. 'Hey, princess.' I pat the couch and she pads over, dropping a kiss on George's head as she lowers next to me.

'What are you doing in here?' she asks.

'Me and George needed a time out.'

'So you could teach him some tricks of the trade?' She produces the silver coin from behind my ear, twiddling it between her fingers on an accusing hum.

I grin. 'It's just magic.'

'And God knows where it could lead to.'

'Maybe he'll be the next Dynamo.'

'More likely the next Becker Hunt.' She nudges me playfully. That'll never happen. I won't let it. George will run the Hunt Corporation one day, but only the legitimate side of the business will exist by then. I promised Eleanor that, and I don't plan on breaking it. 'I need to get him bathed and in bed,' Eleanor says, just as George yawns loudly.

I pout and dot his face with kisses before reluctantly passing him over. 'Has everyone gone now?'

'All except Dorothy. She's helping Gramps to his room.' Eleanor stands and sits George on her hip.

My smile is instant. And so is the blood rushing to my cock. My eyes drop and she turns teasingly, sauntering out of the library with a purposeful sway with my boy in her arms. Today has been amazing. The courtyard of my Haven has been transformed into something even more spectacular than what it already is, marquees erected, flowers everywhere, champagne flowing and the people we love flooding the space. But this time, *our* time, is what I've been looking most forward to.

Consummation. My palms tingle with excitement. 'Be quick,' I order, adjusting my straining trousers.

She tosses a coy look over her shoulder as she disappears through the door, causing all kinds of chaos to erupt in my groin area. 'It's going to be a good-fucking-night,' I say to myself, rising to my feet.

Deciding to check up on the dogs and get myself a drink before I head for our private space, I wander down the corridor towards the kitchen, relishing in the peace surrounding me. I flip the top buttons of my shirt open and push my way into the kitchen, finding the dogs curled up in their basket. Winston gives me a moment of his attention before returning it to Clementine, licking her ear affectionately. 'Hey, boy,' I coo, wandering over to them and crouching. Winston gives me droopy eyes, and I swear I see concern in them. I look at a sleepy Clementine, her belly swelling massively. She's due any day now, and while Eleanor's girl is taking pregnancy in her stride, just like her owner did, Winston isn't so serene. He refuses to leave Clementine's side. Hasn't for weeks now. I reach forward and stroke his sad face. 'I know how you feel, buddy,' I soothe him. 'She'll be fine. Stop worrying.' I'm a fine one to talk. I didn't leave Eleanor's side in the last month either, and I was good for nothing when she was in labour. I've never felt so helpless.

I fill their water bowl and try to distract Winston from his fretting with a pig's ear. He turns his nose up and nuzzles Clementine. 'You should eat. I've only got *one* ankle biter and it's fucking exhausting. You need to keep up your strength, because something tells me there's more than one pup in there.' Jesus, looking at the size of Clementine, there could be an army of them. I place the treat next to his paw and get myself a whisky. 'See you in the morning, guys.' I flick the light off and bump into Dorothy on my way out the kitchen. 'Gramps okay?' I ask.

'Tired,' she confirms, pulling her fascinator from her hair. It's about time. Her vibrant headwear – a mix of a million different coloured spring flowers – clashes terribly with her blue rinse. I've had to put my shades on every time I've looked at her today. 'It's been a long day, but so wonderful!'

'It has,' I agree. 'Thank you for keeping tabs on Winston and Clementine.' She's been fussing over them all day, going back and forth to the kitchen to make sure both are well.

'She's glowing,' Mrs Potts remarks. 'Positively glowing.'

'Winston isn't.' I laugh, taking a swig of my Haig.

'He's a worry-wart.' She waves a hand flippantly and pulls her giant carpet bag onto her arm. 'I should be going.'

'It's late, Dorothy.' I'm not letting her get herself home at this hour, and I've drunk too much to drive her. 'Use the spare room, please.' I walk past her before she can refuse.

'If you insist,' she sings happily as she gets on her way to the spare room. 'See you in the morning.'

'Good night, Dorothy.' I take the stairs to our private space, rounding the steps quietly, listening for any signs that George might delay my plan. It's quiet. Beautifully fucking quiet. I grin and knock back the last of my drink, pushing through the door. I spot her immediately, standing at the foot of the glass wall looking over our grand hall, the train of her dress spread perfectly around her. She looks like a fucking goddess. Good God, just look at her. My wife. The mother of my boy. 'You're a lucky fucking man, Becker Hunt,' I whisper to myself, placing my glass down blindly and approaching her quietly, seeing her shoulders rise as I near. She feels me.

'Boo,' I whisper, slipping an arm around her waist and tugging her back. Our bodies meet and mould together, her perfect arse pushing into my groin. 'I have something for you.'

She pushes her backside into me further. 'I can feel it,' she replies huskily.

Biting at her ear, I lick the outer shell and relish in her

shudders. 'Soon,' I promise. 'Come.' I take her hand and pull her towards the door.

'Where are we going?' she asks, looking back to George's nursery area.

'Somewhere.'

'But he might wake.'

I grab the intercom as I pass the shelving unit that separates our bedroom. 'He'll be fine.'

She comes willingly, following a few steps behind as I lead her back down to The Haven and through the corridors towards the underground garage. 'Becker, where are we going?' she asks again, but I ignore her pleas for information, pulling her on silently. When we reach the door to the garage, I let us in and smile as I hold it open for her. She's frowning. Picking up the bottom of her dress, she wanders in, keeping suspicious eyes on me. 'What are we doing in the garage?'

'Shhhh,' I order, holding my finger to my lips. I see the hollows of her cheeks pulse on an impatient bite. 'This way.' I position her carefully at the back of the only car in the garage that's concealed by sheeting.

'Wait,' she says, looking to the side and noticing Gloria and my gorgeous vintage Ferrari uncovered. 'If your favourite women are there, then what's under here?' she points to the car before her.

'This, princess, is your wedding present.' I take the sheet and pull it off, relishing in the gasp she releases. 'Happy wedding day, Mrs Hunt.'

'You bought me a Ferrari?' She looks at me with wide eyes. 'Becker!'

'Yes, and it's black.' I point out the obvious. 'Because, you know, my red one clashes with your hair.'

She laughs and runs to the driver's side, peeking inside. 'You trust me with it?'

I roll my eyes. This gorgeous woman has managed to scratch

every car I own getting them in and out of the garage. It got to the point I had to ban her from driving all except the Audi. I never did get it repaired. There was no point until she got the hang of the hydraulic lifts. I think that day has finally come. There's been no new scratches on the Audi for over a year, and she's nagged me constantly to drive my pretty red Ferrari. My face each time she asked told her the answer. 'I trust you with it,' I confirm, joining her by the car.

She turns and throws her arms around me. 'I love it. Thank you.'

'Welcome.' I accept her appreciation for just a second before I whirl her around, pushing her front-forward onto the bonnet. She gasps, shocked. It makes me laugh on the inside. She didn't honestly expect me to pass up this opportunity, surely? But first . . .

I pull her dress aside by her shoulder blade, tugging it down until I find what I'm looking for. I smile at the ink, the art incredible.

The missing piece of the map. I dip and kiss her tattoo, before licking up her spine to her neck.

Her hands slap on the paintwork, my front meeting her back, pressing her into the hard metal. Her body is throbbing along with mine. 'Time to consummate your new car, princess.' I pull her up and her hands wedge into the paintwork. I've fucked her over the bonnet of each of my cars. I'm not about to break tradition.

I thrust my groin into her bum, moving her hair from her neck. 'Your arse looks fucking divine in this dress.' My palms work up her inside thigh, and her hands ball into fists.

'Oh, Jesus.' Her head falls back on her shoulders, the bright, florescent lights of the garage forcing her to close her eyes. I smile wickedly and reach down, gathering up the pool of white satin and pulling it up to her waist. My fingers slip between her legs and sink into her wetness, making that delectable arse fly back. I'm solid. Ready. But I continue priming her, my fingers massaging gently as I suck at the creamy skin of her neck, my hips rolling expertly into her backside over and over, driving her wild with impatience. 'Becker,' she whimpers.

'It's coming, princess.' I begin to fuck her with my fingers, plunging deep, circling wide, withdrawing slowly, as her moans ring out loud. The sound, good Lord, the sound.

I unzip my fly, feeling her internal muscles tightening. 'Someone's being greedy.' I bite her cheek and break away, pulling my fingers free and stepping back. She shouts her frustration to the ceiling, squeezing her eyes closed. Then I skate a steady palm across the smooth skin of her arse, *my* arse, admiring the perfect curve that's more pronounced since she carried my son. I didn't think I could love her arse any more than I did. Didn't think it could be any more perfect. I was wrong. I raise my palm, and she stills, snatching some air in preparation, bracing herself. She's never prepared. I bring my hand down swiftly, slapping her arse on a piercing crack. The instant sting that spreads across my palm makes my cock bulge more, the pink of her skin a sight to behold.

'Fuck!' She jolts forward, and her eyes spring open. I watch as she looks back and searches me out, her soft eyes lazy and appreciative, her hair wild and damp. I remove my glasses and slip them into my pocket, giving her direct access to my appreciative stare. It doesn't matter that my vision is suddenly blurry, because I won't be able to see straight soon, anyway.

'Good?' I ask, starting to tenderly stroke her burning arse, leaning in and giving her cheek an equally tender kiss.

'You're a depraved holier-than-thou twat, Becker Hunt,' she puffs, making me smirk.

I slowly position myself behind her. 'I'm making no apologies,' I say under my breath. 'I'm going to fuck you to the Pantheon and back, Eleanor.'

She laughs, and I growl, positioning the head of my wet

cock at her opening. I don't slip in slowly. I don't tease my way through her soaking pussy. It's been a long day waiting to get my hands on her properly.

I thunder forward, smashing into her brutally on a bellow that echoes around the stark garage. Her scream follows suit, bouncing off the white walls, and my world spirals into beautiful, desperate chaos, the power of our connection sending me descending into a haze of unadulterated bliss. Her sweaty palms slip over the paintwork of her new car, trying to find the anchor they need to hold her in place while I pound into her. I groan, striking hard and fast, yelling each and every time. I begin to gulp down air, taking long, deep breaths. The depths I'm achieving and the force behind my drives are building me up quickly, my balls aching. 'Fuck, yeah,' I yell, shifting one hand to her shoulder, clawing my fingers into her flesh. 'Feel good, Mrs Hunt?' Another brutal drive sends her up onto her tiptoes, her head going limp on her shoulders and hanging lifelessly. I delve my fingers into her messed-up hair and tug her head up. 'Do. I. Feel. Good?' I bark. I'm going out of my fucking mind. Everything is spinning. I feel spaced out, yet totally compos mentis. Completely with it. All the nerve endings I possess are zinging, screaming, raring to burst. 'Eleanor!' I roar.

Bang!

'Yes!' she cries, the word literally hammered out of her.

My cheeks puff out, the tip of my cock starting to spasm in preparation, every drop of blood rushing to my head. I'm going to come, and the power of it is going to make me collapse. Or pass out completely.

'Becker!'

'Hold on,' I shout, jacking her onto me, causing her hands to slip from the car. My stone dick starts swelling, pushing further into her soft, convulsing walls, sending me over the edge. She flips out, throwing her head back, screaming an insane torrent of nonsense into thin air. And then I literally feel her shatter, her body going slack, making it impossible to keep herself up any longer. 'Motherfucker,' I choke, coiling my arm around her waist to keep her in place. With one last mind-boggling plunge, I gasp, pushing my hips upward and releasing everything I have in consistent, steady pulses. I moan, groan and curse as I stagger back, taking her with me, literally crumbling to the floor, catching Eleanor as she comes down. I'm fucked, gasping for oxygen, my cock throbbing uncontrollably with the aftermath. I give into my heavy lids and close my eyes, her wet dress-covered back stuck to my chest and the back of her head falling onto my shoulder.

I sigh my satisfaction, letting my hands creep around her tummy and lock down, keeping her secure to me. The pounding blood in my ears is joined by the sound of Eleanor panting. It's the sweetest sound, and I nuzzle into her ear, nipping at her lobe. She exhales happily and grumbles her protest when I break away. 'Bed,' I order as I drag myself to my feet, smiling at her slighted face when I fasten my fly. Without another word, I bend, gather her into my arms, and stride out of the garage with my wife draped across my arms. Her head settles on my shoulder, and I look down at her glowing face.

'Do you think you can stand?'

'No,' she answers quickly. 'Why? Is my arse getting too heavy these days?'

'Your arse is just perfect.' Let's get that straight before she takes it away from me. 'Leave my arse alone.'

'It might grow even bigger soon,' she whispers quietly.

I pull to a halt, my eyes shooting down to hers. I find her grinning. 'Are you playing with me? Please don't play with me.'

'I did a test this morning.'

And just when I thought I couldn't be any happier. I exhale and sink my face into her hair. 'How many weeks?'

'Just twelve.'

'God, woman, you make me so happy.'

'Me or my ever-increasing arse?'

'You. Your arse is just a bonus.' But the sight of it when Eleanor was at full term with George is suddenly riddling my mind. I grin into her neck. 'I can't fucking wait. But I wanted to be there when you did the test.'

'I wasn't certain. And I didn't want to get your hopes up. I know how much you loved my massive arse when I was expecting.'

'Not massive. Perfect.'

'Yes, because there's more area for you to slap stu—' Eleanor's head shoots up. 'Was that Clementine?'

'What?' Just as I ask, I hear another whimper.

'That.' Eleanor is out of my arms in a flash, picking the bottom of her dress up and running out of the garage.

I grab the baby monitor and slip on my glasses as I follow, a little less urgently than Eleanor.

'I'm coming,' she yells. 'Where's Mrs Potts?'

'So she can use her feet for her dog?' I grumble. But I'm still grinning. Boobs, belly and arse. I wish she could be permanently pregnant.

Mrs Potts appears from the spare room, as if by magic, rollers in her hair, a floral nighty drowning her short, plump body. 'Is it time?'

'You'd better get the blankets.' I push my way into the kitchen and find Eleanor crouched by the dog bed, her dress a mass of bunched-up satin puddled on the kitchen floor. She has Clementine's jowls in one palm, her hand tenderly stroking her head with the other while Winston circles close by. 'Well?' I ask, joining her and trying to settle Winston.

'She's in labour,' Eleanor says without looking at me. 'It could be a long night.'

'To go with a long day.' I sigh, just as Mrs Potts bursts through the door with arms full of blankets.

'I'm here!' She wobbles over and dumps the pile next to the

dog bed, assessing Clementine. 'Look at that face,' she says happily. 'Oh, I can't wait to have The Haven full of puppies.'

I take Winston by the collar. 'C'mon, boy. Let's leave the ladies to do their thing.' I gently coax him towards the door, looking back as I go on a smile. A wife, *two* kids, two bulldogs and puppies to boot. Fucking crazy.

Winston grumbles a little as I lead him to my office. 'You'll just worry more,' I tell him. 'It's not pretty. Best to try and relax a little. Get some rest. She'll need you soon, you know.' I push the door to my office open and usher him inside, and he looks up at me and barks in agreement, ambling over to the chair and jumping on. He curls up as I sit the baby monitor on the drinks cabinet and pour myself a Haig, taking a quick swig before placing it on my desk and wandering to the foot of my book-case. Scanning the shelf before me, I locate the book I need and tilt it, standing back as the shelf creeps open, revealing my safe. I bend a little at the waist, presenting my eye to the scanner before twiddling the dial the few times needed and getting the key from my pocket. I slip it in the lock and turn, getting my usual thrill from the clicking that indicates the release of the locks. My tummy actually flutters. It never gets old.

Reaching inside, I gather the bundle into my hands and wan-der over to my desk, placing it down with the care it deserves.

Then I pull off the cover, take a seat, kick my feet up, and grab my drink.

And I relax back and admire it for a while, smiling to my-self when I think that Brent Wilson probably does this very thing each day. Except he admires a fake – another fake that I masterfully crafted and buried under a slab on the porch of the Pantheon before I dug it up again. I smile at the thought. I'm not sure what I took more pleasure from: discovering that the real sculpture had been in Rome all along and my girl found it for me, or watching Brent run away with another fake. It's a close call.

I look up when the door knocks, and a second later, Gramps pokes his head around. His eyes fall straight to *Head of a Faun*, a knowing smirk pulling at his old lips. 'Why aren't you in bed?' I ask, getting up and pouring him a whisky.

He walks slowly to the chair on the other side of my desk and lowers on a little grunt, accepting the tumbler when I hand it to him. He tosses a newspaper on the desk, and it lands next to the sculpture. I look down, smiling.

Brent's face graces the front page, and the headline is telling the world that he's been sentenced to ten years for stealing an O'Keeffe from Sotheby's. I'm not going to feel too bad for setting up the prick. I needed justice for Mum and Dad. I smiled my fucking arse off as I smothered the painting with his finger-prints, thanks to the glass I stole from his suite at The Stanton. God, I would have loved to have seen the look on his face when the police found the O'Keeffe in the vault of his hotel. Framing Brent was one of my finest moments. I'm still buzzing.

'He'll be gunning for you when he's out,' Gramps muses.

'I've got a good five years before I need to worry about that.'

He reaches for the sculpture, swivelling it until it's facing him. Then he leans back on a smile and stares at it.

I watch him, getting as much pleasure from studying my granddad as I do the long-lost treasure. 'Gramps?' I say, winning his attention. I hold up my tumbler and toast the air above *Head of a Faun*. 'To Mum and Dad.'

He nods, and we both knock back our drinks, slamming the glasses down on the Theodore Roosevelt desk in unison.

Gramps smiles, getting comfortable as best as his old bones will allow. Then he breathes in and lets the air out on a wistful sigh. 'I love you, Becker boy.'

'Love you more, Gramps,' I reply quietly, reaching forward and swivelling the sculpture back to face me before refilling our drinks and passing his over. 'Love you *way* more.' I relax back in my chair.

'To the Hunts,' he says. 'Best bleedin' treasure hunters that ever lived.' He stares at the sculpture, and I see peace in him as much as I feel it in myself. 'Did you hear they're having the Mona Lisa removed to be cleaned?' he asks, his eyes still on *Head of a Faun*.

'Oh?' I try to stop my veins from tingling with excitement. Honestly, I do.

He peeks up at me. 'Next month, apparently.'

'Interesting.' I muse, rolling my tumbler across my bottom lip.

'I thought so, too.' He reaches for the sculpture and swivels it back to face him. 'But, you know, you're retired now.' He lifts his glass and swigs.

'Yeah,' I muse, our eyes locked across the desk. 'I'm retired.'

My dear old granddad's mouth slowly stretches into a grin.

And damn my thirst for adventure, I grin right back.

Acknowledgements

And here I am again wondering what to write and how I can express my appreciation for so many people in a different way. To my people at Orion, my UK publisher, thank you for giving my stories a home in the UK. I look forward to many more years working with you. To my agent, Andy, you're fierce, loyal, and an inspiration to me every day. I adore you. Thank you for being you.

And to my readers out there who have been waiting for the conclusion of Becker and Eleanor's story, you are absolutely not ready for this thrilling ride. Hold tight. The adventure continues. Thank you for being here with me.

JEM xxx

About the Author

Jodi Ellen Malpas was born and raised in the Midlands town of Northampton, England, where she lives with her husband, boys, and a beagle. She is a self-professed daydreamer, a Converse and mojito addict, and she has a terrible weak spot for alpha males. Writing powerful love stories and creating addictive characters has become her passion – a passion she now shares with her devoted readers. Her novels have hit bestseller lists for the New York Times, USA Today, Sunday Times, and various other international publications and can be read in more than twenty-four languages around the world.

You can learn more at:
JodiEllenMalpas.co.uk
Facebook.com/JodiEllenMalpas
Twitter @JodiEllenMalpas

If you can't get enough of Eleanor and Becker's sizzling love story, go back to where it all began ...

An irresistible connection, a desire that won't let go ...

When aspiring antiques dealer Eleanor Cole is handed the chance of a lifetime to work for the Hunt Corporation, the renowned antiques dealers, she doesn't think twice. Only then does she discover she'll be working up close and personal with the notorious and insanely irresistible Becker Hunt. He is a man famous for getting what he wants, and Becker wants Eleanor.

But as Becker pulls her deeper into his world, she discovers there's more to him than meets the eye.

And falling for Becker goes from being foolish to dangerous ...

Available in paperback and eBook now

Discover an unforgettable love story that will take your
breath away . . .

**Giving into desire could destroy them, but denying their
passion is impossible . . .**

Hannah Bright has finally found a place to hide from her
past, in the quiet town of Hampton. But the peace she needs
is disrupted when she meets Ryan Willis. Insanely handsome
and highly dangerous, Ryan is exactly the kind of man Hannah needs to avoid . . .

Reconsidering his career in private protection, Ryan is home
to figure out his next move. Meeting Hannah is definitely not
part of his plan, yet Ryan can't resist her. But Hannah has a
dangerous secret, and Ryan won't stop until he finds out what
she's hiding. Nothing prepares him for what he discovers.

Can Ryan keep Hannah safe? Or will her past destroy any
chance they have for a future together . . .

Available in paperback and eBook now

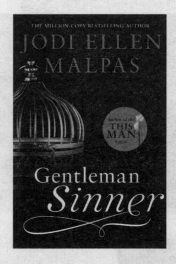

Discover the international phenomenon of *This Man* ...

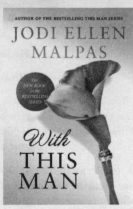

Available now

ONE NIGHT *– the hottest*
pulse-pounding trilogy . . .

Available now

'The latest queen of erotic literature'
Sunday Times

Two stand-alone novels from the Sunday Times
and New York Times *bestseller*

JODI ELLEN MALPAS

Credits

Jodi Ellen Malpas and Orion Fiction would like to thank everyone at Orion who worked on the publication of *Wicked Truths* in the UK.

Editorial
Victoria Oundjian
Olivia Barber

Copy editor
Justine Taylor

Proof reader
Laetitia Grant

Audio
Paul Stark
Amber Bates

Contracts
Anne Goddard
Paul Bulos
Jake Alderson

Design
Debbie Holmes
Joanna Ridley

Nick May

Editorial Management
Charlie Panayiotou
Jane Hughes
Alice Davis

Finance
Jasdip Nandra
Afeera Ahmed
Elizabeth Beaumont
Sue Baker

Production
Ruth Sharvell

Sales
Jen Wilson
Esther Waters
Victoria Laws
Rachael Hum
Ellie Kyrke-Smith

Frances Doyle
Georgina Cutler

Operations
Jo Jacobs
Sharon Willis
Lisa Pryde
Lucy Brem